A SERIES OF MOMENTS

MOMENTS

Beautifully Broken Moments

M.L. BROOME

TERRACOTTA DRAGON ARTS

A Series of Moments
Beautifully Broken Moments
Copyright © J. E. Soper 2019
All rights reserved.

Digital Edition MARCH 2019 ISBN: 978-1-7338964-6-7
Print Edition ISBN: 978-1-7338964-7-4

Publishing by:
TerraCotta Dragon Arts

Cover Art by:
Suzana Stankovic, LSDdesign

Editing by:
Emily Tamayo Maher

Interior Design & Formatting by:
Suzana Stankovic, LSDdesign

Your body is away from me, but there is a window open from my heart to yours.

~ **Rumi**

Dedicated to my dear friend Mike, who has been a huge advocate and support throughout this process. Even when I didn't believe in myself, he pushed me through with his friendly banter and encouragement.

Thank you, for everything.

CONTENTS

Recap of the first books in A Series of Moments

From the Moment We Met, Book One

Jacob Edmonton has a plan for his life, but it doesn't include love. He was Hollywood's quintessential golden boy—until a flash-in-the-pan fling with a high-profile singer upended his world—and his reputation. Now he's nursing more than a wounded ego and his only goal is to repair the damage.

But his return to superstardom is shot to hell when his sister winds up undergoing emergency surgery. There he meets Lilly Staver, a straight-shooting nurse who's as brutally honest as she is beautiful. She sees through his suave façade and he wants to hate her, until he realizes he can't resist her.

Lilly knows all about men like Jacob Edmonton—if you've seen one pretentious, egocentric celebrity—you've seen them all. She's unimpressed with his Hollywood pedigree and his belief that love is reserved solely for maniacs. So why can't she stop thinking about him? Her mind tells her to run as fast as she can from Jacob…but her heart isn't listening.

Love as they know it just took a hairpin turn into uncharted territory, but when Jacob's former girlfriend shows up with an opportunity to salvage his career, will he choose the life he knows or the love he never knew existed?

Unguarded Moments, Book Two

Jacob made a choice, but now he realizes he made the wrong one. The lights of Hollywood dim in comparison to the love he left behind, the love he found with Lilly. He's ready to fight tooth and nail to bring Lilly back into his life but is it too late to undo the damage?

Lilly saw the writing on the wall when she met Jacob, but she chose to follow her heart instead. Her foolish, naïve heart. She's learned her lesson many times over—loving Jacob Edmonton was a bad idea in every sense of the word. She gave him her love, but instead of loving her back, he watched her walk away. She vows to never make the same mistake again...but can she resist the one man who still holds every piece of her shattered soul?

Thousands of kilometers lie between them now, but the distance isn't Jacob's biggest hurdle. He has to convince Lilly that loving him wasn't the gravest mistake she's ever made.

The heart wants what the heart wants—but can Lilly believe in Jacob again, or will her fears end any chance of reconciliation?

Excerpt from
"Unguarded Moments"

A chill ran up Jacob's spine, but he shook it off as he escorted Victoria to the door. "I'll meet you at the press conference."

A crowd of reporters gathered in the hotel conference room, all vying for a prime spot.

Jacob rang Lilly on his way out of the suite, wanting to give her a heads up to the situation but his call went straight to voicemail.

He felt an unease as if something untoward was about to happen, but he surmised it was nerves. Victoria, on the other hand, was glowing. She seemed joyous to attend this press release.

"Good evening everyone," Victoria began, waving graciously at the crowd. "Thank you for gathering here on such short notice. I know we all lead busy lives, so I'll get right to the point. The first announcement is a surprise even to Jacob. He has been offered the lead role in Milieu of Madness!"

The journalists clapped while Jacob sat there, stunned. *What the fuck? Why didn't Albert call me about the role?*

As if on cue, Victoria continued, "Albert was going to speak to Jacob today, but I begged him to let me have the fun of informing him that he's landed the most coveted role in Hollywood!" The applause continued, but Jacob felt as if his world was about to be upended.

Victoria's smile oozed warmth, but Jacob wasn't fooled. "The second announcement is on a much more personal note. Jacob and I are expecting our first child together!" The room erupted into a tizzy, and it was everything Victoria could do to calm them down. "Hold on folks, I'm not done yet. Jacob and I went our separate ways a couple months ago, but with our impending arrival, we decided to get married within the next few weeks. This baby rekindled our love in the best possible manner." Her smiled beamed as her eyes found Jacob. "I'm going to Mrs. Edmonton!"

Just like that, the room fell away, and Jacob thought he might lose consciousness. The noise was dizzying, with cameras flashing and reporters buzzing like a nest of hornets at the news.

He closed his eyes, swallowing back the nausea that threatened to show itself in front of members of the international press. Game, set, match. There was no easy way out of the monstrous lie Victoria fabricated. He didn't give a shit about his reputation, but he knew the media and Victoria's army of fans would have a field day if he contradicted her statement. Lilly would become the harlot and homewrecker, her reputation and safety ripped to shreds.

His mind reeled trying to rectify the situation, but he blanked. He felt

Victoria watching him, waiting to see how he would play against her latest hand. She planned this from the beginning, knowing he would walk willingly into her web.

One journalist looked particularly perplexed by the news. "Well, first congratulations on your...news. However, Mr. Edmonton, there have been rumors around London that you are engaged to another woman. I guess there isn't any truth to that story?"

Jacob's head throbbed as he sighed, summoning all his resolve to not overturn the table and smash the room to bits.

If he admitted his love for Lilly, she would be massacred by the press. If he denied any involvement between them, she would be protected from everything except a broken heart. *What kind of choice is this?*

A few more journalists chimed in, demanding to know his business with this other woman. He wanted to scream that she wasn't the "other woman", she was the love of his life, but he remained silent.

Lilly was an innocent soul whose integrity would be forever torn apart if he didn't take steps now to protect her. All her tireless work for the betterment of others would be destroyed in a flash and faith in her actions might never recover. She almost certainly wouldn't get the funding for the sanctuaries she held so dear to her heart, and that would be devastating.

Beyond her charity was the question of her basic safety. If Victoria was this ruthless, he didn't doubt she would hurt Lilly if he didn't play along. The thought of his angel coming to physical harm because of him was beyond comprehension. He couldn't do it, he couldn't put her in danger. He wasn't worth that risk.

Jacob blinked back tears, cleared his throat and told the biggest lie of his life. "There is a woman in London, a dear friend who needed my assistance after a recent injury. However, there is no romantic situation between us." He paused, realizing the press had obtained pictures of him and Lilly kissing while in London. "We dated briefly, but when I learned of Victoria's pregnancy, we decided to part ways as friends. I wish her nothing but the best."

Ben and Sabina flanked Lilly in her office that afternoon, as soon as the press release hit the airwaves. Due to Victoria and Jacob's immense popularity, it was all any news channel could talk about—a baby of paramount importance. *And to think the day started on such a high note,* Lilly considered as Sabina hugged her for the millionth time.

When they first told her, she scoffed, claiming it was a fabrication. After all, the media had often twisted things in the past. Granted, Jacob never mentioned holding a press release with Victoria, but perhaps he didn't think he needed to disclose information Lilly already knew.

Sabina brought up the video release, her hands shaking as she pressed play. Ben positioned himself behind Lilly, rubbing her shoulders.

Lilly surprised herself when she didn't scream or throw the computer monitor across the room. Instead, she watched Jacob state that he was going to marry Victoria and his dalliance with Lilly—'the unnamed woman in London'—was only a fling and meant nothing long-term.

She didn't say a word as she clenched her jaw, letting her heart process what her mind suspected since she first allowed Jacob into her life. She was a passing fancy, secondary to his career and his ex-girlfriend. It was exactly what had happened with the last man she loved as well. She gave everything she had but, in the end, it didn't matter. She wasn't important enough, pretty enough or valuable enough to come first. It wasn't a surprise, some part of her always knew this truth about Jacob.

He had left her with only one choice. Lilly needed to find a place where Jacob couldn't hurt her anymore.

CHAPTER ONE

Jacob

"You have visitors." Miriam's tone was biting, but Jacob couldn't blame her. He'd been a disaster since the press release aired and his engagement to Lilly screeched to a halt under Victoria's truckload of lies. Everything he ever wanted, with the woman of his dreams, destroyed by his ex-girlfriend's quest for control and vengeance.

The details of the press release remained fuzzy, not surprising considering the copious amounts of alcohol Jacob now consumed around the clock.

"Did you hear what I said?" Miriam snarled, snapping her fingers under Jacob's nose. He deserved such treatment, and he knew it. It was anyone's guess which infuriated Miriam more—his maltreatment of Lilly or his consistent state of inebriation.

He grunted in reply, his head thumping from his whiskey breakfast. "Let me guess—"

"No, it isn't the devil herself." Miriam regarded her friend with a mixture of disdain and disgust. "Jesus, Jacob, go splash some water on your face and brush your teeth. You reek like a brewery. I can't keep you on set if you continue showing up like this, you know that."

Jacob shrugged, taking another swig of liquor from his glass. "You can always fire me."

"Cut the shit, this isn't you."

Jacob laughed dryly. "No? This"—he shook his beverage—"is the only thing keeping me from killing myself to escape the hell that is now my life."

Miriam rolled her eyes in frustration. "Your sister and Roger are waiting in your trailer. Take the rest of the damn day, maybe they'll know what to do with you."

Jacob dragged himself to his trailer, the gleaming white buildings and azure waters that formed the backdrop of the movie set a mocking reminder of what he'd lost. With a labored breath, he glanced over at the sea. He'd selected a spot in Perissa for his wedding to Lilly, he thought it was the most breathtaking locale in all of Santorini. The black sand beaches were exquisite, but they'd pale in comparison to his angel. "I miss you, Lilly," he whispered, each syllable spearing him in the heart.

Turning away, he stumbled up the two steps and pulled open the trailer door, offering a pitiful wave to Janie and his best friend. "Family."

Janie exchanged a glance with Roger. "Are you drunk?"

"Not quite, but don't despair Lil Bit, I'm no quitter. I'll be snockered soon enough." He fell back on the sofa, taking another pull from his ever-present whiskey glass.

Janie grabbed the glass, unscrewed the lid and dumped the contents down the sink, ignoring Jacob's loud protests. "Oh, shut up, Jacob! What the fuck is going on here? You never drink on set. You look—and *smell*—appalling."

"So sorry I'm not dressed in my best tux for you, Janie. I'm not exactly having a banner couple of weeks," Jacob choked out, willing back the ever-present nausea.

"*You're* having a bad couple of weeks? My apologies." Damn, but his sister could lay the sarcasm on thick. "Pray tell, why would that be?"

Was Janie seriously asking him this question? "You know damn well why," Jacob gritted out.

"No, we don't." Janie wasn't backing down either, her blue-eyed glare matching his own.

"What do you want from me, Janie?"

"I want answers! We all do. We deserve an explanation for this stunt you and Victoria pulled. Why did you break Lilly's heart? It's obvious you're unhappy with the decision."

Talk about the understatement of the century. "I'm miserable."

"That much I can deduce on my own." Janie yanked a bottle of water from the mini fridge and shoved it into her brother's hand.

"Why haven't you called me?" Jacob inquired, changing the subject. He wasn't ready to broach the topic of Lilly yet.

"Because I'm furious with you, Jacob! I'm sick of watching you hurt my friend, all because of some fake-titted floozy and your precious career."

"That's not what happened," Jacob choked out, his throat tightening.

"So why did you do it?" Janie beseeched, her voice imploring.

"If you hate me so much, why are you even here? To rub it in my face how horrible my life is now? How I threw away the only person who ever mattered to me? Why are you here?" Jacob's voice increased in decibel with every question.

Roger, who had been silent until that point, sat next to his friend. "Right after the press release aired, Janie and I made plans to fly here and throttle you soundly, but Lilly asked us to leave the situation alone. She said you'd made your choice—and hers. Honestly, we believed you *were* in cahoots with Victoria since you never reached out to either of us to explain your actions... until Miriam rang me a couple days ago."

2

"Miriam called you?" Jacob shook his head, his fuzzy brain wishing he had imbibed a bit less whiskey.

Roger nodded, his gaze focused out the small trailer window. "I'm friends with her too, remember? Miriam told me you were a disaster. She didn't know what to do with you."

"How is my behavior your problem? You despise me, remember? I know what I've done…and I know why I had to do it," Jacob muttered, downing a sip of water. The liquid burned more than the whiskey as it traveled down his aching throat.

Janie sat on the other side of Jacob, gingerly clasping his hand. "We don't hate you, Jacob. As soon as Roger heard from Miriam, we started putting the puzzle pieces together and realized we needed to get down here and find out what the hell really happened."

Jacob blinked back tears. "Does Lilly hate me?"

Janie's eyes widened in disbelief. "Are you trying to be funny? No, she's your biggest fan, every woman loves having their hopes and dreams ripped apart by their fiancée via international media."

Jacob buried his face in his hands. He deserved the pain, every ounce of it, and there seemed no end to the heartache.

But Roger wasn't going to let Jacob slide without full disclosure. "This isn't like you Jacob. On your worst day, you've never treated another human being with the blatant disregard you showed Lilly."

The tears rolled down Jacob's face, no longer willing to remain locked away, but he didn't care; he couldn't drink away the emotions any longer. "I know."

Roger stood up, clenching his fists in aggravation. "Well, as long as you're aware—"

"Sarcasm isn't helping, Roger," Janie chided, placing her hand on her friend's arm.

"Just tell us, why did you do it? Christ, you sure had us all fooled. We thought you adored Lilly—"

"I *do* adore Lilly."

"So why instead of loving her, did you rip her apart? Jacob, of all the people I know, she is the *last* person who deserved that."

The nausea was going to win. Jacob didn't know how much longer he could sit there without emptying the contents of his stomach on his friend's shoe. "You think I don't know that?"

"We don't know what to believe anymore, Jacob," Janie interjected. "Lilly thinks you enjoy cruelty as sport with her, but Roger and I know you better than that. We know *you*, Jacob." She knelt in front of her brother, her voice softening. "Please, help us understand. Help us to help you—and Lilly. Explain why you and Victoria opted to hold a press release instead of speaking to her first. Why would you destroy her in such a manner?"

Her soft but insistent questions broke through his emotional armor and the pain overtook his body as Janie's arms wrapped around him. He sobbed against his sister, the mental anguish and exhaustion finally set free. He hadn't slept in days except for fitful nightmares where he awoke drenched in sweat and crying out for Lilly.

When his sobbing waned, he took a few gulping breaths, readying himself for the explanation. "Victoria wanted to announce the pregnancy early. She claimed Edward threatened to sell his version of the story to the tabloids. I agreed, thinking it made sense and Victoria seemed reasonable at the time. I didn't see it coming. She blindsided me with the statement about our impending marriage. I wanted to recant her lie but I knew Lilly would be at the mercy of the media and Victoria's psychotic fans, thinking she was somehow the reason Victoria and I weren't together."

"You lied to protect her?" Janie prompted.

Jacob nodded. "It worked out well, didn't it? The next day I had a statement prepared and I went to Victoria with the document. I told her I was going public about my engagement and Victoria sat there, filing her fucking claws and without so much as a glance, said it would be terrible if something unfortunate happened to Lilly. She threatened to smear her name, portraying her as a harlot and homewrecker. The lies would destroy her credibility with her job and charity work."

Janie nodded, placing a reassuring hand on his knee.

"It was the most awful choice, but I didn't know what else to say at that point. The press only referred to Lilly as this unnamed woman in London, and I knew as long as she maintained anonymity, she would be safe. She's already been attacked once, I would never forgive myself if any harm came to her because of Victoria or her crazed fans."

"Even if Victoria isn't personally crazy enough to pull such a stunt, there's no telling what her fans would do," Roger lamented.

"You're being kind, Roger. She's a psychopath, a hormonally pregnant psychopath," Janie growled.

"It certainly wasn't the optimal choice, but Victoria didn't really leave you with one." Roger patted his friend on the shoulder. "Do you even know if the baby is yours? And this garbage she's spouting about Edward, he's been nothing but kind towards Lilly since the news broke; sending her flowers and calling her to check in. I don't get the impression he planned on releasing any information. In fact, he seemed as shocked as the rest of us when the news broke about your upcoming marriage to Victoria."

"Edward is checking on Lilly? Wonderful. He probably wants to step right into my shoes. I suppose she would be happier with him anyway. God knows I don't do anything but hurt her." His hands trembled as he wiped his face again. "I have no clue if the baby is mine, she claims it fits our timeline. I've requested a paternity test, but she fed me some rigmarole about dangers to the fetus. I don't know what's the truth anymore."

"'That's assuming her timeline *is* the truth. She could easily lie to you about the conception date by a few weeks, you need a paternity test," Roger insisted.

Jacob nodded. They weren't telling him anything he didn't already know, but the fight was gone from him. Victoria had gotten in too many licks this round. "I'm trying but she's balking at the idea. What does it even matter? My life is in the toilet, why bother?"

Janie stood, pacing the trailer floor. "Nonsense. You don't sit back and let her win. Victoria's played a tremendous hand, but you may have some aces up your sleeve."

"If you know a way out of this hell I'm living, I'm all ears, Janie."

"If we narrow down the conception date, then we'll have a better idea about whether or not the baby is yours. If it is, you wait a month and then publicly break up with her, stating your role strictly as the child's father. If it isn't yours, the media would be shocked if you didn't break up with Victoria immediately."

"'It's an idea, I guess," Jacob mumbled.

"Well, it's better than sitting around here soused and miserable."

Jacob shrugged. "Even if I determine the baby isn't mine, it doesn't matter. None of that brings back my Lilly."

Roger shook his head. "Let us worry about that part."

"She won't even return my calls. I've called and texted hundreds of times. I figured she would reply just to shut me up."

Janie and Roger exchanged a glance. "She blocked your number, she isn't getting any of your calls."

Jacob groaned. "Of course she did, why wouldn't she? I'd block my number too."

Janie hesitated before reaching into her bag, pulling out Lilly's necklace and his grandmother's emerald ring. "Lilly wanted to make certain you got these back. She left the clothes and other items at your house, but she asked me to hand deliver these pieces."

Jacob's jaw clenched as he took the items, an errant tear splashing the metal. "Christ, it's really over. What am I supposed to do now, Janie?"

Janie hugged her brother again. "Sober the fuck up. You can't fight Victoria half in the bottle. Get your damn paternity test or hire someone to figure out who is the father of her baby. You always used protection with Victoria?"

Jacob nodded. "Always, I never trusted where she'd been. I'm not a total moron,"—he met their reproachful glances and released a long sigh—"at least not in that department. Hell, the last time we had sex was before I left for Santorini."

"Nothing happened when she came to visit the set?"

Jacob rolled his eyes. "Oh, she tried to seduce me. It was like being courted by a serial killer."

Roger offered up a smirk. "Is that a no?"

"'That's a no way in hell. I kicked Victoria out the door almost immediately after her unwelcome arrival in Santorini."

"So," Janie began, looking at a calendar on her phone, "the last time you were intimate was the end of February?"

Jacob nodded, shuddering at the memory. "Right before I arrived here."

"I take it you don't want a repeat performance?" Roger gave his friend a smack on the arm. "Hey, at least you're conversing like a human being again."

"Can we focus please?" Janie butted into the moment of camaraderie, earning a chuckle from Roger. "So, if the black widow isn't lying, she should be about nine or ten weeks at this point."

Jacob scrubbed his face, feeling his frustration build. "Is that supposed to mean something to me?"

Janie shrugged. "No, but when you speak to Victoria, you might ask how far along she is and see if the numbers match."

"This is ludicrous," Roger declared, thumping his fist on the countertop. "Enough of playing this woman's games. He needs the damn paternity test. She has to consent to one."

"She's claiming it'll hurt the fetus! What do you want me to tell you, Roger?" Jacob bellowed, raking his fingers over his scalp. "I have no clue if she's lying about the dangers. I'm a bloody actor, not a medical professional."

As soon as the words left his lips, the threesome met gazes.

"You're not," Roger murmured, "but Lilly is. Hell, this is her arena, she would know better than we would."

"I can call her," Janie stammered.

Jacob's heart stopped beating in his chest. He might get to hear Lilly's voice again. "Can I speak to her?"

Janie replied with a brusque shake of her head. "One step at a time, big brother." She went outside the trailer and returned a few minutes later. "Lilly said this isn't her 'arena' as you so eloquently put it Roger, but risks associated with paternity testing are relatively rare. She then pointedly inquired if I was asking for my brother"—Janie glanced at Jacob—"and I said no, it was something that Audrey and I were discussing. Which might have been more credible if one of us had a penis."

Jacob laughed in spite of himself at his sister's words. "I don't want to know if one of you has a penis."

"I second that emotion," Roger added.

The three shared a chuckle, and for a moment Jacob almost felt human. "So, there's a good chance I can force Victoria's hand with this paternity test?" He breathed a sigh of relief. "How did Lilly sound? How is she holding up?"

"Jacob," Janie began, but her brother cut her off.

"Please, Janie. I'm in agony here."

Janie licked her lips nervously, catching Roger's gaze. "She's surviving…I guess. I've called her dozens of times, but this morning was the first time she actually answered her phone."

Jacob felt the last remnants of his heart seize. "I did this to her. I caused this pain."

"This time, mate, it wasn't you," Roger replied.

"Lot of good *that* knowledge does me, she hates me regardless." Jacob couldn't fight the urge anymore. He grabbed Janie's phone, laying on the table, and dialed Lilly's number, putting the call on speakerphone.

"What the hell do you think you're doing?" Janie hissed.

"I need to hear her voice." He knew he sounded like a madman, but no matter. Lilly was his lifeline and she was drifting further and further away from him.

"What am I supposed to say—" Janie's question was cut off as the line connected.

"Janie, you're killing me over here. I've had to leave this meeting three times." Lilly's voice was dry but friendly. "What's up?"

The glare his sister sent him could shoot holes through granite, but Jacob didn't care. Lilly's New York accent was the sweetest sound he'd heard in weeks.

"Lilly…sorry to bother you again…I had another question…"

Lilly cleared her throat. "About the paternity test you—and

7

Audrey—need?"

Janie rubbed her eyes and Jacob knew he'd pay later for this stunt. "Well…"

"Janie, what is this really about?"

"I'm with Roger."

"Okay," Lilly hedged.

"In Santorini."

The seconds of silence screamed out like hours, the silence deafening from Lilly's end. "What do you want?" Her voice, strong only moments before, now resonated with defeat.

"Victoria is claiming the paternity test will hurt the baby, so she's fighting having it done until after the birth."

"How is this my problem?"

"Is there a non-invasive method, Lilly? Jacob needs to know the truth because what Victoria did to you both—"

Lilly's harsh laugh barked through the phone. "What *Victoria* did to us both? Let's not forget your brother's role in this hellish nightmare, they're equally guilty."

This was killing Jacob. He inched forward in the chair, opening his mouth to speak on his defense but any thought of that was shot down by his sister's glare.

"Lilly, I know what you must think—" Janie began.

"No Janie, I don't think you can even begin to imagine what I'm thinking or feeling." Lilly heaved a huge sigh. "I'm not his nurse for hire, but a blood test will be sufficient. They don't have to do an amniocentesis anymore, a blood test can identify DNA structure. It's expensive, but those two have more money than God so I'm sure they can afford it. Was there anything else?"

Jacob caught his sister's gaze and mouthed, 'Tell her why I did it.'

"Janie, I don't have all day," Lilly reminded her.

"Jacob doesn't believe the baby is his, he always used protection with Victoria. Hell, he never even wanted kids before he met you." Janie's face was lined with tension, this phone call was painful for everyone involved.

Silence, then a sigh. "Congratulations? I'm sorry? Whoo-hoo? Which emotion am I supposed to be passing along to your brother?" Lilly's tone was flat, but the undercurrent of tension was evident.

"Lilly, there is so much to explain. The truth is Victoria backed Jacob into a corner. He went along with her game to protect you—"

"By throwing me under the bus? I don't buy into his brand of protection. The only thing Jacob excels at with regards to me, is making me feel worthless."

Jacob blinked back tears at this blatant hostility from his beloved. Even worse was knowing he was the reason behind her icy exterior. "Lilly—"

The word left his lips before his brain had time to rein it back in and the incredulous glare from his sister summed up the stupidity of his action.

"Janie, am I on speakerphone?" Lilly growled, her voice quivering with intensity.

"Um—" Poor Janie, she was going to get the brunt of this mess.

"Take me off speakerphone. *Now.*"

The disgust and anger in Lilly's demand was evident and Janie wasted no time scooping up the phone and exiting the trailer to finish the conversation.

"I just keep fucking up, don't I?" Jacob agonized, letting loose with a quick jab to the wooden table in front of him.

"Breaking the furniture isn't going to help," Roger admonished, sending him a knowing look.

"Thanks for reminding me…after the fact," Jacob scowled, shaking his hand. That would leave a mark. The table was, not surprisingly, fully intact. The only saving grace was he had enough alcohol on board to not feel the full extent of the pain…yet.

Janie walked back in, her mouth a thin, angry line. "Well, that was fun. Thanks Jacob, I'm beginning to understand how Lilly feels being thrown under the bus."

Jacob stood and wrapped his arms about his sister. "I'm so sorry Lil Bit, I honestly didn't realize I said her name aloud. It just broke me, hearing how she thinks she's worthless. I hope she isn't too angry with you."

"I'm not her favorite person right now, but I'll mend fences later. Give her some time to calm down and process everything." Janie released a sigh before returning Jacob's hug. "I know you're hurting, Jacob. It's an awful situation." She pulled back and caught sight of Jacob's swelling digits. "What in hell did you do?"

"Compounded an already horrendous morning," Jacob muttered, rubbing his injured paw. "This pain is nothing. Knowing how much Lilly despises me, that's more than I can handle."

Janie turned on the tap and pulled Jacob's injured hand under the cold water. "She doesn't despise you, but her heart's been smashed into a million pieces. You fucked up big time, whether you intended it or not, and it's going to take some time for her to even consider forgiving you."

"Like we said, you get the paternity test, and we'll work on Lilly." Roger helped his friend to his feet. "For now, Miriam said we have the day to get you back to rights. First shower, shave and clean clothes. Then a diet which doesn't consist of alcohol and some sleep in a room where Victoria can't find you."

"Victoria isn't here," Jacob mumbled.

"Trust me, she will be soon. Especially when she realizes we've flown here to speak with you."

"How am I going to convince her to do the test?" Jacob inquired. "She's crafty, she won't make it easy."

"Simple," Roger replied. "She wants to play a game? Up the ante. Tell her she gets the test, or you'll let it slip to the media that she's been unfaithful and you're questioning paternity. If *she* doesn't want to look like a harlot, she'll agree."

Jacob smirked. "Let's hope so. But what about Lilly?"

"I told you, let me and Janie handle it—"

"I mean her safety. Victoria dropped hints that she might hurt my angel. I can't just let that threat slide."

"Hire an assassin?" Janie volunteered, shrugging and letting loose a chuckle. "It was a joke…kind of."

Roger sighed, shaking his head at Janie's poor attempt at humor. "She's crazy, but I doubt she's reached that level of insanity. She figured a veiled threat would coerce you into playing along, and she was right."

Jacob nodded his agreement, but he wasn't so sure. He didn't know where Victoria drew the line anymore.

"Jacob, we'll keep an eye on Lilly." Roger threw an arm around his friend's shoulder. "Mate, you need a shower immediately. I'm getting drunk off your fumes."

"Sod off, Roger."

Roger chuckled, garnering a sick amusement at his friend's dilapidated state. "I know it's not the best time, but I must offer my congratulations."

"Are you kidding me?" Jacob hissed in response.

Roger held up his hands in mock surrender. "Easy. I meant, congratulations on landing the role in Milieu of Madness. The part of your dreams, right?"

Jacob grunted. "I have to talk to Albert. I've decided not to take the role. I don't want anything Victoria has to offer, not after what she did to me…and Lilly."

Janie wrapped her arm around her brother's waist. "You should write Lilly love letters, like they used to do before everything went electronic."

Jacob gave her a small, sad smile. "If only that would work."

"She won't speak to you, so it doesn't leave many options, does it? If you have things you want to say, I suggest you consider my idea."

"I'll consider any idea that ends with her not hating me, although I hate myself enough for the both of us." He contemplated the idea further. "You think it could help the situation?"

Roger clapped his friend's shoulder. "Chin up mate, the war isn't over yet. You lost a momentous battle, now it's time to regroup with a new plan of action."

"Thanks, Napoleon," Jacob grumbled.

"You know Napoleon wasn't actually short? All a farce. He was round as a penguin but definitely average height."

"For a penguin?" Janie added.

Jacob couldn't hold back the smile as it spread across his face. His heart was smashed beyond recognition, but perhaps with the help of his family and friends, he might still win back his freedom. Winning back Lilly, however, was an entirely different matter.

Lilly

"Whiskey, neat," Lilly mumbled to the server, forcing a smile that made her face want to crack.

"Would you like a menu?"

Lilly shook her head.

"Anyone else joining you?"

The server's questions were innocent, but they only compounded Lilly's loneliness. "Nope, just me."

"No problem, miss. It'll be just a moment."

A well-known blues song blasted through the pub speakers, the singer crooning about betrayal and broken vows. Christ, it seemed unhappiness followed her like a shadow. She normally drowned her sorrows safely within the confines of her cottage, but after hearing Jacob's voice earlier that day, she knew she wouldn't make it that far.

It was ludicrous. The man only uttered one word, her name, and yet it turned her inside out. Those two syllables dripped with such longing that Lilly felt it thousands of kilometers away.

But her mind took control as soon as she realized she was on speakerphone, her private pain echoing out for all gathered around the phone to hear. She let Janie have it once she realized that Jacob could hear her statements, and her friend was so morosely sorry that Lilly was finding it difficult to remain angry.

Janie was a dear friend, but she was also the sister of the enemy—the enemy of her heart and soul—and Lilly didn't know how that would ultimately play out with their friendship. Blood was thicker than water, except in Lilly's case. Lilly's only family *was* her friends and now she felt more alone than ever before.

Leaving New York eight months earlier was a cakewalk compared to the hell she was currently enduring.

"Mind if I join you?"

Lilly looked up to see Enrique, his hands gripping the edge of the table, his brow creased with concern.

"I'm afraid I'm terrible company at this point," Lilly responded, "but if you want to risk it, have a seat."

"I'll take my chances." He flagged the server and ordered a drink before sliding into the booth and turning his dark gaze to Lilly. "I've wanted to call you, or stop by—"

"Why?" Lilly interjected, chewing her lip as she ripped tiny pieces off the edge of her napkin. "To tell me you knew this would happen? To remind me what a fool I am for believing him? Don't bother, I already know I'm a fool. I don't need your help." The tears, reined in so tightly, slid down her cheeks.

Enrique sighed, running his hand through his hair. "I wanted to apologize."

Her eyes widened like saucers. This was an unexpected turn in the conversation. "Why? What did you do?"

"I behaved like a jealous asshole. It doesn't matter if my words were true or not, I should have handled the situation differently. I should have been kinder to you, more understanding of your feelings."

Lilly wiped her tears with her palm, offering a sad smile to her friend. "Thank you, but no apology is necessary. You were trying to protect me—"

Enrique scoffed. "Don't give me that much credit. I was angry because you didn't want me, and I damn well didn't want you with him. I hated Jacob for the hold he had on you and the way he treated you when all I wanted was a chance—"

Lilly's head throbbed, she was too battle weary to go another round with the surgeon. "Enrique—"

"Let me finish. You remember the argument we all had at your house the morning after the attack?"

Lilly nodded.

"When you told me that you were in love with him, I was so furious that I went home and kicked a hole in my wall—right through the drywall. And for a brief moment, I felt vindicated when he pulled that stunt on live television. But that vindication was short-lived because I realized an amazing woman was crushed by his actions. And that, crushed me."

Lilly studied her whiskey, unable to come up with a single retort. She wasn't certain at this point which hurt worse—that Jacob had ripped her dreams to shreds or the fact that Enrique derived some sick sense of satisfaction from her pain.

Enrique shifted in his seat, his fingers drumming the tabletop. "Ben and Sabina wanted me to come with them to your house the day the press release aired, but I thought I should give you space, and give myself space to figure out what the hell to say to you."

She couldn't stare at her whiskey forever, the answers weren't hiding in the bottom of the damn glass. Raising her tear-stained face to him, Lilly choked out, "You're a bastard for gleaning any happiness from my torment."

Enrique focused his dark eyes on the wall, a muscle in his jaw twitching. "I know," he mumbled.

Lilly held his chin, directing his gaze back to hers. "I didn't catch that."

He clasped her hand, giving it a warm squeeze. "I was a complete and utter jerk. You never deserved any of this pain and I am so sorry that I believed, for one second, that you did."

She let her hand drop back to the table. This man knew how to apologize—and mean every syllable. Jacob could take a lesson or two from Enrique. "I've missed you. You're my friend and I need my friends now more than ever."

"Oh Lilly, I never wanted to be your friend—"

A fresh batch of tears surfaced. "Wonderful," Lilly choked.

"What I mean is that I wanted more from you, but the timing was never right, and the truth is that you've been in love with Jacob since the day you met that maniacal moron. I saw it, everyone saw it."

Everyone indeed. It seemed the whole world was parlay to her dance with unrequited love. "Doesn't matter, Jacob doesn't love me back."

Enrique grasped her hands again. "As much as it pains me to admit this, Jacob loves you."

"Oh right, his affections are totally obvious considering recent events." Lilly sniffed before downing a swallow of whiskey.

"They were pretty damn apparent the day I berated him at your house. It was written all over his face—the man worshipped you—and he was willing to take me out if I stood in his way. I don't know what the fuck happened or why he and Victoria pulled that stunt at the press release, but I know he loves you." A pause, the silence filled only with the sounds of yet another tragic love song and Enrique's tapping fingers. "Have you spoken to him?"

Lilly shook her head. "I blocked his number. I have nothing to say to him."

"Don't you want answers?"

Now the tears fell in earnest, she was a sobbing mess. "No, I don't! I don't want to know why he felt he had to hurt me in such a cold and calculating manner. We all think the truth makes things better, but the reality is that the truth hurts...and I've hurt enough for one lifetime." She slugged back her whiskey, feeling the burn trickle down her throat. "I was a fool, I should have listened to you."

"You were in love, love makes fools of us all."

"Fuck, now you sound like Jacob."

"Heaven forbid," Enrique scoffed, thanking the waitress as she brought a refill before leaning against the seat and studying Lilly. "How are you holding up?"

Lilly released a forced laugh. "Oh, I'm grand. Can't you tell?"

"Seriously."

She shrugged. "I'm existing, which all things considered, is pretty damn impressive. Work, animal shelter and home. That's my life now."

"Sabina told me that you've refused to go out, even for a movie or coffee."

"I told you earlier, I'm not good company. I'm best left by myself, to my own devices."

"That's a load of garbage. You have to rejoin the living sometime, Lilly." The young surgeon cleared his throat. "Why don't you take a vacation? Get out of London for a while. Go get laid."

Lilly's eyebrows rose at his statement. "Are you offering?"

Enrique chuckled. "Afraid not. I'm no longer a single man."

Lilly brow quirked, a look of surprise crossing her face. "Really? Have you finally caved and given Emma a second chance?"

"No, I ended things with Emma. She cried for all of a minute before consoling herself in the arms of another barrister."

"Wow."

"It's fine, I'd been over Emma for ages. I'm actually dating a nurse from the hospital. She's fabulous and I never saw her coming...now I can't imagine not being with this woman."

Lilly pondered his words. Who in the world was he dating? St. Luke wasn't that large, she must know her. "Are you going to tell me, or do I have to guess?"

"Guessing is more fun for me." He let loose with a hearty laugh at Lilly's scowl. "You know her, quite well, actually."

Lilly chewed her lip, running over the names of the pretty young nurses on the floors. *Who the heck could it*—Lilly's jaw dropped. "You're *the guy*! The one that made Sabina all giddy and giggly." When Enrique nodded, she chuckled. "That's absolutely fabulous. Good for you! She's an amazing woman."

"That she is, but we hesitated to tell you."

"Why?"

A repentant look crossed Enrique's face. "Remember I said I never saw her coming? It happened right after your attack, when I discovered Jacob had flown back here to rescue you. I knew he was going to propose, and I knew you were going to say yes. So, I was drowning my sorrows and asked Sabina to join me. One drink led to another and one thing led to another...I'll let you fill in the blanks. Sabina was convinced it was nothing more on my end than drunken sex—some roundabout way of getting even with Jacob—but I knew immediately that wasn't the case. I realized how very much I enjoyed her. So, I asked her to dinner and during that meal, I told her I wanted more than drunken sex. Lucky for me, so did she."

"Classic; I love that story so much. Mazel Tov." Lilly squeezed his hand. "You look so happy when you talk about Sabina."

"I am extremely happy. It's totally unexpected."

"The best things always are." Lilly grinned, biting her lip. "Where is my darling friend, anyway?"

"She's with her daughter. I think she was terrified of your reaction."

"Tell her I'm thrilled, and I expect to see both of you together soon."

Lilly and Enrique left the bar an hour later, his hug a welcome respite after the last couple weeks of lonely nights.

She arrived home and sent Sabina a text, congratulating her on her new relationship. It lightened her spirit to know that people she loved were experiencing happiness, even if she was never to be that lucky.

She spent the next hour soaking in the tub, sipping whiskey and ruminating over recent events. Enrique was right, she did need to rejoin the land of the living...even if she would be perfectly content to stay at home, hidden under a blanket.

She settled on the couch and grabbed her phone. Janie had left countless texts and voicemail messages during the last couple weeks, but Lilly had ignored them all. This afternoon was the first time she had spoken with her friend and her emotions were still swirling from their earlier argument.

Another voicemail from Janie. What could she want this time? "Lilly, please call me back. I have something important to tell you. It's about Elizabeth."

Lilly's blood ran cold. Was something wrong with Janie's daughter? She dialed her friend immediately.

"Lilly! I'm so glad you called!" Janie exclaimed.

"What's wrong with Elizabeth? Is she okay?"

"I never said there was anything *wrong* with her. She misses you, we all do."

Lilly glared at the phone. "So that bit about Elizabeth was a strategic maneuver on your part?"

"I didn't want to grovel via text or voicemail message, so I had to coerce

16

you onto the phone somehow," Janie grumbled.

Lilly chuckled despite herself. It was impossible to stay mad at this woman, her heart was always in the right place. "Well played."

"Are you still angry with me?"

What was the point? It wasn't Janie's fault that Jacob broke her heart. Hearts got broken every day, Lilly was no exception. "I suppose not."

Janie's sigh of relief was audible. "Oh good, I was so afraid I'd lost my friend. Even before today. You just shut me out."

"I'm sorry I haven't returned any of your calls. I needed to get my head clear...or clearer anyway."

"I understand why you sought solitude, but I need you to remember that I love you and I'm here for you."

"I appreciate that, Janie."

"Who are you talking to, Lil Bit?"

Lilly's heart raced when she heard his voice through the phone. It was Jacob. His voice for the second time that day. The thumping in her chest continued—apparently no one had given that organ the memo that the man was a diabolical cad.

"Give me a moment, Lilly," Janie stammered.

The voices became muffled and Lilly surmised that Janie had covered the receiver. No matter, it gave her a moment to calm herself before her heart burst out of her damn chest.

"Lilly? Are you there?" Janie asked. "Sorry about that interruption, I'm on the balcony now. I told him not to interrupt me, but you know how big brothers are..."

"Actually, I don't." It took everything in Lilly's being to force those three words from her throat. Was she being toyed with again? Was this a repeat of earlier?

"They're a pain in the ass. Never do as they're told."

"Why do keep calling me from Santorini? I'm sure you and your brother are busy...there must be a ton to discuss with his upcoming...nuptials." The last word was strangled as Lilly forced it past her lips.

"I wanted to speak with you about those supposed nuptials."

Who knew you could feel a punch in the gut without any physical contact? Lilly tried to breathe, but the oxygen just couldn't find its way to her lungs. She didn't know if she wanted to hurl something, vomit or break down into a puddle of tears.

"Lilly, are you there?"

Lilly's mind screamed, *why would you call me to discuss the upcoming marriage of the love of my life...to someone else? How much more torture can I handle?* Her mouth managed two words. "I'm here."

"Roger and I flew down here to find out what the hell was going on, to get answers. Lilly, I need to explain the situation to you. There's so much that none of us knew—"

"No." Lilly cut off Janie's statement. "I don't want to hear it. I don't care what his reasons were."

"Lilly, it's really complicated—"

"Is that your family's excuse for when people do fucked up things? Your brother used that term a myriad of times with me." Lilly paced the rug, willing her anger to settle. "This was a bad idea. I knew I shouldn't have returned your call—"

"Hey! I'm *your* friend too. I've missed you, Lilly. I've been worried sick about you. We all have."

Lilly wiped away the tears, but it was pointless, there were buckets more where those came from. "I can't do this, Janie."

"Please don't hang up," Janie implored.

"One condition. Can we not mention Jacob?"

"I have to relay what I've learned and then, if you never want to mention Jacob again, I understand. But please, you need to hear this."

A deep exhalation sounded from Lilly's chest. She could do this, she could survive this situation. "Go ahead."

"I was so angry at my brother that I couldn't see straight when I landed in Santorini. I was all set to beat him about the head and neck with a blunt instrument—so was Roger—until we saw him. He's not doing well. That's an understatement. He's a bloody disaster."

"I don't care!" Lilly choked out, her voice cracking. "I'm so fucking tired of hearing about poor Jacob and how complex his life is and how I need to understand! He broke my heart—on international television—and now I'm supposed to feel sorry for *him*? No. Way. In. Hell." Her entire body shook with the force of her narrative.

"It's not what you think. This whole debacle is *not* Jacob's fault. He was trying to protect you—"

"You've got to be kidding me. I'm not listening to any more of this, Janie. I'm clean out of love and understanding, so if you don't have anything else to say..."

Silence echoed out loud as thunder from the other end of the phone.

"That's what I thought. I have to go," Lilly mumbled, wiping the tears from her face.

18

"He worships you, Lilly. He loves you more than life itself," Janie whispered, so low Lilly could barely understand the words.

"No, he doesn't. If he did, he'd be here." Lilly disconnected the call before throwing her phone across the room and collapsing onto the bed.

CHAPTER TWO

Jacob

"I wondered what you were doing in here."

Jacob turned to see Miriam strolling down the shop aisle, a curious grin across her face. "Hey there."

"This store is amazing. How did you find it?"

The store *was* amazing. It was tiny, hidden down a narrow alleyway, the door blending into the stucco. But once you found the door—if you found the door—inside was a magical blend of local jewelry and artisan crafts.

Jacob returned his attention to the bracelet in his hand. It was a dainty white gold chain with turquoise stones throughout.

Miriam glanced at the bracelet and cleared her throat. "Which special lady is that for?"

He swallowed, willing back his emotions. "There's only one special lady."

"Have you and Lilly reconciled? That's fantastic. I'm shocked but—"

"No," Jacob cut her off, "we haven't. She's not speaking to me, not that I blame her."

Miriam clicked her tongue against her teeth. "Roger and Janie filled me in on the situation. I'm sorry I was so hard-hearted in the days immediately following the press release. I was so angry at you—"

"You had every right to be. I hate myself."

"I really believed you and Victoria had reconciled, and I wanted to bash your skulls together for being so ridiculously stupid."

Jacob nodded, hoping this wasn't supposed to be a pep talk.

"I should have known that she cornered you. Roger mentioned that she threatened Lilly?"

Another nod. "Yep. Indirectly of course, because she's as devious as she is diabolical. She knew I'd cave once she intimated harm might befall Lilly."

"Would you like to have dinner?"

It was the first time in weeks that Miriam had invited him to dinner, hell it had been days since she'd said more than two sentences to him. "I'd like that. I've been…ordering room service."

"Is that code for drinking your dinner?"

"Pretty much."

"How about we change it up a bit? Introduce some actual food into your diet?"

"I don't have much of an appetite."

"Well, something is better than nothing." Miriam linked arms with Jacob, squeezing his arm. "Are you buying that?" She indicated the bracelet.

"I send Lilly something every day. A letter or card and some token of affection. I've been doing it for a week now."

"She hasn't responded, has she?" Miriam sighed when Jacob shook his head. "Come on, let's go eat. We can chat some more. I've missed my role as therapist."

"I don't think there's a therapist in the world who can fix this disaster," Jacob lamented.

"Always the optimist, aren't you?"

Jacob released a dry chuckle. "It's my trademark."

"Ha! Here I thought humble self-deprecation was your motto."

The friends strolled to a local restaurant and found a seat overlooking the ocean. As Miriam chattered on about filming, Jacob's gaze focused on the blue Aegean.

Even though Lilly had never set foot on Santorini, he saw her everywhere. He carried her mental image like a security blanket; without his constant memory reel of his angel, he would cease to function.

"Are you hearing a word I'm saying?" Miriam inquired.

Jacob startled back to the present, shooting Miriam a sheepish grin. "I'm sorry. I was just thinking…"

"About Lilly." It was a statement, not a question.

"Always about Lilly."

"So, you're going to leave it like this, then?"

"Like what?"

"You and Lilly living separate and miserable lives."

Jacob ran his hand over the back of his head. "I don't *want* to, but I don't see many options here. I did what I did to protect Lilly, but it doesn't matter, she hates me, regardless of my reason."

"No, she doesn't." Miriam leaned back, a smirk on her face. "Here I thought I was making headway with my best pupil."

"What the hell are you talking about, Miriam?"

"Remember the last time you fucked up and had to fight to get her back?"

"How can I forget? Yet another of my shining moments."

"Hey, you stepped up to the plate and fought…and you won."

"It's different this time."

"Yes, it is, this time you actually weren't the asshole. She only thinks

21

you're the asshole."

"Is that supposed to make me feel better?"

Miriam nodded. "Absolutely. When the truth comes out, as it always does, and emotions have settled, Lilly will know you only hurt her to save her. And if she loves you one iota as much as you love her, she'll run back to your arms."

Her words woke up Jacob's heart with an emotion he hadn't felt in weeks—hope. "You really think so?"

"I do. The cards and gifts are a nice touch, but the truth will be the only thing that can truly undo the damage."

"I miss her so much, Miriam," Jacob whispered, taking in a shaky breath. "All I want is to spend my life making her happy…all I want is that chance."

"Best way to ensure that outcome is to get things straightened out with Victoria. Avoid dramatics and stifle your anger, righteous though it may be. You don't need Victoria causing any more problems."

"What do you suggest? Sleeping with the enemy?"

"God no! But berating her will only make her more dangerous…to you and Lilly. Best to err on the side of caution with that one."

What in the world was his director driving at? "So, I shouldn't demand the paternity test?"

"Oh, hell yes, and be firm about your demands surrounding it. But do it with your good old English charm. I know you can be charming. I've seen it… once or twice."

Jacob walked Miriam to her room a couple hours later. The dinner had been a welcome distraction, but he needed to ready Lilly's package for the post tomorrow.

He stepped off the elevator and stopped dead in his tracks. A settee sat against a wall in the corridor, but Jacob surmised no one ever sat in the thing, with the exception of the stray drunk teenager who'd forgotten which room belonged to them. He was wrong.

Victoria perched on the edge of the cushion, wearing a patterned sundress and demure expression, looking every bit like innocence lost. *What a crock.*

He readied himself with a biting comment, but Miriam's advice echoed in his mind. Jacob drew in a steadying breath, pulling out his key card and walking to his door. Perhaps if he ignored the problem, she would go away.

Perhaps not.

Victoria wasted no time closing the gap between them. "There was a horrible smell at my hotel. I couldn't stay there. I hoped you might—"

"No way in hell, Victoria."

"But—"

Jacob leaned his forehead against the door, releasing a resigned sigh. "Isn't there anyone in all of Santorini whose door you could darken but mine? Why are you here anyway? Another convenient video shoot?"

"No, I came to see you. I may not be your favorite person at the moment, but you are the father of my child."

"That is yet to be determined."

The door of the suite across the hall cracked open, and Jacob saw two beady eyes surveying the scene. Their conversation was drawing attention and Jacob had enough eyes on him.

Pushing open the door, Jacob snapped, "Get inside." Once his suite door was safely shut to the outside world, he whirled to face his ex, his eyes ablaze. "What are you doing here?"

Victoria glanced around the suite, avoiding his gaze. "Where's Roger and Janie? I expected to run into them on this beautiful island paradise."

"They returned to London a few days ago, but you know that already, don't you?" He crossed his arms and stared holes into Victoria's visage. "I repeat, what are you doing here?"

Victoria didn't bother with a syrupy act as she jutted out her chin. "You won't return my phone calls—"

"I have *nothing* to say to you. You ruined my life." *So much for not letting my anger get the best of me.*

"But—"

Jacob held up his hand. He was done with this vixen's propensity to bend the truth to suit her needs. "No. I've told you several times that I want a paternity test. Any other details will be handled through our attorneys."

"Is it really healthy for our child to be born into such contention?"

"Our child? I don't even know if it's my child! You fucked half of Hollywood, most of them during our relationship!" He clenched his fists, willing his rising fury down before he threw something heavy in her direction. "I want you to submit to a blood test to determine paternity."

Jacob noted the color drain from Victoria's cheeks. "I told you, there's dangers with that type of testing—"

"No, I'm not asking for an amniocentesis, just a vial of blood."

Any shock was quickly swept behind her well-practiced smile. "I can only imagine where you learned that piece of information…someone in the medical field, I surmise. I suppose I can look into the details…"

"If you don't then I won't have anything to do with you—or your child."

"Won't that play out well in the rag mags? Jacob Edmonton deserts his pregnant girlfriend—"

"You're not my girlfriend! You'll never be anything to me but a mistake," Jacob thundered, his fists clenching and unclenching. "If you agree to the blood test and the child is mine, I will be an active part of their life. Otherwise, there's the door. Don't let it hit your ass on the way out."

Victoria held up one hand. "I can see the headlines now—"

"That's it. Get out."

Victoria sighed and crossed her arms across her chest. "I want us to be cordial with each other, there's no need for anger—"

"You should have thought of that before you ripped away the only thing that matters to me."

Her eyes narrowed as drummed her nails against the wood credenza. "I assume you and Lilly are no longer in contact?"

God damn it, if she wasn't a woman. "You *assume* correctly. Another correct assumption is that you're the cause."

"I doubt it would have worked out regardless. You're so different."

"Not another word about my Lilly," Jacob growled.

Victoria paused for a beat, her tongue circling her red lips like a lion about to devour its prey. "I don't think she's *your* Lilly any longer."

His patience was at an end, if he stayed near Victoria much longer, he wouldn't be responsible for his actions. "I will ask you one last time, what do you want?"

But Victoria acted as if she hadn't heard him, her eyes examining her nails. "I hear she's become quite withdrawn, not doing anything beyond work."

"Victoria." The low tone rolled out of his throat, her final warning. He marched the two steps to the suite door, this conversation was over. As his hand gripped the knob, a wave of foreboding washed over him. How the hell did Victoria know anything about Lilly? Was she scoping out his angel, ensuring that she stayed far away from Jacob? "What did you say about Lilly?"

Victoria's green eyes flitted to Jacob's face as a small chuckle fell from her mouth. "What? I've been worried about her state of mind with all the recent events."

What a load of bollocks. Jacob stalked over to her, leaning his face within a few centimeters of Victoria. "If you touch one hair on my beloved's head—"

"You'll what?" Victoria wasn't backing down either. "You'll do nothing, just like every other time."

The air was turning noxious as Jacob struggled to retain any semblance of sanity. His mind whirled at Victoria's inferred threat. It didn't matter that he had let the love of his life go, she still wasn't safe from this maniac. "Stay away from her, she has nothing to do with our situation. You don't want her—"

"But you do, don't you Jacob?"

Want her? He didn't want Lilly. He craved her, he adored her, he worshiped her. Want didn't come remotely close to describing his level of devotion. He scrubbed his face with his hands. Victoria was always one step ahead. She knew he would play her game so long as Lilly was vulnerable to her plots.

Victoria let out a sigh. "That's what I thought and that is unacceptable to me."

"I'll go to the police, Victoria. I won't let you hurt her."

Victoria's green eyes widened in mock innocence. "When did I ever say I was going to hurt her? Jeez, Jacob, I'm not a monster. Perhaps I'm just hormonal…or heartbroken that the man I love is denying his only child."

She was indeed a psychopath. A brilliant, insane psychopath. She'd thought of everything. No matter what path he took, she was ready and waiting with a counterstrike. "What the fuck is wrong with you?" Jacob hissed.

"I want you…and I want you to give us another chance. We could be really great together—"

"No way in hell."

Unfazed, Victoria switched gears. "When do you start filming Milieu of Madness?"

Now the bitch was making small talk? "None of your business. My life is none of your business."

She ran one sharpened nail down his cheek. "That's where you're wrong. Your life is entirely my business and thanks to our child here, it always will be." She pressed her lips against his, smirking when he recoiled. "I hoped you would have forgiven me by now, but I see that isn't the case. I'll give you a bit more time but remember, there's a lot riding on your behavior. It would much easier to simply give us another go—"

"Get. Out. Now." Jacob didn't move, he couldn't. If he did, he might be led away in handcuffs.

"I'll leave, for now. But darling, I do hope you'll reconsider your stance on our reconciliation." Victoria cupped his crotch, giving it a firm squeeze before strolling out of the trailer.

The door had barely shut when Jacob grabbed his phone and called his manager. He had an urgent request he needed filled.

After the call, Jacob opted for a second dinner, one consisting of whiskey and a glass. He'd lost his appetite for anything else.

He dialed his sister, hopeful that she had seen Lilly in the days since she returned to London. He knew their phone conversation the other night had been anything but successful, but perhaps a few extra days had softened Lilly's stance.

"Jakey, how are you?" Janie's voice bubbled with concern.

"Don't ask."

"Are you drinking?"

Jacob gulped back a swig of whiskey. "Yep, but I've made strides forward. I'm sober on set now. I wait to consume my pint of whiskey until after we wrap for the day."

"Jakey—"

"Have you spoken to Lilly?"

Her silence was the only answer he needed, and he hung his head as the throbbing returned.

"Janie?"

"I've called her several times, but she hasn't returned my calls. I know you're desperate to speak to her, but she isn't even letting me tell her the full story. She's so wounded from all of this and I don't know when she's going to be willing to talk to you."

Jacob felt the claws of desperation. He couldn't breathe without Lilly. "What if I fly to London—"

"Jacob, stop," Janie interrupted. "She won't see you. Hell, she won't even see me."

His heart shredded a bit more at the idea of Lilly pulling away from the people she loved, knowing he was the cause of her self-inflicted seclusion. "Remember how you told me to write Lilly love letters? There's this little row of stores and they have the most beautiful handmade jewelry and trinkets. I write her a letter and send her one of the items every day."

"That's really thoughtful, Jakey."

It wasn't thoughtful, it was a desperate ploy for contact—and he knew it. "Do you think she's even opening them?"

"I can't answer that, but I doubt it."

Jacob collapsed into a chair, catching sight of his reflection in the mirror. He looked haggard—dark circles rimmed his blue eyes, new frown lines marched around his mouth, his clothes hung off him. He'd aged a decade in three weeks. "I don't want to stop sending the gifts, because at least she knows I'm thinking of her. I can't do this, Janie. I can't go on without her."

"Have you spoken with Victoria at all? Any progress there?"

"She was waiting for me outside my suite."

"What the hell did she want?"

Jacob kicked back some more whiskey. "She wanted to apologize for her bad behavior. What do you think she wanted? She wanted to reconcile, seemed shocked that I didn't take her up on the offer."

"Has she granted you a paternity test?"

"Not yet, she claims she'll look into the blood test…it's all a load of crap."

Janie released a loud sigh. "She's not still there, is she?"

"Are you insane?"

"Just checking. You've fallen into her web too many times in the past."

"Not this time. Lilly is the only thing I care about, without her, nothing means anything." He downed the remaining contents of his glass, realizing it didn't burn him anymore. *Huh, at least there was one positive.* "I just hired a security team for her."

"Really? Do you think she's in danger? From Victoria?"

Jacob rubbed a hand over his eyes. Christ, his head pounded. "Victoria knew Lilly's whereabouts, admitted to keeping tabs on her. I wouldn't put it past her, so I hired a team. I have to keep Lilly safe, she's so tiny—"

"Jakey." Janie's nickname resonated with feeling, wrapping around him like an embrace.

"It's the only thing I can do for her right now. And I'll move heaven and hell to do that." Jacob felt the anguish rising again. "I have to go, Janie."

He hung up the phone and poured another glass of alcohol.

Lilly

he postman is going to expect a ridiculous Christmas gift this year, Lilly thought as she pulled two boxes from her mail. Packages and envelopes arrived daily—often more than one—all postmarked from Greece.

Lilly placed these packages with the rest of the gifts in an empty laundry basket shoved in an unused closet in the living room. Initially, she considered throwing them in the garbage, but her heart screamed in protest, and over the last several weeks she stopped tossing the packages with such contempt and began placing them gently in the now overflowing basket.

An urgent knocking brought Lilly back to the present and she opened the door, smiling at Janie and Elizabeth on the stoop.

"Well, you are still amongst the living." Janie offered up a smirk before embracing her friend.

"I suppose one could call it that," Lilly murmured, making way for them to enter the cottage. "To what do I owe the pleasure of your company?"

"We missed you and wanted to see if you were up for a nice dinner. I refuse to let you remain a recluse any longer." Janie embraced Lilly. "Nice haircut."

Lilly ran her hand through her dark hair, recently cut into a short bob. "You know what they say, get a haircut after a breakup. Besides, I've no interest in looking attractive."

Janie smiled as she fingered Lilly's short strands. "You failed miserably there, then, you look like a sex goddess, as always. Damn, if my brother saw you now—"

"Jacob would hate it, I've no doubt, not that it matters."

Janie laughed. "Hardly. He'd approve all right and you look gorgeous."

Lilly felt her cheeks flame at the notion that Jacob might find her more attractive now than with her long, flowing hair. "I'm sure you didn't come here to talk about Jacob."

"Yes and no. I missed my friend and since it was apparent you weren't going to be social, I came to fetch you. Jacob called right before I left and pleaded with me to come speak with you."

"What about?" Damn, she sucked at appearing disinterested.

"He asked if you had gotten your packages, which I assume is the basket resembling Santa's sleigh on Christmas Eve?" She motioned to Lilly's stash peeking out from the partially open closet door. "He figured you hadn't opened any of them, but there was one that needed immediate attention."

Lilly motioned to the basket, feeling a niggling sadness that his request was so trite. "Which one?"

Janie giggled. "No idea."

"Fine, you got me. What do you say to wine, takeout and Uncle Jacob letter exploration?" Lilly asked, the last part aimed at Elizabeth, who dissolved in a fit of giggles when Lilly tickled her foot.

The women chuckled as Lilly hauled the basket from the closet, placing it on the floor by the sofa.

"Admit it, you missed us." Janie offered up a smile, wrapping her arms around her friend.

"I did. It's been lonely the last several weeks."

"Lilly, you were in a self-imposed exile! I've asked you to hang out at least fifty times and every time was a definitive no, if you even bothered to answer the call."

"So, I've been antisocial. Time to rejoin society, I suppose." Lilly smiled, enjoying the camaraderie. It was a departure from her strict focus on work and charity the last several weeks. Her dedication to her cause was paying off, a great deal of funds had been raised, and it looked like there was a parcel of land that would work perfectly for the sanctuary.

But at night, as she lay alone in bed, her brief courtship with Jacob played on a loop in her mind. Lilly knew eventually it would become less painful, but she wondered if she could survive that long.

A few hours later with full bellies and a few glasses of wine apiece, Lilly and Janie had opened the majority of the packages, while Elizabeth had passed out an hour earlier from all the excitement. Scattered across the coffee table was several pieces of jewelry, local artwork, pottery and all manner of crystals. Each piece was lovingly wrapped, and a card or letter accompanied every package.

Lilly wasn't sure if it was the wine, his letters or her loneliness, but she felt tempted to call Jacob and forget the debacle of the press release.

Thankfully, her head still maintained control of the situation, though her heart was gaining momentum.

Janie cooed from the armchair, and Lilly looked at her expectantly. "I had no idea my brother was such a romantic sap, that bastard has got me crying."

"He's very talented, in more one ways than one." Lilly attempted to look absorbed by the wine glass, but it was futile.

29

"Okay, I don't need to know that much about my brother." Janie tossed the letter in her lap. "Here, read that, it's beautiful."

"I really don't care to—"

"You absolutely do care, now read it." Janie pulled a blanket over Elizabeth's sleeping form.

Lilly glanced at the letter and began to toss it back onto the table, but a glare from Janie made her refocus on the words.

'I wish there were a term to describe what you mean to me. Beloved is the closest word in the English language, but it can't begin to encompass all that you are in my heart. You are the goddess that lit up my soul and breathed life into my body. You don't know the strength you possess when you smile. I still remember the first moment I saw you, although I'm sure you're not aware of it. You had yet to introduce yourself but when I saw you across that waiting room, and you smiled, I was struck. I knew things were right with the world.

You questioned why I loved you or how it was possible, what you failed to ask was how was it not possible? You are irreplaceable in every way, from the way you kissed me (which I yearn for) to your dedication and unbridled love for those around you. I see you in everything—every sunrise, each rainy night, the dew on the flowers in the morning. You are still with me, and I feel your presence as strongly as though you stood next to me. It is the only thing that keeps me going, adoring you from afar.

Until this nightmarish situation is resolved, I am dutiful for I know you would expect no less of me and I strive daily to be worthy of you. You live on a higher plane that we mortals strive to reach, your capacity for love and forgiveness diffuses through every pore on this planet. I doubt ever to achieve that height.

Perhaps my actions are unforgivable, but please understand I did what I had to do to protect you. I acted out of love. I would rather spend the rest of my days in agony and know you are safe; than to know harm befell you because of an impetuous decision at the press release. I tore my own heart apart that day, and the pieces have scattered to the winds. The only one who can collect them again is you.

You're likely wondering what is in the box marked 'Open Immediately'. It's a Roman Orchid. I've never seen this species before, and despite its delicate appearance its strength and tenacity are beyond measure. It reminds me of your warrior spirit encased in the visage of an angel. I know your love of all living things will result in you not throwing it against a wall but setting it somewhere in your home. Perhaps when you look at it, you might feel some of the love I send to you every moment.

'En sa beauté gît ma mort et ma vie.' The words aren't mine, but his longing echoes my heart, and I pray one day you might believe me.'

Lilly realized she was crying when she noticed the teardrops on the paper. "I remember that last line. He quoted it during our day in the English gardens, but he never told me what it meant."

Janie took the letter and typed the quote into her phone. "This is why I love the internet." She found the translation and gasped, her hand over her mouth.

"What does it mean?"

"In her beauty resides my death and my life." Janie handed Lilly the phone for confirmation.

Tears welled up again, but she blinked them back. "What am I supposed to do, Janie? What does Jacob want from me?"

"He wants you to love him."

"This was never about my ability to love him, and he knows that. This has always been about the fact that when Victoria wants him, I'm tossed like yesterday's garbage. I don't understand! I really believed Jacob loved me—the house, the proposal, wanting to have a baby—" Lilly broke off, tears running down her cheeks.

"He does love you. He worships you!" Janie hugged her friend. "Look around you, what little free time he has is spent writing you or buying gifts—"

"I don't want the damn gifts."

"I know," Janie said, wiping Lilly's tears. "It makes Jacob feel some small degree of happiness buying things for you. He told me that's the highlight of his day, aside from when he dreams about you. He calls every day to check on you. He hopes I'll tell him one day that you'll be calling him, but I never do."

"This situation is such a disaster," Lilly remarked, huffing in resignation. "How did we end up here?"

"One word: Victoria. I wish it were legal to kill humans because she is truly malevolent."

"Does he still love her?" Lilly choked out.

"Are you insane? She stripped away the only person that ever brought him happiness. He hates her but he's playing her game—"

"For that fucking role?"

Janie smoothed Lilly's hair, tucking a short strand behind her ear. "No, he's doing it to protect you. He told me until he's back in London, he'll go

31

along with her charade because he isn't close enough to physically protect you."

"What's he planning to do? Camp outside my cottage?"

Janie giggled. "I wouldn't put it past him, anything to be near you. But for now, he feels you're safer if Victoria thinks she's won. He's terrified she might hurt you."

Lilly guffawed over her wine glass. "Too late; she destroyed me."

"She destroyed him, too. He's a shell of a man now. He never smiles or laughs anymore. It would do him a world of good to hear your voice—"

"What would I say? There's nothing left of my heart, Janie." *Christ, I thought time with a close friend would be therapeutic.*

"He never meant for this to happen and even though it was atrocious, I understand why he feared for your safety. Victoria threatened your reputation in the press, which would destroy everything you've built up with the animal sanctuary. I don't put anything past Victoria, especially when it comes to you. You are her biggest obstacle. She's like a cornered animal, and she'll take any route necessary to win the fight."

Lilly nodded. Suddenly Jacob seemed less the villain and more a victim himself. The quote 'the road to hell is paved with good intentions' seemed aimed in his direction. "Perhaps I can understand why he went along with the farce, I just don't know why he didn't call to explain the situation. It's like it didn't even bother him, he rolled with the punches."

"You couldn't be further from the truth." Janie cleared her throat. "I hate to admit it, but Jacob was fall down drunk—around the clock—for the first couple weeks. The only reason he didn't get kicked off the movie set was because of his friendship with Miriam. Roger and I staged an intervention when we got to Greece, he was trying to drink himself to death. He would have succeeded."

Lilly's throat went dry as her mind leapt into overdrive. The idea of Jacob in that level of agony stole her breath. "Why didn't I hear about this?"

"Would you have cared?" Janie's question was pointed but non-accusatory.

"How could you ask me that?"

"It's been several weeks, and tonight is the most I've been able to disclose about what really happened during the press release. Lilly, you wouldn't *let* me—or anyone else—tell you Jacob's side. I honestly thought you wouldn't care what was happening to him...or worse, consider it poetic justice."

"Janie! You know me better than that." Lilly began pacing circles into her rug, her arms crossed to ward off the chill emanating from her body. "Of course, I would care! I was furious with him, but I didn't want him dead!" She sank into one of the chairs. "I spent the first couple weeks thinking he was not only fine with the decision, but an active participant. I had no inkling he was taking things so hard."

"That's an understatement. Jacob's devastated. He never believed love like this existed, and the moment he finds it, it's stolen from him. He knows you won't forgive him, but that hasn't stopped him from trying and this time it truly wasn't his fault. I don't know how any of us would have handled that situation. Victoria is a one-woman manipulation army."

"I'm letting her win by staying away from Jacob, aren't I?"

Janie nodded. "That's one way of looking at it. Another is that I've never seen two people more miserable being apart. My brother told me he would give his life for you and I believe him. He gave up his happiness to keep you safe."

Lilly was left staring out the window, contemplating her friend's words.

Janie roused Elizabeth, who stretched and cooed. "It's time to go, sweet one." They walked to the front door, but Janie paused on the threshold. "He'll be back in a few days, you know..."

Lilly nodded, noting a familiar car parked down the street and biting back a feeling of unease. "That car, I see that vehicle everywhere. Do you think it's Victoria?"

"No, it's the men Jacob hired. He hoped you wouldn't notice. He didn't want to scare you."

"He hired bodyguards? For me?"

Janie nodded. "He loves you, Lilly. He'd do anything for you. I know you don't believe me—or him—but it's the truth. Goodnight, beautiful goddess. I can't wait until Jacob sees you."

Lilly nodded and offered up a chuckle, kissing them both and watching them drive away. She held up a hand in greeting to the car down the street, receiving a flash of lights in response. Janie was telling the truth. With a confused heart, she closed the door on the evening and cleaned up the living room, placing the orchid on the windowsill. She bound the letters with ribbon and put them back in the laundry basket, along with the presents he sent from Greece.

After she was finished, she sank into one of the chairs, noticing his most recent letter still on the table, beckoning to be read again. She perused the lines, her fingers tracing the words.

Lilly glanced at the clock. It was after midnight, and after two in Greece. It was too late to call him. She changed for bed as her heart and head engaged in a battle of wills, the wine allowing her heart to overtake her last vestiges of common sense.

He won't be awake...I'll call, thank him for the flower and protection and hang up. Quick and painless.

She grabbed her phone and unblocked his number, her fingers shaking as she pressed the digits. She took a deep breath, one ring, two rings...his voicemail had to pick up soon.

"Say something so I know I'm not dreaming, Lilly." Jacob's voice was thick, and Lilly wondered if it was with sleep or emotion.

Lilly's breath caught in her throat hearing his deep, sensual voice. "Something."

CHAPTER THREE

Jacob

"I was dreaming about you," Jacob sat up in bed and flipped on the light, ensuring he was actually awake.

"Sure it wasn't a nightmare?" Lilly's voice sounded hesitant, almost timid on the other end of the phone.

Jacob closed his eyes as he relived the dream, his mouth loving every inch of her body, feeling her come alive under his hands. "Definitely not."

"I know it's really late there. I shouldn't have called—"

"I pray every day you'll call."

Lilly paused. "I didn't consider whether you might have company. That would make for an awkward conversation."

Jacob started at Lilly's comment. "Company? Unless you count the cricket in the corner, there's never any company. I can't fathom that idea, actually."

"I wasn't certain if someone was keeping your bed warm—"

Jacob felt sick at her words. How could she think he was sleeping with another woman? "There's only one woman."

She fell silent for a few seconds, but he heard the tears in her voice when she spoke. "Oh, so you *have* moved on—"

Christ, but he was talented at saying the wrong thing. "Lilly, you're the only woman, there's no one else."

"Victoria—"

Jacob sighed audibly. "There's *nothing* between Victoria and me, apart from the baby. I'm waiting on the last legal hurdles to obtain DNA testing because I have serious doubts the child is mine." He fell silent, trying to rein in his galloping emotions. "But any romantic inclinations? Absolutely not."

"Janie told me the engagement was all a ruse concocted by Victoria, that you two were never really engaged."

"Never, I'm desperately in love with the most amazing woman in the world, and I buggered it utterly; but I only want her, no one else. The idea of touching someone else sickens me." He swallowed around the lump in his throat, dreading his next question. "Are you seeing someone?"

Lilly laughed dryly. "I am, his name is Bob."

Her words hit like a punch in the gut. "Oh, that's…that's…damn—"

This time her laugh was genuine. "Battery operated boyfriend, you wanker."

Jacob released the breath he'd been holding and laughed with her. It was the first time he laughed in weeks. "Good relationship?"

"The best one I've ever been in. He makes no demands and when I'm done with him, I stick him in the drawer." Lilly giggled, and Jacob imagined her biting her lower lip like she did when nervous.

"Is that our song playing in the background?"

"Yes, I always think of you when I hear this song. I considered burning all his records, but that's a terrible waste of vinyl." Her voice was tinged with sarcasm, but he suspected she was only partly kidding.

"I'm glad you didn't. This phone call nonsense seems so impersonal. Would you like to video chat?"

The pause was so long he thought the line disconnected. "Sure. I have to warn you, I look different."

"You finally got those facial piercings?"

Lilly guffawed. "Those are next week. I'll call you in a few, let me grab my laptop."

Within thirty seconds his laptop rang with the video call, and he got to set eyes on Lilly for the first time in six weeks. Christ, there had never been a woman more beautiful, her brown eyes wide and questioning, her pale skin glistening in the low light, her lips tinted from wine. "You cut your hair."

Lilly laughed nervously. "Yeah, I did."

His mouth twisted slightly. "Did Janie talk you into that?"

Now her self-consciousness was evident. "No, it was my own dumb decision. Would you prefer I put a bag over my head?"

Jacob chuckled. "Definitely not. You look amazing." He realized he was getting turned on looking at her and adjusted himself slightly.

"So, I looked awful before?"

"I'm batting a thousand here. You were gorgeous before, you're gorgeous now and...sexy as hell." His last words trailed off to a whisper.

Lilly's eyes held a glint of mischief. "What was that?"

Jacob blushed, his erection throbbing and his fingers twitching, desperate to touch her. "I said, sexy as hell, you look sexy as hell. Fuck. Can we change the subject?"

"Why would we change the subject? You're telling me how gorgeous I am. I'm all for this discussion."

Jacob laughed. Lilly was a bit inebriated and for that, he was thankful. It took her guard down a few notches. "I could talk about your beauty forever. How much time you got?"

Lilly chuckled. "You don't look so bad yourself. Janie says you're better now. She told me you fell into the bottle for a while."

Jacob nodded absently, staring at slender lines of her exposed neck and wishing he could climb through the screen and shower her body with kisses. "I guess better is a subjective term. Every day without you is torture, but the first couple weeks were especially ugly. I wanted to die."

Lilly shifted, laying down on her side. "I'm glad you didn't, the world is a better place with you in it." Before he could respond, she continued. "You need to sleep, so I'll get to the point. I read your letters and unpacked the orchid. I read them all today. I wasn't able to look at them until now."

"I understand. Do you like the orchid?"

She bit her lower lip and Jacob's heart flipped. Her simple gestures filled him with such happiness.

"It's beautiful." Lilly smiled, glancing off screen. "It's in the windowsill. I wanted to thank you for the plant but mostly for the letters. Did you mean what you said in that last letter? That's not the first time you've said that to me."

Jacob's heart raced as he nodded, his voice barely a whisper. "En sa beauté gît ma mort et ma vie—you're my irreplaceable angel."

Tears dripped down Lilly's cheeks as she shook her head. "You cannot keep breaking my heart—one wonderful week is not worth six weeks of torture."

"It's torture for both of us. This isn't a one-way street, but the moments we shared are worth any degree of madness I'm suffering now."

"Are they? I don't know how to fix my heart, how to move on from loving you."

Jacob closed his eyes at her agonizing words. She wanted freedom from the claim he held on her. "All I've ever wanted is your happiness. I don't want you to move on, Lilly. I know that's selfish, and you deserve—"

"I deserved you."

Jacob's intake of breath was sharp—he didn't expect such a direct response. "You still have me."

Lilly shook her head sadly. "I never had you."

"How can you say that? I proposed marriage, bought us a home, desperately wanted a baby with you—"

"I didn't need those things. I needed you. Just you." Tears streamed down her cheeks. "I don't want to be your dirty secret, some anonymous woman in London you have to hide. I know the reasons you felt it necessary to conceal our relationship, but it doesn't make the knife cut any less deep."

"You were never my dirty secret, you're the love of my life."

"The one no one knows about, the one who has to pretend our plans never existed, so that your ruse with Victoria can continue," Lilly gritted out, her words biting.

Jacob felt desperation, he was losing Lilly. "Once I return to London, the whole world is going to know about you."

"That's not the point—"

"Let me finish, my angel. Once I return to London, nothing in this bloody world will stop me from being near you, not even you. I know you're scared but I will bash the hell out of those walls you've erected, and I will love you until the day I die. But Lilly, I had to protect you while I was so far away."

She took a slow inhale, as if considering his statement. "Hmm, I waved to my security detail, felt a bit like the President. Were bodyguards really necessary?"

"I hoped you wouldn't notice them, but I should know that nothing escapes you. I would have told you Lilly, but you blocked my calls."

"Do you really think I'm in danger?"

Jacob swallowed audibly. "I'm not willing to take that chance. You're too precious." He reached out, tracing the curves of her face on the screen. "I'd do anything for you."

"And you think once you return to London I'm just going to fall into your arms, after everything we've endured?"

"I'm hopeful after showing you every day how much I adore you you'll either give in because of love or cave because of annoyance." He joked, but he felt the fear spark in the back of his mind. What if reconciliation wasn't something Lilly could consider?

Lilly propped her chin on her hand, her full breasts overflowing out of her tank, her sexy smirk playing about her lips. "And what would this daily adoration look like?"

Her questions were making his erection throb. "Anything your heart, mind or body desires, Lilly."

"Tempting." Her tongue darted out to lick her lower lip as she pushed her hair from her face.

"You're the temptress. Do you have any idea what you're doing to me right now?"

"What am I doing?" Lilly breathed, her voice innocent but her eyes twinkling. This woman knew how to drive him out of his skull with desire. "I do have one question."

"Anything."

"Would you be able to promise less madness and more exquisiteness in the future?"

Jacob's breath caught in his throat. "What are you saying?"

Lilly released a sigh. "I'm saying this person you love so much…she loves you so much too." She looked away, blushing as if she'd revealed too much. "I've got to go. Sweet dreams, Jacob."

"Wait, Lilly!" But she'd ended the call and he was left staring at a black screen.

Jacob's heart beat wildly. She told him she still loved him, intimated there was a chance. He could not leave it like that and dialed her number, but it went to voicemail. He hung up and tried again, determined to reach her. He would call a thousand times if needed.

"What?" Her voice finally answered softly, as if her mouth were pressed against a pillow.

"You cannot leave a conversation like that."

"Why not?"

Jacob leaned back against the headboard, his voice lowering a notch. "It's an unacceptable action. I can only tolerate so much madness in my days before I'm beyond reprieve."

"How would you prefer I end the conversation?" Lilly purred.

"Not at all is my preference."

"Well, whet my appetite sir. Tell me what you're thinking right now."

Jacob scooted back down in the bed, closing his eyes and imagining her next to him. "How gorgeous you are and how desperately I want you naked in my bed right now. I didn't think it possible, but you look sexier now than you did."

She released a low gasp. "Really?"

"Yes Lilly, you're mesmerizingly beautiful." He smiled at her husky giggle; he had her. "But that's not *all* I'm thinking about."

"No?"

How do you select a single memory when every one represents the most magical moments of your life? "I had just gotten off the phone with the fertility clinic and I rushed outside to tell you the results of our testing. You were walking in the gardens of our country home and when I caught sight of you…there was a moment that I couldn't breathe. I couldn't believe that out of everyone on the planet, the most perfect woman in the world chose me. All I wanted was to lay you down on the grass and make love to you—love you until you promised never to leave me, love you until we made a baby."

"I like that memory. I wish you had made love to me that day in the

39

meadow," Lilly whispered.

"I think about that day all the time. Who am I kidding? I think about *every* day I spent with you." He sighed. "I wish it were you having my baby, I wish it every day."

He heard her soft cries, muffled as she tried desperately to keep them quiet. "If wishes were horses, beggars would ride."

"I'll beg forever for another chance with you." Jacob realized any deep romantic connection was so difficult for Lilly now, but he prayed one day she might let down her guard again.

"You told me what your favorite memory was—"

"One of millions of memories," Jacob interjected.

"What would be your favorite memory tomorrow morning if I was there with you right now?" Her deep voice rolled over him like molasses.

Jacob damn near exploded at her intimate question. Christ this woman bewitched his every cell. "We would still be making the memory tomorrow morning."

"This sounds interesting."

"I would hold you down and kiss every inch of your body. I would start with your lips and then travel down your neck to those gorgeous breasts and down your stomach to your hips." His breath hitched as he pictured Lilly naked in his mind, his hand gripping the sheet. "Then I would wrap my tongue around your clit"—Lilly's soft moan only goaded him on—"and kiss you until you exploded. Then I'd start at the top and do it all over again." He realized he was writhing in the bed, his desire at a boiling point.

Lilly's voice was breathy on the end of the phone. "Wow. When are you getting home?"

"Two days. But if you want me sooner, I'll be on a plane tomorrow."

"I miss you. I wish things were different."

Jacob's throat closed at her statement. "I love you so much, Lilly. Please let me fix this—give me twenty-four hours. I'm begging you, just give me twenty-four hours."

"For what?"

"You'll see, I'll fix this mess. Then I'm marrying you. I've got the license, and nothing will stop me from doing what I've wanted to do since the day we met. Then I'll spend the next fifty years making all this up to you."

The silence from her end of the phone was agonizing. He could almost hear the myriad of emotions—disbelief, anger, resignation, hope—flit through her brain, searching for an answer…searching for the *right* answer.

"I must be insane to even consider your request."

Jacob's heart hammered in his chest. "Or in love."

"You have twenty-four hours. Goodnight," Lilly replied as she disconnected the call.

Jacob stared at phone, his mind racing. He was a man with a plan. He texted Victoria, telling her he was about to connect via video chat. He warned that if she ignored his call she would find out about his statement at the same time as the international media.

His plan worked. Victoria appeared panic-stricken on the video. "It's the middle of the night in Greece. What's going on sweetie? Did you miss me?"

"Cut the shit. Now listen—"

Victoria began to speak over him, but Jacob was finished with her control antics.

"I said listen! You will not speak over me again, do you understand?" Jacob waited as she nodded mutely. "My barrister has the order for DNA testing, and it will be sent via courier to you. As a legal document, you are obligated to respond, and the test I'm requesting is not invasive in any manner. I hoped to avoid this route, but you have seen fit to be as uncooperative as possible, so I'm letting my legal team handle this situation."

Victoria opened her mouth, but Jacob held up his hand. "Second, I am releasing a statement to the press. It states you and I are not engaged, and although we are dedicated to this child, there is no romantic future together."

"You're kidding."

"Not a whit and if you don't agree to the DNA test now, I will release a second press clip, this time referring to your notorious bedroom habits and my suspicion that I'm not the father."

Victoria gasped in shock. "You wouldn't dare."

"Sweetheart, you have no idea. Two can play at your game. And, so you can't throw Milieu of Madness into my face one more time, I've placed a call to Albert, respectfully declining the role."

Her green eyes narrowed and attempted to pierce his armor, but this time, he was impenetrable. "I'm flying to Greece tomorrow to discuss our situation."

"Don't bother. I'll be in London."

"Let me guess, another round with your little nurse?" Victoria spat.

"I don't know if that wonderful woman will ever forgive me for what happened. What I do know is this: if that baby is mine, I will be a doting father, but the relationship ends there. I will spend the rest of my days fighting to get back the love of my life, and if you *ever* threaten Lilly's reputation, safety or our relationship again, I will dig up the darkest dirt from your past and plaster it across every tabloid around the globe. Do I make myself clear?"

Victoria looked shocked by his diatribe. Jacob was usually calm and collected, but now he was on fire. "Aren't you acting a little reckless with so much on the line?"

Jacob guffawed as the realization hit him. "You're right, I am. I'm finally putting the person I love the most before everything else." He brought his face right to the camera. "And it feels fucking amazing."

By the time 6 a.m. rolled around, Jacob had changed the entire trajectory of his career and social life. His publicist issued the press release per Jacob's request, his barrister finalized documents regarding the DNA test, and Albert would be receiving his message regarding Milieu of Madness within the next few hours.

As Jacob ambled down to breakfast, he encountered Miriam with a look of delighted shock on her face.

"Good morning, love." Jacob gathered her into a hug, kissing her on both cheeks.

"Who are you and what have you done with the moody bloke that's existed here the last six weeks?"

Jacob laughed as he spun her around. "I issued a press release, telling the truth about Victoria and me."

"I saw, well done you." She stopped, looking at him deeply. "But that's not why you're so happy. You spoke to Lilly."

"Is it that obvious?" Jacob smiled. "I'm flying back to London and begging her to marry me. I think she might consider my proposal."

Miriam smiled. "I don't even know this woman, but I love her for the amazing amount of crap she's put up with in regard to you. Don't you dare hurt her again."

"I plan to spend the rest of my life making it up to her."

Lilly

illy spent the next morning cleaning cages and walking dogs at the animal shelter. It was noon before she glanced at the clock.

They say the key to quieting the mind is keeping busy. What a load of garbage. She was physically busy, but her mind was pummeled by repetitive thoughts of all his promises the night before. Would anything come to fruition or would they wither and die like they had in the past? He told her he was going to marry her, but she had walked this path before, and the outcome nearly broke her—heart and soul.

After a quick shower and change, Lilly headed for the Tube. She didn't know if Jacob meant what he said, but just in case, she wanted to be home and ready.

She was walking through the Tube cars when a familiar voice rang out. "Lilly!"

Spinning on her heel, she saw Roger, patting a seat next to him. "What a surprise! What are you doing here?"

"It's a little-known secret that I prefer the Tube to London's hellish traffic. Did you see the news this morning?"

Lilly shook her head. "Let me guess, Jacob and Victoria eloped last night, and they're having twins." Her laugh lacked any mirth.

Roger smiled and shook his head, bringing up the press release on his phone. "Not even close."

Lilly read the release, her eyes widening. Jacob publicly stated that he and Victoria were no longer a couple and a DNA test was pending as a result of Victoria's ignominious past. "I can't believe he released this publicly!"

"And, Jacob's flying back to London today. In fact, he may have already landed. He has an interview on the Brad Taylor show."

"How do you know that?" Lilly's heart was pattering at the bevy of information she had just been handed. *You had a busy night Jacob, maybe you were telling the truth.*

"He called me and told me he's arriving early. He also sounds more chipper than I've heard in the last six weeks. You wouldn't know anything about that, would you?" Roger asked, flashing Lilly a knowing smile. "Your hair looks fabulous by the way, you should have cut it ages ago."

Lilly smirked. "I wish someone had told me I looked so awful with long hair."

"Hardly, but this," Roger motioned to her hair, "is a fantastic look for you. Jacob's going to love it."

"He didn't seem to care either way last night," Lilly lied.

"A-ha, the truth emerges! I knew you two were talking and trust me when I say that man won't be able to keep his mitts off you."

"I believe his preference runs toward willowy blondes."

Roger chuckled. "Keep telling yourself that dear, doesn't make it true."

Lilly glared in Roger's direction, but he scrunched up his face, causing Lilly to collapse in a fit of giggles.

Roger and Lilly spent the next several minutes discussing family, friends and her plans for the animal shelter.

"You think you've found land for the first sanctuary? That's bloody amazing, Lilly. I'm in awe of the dedication you've given to this project."

"I hope I can get it completed before the term on my job runs out."

"What then? You're not leaving England, are you?"

Lilly smiled, somewhat sadly. "If I don't have a job here, I have to return to the States. But it's okay, it will be nice to see home again."

Roger gave Lilly a hug. "You belong with Jacob. This is home."

Tears welled in Lilly's eyes. "Is it? I'm not so sure anymore."

"Give him a chance to prove it to you, you both deserve that happiness. Do you have some time this afternoon for lunch and shopping?"

Lilly considered his invitation. "I don't see why not."

"I have to pick up a gift for Jacob's birthday, and I could use your expertise."

"I doubt I know Jacob better than you do."

"You know him better than anyone." The Tube slowed, and Roger stood up, giving Lilly a questioning look. "Are you coming?"

As they exited the train, Lilly's phone rang. It was Edward—he had become a good friend over the last several weeks, making her smile on more than one occasion. In fact, he was the first one to drag her out of the house and back into the world of the living. "Good afternoon, sir."

"Are you hungry? I thought we might get some grub and a pint," Edward suggested.

"I'd love to but I'm actually on Bond Street."

"Fancy digs."

Lilly giggled. "I'm with Roger. We're looking for a birthday gift for Jacob."

Silence from Edward's end of the conversation.

Well, shit.

"Hello?"

"You're speaking to Jacob again?"

Lilly groaned, this was not a topic she wanted to discuss with him. "Long story, I'll tell you later."

"Okay, well enjoy your afternoon."

Lilly stared at her phone after the call ended. Edward seemed less than thrilled at the concept of her reconciling with Jacob.

"Who was that?" Roger inquired.

"Edward, he's become a close confidant."

Roger regarded her soberly. "Be careful there."

"Why?"

Roger shrugged. "He has some questionable connections to one of your favorite people."

Lilly nodded, aware of Edward's friendship with Victoria. "Noted. On a happier topic, what's good for lunch?"

Roger chuckled. "It's Bond Street, everything is delicious here, and it'll only cost you a kidney."

"Good thing I have two," Lilly retorted, smiling, as they entered a small French restaurant.

An hour later, the two friends strolled up the street toward Daniel Prince Jewelers, and Lilly stopped in her tracks.

"What's wrong?" Roger inquired.

"It's the jewelry store where they designed my ring."

Roger nodded as if he already knew this fact. "Good, you can pick that up, too."

"You're hilarious," Lilly muttered, following him into the store. A jeweler approached them, and Roger explained what he wanted—a pocket watch with visible internal workings, preferably in platinum that could be engraved. The jeweler led them to a case of watches and Roger perused, asking Lilly her opinion on various options.

But Lilly was distracted by a figure walking in the door—Victoria, in all her high-heeled, bedazzled glory. "Roger," Lilly whispered fiercely, motioning to her left.

"Oh, bloody hell!" Roger muttered as Victoria strolled toward them. "Victoria, what a surprise, what are you doing in London?"

Lilly felt Victoria's eyes on her but maintained her focus on the jewelry counter.

"Jacob arrives home today, and we have plans to see each other. He's excited about the baby. He's so cute." Victoria patted Lilly's arm. "Sorry, I know this must be difficult for you."

"It's a walk in the park, Victoria," Lilly snapped.

Victoria snorted, taken aback by Lilly's retort. "Aren't we snippy today? I'm sorry things didn't work out between you and Jacob—"

"Au contraire, according to the press, things didn't work out between *you* and Jacob," Roger interjected.

Victoria's face split into a disparaging smile. "You can't always believe what you read." She fixed her contemptuous gaze on Lilly. "I wanted to apologize, people like you—"

"Apologize?" Lilly gaped.

"—don't understand our lifestyle, how it is living in the public eye. I saved you a ton of heartache. Jacob and I understand each other. He needs someone who won't distract him from his goals. Did you know he's pulling out of Milieu of Madness because of the situation with you? Look at what you did to him, you got his priorities all screwed up."

"You're ridiculous! This woman straightened out his priorities. He finally knows what love is because of Lilly. You have done everything in your power to destroy their relationship, but according to my best mate, this woman at my side will be Mrs. Edmonton within the month," Roger hissed.

"I believe I heard that same story a couple months back—is this a re-run?" Although Victoria maintained a cool exterior, it was a facade, her eyes raged in anger.

"Wait and see. You're jealous of how much he adores Lilly, and the fact that you couldn't buy his affection."

Victoria's eyes narrowed. "Don't forget, Roger, I'm carrying his child."

Roger snorted with contempt. "We'll see how that DNA result plays out before we start selecting nursery furnishings."

Lilly's head thumped at the verbal ping-pong, she needed to end the argument and escape, away from the woman who represented everything she lacked in her life.

Then a thought occurred to her, and Lilly's heart dropped. "How did you know Jacob was coming back into town today?"

Victoria shrugged nonchalantly. "I spoke with him yesterday before I left Greece."

"You were in Greece?"

A malicious sneer was Victoria's only reply.

Lilly put her hand on the counter to steady herself. Was Jacob lying again? Had he been with Victoria yesterday, only hours before professing his love to her? "I suppose it's also a coincidence that you're at this jeweler?"

Victoria flashed a diamond and sapphire bracelet under Lilly's nose. "A little bauble from the man of the hour. Jacob frequents this store. I'm assuming this is where he took you as well." Seeing the look of despair cross Lilly's face, she feigned concern, putting her hand on her shoulder. "Don't feel bad, you're not the first girl who fell for his charms."

"Nice seeing you, Victoria." Roger cut off the conversation as the blonde departed, eyes ogling her from every angle as her long legs disappeared out the door. "Lilly, don't believe a word coming out of her mouth."

Lilly felt sick. Her intuition, once her guidepost, was in a permanent state of disrepair. She had no idea what to believe anymore. "If they're not in contact, how did she know he was coming home today? I'm an idiot, I almost fell for it again."

Roger grabbed her shoulders, forcing her to meet his gaze. "She plays games. She's a master manipulator, and she has eyes everywhere. I guarantee Jacob mentioned to someone—anyone—that he was flying home today, and they passed along the information."

"He bought her a bracelet—"

"He did *not* buy her anything of the sort. I told you, it's all lies."

"Why is she doing this? I don't think she even loves him."

"I doubt Victoria loves anyone, but she's a control freak, and she had Jacob firmly under her thumb until you came along. You're her biggest threat and what's even more damaging to her ego is you're not some celebrity socialite. But even with all her money and power, she could never make him love her like he loves you. I doubt anyone has ever loved her like that. You're Jacob's world. You need to believe me."

"Then why was she in Greece?" Lilly couldn't sweep Victoria's words under the rug, there was no way this was just another coincidence.

"It's a country, Lilly, she could have been doing a lot of things there. Likely, she never set foot in Greece but knew it would drive you mad to hear they were together. She knows how he adores you and that makes her sick with jealousy." Roger ran his hand through his hair, exasperated. "I know it's difficult to see past everything that's happened, but you don't know Victoria like I do. You don't know what she's capable of. Victoria makes a game of hurting people and twists it to be someone else's doing. I'd admire her if she wasn't such a nefarious beast."

Lilly chortled at Roger's last statement. "A nefarious beast—Victoria World Tour—we need t-shirts." She turned back to the counter. "Have you selected a timepiece for Jacob?"

47

Roger chose a vintage Patek Philippe pocket watch and asked for Lilly's input with the engraving. She decided on a Tennessee Williams quote, *"Time is the longest distance between two places,"* and they agreed it held multiple meanings that would resonate with Jacob. Roger left a deposit on the watch; it would be ready for pick-up in two weeks.

They were about to exit when Clive caught sight of them, making a beeline across the store. "Good afternoon, Miss Lilly, you look lovely. You cut your hair?"

Lilly nodded and laughed. "About a foot of it, yes. How are you?"

"I'm wonderful. You just missed Mr. Edmonton. He picked up your ring not an hour ago."

"He did what?" Lilly stammered.

"He picked up the ring. If I'd known you were coming in, I would have waited to ensure the size is correct."

Lilly's thoughts raced. There were two options—Jacob meant every word last night or Victoria meant every word today. One made her heart sing and the other made her heart sick.

Err on the side of caution, Lilly. Don't assume anything where Jacob is concerned.

"Jacob and I aren't together anymore."

The jeweler looked bewildered. "Are you quite sure?"

"Maybe he means to give it to someone else," Lilly stammered.

Roger snorted at the idea. "I doubt that very much."

"Why? He did announce his engagement on international television," she countered.

"It's not like that, and you know it," Roger stated firmly.

Now Clive looked stunned, as if he'd stepped into the middle of a soap opera drama and wasn't certain how to escape.

Lilly forced a smile and patted Clive's hand. "It was wonderful seeing you. We have a train to catch."

Lilly and Roger jogged toward the Tube track but missed the train by seconds.

"No worries, there will be another one in ten minutes," Roger remarked, fetching them some tea from a local vendor. "Is that wedding bells I hear?"

Lilly shrugged. "Not mine. Jacob and I aren't engaged."

Roger smiled mischievously. "Yet."

Lilly glared at Roger.

"I'm serious! Within a week you'll be engaged, married within a month, and having a baby within a year."

God, I wish. "You're incorrigible. Last night was the first time I spoke to Jacob in six weeks. I don't know who to believe—Jacob or Victoria. I'm not certain he wants me back."

"Your nose grew with that statement. You know Jacob wants you back."

"We're not together, but he picked up an engagement ring—"

"Your engagement ring."

Lilly shook her head. "It's not mine, it never was. Perhaps Victoria is telling the truth."

Roger ruffled Lilly's short hair. "You're being daft as a door, and you know it. It was *always* your ring. I wager he's got something grand planned."

The Tube rolled up, and the two friends boarded it, finding seats in the closest car. They kept discussing Jacob's upcoming birthday and his arrival back in England. Roger was convinced Jacob only had eyes for Lilly and she caught herself almost believing his words.

Then a sound roared up from nowhere, so loud it shook the cars and cracked the windows. Lilly only had time to shoot Roger a terrified glance before the impact hit and the world went dark.

CHAPTER FOUR

Jacob

Miriam's jet landed at Heathrow a little after 10 a.m. and Jacob wanted to kiss the ground when he set foot onto the tarmac. Instead he opted to embrace his friend before jumping into the waiting limousine.

The driver dropped him at his house where he showered and changed, debating on whether to shave or keep the few days of stubble on his face. Deciding on the prior, he strolled downstairs, patting Charlie on the head before meandering into the kitchen.

"Hello, darling, it's so nice to have you home." Hannah, his housekeeper and second mother, set down the vase of fresh flowers and hugged him fiercely. "You look so handsome, I always did like you cleanly shaven."

Jacob smiled and returned the hug. "I'm headed to an interview."

"Where?"

"The Brad Taylor Show."

"Fancy pants, aren't you? I wondered what you might like for dinner, perhaps a Tuscan meal?"

Jacob chuckled; Hannah knew him better than his own kin. "Sounds fabulous."

Hannah nodded, a glint in her eye. "The jeweler left a message, said the engagement ring is ready to pick up. Is there something you'd like to tell me? Please tell me it doesn't involve Victoria."

Jacob smiled. "Not in the slightest."

"Any news on the paternity test?"

"My legal team sent the documents today, so we'll know the answer soon."

"What are you hoping for?"

"Pardon?"

"Are you hoping it's your baby or not?"

Jacob considered the question. "I want to have children, just—"

Hannah's eyes held a knowing glint. "Just with a certain brunette nurse that captured your heart. One that greatly appreciates fine Italian dining?"

"That would be amazing. We're not there yet, but I'm working on it. It feels so right this way."

"It's about time Lilly came first in your life."

He nodded in agreement, Hannah spoke the brutal truth. He'd just been too dumb to realize it. "God, I know. I spoke with her last night via video chat. I miss her so much, Hannah."

Hannah squeezed his arm. "I hope you two can work things out."

Jacob smiled. "Not nearly as much as I do." He glanced at his phone. "I've got to run. I'll see you tonight, hopefully with Lilly and the ring, in tow."

"I knew you were planning something," Hannah called after him.

Jacob arrived at the studio and the host, Brad Taylor, met him outside the dressing room. Brad's show had become a sensation in the last few years, and it was no wonder. He blended the humor of Johnny Carson with the investigative reporting of Dan Rather. To put it mildly, the man pulled no punches, but his stories always resonated with truth, and truth was exactly what Jacob was ready to share with the world.

"Jacob, what a nice surprise. Perfect timing with the award nominees being announced and your press release this morning. So…" Brad leaned in and whispered, "I wager you have something up your sleeve for the show tonight."

Jacob flashed his million-dollar smile. "Yes, I do." He fingered the small box in his pocket, the one that cushioned Lilly's ring, and felt a flash of nervousness. He was putting his entire reputation on the line, but he needed to come clean about the real woman who stole his heart.

"Fabulous. You know the drill. You're on right after this…whatever this boy band is called."

"Nothing like being informed about your guests, Brad," Jacob chuckled.

"I can't keep up with them, mate. These boy bands are everywhere and by the time I can finally match their face with their name, the bastards have gone through puberty and I have to start all over again." He shook Jacob's hand, patting him on the shoulder. "It's hell getting old. I'll meet you out there."

Jacob spent the last few minutes in his dressing room before being escorted to the stage. The applause of the studio audience was thunderous, he only hoped they wouldn't be throwing things by the end of his segment.

He took a seat next to Brad, as the host opened the interview with a few jokes about the rigors of acting life and Jacob's award nomination.

Just as Jacob began to relax into the rhythm, Brad switched gears, segueing into more intimate topics.

"The press release heard round the world. Care to speak to the validity of those statements?"

Jacob cleared his throat. *Here we go.* "What can I say? They're all true."

"You're saying that not only is there no engagement between you and Victoria, there is no romantic attachment."

Jacob nodded. "That's exactly what I'm saying."

"But she is pregnant?"

"As far as I know. I haven't examined her." Jacob's quick-witted retort earned a chuckle from the audience. Thank God, they weren't jumping out of their seats...yet.

"The release also mentioned that the child may not be yours. Do you care to address that subject?"

Jacob laughed, giving himself a moment to determine how to answer diplomatically. "It's too soon to tell, there is a DNA test pending."

"What are you hoping for?"

I'm going to kill you for asking that question. "A healthy child, whoever the father may be."

"Good answer. I commend you for that one." Brad tapped his note cards, as if unsure how to proceed. "Your press release wasn't the only item of interest this morning. There is a subject that your fans are desperate to know the truth about, if you're willing to have the conversation."

Brad handed Jacob a magazine, photos of him with Lilly plastered on the first few pages, and a title stating, '*Jacob's Real Love Lives in London.*' It was the first time Jacob had seen the article and his heart leapt at the love so obvious between the two of them.

"Well, that smile says everything. Who is this mystery woman, Jacob? Is she the same one you admitted to having a fling with when Victoria announced her pregnancy?"

Jacob swallowed, here goes nothing...and everything all at the same time. "Her name is Lilly, and she wasn't a fling."

Brad's eyebrows raised. "No?"

Jacob shook his head. "I met her when my sister required surgery. I fell in love with Lilly the moment I saw her, and it scared the hell out of me. I never felt that way about anyone in my life."

"Not even Victoria?"

"Not even close, no offense to Victoria. I tended to keep people at a distance, but Lilly busted through my barriers without even trying."

"What was your relationship with Lilly when the news of the pregnancy broke? Were you together? If these pictures are anything to go by—"

"We were most definitely together. I flew back to London from Santorini—where I was filming—when I realized I couldn't live without Lilly and proposed marriage. I attempted to bribe the British consulate to let me marry her that same week, but Brits are so stringent in their rules."

Brad laughed in agreement.

"When I returned to Santorini a week later, on the day of that press conference, I was engaged to Lilly and had every intention of marrying her as soon as the paperwork was approved."

"This was not a fling by any means."

Jacob shook his head.

Brad leaned forward. "So why the ruse? Why did Victoria state you two were getting married?"

"You'd have to ask Victoria that question. She made that statement without even consulting me," he retorted with a grimace.

"Was Victoria aware of your relationship with Lilly and your pending marriage?"

"Absolutely. She also knew, regardless of the pregnancy, that Lilly and I had decided to continue our engagement. I suppose that didn't sit well with her."

Brad scratched his chin thoughtfully. "Victoria wanted to reconcile?"

What she wanted was to ruin my bloody life. Mission accomplished... almost. "If the press conference is anything to go by, she wanted more than a reconciliation."

"She sabotaged you."

Jacob almost bit through his tongue, holding back all the venom he wanted to spew about Victoria. "One might say that, the only thing I know for certain is my heart broke that day. I was afraid Lilly would be ripped apart in the media and construed as a mistress and homewrecker. That is the furthest thing from the truth. Lilly was never the other woman, she was the *only* woman."

The audience let out a collective sigh of approval, and Jacob released a sigh. This was moving along quite smoothly.

"Why don't you describe the real Lilly for all of us, nip any false rumors in the bud."

Jacob smiled, his mind drifting to a memory of their bodies pressed together, lips locked, and limbs intertwined in a loving embrace. "Where do I start? She's passionate about everything and everyone she loves, and she loves everyone. And she's compassionate—so giving of her heart and time. Lilly's ethereal, too perfect for this ugly world. She's the single greatest thing that's ever happened to me."

Brad couldn't hold back the grin crossing his face. "It sounds like you're still head over heels."

"I'm utterly in love with Lilly Staver. I have the engagement ring we designed, but she never got to wear it…" Jacob fished the box out of his pocket and handed the box to Brad, who admired it, looking surprised at the turn in the conversation.

"Wow, that is exquisite, very unique. Do you mind me asking why you have it with you now?"

Jacob released a nervous chuckle. "I plan to beg Lilly to marry me tonight before this airs. If she says yes, I intend on having her in front of a minister within forty-eight hours."

"I know before she does? I love that." Brad faced the cameras. "Lilly, if you're listening, I hope you're bound for the altar as Mrs. Edmonton. I can tell you with no uncertainty this man adores you." Turning back to Jacob, he shook his hand. "Best of luck, keep us posted. We'll have to do a whole wedding and marriage segment on you two."

"Let's hope so."

The cameras turned off, and the two men walked offstage. Brad turned and gave Jacob a friendly punch in the arm. "That was some good shit. The public is going to go crazy, in a good way."

"Hopefully I'm not drawn and quartered for dumping Victoria. She has some…enthusiastic fans."

"Not as many as you think, Jacob. Besides, the studio audience ate up the segment. You heard the applause. They love nothing more than a good Cinderella tale."

"Let's hope Lilly agrees."

"She sounds like one hell of a woman."

"She's my everything," Jacob admitted. It was oddly comforting to bare his soul in regard to Lilly.

"Victoria, I've heard rumors about her. I'm assuming she threatened you. Threatened your career?" Brad leaned against a hallway wall, a discerning smile on his lips.

Jacob offered a nod, aware he was not Victoria's first victim. "That seems to be her M.O., she has the face of an angel and the heart of a viper."

"That's insulting the viper, mate."

Jacob was about to answer when a group of people beelined for the men, pulling Brad aside.

Brad returned a few moments later, his face ashen.

"What?" Jacob asked, sipping his water.

"There's been an explosion on the Tube, they think it was a terrorist attack. It's bad."

Lilly

illy's body ached as she opened her eyes, at least she thought they opened, the world around her was black. She choked on the stagnant smoke, a pain in her side and leg slicing through her body like a shotgun blast.

Lilly tried to focus, but her mind was fuzzy. Where was she before the world went black?

Where am I? I'm on the Tube, there was a noise, some horrifically loud booming sound…

She struggled to stand, but soon realized her right leg was pinned under a set of dislodged seats. Lilly shrieked as she pulled her leg free, collapsing in pain when she attempted to stand. Struggling to assess the damage, she noted her jeans were torn and bloodied but couldn't identify any bone damage.

Roger…where's Roger? He was right next to me…

Nothing looked the same.

Her eyes started adjusting to the dark, and she could barely make out the mangled metal and plastic interior bent at odd angles, a layer of soot covering everything. It appeared that the windows of the Tube now rested against the ground. *The Tube must have derailed. We were sitting on the left, so we got thrown down to the other side when the crash occurred.*

"Roger?" she rasped. "Roger, where are you? Can you hear me?"

Gagging on the noxious fumes, Lilly half crawled, half dragged herself in the direction where she believed they were seated.

"Roger! Roger, where are you?" Lilly tried to scream, but her voice emerged a whisper, her lungs burning in the acrid smoke. "Roger! I can't see you, say something!"

From her left, she heard a scraping sound and struggled to hear anything that sounded remotely like his voice. Finally, a faint whisper came from that general direction. "Lilly…Lilly…"

All around her were bodies, some coughing and struggling to stand, a few contorted into positions not compatible with life. Ignoring the carnage, she slid forward.

A woman held her young son against her breast as he screamed—whether it was from pain or terror, Lilly didn't know.

"Miss, let me help you." A stranger with weary eyes offered her a hand, but she shook her head, intent on reaching Roger.

In her haste and the unnatural blackness, Lilly slid over something sharp, cutting a gash into her leg. She writhed at the pain but didn't slow down on her trek to Roger's side.

She found him pinned under a set of seats, his face white as a sheet save for the blood specks littering his cheeks.

"Roger, I'm here." Lilly assessed the damage. "Can you move your legs?"

Roger shook his head weakly. "Can't move them, can't feel them."

Lilly ignored the thrashing pain in her body and pulled herself to a standing position, throwing her body weight against the set of seats in a futile effort to move them off Roger's lower body.

His scream of agony stopped her cold and she recoiled in horror; twisted metal shards protruded from his body, one from his chest and the other from his lower abdomen. Her years of nursing summed up the situation, a punctured lung and ruptured spleen. He would bleed out or drown in his own blood if he didn't get help fast.

She collapsed by him as he struggled to breathe, placing his head on her lap and screaming in vain for help that wasn't coming.

A young man kneeled by them, his face black with ash. "Let me help you move the seats."

"No! You can't." Lilly motioned to the metal shards rising up like daggers from Roger's body.

"Right. They've managed to pry open one of the doors. I'll get help down here immediately." The young man stopped for a moment, his eyes widening in recognition at the famous actor.

But Lilly was done with the conversation, turning her attention back to Roger. Using her most convincing nurse voice, she smoothed his bloodied hair from his eyes and offered a smile. "Help is on its way; you just hang on Roger, we're going to get you out of here."

Roger's hand struggled to find hers, his grasp weak. "I'm not getting out of here, Lilly." Lilly began to protest, but Roger continued. "It doesn't hurt. You need to get out of here." His eyes focused enough to see others struggling in the debris.

She shook her head, tears streaming down her face. "Absolutely not, we arrived together, we are leaving together." Coughs racked her body and she spit out blood-tinged mucous.

"Go," Roger's voice was as forceful as his mortally wounded body would allow, but Lilly remained firm in her decision.

"No way in hell, rescue crews will be here any moment. You heard that young man, he's going to fetch help personally." She noticed blood pumping steadily from his arm and slipped off her belt, wrapping it around his arm to form a makeshift tourniquet. "There, that'll hold until help arrives."

Roger groaned, his skin ashen as his breathing became shallow and reedy. "Tell Sophie—tell Sophie I love her, and I'll always be with her. Tell her to look in every sunrise—"

"You're going to tell her yourself."

Roger's face took on an odd light. "Please, Lilly, please do this for me. Let me tell you these things."

Roger had accepted his fate and Lilly needed to accept it as well, she nodded as her eyes clouded with tears. "Go ahead, tell me everything. I'll make certain they know."

Roger's breathing was gurgled now, and Lilly knew the end was imminent. She prayed he would have the chance to express his thoughts before he left this world. "Every sunrise, every beam of light will be another way I send my love to her. Tell my daughter every star in the sky was hung for her—" He broke off in a fit of choking, blood trickling from the corner of his mouth.

Lilly wiped the blood away and adjusted his head slightly. There was no comfort to be found, not for either of them. A massive creaking sound erupted, and part of the car collapsed not more than ten feet from them.

Lilly threw her body over Roger's to shield him, and a piece of shrapnel slid into her already injured leg, causing her to scream in pain.

Roger's eyes were fading now, but he held her gaze. "Get out of here before you lose your chance."

Lilly shook her head and kept stroking his hair. "You're not done telling me everything." Her voice was gasping and strangled in the caustic air and every breath felt like she was inhaling nails, but she would not leave her friend.

"Stubborn ass," Roger whispered, and Lilly laughed through her tears. Another creaking sounded and Lilly looked in the direction, half expecting another collapse, but it never came. She began hearing muffled voices outside the car and knew rescue crews were close. "You hear them? They're coming— the rescue crews are here."

Roger's eyes closed, his breathing so shallow it was difficult to detect any chest rise. Finally, he struggled to open his eyes and said, "Tell my Mum she gave the best hugs…and Jacob, tell him he's my best mate and love is always the answer. It's my Dad, I see him there." His hand weakly pointed in a direction off to the right, and Lilly nodded.

"You go see him, go be with your Dad. I love you, my friend." Lilly kissed his head, keeping her lips pressed against his hair.

One last small smile crossed his lips as his eyes closed and his last breath whooshed through his body. Lilly collapsed over Roger, cries wracking her body as grief took hold.

The voices of the rescue workers got louder, and then they were right next to her, asking if she could walk. Lilly shook her head, and two men lifted her onto a stretcher.

She saw another kneel by Roger, checking a pulse and shaking his head. "Be careful with him, that's my friend! I promised him we would leave together."

The rescue worker shot her a sympathetic smile. "We'll help him, I promise, but you need medical attention. Your friend would want you to get treated immediately." He slipped an oxygen mask over her face and eased her down onto the gurney.

Another creaking sound thundered as if it were right on top of them, and all Lilly heard was screams to evacuate before everything went dark.

CHAPTER FIVE

Jacob

He and Brad watched the live news feed at the studio, shocked. When he returned to his dressing room, there was a litany of calls from Janie.

He assumed she wanted to ensure his plane landed safely but her sobs told him otherwise. "Jesus, Janie, what happened?"

"He's gone. He's gone, Jakey."

"Who's gone? What happened?" Jacob bellowed, his heart pounding.

"Roger," Janie sniffled, "Roger was killed in the attack. I'm so sorry, Jakey. I needed to tell you before the news broke."

Jacob's phone fell from his hand as Janie's voice echoed out the most devastating words; his best friend was among the dead in the terrorist attack.

He couldn't remember his reply to Janie or if any words actually left his mouth. He hung up the phone and threw it across the dressing room, sliding onto the floor, chills wracking his body.

He wasn't sure how long he remained in that position, but Brad was soon at his side. Jacob somehow relayed the terrible news.

"Oh, Christ"—Brad kept repeating—"not Roger." Although the entertainment field was vast, Roger and Jacob had both attended several London events with Brad, and the talk show host was always a fan of Roger.

"I have to go," Jacob declared, pulling himself to a standing position and searching for his keys.

"Jacob, you're in no shape to drive. It'll be a madhouse with all the roadblocks. Wait a while, leave in a couple hours."

Jacob held his keys firm, his gaze steely. "I don't have a couple hours. I need to get to Sophie."

It was only 9 p.m., and yet it had become the longest day of Jacob's life. Every room at Roger and Sophie's house brought on a new wave of despair, although he remained stoic for Sophie. She vacillated between unearthly quiet and sobbing in Jacob's arms, not knowing how to tell her daughter her daddy was gone.

She couldn't do it. How do you tell a four-year-old daddy isn't ever coming home?

Jacob volunteered for the wretched task and searched out Roger's daughter, Martha. He found her in her bedroom playing with her stuffed cat. The little girl sensed that something had occurred, but she couldn't grasp the gravity of the situation.

Jacob knelt by Martha and stroked her hair, and she rewarded him with a smile.

"Who's your friend?" Jacob's voice faltered as he forced a smile.

"His name is Oliver, my Daddy gave him to me. Where's my Daddy?"

Tears sprang to Jacob's eyes, this was going to be agonizing. "Your Daddy got hurt today."

She stopped playing with Oliver and cocked her head to one side, a curious look on her face. "Is he okay?"

"No, he's not okay, honey."

"When is he coming home?"

"He's not," Jacob choked out, covering his mouth with his hand.

Tears brimmed in Martha's eyes. "Where's my Daddy. I want my Daddy!" she cried out, and Jacob pulled her to his chest, holding her as she wailed for the father that was forever lost to her.

When the little girl's cries had ebbed, she rubbed her eyes with the heel of her hand, sniffling. "I didn't get to say goodbye to him before he left."

Neither did I, Jacob bemoaned internally. He stood and offered a hand to Martha. "Take a walk with me?" He held her hand and walked onto the patio where the bright starlit beauty belied the devastation of the day. He knelt by her, wrapping his arm around her waist. "You see all those stars? Did you know when someone goes to heaven, they get a star so they can see the people they love and the people they love can see them?"

The little girl turned to him. "Is Daddy in heaven?"

"Yes sweetie, your daddy's in heaven. But look up, see that star? That beautiful bright one?" The little girl nodded, and Jacob took a moment to control his cries silently. "That star belongs to your Daddy now, so whenever you miss him, or need to talk to him, you come out here, and he can hear you. Do you want to try now?"

She nodded and turned her face up to the stars. "I'm sorry I didn't hug you today. I love you Daddy." She held her stuffed cat to the sky. "Mommy washed Oliver, so he isn't dirty anymore."

It took every ounce of strength in Jacob's body to hold it together as the little girl attempted to process the news. After a few moments, she asked to go to her Mum. Jacob remained with them until they fell asleep, their emotions usurped by the immense exhaustion of the tragedy.

As Jacob walked to his car, he saw that his phone was full of messages and voicemails. Victoria called numerous times once the news of Roger's death hit the airwaves, her messages sweet and concerned. She informed him she was in London and would meet him at his house that evening. She ended with a declaration of love, telling Jacob she was heartbroken for his loss, and Jacob almost believed her sincerity. It sounded as if she too had been crying.

But Jacob wasn't heading home. He was bound for the one person who could bring him some semblance of peace. He needed to feel Lilly's arms around him, perhaps then the world might make sense again.

Sabina opened the door to Lilly's cottage, startled to see Jacob on the stoop. She enveloped him in a huge hug, murmuring condolences about Roger, and when they pulled apart, both had tears in their eyes.

"Is Lilly here? I need to—I need her."

"She's in the hospital."

Jacob nodded. "Makes sense with the—with what happened."

Sabina's face took on a strange expression. "No, she was on the Tube."

Jacob stumbled against the porch column, Sabina reaching out to steady him. "What?" His mind raced in a million directions, he obviously heard her wrong. "What did you say?"

Tears slipped down Sabina's face. "Lilly was injured in the explosion. I'm collecting some things for her—"

"Where is she? What hospital?" Jacob bellowed, his heart pounding in his ears.

"St. Luke, wait, I'll take you! You're in no condition to drive!" Sabina's words clamored as Jacob raced to his car, backing out of the driveway.

He didn't know how he made the hospital in ten minutes but surmised he had run several lights and gone the wrong way up a one-way street. He screeched into the front drive, handing the keys to the valet before turning toward the entrance.

"You need your ticket, sir," the valet yelled after him.

"I'll figure it out later."

Jacob took the stairs to the fourth floor three at a time. The elevator simply wasn't moving fast enough.

He saw Janie when he entered the unit and she threw her arms around her brother, her face mottled with sorrow. "You're here. I just left you a message. I only found out about Lilly. She was brought in without identification, but an employee recognized her and notified Sabina." She hugged him again. "I'm so sorry, Jakey."

Jacob pushed Janie back, clinging to her shoulders. "I have to see Lilly. Where is she?"

"Room 423, end of the hall."

He gave his sister one final hug before running down the hallway.

Enrique stood outside her door and blocked the entrance at Jacob's approach. "No way, you are not going to upset her right now. She has been through too much."

Jacob was in no mood to argue, he would ram through the surgeon if he didn't let him pass.

He opened his mouth to protest when Lilly's voice demanded in a weak whisper, "Let him through, Enrique. I need to speak with him."

"So help me God if you upset her—" Enrique hissed as Jacob squeezed past him.

He took a deep breath and approached the bed. She was pale, her right leg encased in a leg immobilizer, scrapes and cuts running the length of her body.

"Hi angel." The sight of her injured stole his breath and he felt a helplessness he had never known. Pressing a kiss to her forehead, he cupped her face in his hands, her skin like ice.

Lilly pulled off her oxygen mask and struggled to a sitting position. "I'm so sorry about Roger. I'm so sorry."

Her simple apology broke the last dam holding Jacob's tears, and he collapsed on her lap, his body heaving with grief.

Lilly stroked his head, murmuring words of comfort as his sorrow soaked her gown with tears. After several minutes his crying lessened, and he raised his head, looking into his beloved's face.

Jacob wrapped his arms around her in a hug, startling when Lilly whimpered in pain. He released her immediately, and she forced a smile. Jacob examined her face, whiter than before, as white as the sheet on which she lay. "I'm sorry! I didn't mean to hurt you. Can I get you anything? Do you need pain medicine?"

Lilly shook her head, peering at the monitor as it alarmed again. "I'm okay."

Jacob followed her gaze as the monitor beeped and flashed. He lacked medical expertise, but he knew Lilly wasn't disclosing the full story. "Why does the monitor keep beeping?"

Lilly coughed and held the mask to her face, taking a deep breath. The inhalation brought on another coughing fit, and Jacob stroked her hand while praying for it to pass. After settling, she lowered the mask, resting her head against the pillow. "The oxygen sensor doesn't work well because my fingers are cold."

"Well, let's warm them up." Jacob placed the mask back on Lilly's face; speaking seemed to be a struggle for her. He grasped her hands, rubbing her fingers. "Any better?"

Lilly nodded, but the machine kept beeping. She picked at her sheet, not meeting his gaze. "Don't you love technology? Tell me about Sophie and Martha. Have you seen them?"

"They're asleep, thankfully; Martha can't understand what happened, not fully. She cries and then asks when Daddy's coming home, then cries again. I don't think she grasps the permanence of the situation. But who can blame her? Hell, I can't understand the situation. I can't fathom I'm never going to see my best mate again. How did this happen? What kind of world do we live in?"

But Lilly didn't answer, just held his hand, her cold fingers stroking his palm. Her simple touch brought him more peace than he had felt in the last several hours.

"I had no idea you were on the Tube, Lilly. I'm so thankful you're okay. If you had—" Jacob broke off, he couldn't let his mind travel that dark path.

Her own tears rolled down her cheeks as she tongued the cracked corner of her mouth. "I'm so sorry about Roger. Please don't hate me. I didn't know—"

"I could never hate you, Lilly! How could you ever think something like that? You're my everything." He pressed his lips to her fingers, they were like ice. "You're freezing, I'll get you a blanket."

Lilly stayed Jacob's movements. "Don't worry about me. I'm exhausted, I need to sleep."

But Jacob ignored her, grabbing a blanket from the foot of the bed and wrapping it around her petite body before butting the chair against the bed frame. "You sleep. I'm here."

Lilly smiled as well as her abraded lip would allow. "Go home and rest. There's nothing you can do here. I'm in good hands."

Jacob shook his head, kissing her hand and caressing it gently. "There is no way I'm leaving you." Lilly pulled down the mask and began to protest, but Jacob held up his hand. "Just stop. I'm staying, and that's final."

The monitor beeped again, and Jacob knew he needed a second opinion on the situation. Standing up, he leaned in and kissed her gently on the forehead, as soft as butterfly wings. "I'm going to fetch you some more blankets and speak with Enrique. I'll be back in a moment."

Jacob met Enrique and Sabina by the nurses station as they discussed Lilly's injuries and her determination to attend Roger's funeral.

"I'm glad you made it here in one piece," Sabina stated, handing him a valet ticket. "You left this at the valet station."

Jacob shoved the ticket into his pocket. "Thanks. Sorry for leaving you like that."

"Don't worry, I understand."

"Lilly is so cold, she can't seem to get warm. I've put an extra blanket on her, but her fingers are like icicles."

Sabina nodded, as if expecting the statement. "Some of it is likely the shock of the situation."

"Some of it? What are the other reasons? Sabina, what are Lilly's injuries? She looked too exhausted, I didn't want to tire her further." Jacob's body surged with nervous energy, rattling through his feet which tapped compulsively, his arms knotted across his chest.

Sabina cleared her throat. "She has a ton of cuts and bruises, nothing too severe save for a slash on her right leg that required stitches. Her right knee sustained some damage and will take some time to heal—"

Jacob sensed Sabina was glossing over Lilly's injuries, but he needed brutal truth. "What aren't you telling me?"

"What she isn't telling you," Enrique interrupted, "is Lilly sustained a lung injury because of her prolonged exposure following the explosion. She likely wouldn't have been as serious if she left ground zero when she had the chance."

Jacob's mind reeled. "Why didn't she leave immediately if she had a chance?"

Sabina squeezed Jacob's arm. "She wouldn't leave Roger."

Jacob's world started coming apart. "Lilly was *with* Roger? They were together on the Tube?"

"Lilly said they ran into each other and ended up sitting together. When the explosion occurred, Roger was crushed, but Lilly wouldn't leave him until rescue crews arrived."

Jacob's eyes closed as another flood of emotion ran over him. "That's why she asked me not to hate her."

Always his brave warrior, Lilly risked her life to stay by the side of his best friend as he died. Yet despite the selflessness of her act, she worried people would blame her for the outcome.

Sabina nodded. "She blames herself that he died, and she survived.

She claims it was her fault they missed the earlier train, a conversation with Victoria delayed their departure."

Jacob's head spun as he attempted to sort through the shattered pieces of the day. Victoria hadn't mentioned being involved in the attack in her earlier voicemail. "Was Victoria also on the Tube?"

Sabina shrugged. "I don't think so. I believe they saw her earlier that day. That's all I know, it exhausted her to tell me that much."

Jacob grabbed Sabina's shoulders. "I'm worried, Sabina. The alarm on her monitor keeps sounding. Lilly claims it's nothing to worry about, but I don't believe her. I'm staying the night here. I need to be by her side."

"I'm going to look into her…monitor situation," Enrique stated, sending Sabina a purposeful glance before hurrying to Lilly's room.

"Sabina, is she going to be okay?" Jacob whispered, terrified of the answer.

"If anyone can survive this attack, it's Ms. Staver." Sabina offered a somber smile.

"Soon to be Mrs. Edmonton."

"Hmm, is Lilly aware of that proposal?"

Jacob chuckled, embarrassed. "I'm fantastic at groveling. I hope I can convince her by begging and pleading."

Sabina pursed her lips before meeting his gaze. "You could try loving and supporting her—might be a better path."

Jacob nodded. He had spent far more time making up to Lilly and not enough showering her with adoration. But no more. Jacob knew exactly what he wanted from life, and it all centered around the petite brunette in room 423.

Glancing around the waiting area, his eyes fell onto a tabloid laying on a table, featuring a picture of him with Lilly in London. The title read '*Mystery Lady is Jacob's True Love*', and he grabbed the rag, turning to the article. The few paragraphs detailed the romantic tryst, as observed by the author. He claimed the adoration between the couple was evident and believed Jacob's relationship with Victoria was a ruse. Per his deduction, the only woman Jacob loved was the one in the photograph. Overall, it read in a similar fashion to the magazine article Brad showed him earlier that day.

Sabina tilted her head at the magazine. "I'm assuming you'll refute the story?"

Jacob shook his head. "I'll never refute the truth. I know you don't believe me, but I love Lilly more than you can imagine."

"Yes, but do you love her enough?" Sabina shrugged. "You've made so many claims, but the only thing you've mastered is how to break her heart. It will take more than words to convince me—or Lilly—that you mean what you say."

Lilly

illy held out Jacob's phone when he reentered her room. "You forgot this." She bit the inside of her lip, keeping her expression purposely blank.

Jacob glanced at his phone and released a loud sigh as he fell into the chair next to her bedside. "It's not what you think."

Lilly avoided eye contact, her gaze focused on the pilled blanket. "It's not my business."

"She's worried about me after what happened to Roger—" Jacob's voice cracked.

Lilly's heart wrenched at his agonized expression. She knew he couldn't utter the words, couldn't say out loud that his best friend was dead. Not now anyway, perhaps never.

He didn't need any additional inquisitions tonight. "She kept calling, so I finally answered the phone. I didn't want her to worry."

Jacob closed his eyes and groaned. "What did she say?"

Lilly paused, considering her words. "She was cordial and concerned. She wished me a speedy recovery and asked me to tell you that she had dinner waiting for you at home."

Jacob scrubbed his face with his hands, aggravated. "She left a message saying she would meet me at my house, but it slipped my mind. My only goal was getting to you."

Lilly tongued the crack at the corner of her lip, uncertain what to believe as gospel anymore. She opted to play it safe, keep her distance. "You've done your duty. You should return home to Victoria. This stress isn't good for your baby."

His eyes narrowed. "My duty?"

"As a friend. Thank you for checking in on me but you've had an awful day, and you need to rest."

A muscle twitched in his jaw. "I'm not going anywhere. I'm staying right here."

Lilly noticed the tabloid resting on his lap. "Are you reading tabloids now?"

Jacob chuckled, showing Lilly the article. "Not really, but it had an article about me and my 'mystery woman'. They say she's the love of my life."

She took a breath from her mask when her monitor began alarming, then forced a tremulous smile. "You know what they say about tabloids. It's all lies."

"I think what I said was that they usually had the scoop, and this time they definitely got it right." Jacob clasped her fingers, but she drew back, rubbing her hands together.

"Go home Jacob, let me rest. I need my strength for Roger's funeral." Lilly stumbled over the last word, tears in her eyes.

Jacob grabbed her hand, holding it against his lips. "Lilly, you're injured. You need to focus on getting well. Lord knows Roger would understand."

Lilly shook her head. "I made him a promise, and I plan to keep it. Now go, I'll talk to you later."

"I don't want to leave you, Lilly." His bright blue eyes gazed at her, beseeching her to relent and let him stay.

God, she wanted to believe him. But Victoria stood between them, and she would always have a place in Jacob's life. "You're needed at home."

"I'm needed *here.*"

Lilly laid her head against the pillow and shook her head. "No, you're not. I can take care of myself." She watched as her words hit him like bullets. It pained her to say them, she could only imagine how it felt to be on the receiving end. Time to backtrack and soften that blow. "What I mean is, there's an entire hospital of trained professionals to watch over me."

"Fine, you don't want me at your bedside, I'll go sit in the waiting room."

The man was not taking no for an answer, and Lilly didn't have the stamina to go any more rounds. "Don't be ridiculous. Get some rest tonight and then come visit me tomorrow…if you'd like. You can come before dawn if it makes you feel better."

"Staying right here next to you would make me feel better," Jacob grumbled.

"Please, Jacob."

Jacob's jaw clenched but he resignedly rose from the chair. "If you need anything—*anything*—you call me immediately. Do you understand? And since you're so damn stubborn I'll take you to the funeral myself. Being near you is the only thing that will make this bearable."

Lilly considered arguing but thought better of it, offering a sad smile. "Okie dokie. Give Victoria my best."

Jacob kissed her on her forehead, his lips lingering against her skin. "Angel, are you sure—"

"Go home, Jacob."

With a final squeeze of her hand, Jacob walked out the door.

The door had just closed when Lilly's floodgates opened, her tears welling up as she relived the day. Today was the stuff of nightmares. She couldn't wrap her head around the fact that she survived a terrorist attack, or that Roger hadn't.

Pain was increasing throughout her body, but doctors feared giving her narcotics because of her compromised respiratory system. She knew how severe the damage was to her lungs—she knew it when she refused to leave Roger's side—all that could save her now was prayer and time.

"Where's Jacob?" Sabina asked as she entered the room, toting a basin of bath supplies.

"He went home." Sabina shot a look of contempt at the door and Lilly smiled. "Down tiger, it was my decision."

"You'll have to explain your logic to me."

"Victoria was waiting for him, so I thought it best for him to get some rest, or whatever the two of them plan to do tonight."

"According to that press release Jacob issued, they're not together romantically." Sabina filled the wash basin with warm, soapy water and brought it to the bedside table.

"Thanks, I've got it from here." Lilly reached for the washcloth, but Sabina held it tight.

"Like hell you do. I'm not going to allow you to run *me* off. Now lay there and try to pretend this in any way resembles a shower."

"Do I have a choice?" Lilly managed a giggle.

"No. Otherwise, I'll tell my boyfriend you're being confrontational and non-compliant."

Lilly groaned. "You're going to use your boyfriend as leverage? Is that all he's good for?"

The twinkle in Sabina's eyes spoke volumes. "Enrique is good for a myriad of things."

"I'm so happy for you…for you both. Love looks good on you."

A flush crept over Sabina's cheeks as she focused on swabbing Lilly's face and neck with the warm cloth. "It feels good, too. Lilly, you know I love you, and I only want what's best for you."

Lilly knew where this conversation was heading. Sabina didn't pull any punches. "You don't think I should see Jacob anymore."

"I know you love him, and he claims to love you, but sometimes love isn't enough. Victoria is pregnant with his child. Do you think she would even allow you to be together?"

69

A tightness formed in Lilly's chest, but she drew in a deep breath. The words, although harsh, were the truth. "You're right. I thought perhaps I could handle him having a baby with Victoria, but the truth is it shreds my heart. I'll never have that with him, and it seems so unfair."

"I think he would give you anything you wanted, including a baby. I just worry Victoria would make your lives hell and get off on doing it." Sabina paused, running a comb through Lilly's hair. "I give him credit for issuing that public declaration, but he still hasn't mentioned you or what you mean to him. The man should be proclaiming his love for you from every rooftop in England."

Lilly chuckled. "How theatrical."

"It's romantic. Hell, at the very least, he should have stayed with you tonight. Victoria can take care of herself."

"I told him to go."

"And he should have ignored you, just like I'm doing," Sabina retorted.

They finished Lilly's sponge bath and Sabina helped her into a clean gown before handing her a mirror.

Lilly examined the final result, noting the bruise on her cheek, the cut on her mouth and the long scrape down her neck, not to mention the myriad of abrasions covering the rest of her body. "Who am I kidding? Why did I ever think I could compete with someone like Victoria? She's a beautiful, blonde, world famous millionaire and I'm…none of those things." She laid the mirror in her lap, giving a mirthless laugh.

"You could be blonde. I can grab a bottle of peroxide from the supply closet." Sabina quipped, earning a small smile from her friend. "You're perfect the way you are, and the right man will ensure you never forget that fact."

"Starting right now." Jacob's voice carried from the doorway, startling the women. He held a small overnight bag in his hand and a giant stuffed bear tucked under his arm.

"I didn't expect to see you back here tonight," Sabina noted, a cool expression on her face.

Jacob scooted onto the bed next to Lilly, his fingers stroking her hair and neck. "I went home and escorted Victoria off the property. I spent a few minutes with Hannah, she didn't know about you and Roger. I sat down for exactly thirty seconds and packed a bag to return to you, because beside you is the only place in the world I'm happy. I know I have to prove myself and I'll do that until my last day on earth. Just let me be near you."

"Jacob—" Lilly started, but Jacob placed a finger on her lips, silencing any argument.

"I wasn't finished." Jacob nuzzled her neck, playfully nipping her earlobe. "I hope you don't mind me staying, but I'm not leaving unless security drags me out. Am I welcome?"

Lilly nodded and released a sigh of relief. "Definitely."

She started when Sabina chuckled, having forgotten they weren't alone. "I've never been so thrilled to be wrong. If you're staying with Lilly, I'll head home. My neighbor is watching my daughter."

"I'll take care of Lilly, I promise."

Sabina hugged her friend, planting a kiss on her forehead. "You call me if you need anything. Promise me."

Lilly nodded, blowing her friend a kiss as she walked out the door. As soon as the door closed, she averted her eyes to the bedspread, self-conscious about her haggard appearance. Her gown had ridden up, exposing one of many nasty gashes and Lilly slid the blanket up her body to hide the carnage.

Jacob yanked the blanket down, resting his hand on her thigh. "Don't you dare feel ashamed of these cuts, they'll heal. You survived a terrorist attack today. And if I hear you compare yourself to Victoria again—"

"You heard all that?" Lilly closed her eyes, embarrassed.

Jacob grabbed the overnight bag and opened it, his gaze intent on her. "You're superior to Victoria in every way. There will be no more talk of that woman tonight." He started pulling items out of the bag. "Now, on a happier note, I have contraband."

"Whiskey?" Lilly asked, half kidding.

"Hardly, but I do have chocolate, an iPad to watch a movie, a blanket which is actually soft compared to the sandpaper they provide in the hospital and—" Jacob's voice cut off as he peered into his bag.

"And what?" Lilly asked, struggling to look inside the bag. "Really no whiskey?"

"Scout's honor." Jacob set the bag on the bedside table before sliding into the bed next to her. He spread the blanket over them and slipped an arm around Lilly, pulling her against his chest.

But Lilly's curiosity wasn't abated. She wanted to know what was hiding in the bottom of his overnight bag. She snatched it off the table, gasping when a small box tumbled into her lap. She recognized the jeweler's logo and closed her eyes. She knew what the small box contained. Did she dare hope anymore?

Jacob grabbed the box from her lap, his blue eyes crinkling with amusement. "Well, that's one way to ruin a surprise. You're killing me kid."

"Clive told me you picked up the ring this morning."

Jacob sat up, his eyes narrowing in confusion. "You were at Daniel

71

Prince today?"

Lilly scrambled to think of an answer. "Roger was picking up a gift for a friend. The jeweler mentioned the ring. He said you picked it up today. He thought when he saw me that I was there to have it sized. He seemed to think..." her voice trailed off and she coughed.

Jacob stroked Lilly's jaw, his fingers whispering across her skin. "What did he think?"

Lilly swallowed the embarrassment, staring at the blanket. "That the ring was meant for me. I informed him we weren't engaged, and it must have been for someone else."

Jacob chuckled. "Someone else? Silly girl, who else would I pick it up for?"

"I don't—I don't know." Perhaps she was being silly, but her heart would only allow a modicum of hope.

"Yes, you do. I told you last night I intended to make you my wife immediately. Have you forgotten?" Jacob pressed his lips against hers, his tongue licking the seam of her mouth. "You're weren't that inebriated."

Lilly's gaze held his, a smirk playing about her lips. "I was a little inebriated."

Jacob straightened, faking a scowl. "Do you recall what I said?"

This game would be fun to play. "Hmm, I remember you telling me what you planned to do with me when you saw me. Granted, that will have to wait for another time."

"I promise to make it up to you, my angel." Jacob pressed the box into her hand. "I wanted to wait until later because this is not a romantic environment but..." He flipped open the ring box and revealed the facets glistening against the velvet.

Lilly gasped, her heart racing as she stared at the ring. The ring Jacob designed—for her. The craftsmanship was remarkable, the design delicate and intricately woven. It was the most beautiful ring in the world.

"Do you—do you like it?" Jacob's voice wavered as he asked the question.

"It's exquisite." It was more than a piece of art—it represented all the promises Jacob had ever made, all the hopes she had planted in response to those promises.

Jacob's hands trembled. "I swear, every time I plan a proposal for you, it goes to shit. I had an entire evening arranged for tonight—"

"Did Roger know about this?" Lilly had to ask, she needed to know if their friend held a happy secret on the day of his death.

"He knew every last detail."

"Bastard." Lilly smiled as a tear rolled down her cheek. "He knew all along."

"This is not how I planned this evening in my head, but I can't wait any longer."

"What are you talking about?" Lilly felt her heart beating rapidly and put the oxygen mask to her face, willing her lungs to take in as much air as possible. Was he really going to ask her right now? What would she say? Her heart screamed yes, and her mind threatened a permanent abdication if she agreed to the deal.

Jacob knelt down by her bedside, his eyes on hers. "I don't deserve you, Lilly, but I love you more than life itself. I don't want to wait another second. Lilly Gwendolyn Staver, without all the bravado I hoped for, but with more love than I knew could exist for another person, will you be my wife?"

Lilly was dumbstruck, her jaw slack as she pulled down the oxygen mask.

Jacob noted her silence and continued with his rambling. "I know I'm asking you to overlook certain aspects of my life, but I need you as my wife. I want it all with you—the house and marriage and babies—I want everything… with you." He choked up at the end, his face displaying an anxious tension.

"But look at me! You don't want to take all this on. It will take time for me to recover and—" Lilly watched Jacob's eyes grow wide and aggravated.

He shushed her. "Will you marry me? Not a whole diatribe, just a yes or no—please don't say no—answer."

God, she wanted to believe him, and she wanted to say yes. Lilly wanted to marry Jacob more than she wanted her next breath, but there was so many unanswered questions. "What about Victoria?"

"I thought we weren't talking about her anymore."

Lilly reached for his hand, and he obliged. "Jacob, isn't it a bit soon? I saw the press release. You only broke off your engagement this morning."

Jacob scoffed. "There was never any engagement! Victoria blindsided me with that crock at the conference. There's never been anyone but you, it's *always* been you."

A nurse entered the room at that moment, carrying a cup of pills. "Time for your medicine, Lilly." She sent a stern look at the couple laying in the bed, but Lilly waved her off.

"What is she taking?" Jacob asked, his hand still clasping Lilly. It was evident he wasn't going anywhere.

The nurse looked at Lilly for permission before responding. "An antibiotic, mild painkiller and a multi-vitamin. I'm sorry Lilly, I know you've been on the prenatal vitamins, but the pharmacy doesn't carry them. If you want someone to fetch your pills from home, I can give them to the druggist."

The nurse's statement, so innocent, hung in the air as Lilly turned bright red, mortified that Jacob knew she was still taking prenatal vitamins. Hell, she didn't know why she kept taking the pills, she wasn't having sex with anyone.

"That's fine, the regular vitamin is perfect. Thank you." She accepted the pills and swallowed them, her throat feeling as if it were lined with razors.

Not a word was spoken until the nurse left the room, but she knew Jacob had been staring holes into her since the nurse made her untimely announcement.

"Is there something you want to tell me?" Jacob's words fell like ice shards, his eyes hardened on her face.

Lilly chewed her lip, he was angrier than expected. "Not particularly."

Jacob shot out of the bed like a bullet. "Who is he?"

Lilly sat up straighter despite the pain, a confused look crossing her face. "Who is who?"

"Your boyfriend. You're trying to get pregnant so it's obviously serious. Let me guess—Dr. Torres, right? I should have known." He looked positively distraught and yet was so misguided that Lilly laughed. "I don't find this amusing."

Lilly couldn't stop laughing until her breath caught in a coughing fit. "I do."

Jacob shot her a severe look. "No wonder you didn't want me to stay, I'm obviously in the way."

Lilly grabbed his hand, holding it despite his attempt to pull away. "You're not in the way."

"What a load of bollocks. I'm lying in your bed, asking you to be my wife and you're...romantically involved with someone else. When were you planning to tell me?"

God this conversation train had derailed before it ever left the station. "Never."

"Wow, that's big of you. Let go of my hand." He jerked his hand away, gathering up his things.

"I would never tell you there was someone else because there isn't anyone. I feel really foolish right now but I'm taking the vitamins because I still want a baby with the man I love, even though he was technically engaged to someone else, and destroyed my heart on international television. So, if you want to know who the man is Jacob, go look in a mirror."

A look of understanding dawned on Jacob's face, and he smiled, sliding back into bed next to her and peppering her face with kisses. "Lilly, I'm sorry. I'm an idiot."

"Agreed." She could be angry with him for his reaction, but it was so real that it made her heart happy.

"I'm an idiot that's hopelessly in love with you and from what you just told me, you're hopelessly in love with me."

"Hopeless, at least."

He lowered his mouth to hers, murmuring against her lips. "Marry me, Lilly. Let me make you happy."

A tear slid down her cheek. "I want to marry you."

"Then say yes, my angel."

"I need time, Jacob. You broke my heart. I need to know you'll be here, that you won't leave and run back to Victoria."

Jacob pulled her to him, his lips pressed to her hair. "I will never choose that woman over you. I'll give you the time you need, but it won't stop me from trying to convince you, every second of every day." He stroked her back, lulling her into a more relaxed state. "As soon as you're well, I'm making love to you, and I'm not stopping until you're carrying my child. You'll be the most beautiful pregnant woman in the world."

"I'll be as big as a cow."

Jacob chuckled. "No, you won't. A sheep, maybe."

Lilly shot him a fake scowl. "Thanks a ton!"

He dropped kisses along the side of her neck. "You love sheep. Remember the drive to Cotswolds? You made me stop so you could take pictures of every sheep you saw."

"I like sheep, but I don't want to be compared to one. Forget it. I'm not having a baby with you. You'll spend nine months teasing me."

His arms tightened around her. "Yep, and you'll love every second of it. So get used to the idea."

Lilly smiled against his chest, hoping against hope that this time her luck would be different.

CHAPTER SIX

Jacob

acob woke several times throughout the night to Lilly's labored breaths and despite Lilly's assurances that she was healing, his gut told him her health was in serious jeopardy.

"I don't want to leave you." This argument had lasted the better part of an hour—Lilly wanted him to go home and check on Sophie, but he didn't want to leave her side.

"You have so much to do today, Jacob. I promise I'll be fine."

"I'll be back this afternoon. Call me if you need anything."

Lilly chuckled. "I lost my phone in the attack."

Jacob kissed her lips, smiling against her mouth. "I should buy stock in the cellular company. I'll buy you another phone today."

"Don't worry about it, there's too much to do with Roger's funeral this evening. Make sure Sophie doesn't need help and send her my love." Lilly's eyes filled with tears and her monitor started beeping again, her oxygen level a constant 87%.

"Are you going to speak to the doctor about your breathing? If he doesn't advise you to go Lilly, you're not going. I don't want anything happening to you. You're the most precious person in my life."

Lilly nodded in resignation. "I'll speak to the doctor. Now go."

A pall hung over Sophie's house despite the flurry of activity. Jacob found his friend wandering the garden, her face drawn, and posture stooped. He walked up behind her, engulfing her in a fierce embrace, and she collapsed against his chest.

"Jacob," Sophie sobbed, tears wracking her already exhausted body. "The arrangements are done. The funeral director was wonderful and handled all the details. Roger always parlayed a morbid sense of humor and prepaid everything, down to the floral arrangements." She stroked his cheek, giving him a quick peck. "Thank you for being here. It makes me feel closer to Roger, he loved you so much."

Jacob hugged Sophie to him, holding back his own tears. She needed his strength now, he could mourn later. "I'll always be here, for you and Martha. Don't ever hesitate to ask for anything. You're my dear friend, Sophie."

Sophie nodded, wiping her eyes. "How is Lilly? Is she any better?"

Jacob hesitated with his answer. How honestly should he answer that question? How much more could Sophie handle? "She claims she's fine, but I'm concerned about her breathing. She's worried sick about you."

"Poor girl. Did you know she's speaking at Roger's funeral?"

Jacob nodded. "She said it was Roger's request. But Sophie, she really isn't in any condition to attend. She's stubborn though and fighting tooth and nail to be there."

"I don't want her attending if she isn't well," Sophie paused as tears filled her eyes again. "I can't lose her too."

"She agreed to speak with the doctor about attending. I have to trust Lilly is sensible enough to know her limitations."

Sophie offered a short barking laugh. "This is Lilly we're talking about."

"She is stubborn, my stubborn Yank."

Sophie glanced at her watch and rubbed her wrist, looking at the ground. "I'll see you at the church? I hate the idea of walking in there alone, but I suppose I'll need to learn how to do things on my own from now on."

Damn. It hadn't even occurred to Jacob that Sophie lacked an escort into the church. No widow should have to walk alone to their husband's casket. "You won't be alone, I'll escort you to the funeral."

"You've got to take of Lilly."

"She will not only understand but insist upon this. I'll send someone to pick up Lilly, and I will escort you and Martha."

"Are you certain?"

"Absolutely. I'll run home, get dressed and be back by five."

Jacob groaned when he pulled into his driveway and saw Victoria leaning against one of his porch columns.

What part of 'I'm not interested' does this woman not understand?

"Victoria, what an *expected* surprise, to what do I owe the honor of yet another unsolicited visit?"

Victoria rolled her eyes, her hand on her slightly swollen belly. "Could you take the sarcasm down a notch, all things considered?"

Jacob glanced at the ground and nodded, feeling contrite. There was no need for ugliness. "You're right. What can I do for you?"

"I want to help. I know you have your hands full right now."

"My hands full?"

Victoria rolled her eyes again and sighed. "With Sophie of course…and

Lilly. I heard you spent the night with her at the hospital."

Jacob's eyes narrowed. "That's not any of your business, but how did you hear that, anyway?"

"The walls have ears, my dear." Her eyes narrowed on him. "It's a shame you and I couldn't get past the anger of our relationship to really give things a second go, a shame for our baby." She looked away, her face displaying a wistful hope.

Jacob felt a momentary pang of guilt but pushed it down. "If that baby is mine, he will have all the love in the world. The status of our relationship doesn't matter. I'll be a devoted father. I swear that to you."

"I heard you asked Lilly to marry you, but she didn't accept your proposal."

Jacob's jaw clenched. The walls really did have ears. "She needs time to process everything. I can't blame her after the debacle of our prior engagement. You were there, Victoria. In fact, you're the reason behind my failed engagement."

"You don't understand—"

Jacob held up his hand, this conversation was heading down a dangerous path. "I won't discuss this matter any further with you. You're lucky I'm even speaking to you after the stunt you pulled."

"It's kind of you to be so patient with Lilly. I wish you exhibited that understanding with me."

"Victoria, you slept with at least six other men while we were together, then rubbed it in my face and lorded it over me. Lilly has shown me nothing but kindness and love. There's no comparison between you two. I'm in love with Lilly and you're going to have to accept that fact."

Victoria's eyes narrowed. "So, you believe she's been faithful?"

"What the hell is that supposed to mean?"

Victoria lowered her gaze, examining the floor. "She and Edward got cozy while you were in Greece. According to him, they hung out quite often. Do you honestly believe it was only an innocent friendship?"

"Shut it, Victoria," Jacob replied, although her words sent his mind spinning. He never viewed Edward as a threat, hell, he barely knew the man, but Janie mentioned he and Lilly were friends. Per his sister, they became closer after that poker night at Roger's house, but Janie never intimated anything romantic was brewing between the two of them.

It couldn't be, could it? Stop being ridiculous. Lilly is not Victoria, she wouldn't string me along...would she?

Victoria cleared her throat and flashed an innocent smile, but Jacob swore he saw her hid a smirk behind her hand as she walked into his living room. She tapped her watch. "What can I do to help? Time is not your friend."

Jacob glanced at the clock, groaning at the late hour, it was already well past three. "I need to shower and get dressed. I'm escorting Sophie and Martha to the funeral."

Victoria nodded. "That makes sense. What about Lilly? I assume she's not attending because of her injuries?"

"Shit," Jacob muttered, realizing he didn't have enough time to find alternate transportation plans for Lilly, get himself ready and be on time to collect Sophie. "I was going to take Lilly myself, but I promised Sophie. She needs me right now."

"I'll pick up Lilly."

Jacob's eyes widened at his ex-girlfriend's offer. Was she insane? "No way in hell, Victoria. I'll call Janie." He dialed his sister, but the call went to voicemail. No answer from Audrey or his Mum either. "Damn, they're likely busy getting ready for the…funeral."

Victoria was watching him the entire time on the phone, her face unreadable. "No luck reaching anyone?"

"No. I can send a car for Lilly—"

"Jacob, I'll go get her. I'm here, I'm willing to help, and it's pretty apparent you need me…today at least."

Jacob scrubbed his face. Just like that, he was backed into another corner, and the only way out was through Victoria. "I won't allow you to cause issues today."

"Do you really think that little of me?"

"Is that a rhetorical question?"

"I understand how badly I screwed up when we were a couple, but every misguided action since then was out of the hope you might still feel something for me. I'll admit, it was extremely difficult to watch you fall for someone like Lilly when—"

"When what?"

Victoria picked at an imaginary thread on her dress. "When you never showed a morsel of that dedication to me during our relationship."

Jacob sighed, shaking his head. "Victoria, I was crazy about you—rather, crazy about the person you portrayed yourself to be, but that person doesn't exist. The real you cavorted with man after man. What did you expect me to do, sit around and ignore your actions?"

"Did you ever think I did it to see if you actually cared?"

Jacob guffawed. "You were testing me?"

"I've been doing everything in my power to reconcile with you, but you won't even consider it. I don't hate Lilly—"

"Yes, you do. But you don't have a single reason to dislike her, she's done nothing to you."

"She has you. Besides, I don't claim to understand why you would want someone like her. She's so different from us, she couldn't possibly understand our lives."

Jacob smiled as he thought of his precious Lilly. "Exactly, Lilly's nothing like us, she's warm and real and soft. She loves and forgives, and she never plots against people. She makes me strive to be a better man."

Tears filled Victoria's eyes, and she sank down into a chair, burying her face in her hands. Jacob doubted her sincerity until her shaking shoulders made him question the falsehood, and he knelt in front of her, taking her hands from her face.

"Victoria, please don't cry."

The willowy blonde wiped her eyes, her mascara running down her cheeks. The tears, at least, were real. Who knew if the emotion behind them was also genuine? "It's hard when you love someone, and they don't love you back. When you want a future with someone but because of bad behavior, they can't see past your indiscretions." Her bright green eyes held his gaze. "Why didn't you love me, Jacob?"

Christ, was he really going to have to discuss this topic? Now? Best to try to smooth things over, Victoria's mood swings were legendary, and no one needed this superstar acting out today. Jacob called on all his reserves to provide a sugarcoated answer, one that would hopefully satisfy Victoria's need for adoration. "Victoria, despite your abhorrible behavior during our relationship, you're actually an amazing woman. You're a force of nature. You're beautiful, smart, talented, and when we first met, I was in awe of you."

"Am I not any of those things now?" Victoria sniffled.

"You're still all of those things, but a force of nature requires immense energy and time. Our relationship—if you can call it that—was exhausting. Being with Lilly is easier, there's less bravado and need to constantly perform."

"You're with Lilly because it's easier than being with me? So, if things with me were easier, who would you choose?"

Jacob stalled for a moment, unsure how to answer the question without hurting Victoria's feelings. "That's not the case, so I can't answer that question. Can we please discuss this later? I have to get ready for Roger's…"

Victoria nodded and stood, wiping her eyes. "I'm sorry, today is not about me. I'm an utter jerk for asking."

"You're not an utter jerk. It's nice to see the softer side of you."

"Hormones from being pregnant, I suppose."

"Whatever the reason, it's still nice."

Victoria pulled out a compact, grimacing at her reflection. "I look horrible."

"No, you don't, just wash your face and you'll be good as new. You're glowing, Victoria, you look radiant." She actually looked like a half-drowned Halloween clown, but Jacob was treading lightly. He learned his lesson many times over with his ex-girlfriend. If her ego was wounded, no one was safe.

"You're a bad liar," Victoria joked, standing up and grabbing her purse. "Tick tock, what do you want to do about Lilly? It's already almost four."

Shit. At this rate, Jacob would be lucky to make Sophie's house by five. He was out of time—and options. "Do you promise to be nice to Lilly?"

"Jacob, even I can manage to be kind today. I'll run to the hospital now, and we'll meet you at the service."

But could she truly be nice to the love of his life? Could she set aside her insane jealousy and loathing of Lilly to ensure today celebrated a good man whose life ended too soon? "Lilly isn't going to like this—"

"It's either me or she doesn't go to the funeral. But that's your choice. Or…you can let Sophie and Martha walk themselves into the service."

He couldn't do that to Sophie and Martha, they were already drowning in sorrow. He checked his phone, praying for a last-minute reprieve from Janie or Audrey, but there were no new calls. No new messages. Damn it all to hell, Victoria was right. She was his only hope.

"Give me a chance to prove I'm not a total monster."

"Please, I'm begging you. Be kind to Lilly. She's been through too much."

"Of course. I'm going to wash my face and then I'll go fetch her."

Jacob's heart raced, he only prayed he wasn't making the wrong choice. "One last thing—"

Victoria turned, her face bright and expectant. "Yes?"

"Tell Lilly I'll always mean that last line of my letter. She'll understand."

Her face darkened, but she covered it with a practiced smile. "Certainly. I'll be sure to let her know."

Lilly

"Lilly, this is an awful idea. Your oxygen level is barely 87% with the non-rebreather mask. You will decompensate too quickly outside the hospital." The doctor regarded her, his expression stern.

"Doc, this is really important. I promised my friend I would relay his final thoughts and wishes. I'm the only one who can do it, I'm the only one who was there." Lilly snapped the mask back onto her face, willing her oxygen level to get about 90%. She leaned back against the bed, she had never felt such exhaustion.

"Can't you tell them at a later date? They won't hold against you the fact that you were seriously injured in the attack."

Lilly grasped the doctor's hand; the time had come to beg. "I'll hold it against me. I promised him. Please help me fulfill his final wish."

"I hope I'm not interrupting anything."

Lilly's heart sank at the sight of Victoria in the doorway. She looked splendid in a dark dress, her stomach barely protruding with her pregnancy.

Of course, she looks perfect, she looks like a damn angel carrying Jacob's baby.

"Victoria. I'm surprised to see you here."

Lilly tried to control her nerves as her nemesis entered the room. What in hell was she doing here anyway? Victoria must be dizzy with glee that Lilly was injured while she was so...breathtaking.

Victoria crossed the room, shaking hands with the starstruck doctor as she flashed her grandest smile. "I'm here to take you to the funeral service, that is, if you're cleared to attend." She returned her gaze to the doctor, who blushed under her green-eyed scrutiny.

"I'll be attending." Lilly paused, licking the cut on her mouth. "I thought Jacob was picking me up. Did something happen?"

Victoria ignored Lilly's comment and focused her attention on the doctor. "Will it be safe for her to attend the funeral? I would hate for anything to happen to Lilly."

Lilly coughed, uncertain whether it was involuntary or in response to Victoria's forced declaration of concern.

"I highly advise against it," the doctor stated, catching Lilly's look of death. "But your friend is determined to attend against medical advice.

Hopefully her foolhardy determination will be enough."

"Wonderful, then it's settled." Victoria placed her hand on the doctor's hand, patting it gently. "If you don't mind, we girls need a few minutes to get ready. Thank you so much for all your help."

The doctor blushed again before walking to the door. "It's an honor to meet you, Victoria. You're even more beautiful in person." His gaze moved to Lilly, his expression steely. "Say your piece and get back here, that's an order."

The door shut and Victoria walked over to Lilly's suitcase, picking up a black dress and shoes. "I don't think you'll be able to use these shoes with that thing on your leg, do you have another pair?" Her gaze drifted to Lilly. "You cut your hair. What a surprising choice, Jacob's always preferred long hair."

"What are you doing here, Victoria? Come to gloat?" Lilly didn't have the capacity for small talk, particularly with a woman who despised her existence.

Victoria shrugged. "I told you, I'm here to drive you to the service. Jacob was too busy to drive all the way back and fetch you, so when he arrived home, I offered my assistance." The way she said home implied she also considered his abode her sanctuary and it made Lilly's stomach turn.

"He would *never* send you to pick me up."

Another shrug from the vile cherub. "Call him."

"I can't. My phone was lost—destroyed—in the attack."

Victoria reached into her bag, punching in a number and handing Lilly the phone. "Use mine. I insist."

Lilly simply stared at the phone, only taking it when she heard Jacob's voice on the other end of the line. "Jacob? It's Lilly."

"Hi, angel. I'm so sorry. I promised Sophie I would escort her to the funeral...I didn't think I'd have time to pick you up and make the service on time...Victoria offered—she's being nice to you, isn't she? I'll kill her if she's not—" Jacob's words were hastened, his voice rushed, his anxiety over the situation apparent.

Lilly knew Jacob didn't need any additional pressure—not today. He had to bury his best friend today. "Everything is fine. I was just surprised when I saw her instead of you—" Another coughing fit, the pain radiating through her body. God, it hurt to breathe.

She could hear the remorse in his voice. "I should have come to get you. I don't know what I was thinking. Victoria *swore* she would nice and I couldn't reach Janie or Audrey—"

"Please don't worry about it. It's fine," Lilly grabbed the bedrail and used it to steady herself. At this rate she wouldn't reach the door, much less the funeral service.

"Lilly, you don't sound good. I don't think you should leave the hospital—"

"I'm going and that's final. I'll see you in a little bit," Lilly choked out as another cough took hold. "Hug Sophie for me."

"Do you have any idea how much I love you, angel?"

"We don't have all day," Victoria interjected, not bothering to disguise her annoyance.

"Whatever she says, ignore her. Promise me," Jacob demanded. "She's just jealous."

Lilly managed a small laugh. "Of me? I doubt that highly, Jacob."

"It's true. I promise, once you get to the church, you'll never have to see her again...not in person, anyway."

"Promises, promises."

"I love you."

Lilly smiled—despite the pain, the difficulty breathing, Victoria standing not a foot away—Jacob loved her. "You too."

Jacob let loose a little chuckle. "That was almost an admission."

The words dangled on the tip of her tongue, but their torrid past held her back from uttering the proclamation. "Jacob—"

"It's okay, angel. One day. I'll see you soon. Please be careful."

"I will." Lilly ended the call, handing the phone back to Victoria.

"Satisfied?" Victoria arched one perfectly manicured brow.

"Yes, thank you for letting me speak with him."

"I hear congratulations are in order. Well played, Lilly."

"What are you talking about?"

"Jacob asked you to marry him. Granted, it was after you suffered this awful injury, but he's always been a stand-up guy."

"He intimated his intentions the night before the attack." Take that, Victoria.

Unfortunately for Lilly, Victoria was well-versed in the art of verbal warfare, and she hadn't come to battle emptyhanded. Without missing a beat, she let out a small, derisive chuckle. "But did he actually propose *before* the attack? Let's be honest, Lilly. In your current situation you'd never find a suitor and you've been a dutiful and faithful companion, now he's returning the favor and marrying you."

Lilly forced a laugh, but Victoria's words hit her heart like bullets. "You're insane. Besides, I didn't accept Jacob's proposal."

"Then you're a bigger fool than I thought. What I'd give to be in your position."

Lilly's patience snapped, she was tired of acting cordial. "Would you like to be? I'll gladly trade places with you if you think my position is so much more desirable. You can have my broken-down body and smashed heart, and I'll take your perfect life and baby with Jacob."

"At least I'm giving him a child. Can you still have children at your age?" Victoria forced her question to sound innocent, but her tone dripped venom.

"Why do you care if Jacob chooses me? You don't want him—you couldn't—you wouldn't have cheated on a man like Jacob if you respected your relationship. Perhaps I'm not some mythical Hollywood goddess, but I've always been there for him and maybe that's why he claims to love me." *Shit, I do sound like a loyal hound dog.*

"Old faithful, huh?"

Lilly had heard enough. She was in no mood for Victoria's underhanded remarks. Not today, not any damn day. "I need to get dressed. Will you excuse me please?"

"I'll help you." Victoria held up a hand when Lilly opened her mouth to protest. "Remember, today isn't about you, and we need to hurry if we want to arrive on time."

Lilly shook her head in resignation as she struggled to stand with the leg immobilizer. She flinched when Victoria untied her gown and pulled it down her body. "Thank you."

Victoria eyed the abrasions crisscrossing Lilly's body. "Quite a roadmap."

Lilly grabbed the sheet, embarrassed by her body, particularly next to Victoria's tall blonde perfection. "The cuts will heal."

Victoria nodded in agreement, helping Lilly slip on the dress before grabbing a brush to work through her strands. "I think you should know the truth of the situation, things aren't always what they appear."

"What game are you playing now, Victoria? Don't you ever tire of meddling in people's lives?" Lilly's asked flatly, she had heard enough lies from Victoria.

"I'm not playing any game."

"Right," Lilly sneered, a coughing fit wracking her frame.

Victoria let loose a deep sigh, pushing her platinum strands over one shoulder. "I knew you wouldn't believe me, so I brought proof."

Lilly looked at Victoria's phone, her brow wrinkling in confusion. "Your phone?"

"No. This conversation occurred not more than an hour ago, right before

I came to pick you up."

"You recorded your conversation with Jacob? What's wrong with you?"

"I'm trying to do what's right by my baby, by Jacob's baby. I know you think Jacob is hopelessly in love with you, he probably even tells you all the time that he is, but don't you think it wise to know what's said when you aren't around?"

Victoria pressed play on her phone, watching Lilly's face as the recorded discussion played between her and Jacob.

Lilly knew she had the worst poker face in the world, every emotion played out across her features. Her stomach sank at Jacob stating how she was the easier choice, while Victoria was a beautiful, wonderful force of nature. The worst part was when Jacob refused to answer Victoria's direct question about whom he would choose if both women were equally easy; his silence screamed volumes.

"I don't know about you, but I wouldn't want to be with someone because they thought I was the *easier* choice. Of course, he will marry you now, he feels obligated to you for trying to save Roger and saving Janie. I guess you win."

Lilly chewed her bottom lip, Jacob's recorded conversation playing on a loop in her head. His words broke through her battered emotional walls. Was she really the easier choice? She didn't want to be the easier choice, she wanted to be the right choice.

What did Jacob really want? *Who* did Jacob really want? Did he feel some sense of obligation to her, was that why he was so resolute in seeking marriage?

"You're quiet." For once, Victoria's tone lacked malice.

Lilly slid the oxygen mask back on her face, taking a few deep breaths. She didn't have the energy to fight anymore, never mind the fact that she didn't have the desire to continue this battle for Jacob's heart. Perhaps Victoria was always meant to be the victor and it was time to return the crown.

"Do you honestly believe if I was out of the picture, that you and Jacob would rekindle your relationship?"

Victoria regarded Lilly with a mixture of pity and contempt. "He cares for you, I'll admit that, but I believe if you weren't injured trying to save Roger that he would consider a reconciliation. It would be better for our baby. We have a history together, Lilly, and there's a lot of love there, whether he's willing to admit it or not. But you don't have to take my word for it, you heard the recording."

Lilly had one last card up her sleeve, one final hand before she surrendered the fight. "Riddle me this, why would Jacob go to all this trouble to be with me if he really wanted to be with you?"

Lilly's flat tone ignited a fire in Victoria's green eyes. "He's a gentleman and gentlemen never forget their obligations. However, if he were truly devoted, wouldn't he be here right now…instead of me?"

"He said—"

"I know what he said, Lilly. The man is very talented at *always* saying the right thing. Question is, does he mean what he says? Hasn't he always said the right thing where you were concerned? How many of his promises actually came to fruition? In that regard, you and I are quite similar."

Lilly wanted to vomit. She knew Victoria was twisted and jealous, but she was also correct. Every word from her mouth was the truth, even if Lilly was loathe to admit it.

"You're not a bad person, Lilly. But you don't understand our world, our priorities, the immense pressures. You're too busy living a fairytale—the handsome prince falling for the plain Jane. I get it. If I were you, I'd lead him into marriage by whatever means necessary."

Lilly closed her eyes, wondering if this was another of Victoria's games, but how could she fake the recording? She sure as hell didn't want to be viewed as an obligation. Jacob didn't owe her any favors. She wanted someone to be with her because she was their ideal, their perfect partner. She wanted kismet and fireworks, not sacrifice and liability.

"Hello, Lilly—Victoria? What are you doing here?" Edward entered the room, shooting Victoria a sharp glare.

"Hello Edward." Lilly managed a smile as he dropped a kiss on her cheek. "Thank you for the flowers."

"Of course, luv. I didn't know if you had an escort to the funeral, so I stopped by to offer my services."

"Victoria is taking me—"

"Actually, this is perfect. Would you mind giving Lilly a ride, Edward? I have a pit stop to make—for Jacob—so it will be easier if someone else drives her."

"You're making pit stops for Jacob now?" Edward could barely contain his sarcasm. "Why do I find that hard to believe?"

Victoria had the good grace to appear flustered; it seemed Edward possessed some strange hold over the golden goddess. "Well, he's so busy with the arrangements—"

Edward held up his hand. Conversation over. "I could care less about your reasons. But I'd be happy to take Lilly to the service."

"Wonderful." Victoria offered up her cheek for a goodbye kiss, but Edward had no intention on getting that close. After a few seconds, she drew away, a pout drawing up her red lips. "Charming as ever, Edward. Lilly, I do hope you'll consider our chat." With that statement, Victoria grabbed her bag and made for the door as if a literal fire had been lit under her ass.

Edward watched Victoria depart before regarding Lilly's contemplative face. "Why was Victoria here? You two aren't friends now, are you?"

Lilly snorted in disbelief. "Best buddies. Jacob was busy with the service preparations, so Victoria volunteered to deliver me to the church."

"Odd choice, of all the people to pick you up—"

"She also played a recording of a conversation she had with Jacob," Lilly blurted, too tired to cry over the situation. "Apparently, there's love between them that I wasn't aware of, or maybe I always knew it was there, but didn't want to admit it." Lilly held the oxygen mask to her face, each sentence an exhausting burden.

"A recording? I wouldn't put much stock in it, Victoria's very determined when she wants something, and she wants Jacob."

"It makes sense. It would be better for their baby if they were a couple. Victoria believes Jacob feels obligated to help me and if I hadn't been injured that they would reconcile. Do you agree?" Lilly was amazed by the flat tone of her voice, her resignation to the situation. Perhaps her body was too tired to fight, or maybe her heart had finally called it quits.

Edward paused long enough to make Lilly uncomfortable. "They were only hot and heavy for a minute. I don't think what they shared was love in any sense, rather an insatiable lust for each other."

"Wonderful," Lilly muttered, now even more self-conscious of her injuries.

"However, one could argue it would make sense if they reconciled for the baby's sake. I don't know if they would last. I think they'd burn out again, like last time."

"You think Jacob would get back together with Victoria if I weren't in the way?"

Edward stroked Lilly's hair. "What a question! You're not in the way, Lilly."

"Just answer the question."

"I don't know. How do you expect me to answer that?"

"Honestly."

Edward sighed heavily. "Perhaps—and this is pure speculation—if you weren't in Jacob's life, he might take another chance with Victoria and see how they fit as a family."

And there it was, the brutal truth from an honest friend. She had her answer, now she had to explain it to her naively hopeful heart.

Lilly struggled to a standing position, transferring to the waiting wheelchair. "What would you do in my position? Should I walk away?"

"Don't make me answer this question, Lilly."

"I need someone to give me the truth. I'm tired of believing in daydreams."

"As much as it would hurt, I would walk away and give them time and space to grow as a family."

Lilly sighed with resignation. The daydream was over. "I had a feeling that's what you would say. Besides, I'm no one's obligation. I'd never allow Jacob to stay with me out of a sense of guilt." She clasped Edward's hand. "Thank you, for being a true friend. Most people tell you what you want to hear, not what you need to hear."

Edward wheeled Lilly to the parking lot. "Don't doubt Jacob's love for you. His feelings for you are very real, but it's a different emotion than the one he shared with Victoria. It's simpler."

Lilly's jaw twitched. "Easier?"

"Yes, that's a good word for it, but that's not a bad thing. There's something to be said for a love that's even and steady instead of a scorching fire."

"Sure, one consumes you and the other one you bitterly endure." A tear slipped down Lilly's cheek, but she wiped it away, refocusing on the task at hand. "I hate this day. I hate having to speak at Roger's funeral."

Edward helped Lilly into his vehicle, assisting her into the seat. "It's an idea I can't get used to, that I'll never see him again. I keep hoping this service might provide some closure, but I doubt it." He put the wheelchair in the boot and slid into the driver's seat. "I admit I was surprised to learn you were delivering the eulogy. I didn't realize you knew him that well."

"He asked me to speak on his behalf since I was the last one to see him alive."

Edward nodded, a faraway look on his face. "It's strange how life works out. If you two had switched seats, it would be a different funeral."

Lilly swallowed against the lump in her throat. "Don't think I haven't considered that fact every minute since the attack."

Edward patted her hand, his face rueful. "That came out wrong. I'm thrilled you're still with us, Lilly. Don't you dare beat yourself up about situations over which you have no control. All you can do is move forward and make the best decisions regarding circumstances you can control."

"Words of wisdom." Lilly's face echoed a resolve of steel, but her insides writhed with physical and emotional pain.

CHAP SEVEN

Jacob

he limo ride from Sophie's house to the church was the longest of Jacob's life, but he was in no hurry. He dreaded entering that church and seeing Roger's casket, symbols representing the end of a friendship he believed had no expiration date. He imagined he and Roger would grow old, trading tales with their grandkids and reminiscing about the good old days.

But instead of whiskey filled poker games and jovial discussions about their youth, he sat beside Roger's wife and daughter en route to his funeral. A funeral for a young man with decades of unwritten adventures that died right along with him.

Tears brimmed at the back of his eyelids, but Jacob blinked them away. He had to present a strong front for Sophie and her daughter. They needed someone to lean on today and for many days in the future and his focus was to help bear the weight of their bottomless pain.

And yet, in the midst of this dark hour, there was a light. Lilly survived the attack, and a full reconciliation seemed imminent, as soon as Lilly realized the depth of his love.

He could see Roger smiling down at him, making a snide remark that Jacob finally got his head out of his arse by placing Lilly on the pedestal she always deserved. God, he loved her. He was desperate to make Lilly his wife, tomorrow seemed too long to wait at this point.

The church loomed like an imposing sentry as Jacob assisted Sophie and Martha into the church. A crowd of reporters and mourners gathered outside the church gates, many openly distraught. Jacob often resented the intrusion of the media into personal affairs, but he felt warmed by the number of lives Roger touched in his short life.

Jacob escorted Sophie to her seat before returning to the back of the church to wait for Lilly.

"Looking for me?" Victoria whispered, her lips brushing his ear.

Jacob backed away a step. He didn't want Victoria's hands anywhere near him. "Where's Lilly?"

Victoria pursed her lips. "She's not with me."

"What do you mean, she's not with you? You specifically said you were going to pick her up from the hospital." Jacob's voice was low but intense as his anger mounted.

"Lilly said she would rather attend with Edward, so I left. I wanted to get here as soon as possible to ensure you were doing alright." She reached up, smoothing his short curls. "I've been so worried about you."

Jacob stayed her hand, dropping it to her side. "Stop, please." He paced a few steps, exasperated. "Why was Edward at the hospital?"

Victoria shrugged, offering her most demure smile. "I told you, they're always together. I can't blame Lilly, your courtship has been anything but romantic."

"That's rich. The reason our engagement failed was because of you and your games. Let's not play the role of little miss innocent, okay?"

"I know what I want, and I want you. I'm willing to fight for you, even if I have to fight dirty. But Lilly, as you said earlier, isn't anything like us. She isn't used to being away from her lover for months on end. It can be quite lonely and tempting to take up with a local boy."

"Victoria—" Jacob snarled when he spotted Edward wheeling Lilly into the church. He rushed to her side and grasped her hand—it was ice cold. "Angel, are you sure it's a good idea for you to be here? You don't look good."

Lilly shrugged, taking what appeared to be a pained breath. "Too late now, I'm already here. And I know, I look like death warmed over but I'm not here to win any beauty pageants." She looked at Edward, pointing to an easily maneuverable entrance ramp in the back of the church. "The service is about to start. Edward has offered to assist me, so you can focus on Sophie."

Jacob was about to protest, but the pastor walked in, signaling the start of the service. Jacob trudged back to his seat next to Sophie, holding back an exasperated huff when Victoria squeezed next to him on the pew. Her move earned an eyeroll and look of death from Janie, seated across the aisle. Victoria looped her arm through his and laid her head on his shoulder. It was all Jacob could do to maintain his composure.

He glanced to the back of the church, catching sight of Lilly seated with Edward, her ever dutiful friend. Jacob wasn't a jealous man except where Lilly was concerned. He resented the connection Edward shared with his love. Jacob wanted Lilly to need him, to seek him out for help, but he was the last person she sought out in times of need. Although it hurt him to admit it, Jacob wasn't surprised. He had done nothing but wound her at every turn.

The pastor announced Lilly's eulogy and Jacob's heart caught as Edward escorted her to the podium. She looked so frail, even more delicate than before, and all he wanted to do was gather her into his arms and reassure her that everything would be okay. He would protect her from any additional harm and never leave her side again.

Victoria's hand tightened around his arm and Jacob glanced over at her, willing his anger down at her blatant attempts for affection. *I'll bet you're laughing your ass off, aren't you, Roger?*

"I told you they were close," Victoria whispered, watching Jacob with a knowing look.

Shake it off, Jacob. Don't let Victoria get into your head again. Lilly is not the enemy.

Lilly stood at the podium, her face ashen, the cuts standing out in bas-relief against her skin. She was shaky, but Jacob noted her resolve to say her piece.

"I would say good afternoon, but there is nothing good about it. I believe I speak for all of us when I say I never expected to attend Roger's funeral on this day or any other. I'm sure many of you are curious who I am and why I'm speaking. I'm no one important, but I was privy to a heartbreaking and poignant event last Thursday. It was pure coincidence that Roger and I were on the Tube at the same time. We knew each other socially," Lilly glanced at Jacob, "but I will forever treasure our last lunch and the witty banter for which he was famous. I won't speak about the attack—" Lilly broke off, a cough racking her body. Edward leaned in to support her slight frame until she nodded him off.

"I apologize. As I said, Roger and I were together on the Tube and I was the last person to see him alive. I can tell you this, he was not afraid of dying, but he had things to say to certain people, and he tasked me with the delicate job of delivering his message."

Lilly looked at Sophie. "Sophie, he adored you. To him, you were perfection. He wanted you to know that every sunset from now until your reunion, will be hand painted by him and sent to you, wrapped in warmth and love. For his beautiful daughter, Martha, you hung the moon, and every night, when you look at the stars, know he hung them just for you. Roger said he couldn't understand how a human weighing not eighteen kilograms could bring him to his knees with a glance, but such is the power of love."

Jacob started to rise as Lilly struggled, her posture more stooped, her breathing labored. Sophie shot him a concerned look, but Lilly held up her hand as if to wave them down.

"To his Mum, he and his Dad will watch over you constantly and whenever you catch a whiff of whiskey or a cigar, know they're close to you." Lilly's eyes swung and met Jacob's concerned gaze. "And Jacob, his best mate, he never knew a heart more capable of love if only its owner would open the door. To all of you, he sent one wish—tell people you love them, tell them every chance you get. It's a gift to give your love away, even if there's no chance of it being returned." Lilly's paused, tears rolling down her face.

"I've tried to come up with a song, but it's been the most unbelievably hard task because no four minutes can sum up the man that was Roger. So, I chose to sum up his wishes instead." Lilly nodded, and Warren Zevon's 'Keep Me in Your Heart' began playing.

As the music filled the church, Sophie put her head down and sobbed, clutching Martha. Tears streamed down Victoria's face and Jacob pushed aside his anger at his ex for a moment to wrap an arm around each grief-stricken woman. He gazed up at the church ceiling and gave a smile of thanks for the friendship he had found with Roger. Lilly's words hit home with Jacob—he would never again take the woman he loved for granted. Every day would be a new opportunity to shower Lilly with adoration.

When the song ended, Jacob turned, searching the church for Lilly. He needed to go to her, wrap his arms around and tell her that she was the only reason his heart continued to beat.

But she was nowhere to be found and he felt a clutch of panic. Where had she gone?

"She was told to return to the hospital right after the eulogy. Doctor's orders," Victoria whispered, slipping her hand into the crook of his arm as she rested her head on his shoulder.

Jacob nodded, but couldn't shake the feeling of unease in the pit of his stomach. As soon as the service was finished, he would rush to Lilly's side and no one would tear them apart again.

Lilly

illy's body was shot, so weakened she couldn't stand any longer. Edward helped her into the wheelchair, and she fell back against the cushion.

She struggled to sit up in a futile bid to ease her breathing, weakly grabbing the oxygen mask.

"I need fresh air, please." Lilly's voice was a ragged whisper, and Edward nodded, his face contorted in concern.

"You need to return to the hospital."

Lilly shook her head. "I'll be okay." He wheeled her out the side exit, where the damp air hit her like a wet blanket. "You don't have to stay with me. I'll be fine out here," Lilly lied, forcing another breath into her body. The pain was excruciating, each inhalation felt like a thousand knives stabbing her body.

Edward shook his head, patting her shoulder, his brow furrowed. "No way in hell am I leaving you alone out here."

"Stubborn."

"Very. I'm also concerned about my friend." Edward grasped her hand. "You're freezing, Lilly!"

Lilly tried to raise her hand to wave him off, but that simple gesture required strength her body no longer possessed. "Did I do okay by Roger?"

"You were amazing. It was beautiful." Edward's eyes grew wide when his gaze returned to Lilly's face. "We need to get you to the hospital now."

Lilly half heard him through the fog that enveloped her mind and body. Her body felt as if it were made of lead, breathing was entirely too much of an effort now. Someone was shaking her, and she tried to turn her head, but it felt heavy as cement.

A few faint words from people scurrying around her floated to her through the fog, although Lilly barely understood their meaning.

"Call 999! Lilly, can you hear me? We need an ambulance now!"

Lilly struggled to tell the concerned voices to leave her be for a moment. The constant pain since the attack had finally lessened and she felt a peace envelop her that she had not known in days.

The haze around her mind and body thickened as strong hands shook her, hands she didn't recognize. Voices continued yammering above her and she felt a slight prick in her arm.

"She's tanking, call the hospital and let them know we have a respiratory arrest coming in STAT. Hang in there luv, we're going to give you something to let you sleep…we have to intubate, I'm not oxygenating with the bag…"

Lilly felt people around her, lifting and jostling her body, then everything went dark.

CHAPTER EIGHT

Jacob

S omething was happening outside the church as whispers carried amongst the mourners. *Christ, I hope the media isn't pulling some publicity stunt.*

Jacob glanced up to see Janie look at her phone and her eyes widen before catching her brother's gaze. She mouthed one word—Lilly—before jumping up and running out the exit.

"What's happening?" Sophie inquired, her gaze on the side exit of the church.

"Something's happened...I think with Lilly."

Sophie covered her hand with her mouth, releasing a small cry. "Oh my God no! Go, Jacob. Go now."

Jacob didn't need any additional encouragement. He followed his sister outside, his world—and breath—stopping. Ambulance lights flashed in the parking lot as two paramedics knelt over Lilly's unconscious form.

"What's going on? What happened?" Jacob bellowed, his heart pounding in his ears.

"She couldn't breathe, she just collapsed. I called 999 immediately." Edward's hands trembled as he raked his hands through his hair.

Jacob ran over to the paramedics. "I'm her fiancée, what's happening to Lilly?"

One of the paramedics shot him a look of annoyance at the intrusion. "Respiratory arrest. We're taking her to A&E immediately. We have to intubate."

Jacob wrung his hands, not comprehending a word of the paramedic's statement, and losing all patience. "What does that *mean*? Is she going to be okay?"

The other paramedic placed a hand on his shoulder, her smile sympathetic. "She can't breathe, and she can't oxygenate. If we don't take her now, we'll lose her. I'm sorry. We have to go."

They loaded Lilly into the ambulance as Jacob watched helplessly, unable to accept their words—if they didn't take her now, they would lose her...he would lose her. He would lose Lilly forever.

"What the hell happened?" Victoria stepped out the side door, eyes focused on the departing ambulance.

"I have to—I have—I" Jacob stammered, and Edward grabbed him by the arm, tugging him towards his car.

"I'm taking you to the hospital."

Jacob nodded, unable to form even a simple sentence.

Jacob jumped out of Edward's car while it was still moving and rushed into Accident & Emergency, his heart racing as he approached the check-in desk.

"May I help you?" The clerk, oblivious to his terror, asked in a flat tone.

"Lilly Staver, she was brought in by ambulance."

She peered at him over her glasses. "And you are?"

"What?"

"Are you family?"

"I'm—I'm—"

"Family only, sorry."

Jacob felt as if he had been punched in the face. He considered jumping across the desk and throttling the woman but figured he would be of no use to his beloved Lilly in jail.

He jumped when a hand touched his arm, turning to see Sabina at his side. "Where is Lilly? They won't tell me anything."

Sabina shushed him gently, leading him to a chair. Her voice remained calm, but her face was streaked with concern. "They're trying to stabilize her."

The color drained from his face. "Stabilize her?"

"She has ARDS—acute respiratory distress syndrome—it's from the explosion. The air around the bomb zone was filled with all manner of debris, and Lilly inhaled large quantities. It damaged her lungs. The doctors knew there was a good chance this would happen."

"So, what do we do? How do we fix it? I have the money—how do we fix it?" Jacob's voice was shaking as badly as his hands as he pawed at Sabina.

Sabina clutched his hands, her eyes bright with unshed tears. "The doctors have put Lilly into a medically induced coma, and she's on a ventilator. She'll stay on the ventilator for a few days to rest her lungs while they utilize a special type of treatment to open her collapsed lung tissue. The hope is that after a few days, she can oxygenate on her own, without the ventilator."

"And if she can't?"

Sabina's breath caught, but she didn't say the words, she didn't need to say them. "All we can do is pray the treatments work and she doesn't contract any infections. I'm sorry Jacob."

Jacob couldn't breathe as tears rolled down his face. "I need to be with her—"

"You're not family."

"Sabina don't do this to me. I need to be with Lilly. Please. She's my entire reason for being."

Sabina relented, squeezing his shoulder. "When she's transferred to the critical care unit, I'll come get you. I'm going back to check on her now."

Jacob shook uncontrollably as he rocked in the waiting room chair. Victoria and Edward rushed over, concern written on their faces.

"What's happening?" Victoria asked, grabbing Jacob's arm.

Jacob swallowed against the lump in his throat. "She can't breathe on her own...they don't know if she..." He dropped his head into his hands, sobbing. Arms surrounded him but Jacob was lost in his mind, playing a movie reel of the life he'd lived with Lilly. He adored every facet of her—her laugh, her smile, her kisses, her taste, the way she loved him unconditionally—the idea of losing her was more than he could fathom.

Jacob had downed five cups of tea and paced holes into the hospital floor by the time Sabina came to fetch him in the waiting area.

She escorted him to the critical care unit, pausing outside Lilly's ICU bay and giving Jacob a sympathetic squeeze. "You need to prepare yourself. There are a ton of machines and wires in that room, but they're helping Lilly survive. Bear that in mind."

Jacob nodded dumbly, following Sabina into the bay.

Lilly looked so tiny in the bed, the ventilator beeping softly as it regulated her breathing, medications running in through a myriad of tubes and wires in her neck, her skin a stark white except for the cuts from the attack.

Jacob swallowed back the nausea invading his being. He wanted to run from the room and the feeling of death permeating the space that surrounded Lilly. Instead, he took a few shaky breaths and pulled a chair by her bedside.

"Talk to her, they say even in a coma, patients can hear you. Let her know you're here." Sabina walked to the other side of the bed and checked the IV pumps before placing a kiss on her friend's forehead. "I love you baby girl, you keep fighting. This world isn't done with you yet."

"Did she know she was this sick?" Jacob knew the answer to the question, but he had to ask. He needed to know if once again Lilly had shielded him from the harsh realities of life.

Sabina's eyes filled with tears and she nodded. "She knew. She didn't want to worry you. She said you had enough on your plate."

"What my beautiful Lilly doesn't understand is that she is my whole world. I can't lose her, Sabina."

"She's a fighter, Jacob. Remember that. I'll be back soon." She squeezed his hand and exited the room, leaving him alone with Lilly and the myriad of machinery.

Jacob stroked Lilly's hand, noting the delicate veins running just under her pale skin. Physically, she was diminutive, but she possessed a strength of spirit that floored him. His angel was going to pull through this ordeal, and he would be there every moment of every day to help her heal.

"You knew you were sick, but you didn't tell me. You're always protecting people, but you don't let anyone protect you. That's going to change, my angel. From now until the day I die, my one and only goal is to keep you happy and safe." A fresh batch of tears rolled down Jacob's cheeks. "You're stronger than anyone I know, you're going to make it through this."

Jacob's days passed in a haze. He learned the inner workings of an ICU and all the care required for a critically ill patient. Jacob refused to leave Lilly's bedside even for a moment, despite prodding from staff and family. Victoria bombarded his phone with messages, begging him to return to his house so she could take care of him, but he ignored her pleas. He had one focus, getting Lilly well again.

He spent the days engaged in one-sided conversations with Lilly, telling her everything from his childhood fears to his plans for their future. He had the next two decades mapped out by the end of Lilly's second day in the ICU—four children, a country home in London, animal sanctuaries throughout the UK and daily doses of adoration aimed solely at his future wife.

Jacob massaged Lilly's skin with lotion and performed stretching exercises to prevent muscle atrophy. Members of the staff joked that if his acting career didn't pan out, he would always have a job at the hospital.

He wasn't always alone with Lilly. She had a steady slew of visitors and her room was bursting at the seams with stuffed animals and cards. Janie spent hours in the bay daily, playing eighties pop songs and chattering on about all manner of female issues. Ben and Sabina made daily visits to her bedside to ensure she was received optimum care. Lilly was beyond a VIP patient, she was a treasured staff member and friend. Even Sophie dropped by with flowers and warm wishes for Lilly's speedy recovery.

There was one visitor that Jacob didn't recognize, a young man who resembled his director Albert. He didn't introduce himself, just slipped up to her bedside with tears streaming down his face. He held her hand and told Lilly how she saved his life and how grateful he was to her daily. As quickly as he came, the man left, leaving a bouquet of flowers.

Jacob's curiosity couldn't be abated, and he read the card, noting it was from Albert's film company. It made sense that the young man looked like Albert, he was obviously a family member.

But how in the world did Albert's relative know Lilly? Jacob never mentioned Lilly to his director, but perhaps his Brad Taylor interview had aired. If that was the case, the world now knew of his love for Lilly Staver, and that idea made him smile. It was about damn time.

When Lilly woke up, he would ask her about the mystery man and her connection to Albert. If his director had ever met Lilly, he had no doubt she charmed him just as she did everyone else, she came in contact with.

That settled it, he would ask her *after* he was done convincing her to marry him immediately. Perhaps he could get a preacher to hold the ceremony in the hospital—it wouldn't be the first time in history. She might balk but she could be stubborn *and* be his wife. This time, he wouldn't take no for an answer.

"I thought you might like some tea."

Jacob started awake, looking up to see Enrique standing over him. "I dozed off. Thank you."

The surgeon pulled up a chair next to Jacob and raised his own coffee cup. "I thought we might call a truce."

Jacob nodded. He had no desire to argue with Enrique any longer. Lilly's health was paramount, everything else seemed unimportant. "Lilly would appreciate that, I'm sure."

"She would indeed. She hated conflict. A true hippie, in every sense of the word."

Jacob took a deep breath. He needed to ask the question, although he was terrified of the answer. "Sabina has kept me informed of Lilly's progress, but I 'm afraid she's trying to sugarcoat the severity and I need to know…"

Enrique nodded. "There's minimal improvement in Lilly's lung tissue, but any improvement is a step in the right direction. We expect to see further healing within the next day or so, at which point they will attempt to wean Lilly from the ventilator."

"Oh, I didn't know you were here, Enrique." Sabina walked into the bay, a look of surprise on her face.

"Hi sweetie." Enrique stood, dropping a kiss on Sabina's cheek.

Jacob's eyes widened. What had he missed while he was in Greece? "I know I've been out of the country but…are you two…"

"Together?" Sabina giggled and blushed. "Yes, it was a shock for us, too. I spent months trying to set Lilly up with Enrique—"

"But she was in love with you, you bastard," Enrique smirked.

"After you arrived in London after Lilly was attacked, Enrique and I went out for drinks. We fell into conversation and one thing led to another… and here we are."

Jacob smiled, the first one in days. "That's bloody fantastic. Congratulations, you deserve every happiness."

Enrique wrapped an arm around Sabina's shoulder and flashed her a radiant smile. "Sometimes the answer is right in front of you, but you don't realize it."

"Does Lilly know?"

Sabina chuckled. "Of course. She was thrilled when she found out."

"I'm certain she was. I expect an invitation to the wedding." Jacob's smile widened as both Sabina and Enrique flushed and made a hasty exit.

It had been three days. Lilly's lungs showed improvement, no infections were present, and her blood pressure was stabilized. The doctors were cautiously optimistic, but no long-term plan was discussed.

Jacob remained by Lilly's side, thankful for the change of clothes Janie brought on her daily visit.

"How many times do you plan on listening to that insufferable song?" Jacob scowled at Janie as 'Walking on Sunshine' played on repeat through her iPod.

"Lilly loves this song."

"She won't after hearing it ten thousand times," Jacob grumbled.

"Knock knock." Sabina poked her head into the bay, smiling at Janie's dance moves. "May I speak with you for a moment, Jacob?"

"Should I leave?" Janie questioned.

"That's not necessary," Jacob interjected. Whatever Sabina had to say could be said in front of his sister, she adored Lilly. "Please tell us you have some good news."

Sabina smiled. "I do! Her lung function has improved dramatically. They're going to try to wean Lilly off the ventilator tomorrow."

Relief flooded through Jacob. "She's going to be okay?"

"They expect she'll make a full recovery, but it will take time."

"Knowing Lilly, she'll be up and running the halls tomorrow night," Janie joked.

Sabina bit her lower lip, studying the floor. "It's not that simple. If Lilly had only sustained the leg injury, then she would be home and hobbling around on crutches. But the lung injury weakened her entire body. She will heal, but it's going to take time. It will require weeks—if not months—of rehabilitation for her to regain her strength."

Jacob swallowed against the lump in his throat. "I'll get her into the best rehab money can buy. I know my Lilly, she won't let this beat her, she'll be back to her old self in no time."

"Will it be a similar recovery period to mine?" Janie inquired. "I was exhausted the first few weeks, needing to sleep every few hours, and using a cane to help me with balance."

"Everyone is different. Lilly is young and healthy, like you, so that's on her side. But she's not going to be walking for several weeks. She won't have the stamina to utilize crutches so she will need a wheelchair."

"She's going to hate that," Janie gritted, her gaze swinging to Jacob.

"It's temporary, Janie. The most important thing is that she'll be fine. Until then, I'll take care of her. I'll help her with everything." Jacob forced himself to remain positive. As long as she was alive, the rest would fall into place.

Sabina sighed. "Jacob, I know you love her, but Lilly can't handle you walking in and out of her life anymore. I hate to say this, but if you can't hack it for the duration, you should go now. This recovery is going to be really tough on Lilly. Throw in Victoria's pregnancy—"

"Are you mad? You want me to leave her? Now?" Jacob stood up, his blood pressure pounding in his ears. "Lilly needs me for the first time ever, and you want me to walk away? I'm not going anywhere."

"Jakey, please calm down—"

Jacob spun around, glaring at his sister. "I will *not* calm down. I know things have been fucked up in the past, but that woman is my entire life! Do *not* ask me to walk away!"

Sabina rested her hands on Jacob's arms, willing his anger down. "I doubt she'll let you near her. Lilly doesn't know how to ask for help, especially from you. She was self-conscious before, can you imagine how she'll feel stuck in a wheelchair or worse, needing to be carried?"

"I'll carry her around the goddamn world if that's what it takes!" Jacob knew he was getting loud, but he didn't give a damn. The idea of Lilly pushing him away now was more than he could handle.

Sabina shushed him gently. "She won't let you." She rose and headed for the door. "I hope I'm wrong and Lilly accepts your help, that she's willing to let you see her in that condition. But don't be surprised if she pushes you away, it's her defense mechanism."

Jacob buried his head in his hands after Sabina left, her words reverberating with piercing impact.

"I'm afraid Sabina is right," Janie murmured as she wrapped her arms around her brother.

"Why are you all so certain she's going to kick me to the curb?" Jacob inquired, his foot tapping against the floor. "What do you know that I don't?"

"I know you're a handsome, world-renowned movie star who's having a baby with a gorgeous, world-renowned singer, and Lilly is—"

"The most amazing woman, no soul, I've ever met," Jacob interjected.

Janie nodded. "I know that, and you know that, but she"—Janie glanced at Lilly—"isn't going to agree when she does a comparison study."

"Why would she compare herself to anyone?"

"You've got to be joking, Jakey. Victoria reminds Lilly constantly of how little she matters in the grand scheme of things. Think about it, all those lies Victoria told, all the heartache she caused, yet you never once called Victoria out publicly for anything. Even with your press release, you covered up Victoria's abhorrent behavior."

"But—"

Janie raised her hand to quiet Jacob. "I know, you were being a gentleman, but you were a gentleman to the wrong woman. The woman who deserved your courtesy got the short end of the stick every time. Her recovery…having to regain her strength…it's going to send her into a tailspin."

"Would it make everyone happy if I prove her fears correct, do exactly what you all suspect? Is that what you want?"

Janie shook her head, closing her eyes. "I want you to prove us all wrong, but I don't know if Lilly will give you that chance. Jacob, your track record is atrocious." Janie clasped her brother's hand. "You have to respect her wishes, regardless of whether or not you agree with them."

"So, it doesn't matter that I love her and want her to be my wife? That I want to take care of her? It doesn't matter what I want?"

"Up until now, it *only* mattered what you wanted." She hugged her brother, his body tensing against her embrace. "I hope I'm wrong—we all hope we're wrong—one day at a time. Let's get her awake and off the ventilator before we start deciding her future."

Jacob stood silent, glaring at the wall, nodding only at Janie's prodding. The words of both women reverberated in his head. He had long believed that if Lilly pulled through, they would be over the hard part, now it seemed the hard part had just begun.

Lilly

Thehe fuzzy, dreamlike world faded as the pain of reality trickled into Lilly's consciousness and she realized she was breathing through a ventilator. Throughout her nursing career she often wondered how anyone managed to keep their wits about them with a tube stuck down their throat. Now she knew. Luckily, Lilly maintained some level of sanity and within a few hours, the breathing tube was removed.

She leaned against her pillow, feeling as weak as a day-old kitten, her memories smashed together into a giant ball of confusion. How did she get to the hospital? The last memory she had was speaking at Roger's funeral…and watching Jacob embrace Victoria, comforting her as she cried. How perfect they looked together—both long, lean, and golden—they matched.

Her mental movie ended when Jacob and Janie entered the room. Janie embraced her friend, babbling on about the miracles of modern medicine.

Janie prattled on a few seconds before Jacob scooted her out of the way, bending over Lilly as his lips pressed against her forehead, his hand stroking her hair. God, he smelled good, he smelled like home. Lilly breathed in his scent, grateful for anything familiar.

"Hey angel, it's so good to see you awake." His eyes were bright with unshed tears, and he looked exhausted—deep purple bags bruised his eyes and a few days' stubble littered his cheeks.

"How long—" Lilly croaked, her throat throbbing with the effort.

"Four days, the longest four days of my life."

"Jesus." She had been in a coma for four days? What was the full extent of her injuries? Even worse, what would be the full length of her recuperation?

"I'm exhausted," Lilly murmured as Jacob kissed her fingertips. "Stupid, really. I haven't moved in four days—"

"Rest, my angel. I'll be right here."

Lilly shook her head. He needed the rest as much as she did. "Go home and get some sleep. I can tell you need it."

"I want to stay."

Lilly squeezed his hand. "I know, but you need to maintain your strength. It won't do us any good if you wind up in a hospital bed too."

"It's not a bad idea," Janie interjected, kissing Lilly's head. "Go home, shower, eat some real food. Come back this evening. I'll stay with Lilly until you get back."

Jacob shot his sister a glare but realized he was outnumbered. "Fine"—he huffed, pulling himself to a standing position—"but I'll be back in a few hours."

Lilly nodded, exhaustion already getting a foothold as Jacob cupped her face, his lips brushing hers with the gentlest of kisses. She was asleep before the door closed.

The doctors stopped in an hour later to explain her 'situation'. Her body was globally weakened—God, what a term—by the lung injury and it would be weeks of intense rehabilitation before she was fully independent. Then they smiled and told her how lucky she was before moving to the next patient. Lilly was tempted to throw one of her stuffed animals at their retreating forms.

She fell back against her pillow, defeated. Her recovery would take longer than she planned. Her first attempt to the bathroom might be laughable someday, but the coordination required to access a toilet ten feet from her bed was currently the bane of her existence. It took a nurse, an aide, an IV pole, and a walker to get Lilly to the bathroom—she felt like she had run a marathon.

Now what? I can't even go to the bathroom without an entourage, how am I supposed to do everything else?

She had no family and there was no way in hell she would allow Jacob to see her in such a broken-down state. Her situation might be pitiful, but she'd be damned if she took a drop of his pity. She still had her pride.

"Someone sent you a lovely bouquet." Her nurse remarked with a smile, bringing a giant collection of roses and peonies to her bedside table.

Lilly opened the envelope, pulling out the card. She gasped when she read the name of the sender—it was Victoria—the flowers were likely dusted with anthrax.

A picture fell out, a sonogram image of Victoria's baby. *This woman is diabolical.* A twinge of jealousy cut through Lilly as she examined the developing fetus before laying the photo aside to read Victoria's lengthy correspondence.

I knew my presence would only bring you anger and frustration, so I opted to speak with you in this manner. Your friends expect you to make a full recovery in time—I am so glad to hear that news. I don't hate you Lilly, God knows I've tried, it's just we're both in love with the same man.

I'm enclosing the sonogram picture. It seemed surreal to me until I saw my daughter on the screen and heard her heartbeat. I wanted Jacob there, but he was with you, he's been absent the entire duration of the pregnancy. I messed up. I had an amazing man and I threw him away. I hoped he and I might reconcile and be a family, but he'll never leave you after this tragic event. He will spend the rest of his days helping you pick up the pieces. At this point, I only hope he will be actively involved in our daughter's life. A girl needs her Daddy.

Best wishes, Victoria

Tears streamed down Lilly's face as she read the card again, and she wasn't certain which statement hit the hardest. Was she keeping Jacob from being involved in his daughter's life? Wow, he was having a daughter. She would no doubt be a radiant, blonde cherub like her parents. And Victoria's comment about him staying to help her pick up the pieces of her life, fell like a stone on her heart. That wasn't love, that was obligation.

Jacob whisked into her room that afternoon, freshly showered and shaved. He carried an overnight bag and the most beautiful orange roses Lilly had ever seen.

"I know you prefer plants to cut flowers, but these were so beautiful—" Jacob's gaze settled on Victoria's bouquet. "I see I'm not the only fan in your club." He chuckled, setting up the flowers in a vase before settling into bed alongside her.

Lilly kept her eyes averted, focused on the blanket. "Thank you. You're in a good mood."

"The love of my life is on the mend. I'm in a bloody fantastic mood." Jacob smiled, his eyes dancing like a little boy's at Christmas.

His words tugged at her heartstrings. He seemed so sincere. "There's something else, though. Are you going to share?"

His smile broadened, damn he was beautiful when he smiled. "I've been offered a role in Milieu of Madness. It's filming in London, so I'll be right here with you. I pulled myself out of contention for any role in the movie, but Albert called me this afternoon. He really wants my participation, demanded it actually."

Lilly's smile was genuine. Jacob had earned that role in spades. "Congratulations, you wanted that lead so much."

Jacob shook his head and chuckled. "I decided to take the supporting role and it's all your fault."

Lilly's eyes widened with surprise. "How is it my fault?"

"Remember when we first met and you implied I had talents I wasn't utilizing? The lead was another stereotypical part for me, but the supporting role was a leap of faith, a challenge, one I'd never considered before meeting you."

Lilly's heart leapt at his statement, her advice had a lasting impact on Jacob. "It's brave to move outside your comfort zone."

"Well, because of you I've been living outside my comfort zone, and I wouldn't change it for the world." His fingers traced along her jaw, his touch so gentle against her skin. "Enough about me, back to the important topics. How are you feeling? The nurses told me you got out of bed for the first time."

"I'll be ready to run a marathon in a week." Lilly's tone was biting, and she hated herself for the edge in her words.

"I'll bring running shoes with me next time." His eyes fell upon the sonogram photo and his face paled. "Victoria was here?"

Lilly motioned to the flowers. "No, she sent me flowers and a card explaining her…situation."

Jacob's eyebrows shot up. "Her situation? I can't believe the nerve of that woman."

Lilly handed Jacob the card. "It wasn't a spiteful letter. You should read it."

Jacob snatched the card with a huff, perusing Victoria's words. "This is garbage. She never should have sent this to you and saddled you with her issues."

"They're your issues, too. Why didn't you go to the doctor with her?"

Jacob's hand raked over his buzzed head; his jaw clenched. "I don't think the child is mine, Lilly. I've requested a paternity test several times, but she always has some excuse. I laid down the law—until she provides proof, I'm not involved."

"What if you are the father?"

The silence was palpable, beating like the baby's heart inside Victoria's belly.

"What then, Jacob?"

"I know what you're doing, and I know it's because of what Victoria wrote. Don't let her get inside your head. Don't let her tear us apart again."

"Have you ever considered that if you and I were truly meant to be together, it wouldn't be this difficult? It has been one heartbreak after another, maybe the universe is trying to tell us something."

A nurse interrupted their conversation, bringing a wheelchair into the room. "I'm sorry to intrude, but I wanted to leave this here."

Lilly glared at the wheelchair. "I don't want that damn thing."

"Ma'am, you're going to need the wheelchair for the next several weeks. You're not strong enough to get around by yourself."

Lilly clenched her fists, wishing she had the strength to get out of the bed and shove the wheelchair up the well-intentioned nurse's ass.

"I'll leave it here, but remember, you're not to get out of bed by yourself. You need assistance with all transfers—"

"I got it," Lilly gritted out, glaring holes into the nurse as she left the ICU bay.

"It's only for a little while, Lilly. Before you know it, you'll be back to your old self." Jacob cooed, pressing his lips to her hair.

She knew Jacob meant well, but the events of the last few months came crashing down around her—the secrecy, Victoria's baby, broken engagements, her injuries and limitations—it was more than she could bear. She couldn't be around Jacob anymore, it hurt to look at him and know he would never truly belong to her. It was time to send him back to the woman who carried his child.

Staring at the blanket, Lilly took a deep breath. "Get out while you can."

Jacob's arm tightened around her shoulders. "What are you talking about?"

Lilly swung her gaze to meet his, it was time to drive the nails into the coffin of their relationship. "Look around you, this is my life for the unforeseeable future. You have a life of beauty and wealth and fame, I have this."

"You have me."

Those three simple words almost broke Lilly's resolve, along with the love shining from his clear blue eyes. "Go back to Victoria, Jacob."

Jacob drew back as if slapped. "I don't want Victoria. I want you, I love you."

"You—"

Jacob grasped Lilly's chin, forcing her to look at him. "I know our relationship hasn't been easy, but our love is worth fighting for. In the beginning I thought love wasn't a necessity in my life."

"Maybe it's not—"

He nuzzled her lips. "Let me finish, my angel. I met you and realized you're as vital to me as oxygen. I'd never felt that emotion before and it terrified me. I fought it, I didn't want to be weak, to need you so badly. But the truth is that you make me strong. Now it's my turn to give you my strength until yours returns."

Lilly jerked her face back. "That's not love, that's obligation."

"No, it isn't! I want to take care of you, help you—"

"You need to go." Lilly buried her face in her hands, willing the tears away.

"I'm not going anywhere. Baby, what's wrong?" Jacob pulled her hands from her face, pressing his mouth against hers in an unspoken statement of love. "Don't push me away. Let me in, let me help you."

"I love you—"

"And I love you."

"What I'm trying to say is that I love your dedication to me during all this, but it's time to move on. I'm not good for anyone. It will take months—"

"I don't care if it takes years, we can overcome anything together."

"Our paths have moved in separate directions. It's time we accepted the truth."

Jacob's hands dropped to the mattress as he looked off into the distance. "What are you saying?"

Tears filled her eyes. "Please don't make me say it…"

His blue eyes met hers, filled with an anguish she hadn't seen before. "You're going to *have* to say it because otherwise, I'm ignoring this entire conversation. So, if there's something you need to tell me, say it now."

Tears rolled down her cheeks, but she would not bind someone to her out of a sense of duty. She had nothing to offer Jacob, and Victoria carried his world—literally. "You and Victoria should reconcile. You're going to be a family and you two have a connection we don't share."

"Wow, a connection?" Jacob bit out, looking like he wanted to punch something.

Lilly nodded. "I'm setting you free, releasing you from all obligations. You should be grateful—"

"You want me to be fucking grateful? You're pushing me out of your life, and I'm supposed to be grateful?" His voice bellowed through the unit and his entire body trembled. "I need to know, do you want me gone because you don't love me or because you think you're a burden?"

If she answered one way, he would leave forever. If she answered the other way, he would never leave, but she would never know where his love ended, and his sympathies began. Swallowing hard, she whispered, "I don't love you anymore."

Her lie hung in the air between them, and Jacob shook with emotion. "I don't believe you. Say it again. Look me in the eye and say it again."

Willing every fiber of her body to cooperate with the falsehood, Lilly locked with his gaze and stated, "I'm not in love with you anymore."

Jacob stood immobile for a moment, processing her words. She almost believed he might toss a chair through the window. Instead, he grabbed his bag and walked to the door, turning before he left. "You always believed you were second best in my life, but the truth is you never actually let me love you. You never let me near you for long enough!"

He motioned around the Intensive Care bay. "Do you think this matters? This"—Jacob motioned between the two of them—"this matters. It's the only thing that ever mattered."

"You need to go, Jacob." This was agonizing and Lilly wasn't certain how many more seconds she could hold the man she adored away from her heart.

"I don't *want* to go, Lilly," Jacob beseeched.

"I want you to go." It was a total lie, but one that needed to be told. She had to work through this recovery on her own—much like everything else in her life. He had a glorious life waiting for him. It was time for him to resume his role as the Hollywood star.

"Why don't you want me? I really thought we were going to be okay. I thought for once you needed me. It turns out you never did. I was the fool who needed you. I'm not okay with this Lilly, and I—" He smacked the door frame and left, his sentence unspoken, his words forever locked into the void between them.

Her tears, held back by sheer willpower, released the moment he was gone. She had sent Jacob back to the woman before her, the woman who would stop at nothing to own his heart. Victoria had more fight in her than Lilly, it was time to surrender the war and admit defeat.

CHAPTER NINE

Jacob

acob hadn't bothered to return home after storming out of Lilly's room. Instead, he sought out the nearest pub, where he sat slumped in a back booth, half in the bottle, and intent on staying that way indefinitely. Lilly's declaration that she no longer loved him ricocheted through his body like machine gun bullets.

His mind tried to rationalize her words, negate them, deny them, but his heart reminded him that none of it mattered if Lilly didn't want him in her life.

Brad Taylor called earlier in the day regarding the interview he taped a week earlier. The studio was holding off release in light of recent events. The focus of the next few shows would be about Roger's life and career, but Brad promised the interview would air soon. When he asked about Lilly's recovery, Jacob kept his answer vague. He failed to mention that the entire segment was now moot, there was no chance of Lilly accepting his proposal.

"Invitation to this pity party for me?" A female voice inquired, scooting into the booth opposite him.

Jacob looked up to see his director, and close friend, Miriam flagging the server. He grabbed a cigarette and lit the end, taking a deep drag before Miriam grabbed it, putting it out in the ashtray. "Come on mate, I thought you kicked that habit years ago."

He shrugged. "What's it matter?"

"Are you going to tell me what happened, or do I get to guess?"

With a defeated sigh, Jacob relayed the events of the past day, from the joy of Lilly coming off the ventilator to the crushing agony of her pushing him from her life. "She said she doesn't love me anymore."

"She's a liar." A new voice stated from the end of the booth—Sabina had arrived. In his despair, he called every woman who might have some insight into Lilly's mindset and begged their assistance.

Sabina slid into the booth, shaking hands with Miriam and examining the pack of cigarettes. "This is a great new habit."

"Like I told Miriam, what the hell does it matter anyway?"

The drinks arrived and the server fumbled when she recognized Jacob, but his glare sent a stern warning to refrain from photo or autograph requests.

Miriam gave Jacob a knowing look. "You, my friend, are hopeless. After all these obstacles, all these hurdles, you're giving up now?"

Jacob's eyes widened. "What am I supposed to do? She said she doesn't love me and doesn't want me in her life."

"Of course she said that. I told you she would say that," Sabina interjected. "You have to understand Lilly's perspective. You're this world famous, gorgeous movie star who may or may not be the father of Victoria's baby. Throw in Lilly's injuries and you've got a full-fledged emotional meltdown on your hands."

Miriam nodded in agreement. "It's true, she believes she's damaged goods now."

Jacob took a swig of whiskey. "She isn't damaged, she's a survivor. I've never seen anyone fight like her, she's stronger than anyone I know."

"That may be, but she still feels like an invalid stuck in a wheelchair." Sabina smiled sadly. "Let's also not forget the wonderful conversation between you and Victoria the day of the funeral."

Jacob's brow furrowed and Miriam shot him a look of confusion. "What conversation?"

"The one where you claimed to love Lilly because it was easier than loving Victoria and that Victoria was—how did you put it—an exquisite force of nature. Oh, and how radiant she looked carrying your child." Sabina tapped her fingers on the wood table, narrowing her eyes at Jacob. "Don't quote me, I'm going off what Lilly told me today. I'm hoping she imagined the entire scenario, that it was all a horrible dream."

"Jesus! Jacob, did you really say all that?" Miriam shook her head in disgust.

Jacob scoffed in disbelief. "I did say that—"

Sabina's eyes bulged as she glowered in his direction. "What the hell is wrong with you?"

Christ, would he never cease looking like a blundering idiot? "That was a tiny fraction of the conversation! I only said those things to Victoria because she seemed so distraught before the funeral. I was trying not to upset her further and I knew telling her the brutal truth would hurt her feelings."

"Why do we care about Victoria's feelings?" Miriam inquired.

"I don't give a damn about Victoria's feelings—"

"Could have fooled me. Seems the only one whose feelings you don't give a damn about is Lilly," Sabina hurled back, her finger drumming taking on a faster tempo.

"I was between a rock and a hard place. Sophie asked that I to escort her and Martha to Roger's funeral." Jacob paused, those words felt like a dagger in his chest. "I didn't have time to get Lilly from the hospital and make it to the church. I couldn't reach anyone else and Victoria offered to pick her up. Pissing her off would only have made matters worse. Besides, how did Lilly even know about it?"

Sabina smirked. "Apparently your baby mama wasn't *too* distraught. She recorded the conversation and played it for Lilly right before Roger's funeral. I have to hand it to Victoria, her timing is impeccably evil."

His face drained of color, realizing how his situation with Victoria must appear to Lilly. *Bugger, what a shitstorm.* "I also said Lilly was the most amazing soul I've ever met and she makes me want to be a better man, that loving her is easy because she exudes love"—he buried his face in his hands—"and all I wanted was to marry her and spend my life loving her."

"I'm betting that Victoria didn't play her that part," Sabina replied, sipping her drink.

"Trust me, Lilly is the *only* woman I want."

"You throw together your impending fatherhood, Victoria's constant meddling, and Lilly's injuries and you've got one hell of emotional whirlwind. It's more than enough to shut Lilly down emotionally," Miriam added, patting Jacob's arm.

"I issued that press release stating I wasn't with Victoria. I recanted the whole engagement rumor and any notion of romance. Why can't Lilly see how much I adore her? Why doesn't she believe me?"

"Because in all that time, and all your public demonstratives, you never once mentioned Lilly. The closest she ever came to receiving any recognition was being some anonymous woman in London. She feels like your dirty secret, and now she wants to stay that way," Sabina stated, her expression sober.

Jacob's phone rang. His heart jumped at the caller ID. "It's my lawyer. Let's pray he has the results of the paternity test. Will you ladies excuse me for a moment, please?" He walked to a quiet corner of the pub, his body awash with nervous energy. "Mr. Abrams, what's the good news?"

A sigh from the other end of the call. That was never a good sign. "Unfortunately, there's no good news. Victoria's fighting the DNA test. It looks like we might have to wait for the court to order testing after the baby is born."

Jacob's heart hit the floor. That meant another five months of dealing with Victoria and living in limbo about whether or not he was the father of her child. "Please tell me you're joking."

"We can fight it, but I guarantee her legal team will bury us in paperwork and stall until after the baby arrives. You will get your answer, Mr. Edmonton, just not in the timely manner you hoped."

"Christ, what next?" Jacob mumbled out a word of thanks before ending the call.

"Well, it obviously wasn't good news," Miriam winced, throwing an arm around Jacob's shoulder.

"Victoria's fighting the DNA test. My lawyer says I'll get my answer but not until the baby is born." He slurped down the rest of his whiskey. He didn't know what to do. For the first time in his life, he felt utter despair. "Life keeps getting better and better. That paternity test was the only chance I had left with Lilly."

"That's not true," Sabina interjected. "Lilly had every intention of staying with you—even *with* the baby."

"That was then, Sabina."

"You need to keep fighting."

Jacob threw up his hands in frustration. "I would gladly stay by her side 24/7 for the rest of her life but she doesn't want me there."

Sabina grabbed his hands. "That's not true either. She's terrified and frustrated, she feels useless and ugly and—"

"She's beautiful, she will always be beautiful," Jacob growled.

"She's also alone, Jacob. She doesn't have any family. She's spent her life taking care of herself because no one else wanted the job. Now, when she desperately needs help, she's too self-conscious and embarrassed to ask." Sabina chewed her lip, a strange look crossing her face.

"What? There's more, isn't there, Sabina?" Jacob leaned forward in the seat, tightening his grip on Sabina's hand.

"She fell today."

Jacob gasped at Sabina's words. "My God, did she get hurt?"

Sabina shook her head. "She tried to get out of bed by herself. The nurses were busy, and Lilly didn't want to be a bother. She ripped her IV out in the process, but she's okay. I think she wanted to prove to herself that she could still handle things on her own. When she couldn't, it was another emotional setback."

"What do I do? How do I help her?" Jacob wracked his brain for any method of reaching Lilly, but how do you help someone who believes they're beyond reproach?

Miriam gave the table a triumphant smack. "Well, that's easy. I would advise getting her to a private rehab, the real swanky ones that provide optimal care. The focus has to be on Lilly regaining her independence right now."

Sabina nodded her agreement. "She's set to go to St. Luke rehab in the next few days. The plan is that she'll spend a month there regaining her strength."

"Is it one of the best in England?" Jacob inquired.

"No, it's decent. Those luxury rehabs are so expensive. Lilly can't afford anything like that."

Perhaps Lilly couldn't afford it, but money was money was no object for Jacob. "I've got plenty of money, so cost isn't a factor. Sabina, will you help me find the best one?"

"With your deep pockets, the world is our oyster." Sabina finished off the rest of her drink, offering him a sarcastic grin.

"Is that code for you'll help me?"

Sabina nodded. "Of course, I'll help you. I'll do anything for Lilly." She stood up, shaking hands with Miriam and shooting Jacob a pointed stare. "You're not the only one who loves her. Shall we go?"

Within two hours, Sabina had taken him on tours of several physical rehabilitation centers until he found one he thought suited Lilly. It was called Renaissance and provided the ultimate in luxury accommodations, dining and most importantly, rehabilitative therapies. The gardens and labyrinth walking trail were immaculate, and Jacob believed the tranquility of the landscaping would do wonders for Lilly's state of mind.

"Sabina, this is perfect," Jacob declared, earning a smile from Jacqui, the director of Renaissance.

"We pride ourselves on treating our guests to a luxurious recovery."

"I thought this was rehab," Sabina muttered.

Jacqui quirked a brow at Sabina, a wry smile crossing her face. "Indeed, it is, one of great renown. We have a rigorous hiring process, ensuring only the most dedicated and talented therapists work with our clientele. When you couple that with top-of-the-line equipment and a sixteen-acre ground designed not only for physical but spiritual expansion, our guests are ensured the greatest experience possible."

Jacob smirked. Jacqui could certainly sell ice to an eskimo, but there was no need. Renaissance was perfect for his Lilly. "Where do I sign?"

"Jacob," Sabina hissed. "It's over two thousand pounds per day!"

"I don't care what it costs. It's worth every penny to make my angel well again." Jacob pulled out his black Amex card and handed it to Jacqui.

"If cost is a concern, there are smaller rooms. Your friend would still have access to all the amenities."

"I don't need a smaller room, Jacqui. I want the best room you have. Only the best for Lilly."

117

Jacqui nodded and now her smile was genuine. "She must be very special."

"She's everything."

Jacqui ran the card and began filling out the paperwork. "You know, I heard you were engaged. I'm assuming that Lilly is your fiancée? I'm sorry, I shouldn't pry."

"But you are," Sabina retorted with her usual sass.

"It's fine, Jacqui. We're dealing with a few hurdles right now, but I hope one day soon to make Lilly my wife."

Jacqui returned his credit card, offering the paperwork for his signature. "She's a lucky lady."

"No, I'm the lucky one."

They left Renaissance a half hour later and Jacob drove back to St. Luke, pulling into a spot in the car park before turning to face Sabina in the passenger side of his car. "Thank you for helping me tonight."

Sabina reached over, giving his hand a squeeze. "Thank you...for loving Lilly this much. Jacob, I won't lie to you, I didn't want you coming back into her life this time. You've hurt her so much and I'm so protective of her—"

"I didn't want to be a partner or a husband before I met Lilly. I preferred the one-night stands. They were easy. Then I met her, and everything changed. I don't see any other women, there's only Lilly. I'm not saying I won't make mistakes, but I want the chance to love her the way she deserves to be loved."

"Did you pay for Renaissance in the hopes of winning Lilly back?"

"I do pray I win back my angel but, Sabina, I would make the same exact choice if she and I were never to speak again. She deserves it."

Sabina glanced at her watch, clicking her tongue against her teeth. "Why don't we go visit Lilly? We're already here."

"I want to, but she doesn't want me around."

Sabina shrugged and unsnapped her seat belt. "Maybe she's changed her mind."

Jacob watched Sabina exit the vehicle, his hands clenching the steering wheel. He desperately wanted to see Lilly, but she had told him in no uncertain terms that her feelings were not what they once were. *What am I supposed to do here?*

A knock on the window decided for him. "Are you coming?" Sabina inquired.

They walked up to the critical care unit, Jacob's heart thudding like a jackhammer. Sabina went to speak to the charge nurse, returning a few minutes later. "They gave her something to sleep. She's passed out. Would you like to say goodnight?"

Jacob nodded, quietly slipping into Lilly's room. She was still pale, but at least the gray pallor was gone from her skin. Her injured right leg was elevated on a pillow, her hands folded across her stomach.

Then Jacob saw it, the stuffed bear he brought her when she was first injured, tucked under her arm.

Careful not to wake her, he leaned over her, pressing his mouth to her forehead. "I love you, my angel. You're *mine,* Lilly. I'll wait forever for you." His fingers pushed back a few stray strands of hair from her cheek. "Rest now. It's all going to be okay. I promise."

Jacob walked out past the nurses station, earning a smile from one of the full-time staff. "Mr. Edmonton, I wondered where you were."

"Sabina and I have been busy getting Lilly set up with rehab."

"Girl is going to have some fancy digs," Sabina murmured, earning a chuckle from the nurse.

"She deserves it," Jacob reminded Sabina before heading out the door for home.

Lilly

"Come on, let's do one more set of leg lifts."

Lilly glared at Mick, one of the physical therapists at St. Luke. "Mick, I'm tired."

"So am I, buttercup, but there's no rest for the wicked." Mick gave her a wink, he wasn't letting her off the hook.

"Don't forget I know your boss," Lilly scowled, as she began the dreaded exercise.

"You don't scare me, Lilly. Better be nice or I'll throw in an extra set." Another wink, and Lilly was tempted to throw a punch right in his squinty-eyed face.

By the end of the two sets—the bastard wasn't kidding about the added torture—Lilly had one mission. Murder Mick. She had it all planned out in her mind, step by step. No one could fault her decision. It was obvious he was a sadist intent on inflicting as much pain and discomfort as possible with every session.

"You did good, Yank. I'm proud of you." Mick gave her a quick hug, and Lilly grunted in response. "Good luck in rehab."

"I'll see you there. I'm going to the rehab right across the street."

A look of confusion crossed Mick's face. "You are? I thought—" he stopped mid-sentence, shaking his head as if to clear it. "I must have read the chart wrong. I'll be seeing you soon then, Lilly."

Lilly looked at the clock. Ben should arrive within the hour to help her move across the street. It gave her enough time to fumble around the hospital room and collect her belongings. It was amazing how much stuff accumulated inside of a week.

God this is exhausting, Lilly thought as she shoved her clothing into one of a few duffel bags. When she was finished, she leaned back in the wheelchair, eager to get moving from this blasted hospital.

Besides, she surmised that the busier she was, the less time she had to think about Jacob. *What a bunch of garbage. I always think about him.*

Five days had passed since Lilly pushed Jacob from her life, and their argument replayed in her head like an awful infomercial. She knew letting him go was the best decision for his future, but that fact didn't make her heart hurt any less.

Her friends dropped in to visit almost every day—Ben, Janie, Edward, Enrique, Sabina—but they tread carefully around any conversation involving Jacob or Victoria. It was as if they had signed an agreement that mention of either name was a crime punishable by death.

It was hardest when the evenings rolled around and she laid in bed, alone with her thoughts. Had Jacob followed her advice and reconciled with Victoria? Would they marry soon? Lilly didn't know if ignorance was bliss, but her heart was so broken, it likely didn't matter anymore.

"Are you all packed?" Ben inquired as he strolled in an hour later, giving a cursory glance around the room. "Ready for the fun to begin?"

"Oh, aren't you hilarious. Almost as amusing as Mick. I've plotted his demise, by the way," Lilly remarked, forcing a smile for her friend.

Ben chuckled. "I warned him if he gave you extra sets that he'd better sleep with one eye open. So, are you ready to go?"

Lilly nodded, shifting in the wheelchair. She knew the next month would be an experiment in torture, but in the end, it would be worth the pain. At least she hoped that was the case. It was so difficult seeing things as a patient instead of a nurse. As a nurse, she would cajole the patient with reminders that within a month they would make huge strides in their recovery. As a patient, she wanted to smack anyone who came at her with that approach.

She knew the facts, she knew the statistics, and she knew she would get better. But at the moment her body had the strength of a day-old colt and the endurance of an obese sloth, not to mention the scars she would carry as a permanent reminder. At least they could be covered up…if only there was a bandage for the scars on her heart.

"Did Mick get you up and walking yet?"

Lilly shook her head. "He said I should avoid all weight-bearing for ten days, so I'm stuck in this fucking chair."

"It's temporary, Lilly. Don't forget that."

"Yeah, well, you have no idea what it's like to need help pulling off your pants." Lilly smacked the arm of the wheelchair. "I tell you this much, I'm walking out of that damn rehab in a month. Screw this stupid chair."

"I have no doubt, Lilly." Ben wheeled her to his vehicle, catching Lilly's confused stare. "We're not going to the St. Luke rehab."

"Where are we going? Are you kidnapping me? Are we going somewhere fun?"

"It's only kidnapping if I'm taking you against your will. You seem way too excited to come with me." Ben helped Lilly into his car. "We're going to Renaissance."

Lilly's jaw slackened, that was the rehab of celebrities and royalty, and way beyond her pay grade. "Are you insane? I can't afford Renaissance! I can't afford a roll of toilet paper at that facility."

Ben ignored Lilly until he had pulled out of the car park. "It's paid in full."

"Who paid for the rehab?"

Ben snorted. "You know damn well who paid for it."

Lilly shook her head, unclasping her safety belt. "No, that's unacceptable. Turn around. I'm going to the rehab at St. Luke. I don't want Jacob's charity."

"It's hardly charity, Lilly. Besides, what does it matter? You want to get well, don't you?"

"Yes."

"It's the best rehab in London. It's paid in full. Stop your bitching and take advantage of the gift you've been given."

Lilly's jaw slackened at Ben's curt statement. "Are you angry with me? Because I don't want some Hollywood celebrity footing my rehab bill? Because I don't want to be indebted to him anymore than I already am?" Tears rolled down her cheeks—not surprising—her emotions had been near overflowing since Jacob left her life. "Because I don't want him feeling sorry for me?"

Ben pulled the car onto the shoulder of the road and shut if off before facing his friend. "I'm not angry with you, Lilly, but I'm frustrated that you've shut Jacob out of your life. Did you know that he calls four, five times a day to check on you? He's miserable without you. He'd do anything to help you, but you won't let him near you."

Lilly motioned to herself, the deluge of tears gaining the upper hand. "Who would want to deal with all this? I can't take care of myself. Hell, I can barely get my pants on by myself. I'm pathetic." Sobs wracked her body. "Who would want to deal with this mess?"

Ben gripped Lilly's shoulders with firm hands. "Jacob! Jacob wants to deal with 'this mess,' as you so wrongly put it. I dream about having a man who would see my flaws and love me *because* of them—not in spite of them—someone who puts me on a pedestal and adores me."

"I know you do Ben, and I know that man is out there for you—"

"My point," Ben continued, cutting her off, "is you have that man, but you chucked him like yesterday's garbage."

Lilly's eye's widened. How did her close friend have the situation so wrong? "I did what was best for Jacob. He's going to be a father, he and

Victoria should be together."

"Bullshit, Lilly. You did what was easiest for *you* because you're too scared to believe a man like Jacob could love you the way he does, especially after your injury. You can paint it any color you want, but this situation between you and Jacob has nothing to do with Victoria or their child. He chose you over her time and time again."

Lilly's anger flared, since when was Jacob all innocence and light? Had everyone forgotten how he deserted her—not once, but twice? What alternate reality had she slipped into where Jacob was the misunderstood hero and she was the villain? "When did he choose me, Ben? I was his dirty secret, remember? He loved me privately but to the public, I was 'some London fling'. Meanwhile, Victoria spouted lie after lie, and he allowed it. I was supposed to shut up and chin up. Then I finally say enough and I'm the bad guy?" She wiped her face with the heel of her hand. "How long am I supposed to settle for being second best? Being runner-up?"

Ben nodded, considering Lilly's words. "I guess I'm used to keeping things quiet in the romance department. You have a point, Lilly. I didn't realize how the secrecy of your situation made you feel—you never said anything."

Lilly shrugged, blowing her nose into a tissue. "Why bother? It was never going to change."

"You don't think he planned on rectifying everything when he returned to London?"

"I hoped he would, but then the accident happened—"

"And you pushed him as far away as you could—"

"No," Lilly began, her temper rising again.

"Yes, you did. You pushed him away, Lilly." He grasped her hand, giving it a squeeze. "I'm not trying to upset you. I love you dearly, but I don't want you to find yourself alone because you're too afraid to allow yourself to be adored. You are the kindest person I know, to everyone but yourself. If you had to choose your destiny based solely on what *you* wanted, would you have kicked Jacob out of your life? I doubt it, and that's what I want you to consider."

"I gave him an out and he took it."

Ben let loose a guffaw. "No, you left Jacob no choice. The strongest thing you could have done—for both of you—would be to let him love you. Do you have any idea what it's like to want to love someone so much, but they won't let you? That's the definition of agony."

Lilly fell silent as she considered Ben's words, his car eating up the asphalt on the way to Renaissance. Her ex-boyfriend popped into her head, how he always kept her at arm's length, maintaining a safe distance between her love and his heart. He had a myriad of reasons, the main one being that Lilly wasn't his first choice, but his temporary stand-in. Lilly was heartbroken when she discovered the truth of his situation, but it was nothing compared to her feelings for Jacob. Her ex was nothing compared to Jacob—Jacob was the real deal.

But he inevitably broke her heart too, smashed it underfoot with careless lies and abandonment. Yet she longed for him. But his behavior coupled with that of her ex-boyfriend made Lilly realize one thing—unconditional love was a myth and she wasn't cast in that fairytale.

It was far safer to hold everyone at a safe distance—no need to get her heart tangled in any additional fiascos.

"We're here, Lilly." Ben reached across the seat and squeezed Lilly's hand, bringing her back to the present. "This is even fancier than I expected."

Lilly's eyes widened as she gazed out the window at her new home. It resembled a five-star resort, with lush gardens as far as the eye could see. It reeked of opulence and wealth, neither of which Lilly possessed. "This is too much, Ben. I don't fit in here."

Ben came around to her side of the car with the wheelchair, helping her into the seat. "Of course, you do. You're a glorious, gorgeous queen. Don't you ever forget it."

Lilly smiled. "If that's the case, shouldn't you bow to me or something?"

"Don't push your luck, sweetheart."

Inside, they were met at the front door by the director, a tall woman named Jacqui. She accompanied them on a tour of the facilities, ending with the suite where Lilly would live for the next month.

"Here you are, your home sweet home," Jacqui declared, swinging open the door to the apartment.

"Wow, this is amazing Lilly. It's bigger than the cottage."

Lilly said nothing, her mouth agape as she took in the unbridled elegance permeating from every corner. This certainly didn't resemble any rehab facility she'd ever seen. It was decorated with sturdy but stylish furnishings, all easily accessible for someone with limited mobility.

"What do you think, Lilly?" Jacqui inquired, wheeling her over the window. The view beyond was spectacular.

"Is that the labyrinth?" Lilly asked, pointing off to her left.

"Yes, it is, and soon you'll be walking it. Until then, we have a wide range of activities and services for you to utilize in your downtime."

"Lilly, they have a spa here," Ben remarked as he perused a pamphlet of amenities. "Jacqui, sign her up for a massage, facial and mani-pedi. This woman needs to unwind and beautify."

Lilly shot her friend a side-eye. "Who am I trying to impress—the physical therapists?"

The director sent Ben a knowing smile. "Have you seen the therapists? Honey, they're gorgeous. Of course, who needs eye candy therapists when you have a world class actor doting on you."

Lilly's cheeks flushed. It would be a travesty for Jacob if some rumor about them hit the papers. "I'm grateful for Jacob's generosity, but he's not—we're not—"

"He did mention you two had some hurdles recently, but he's highly vested in your care."

Lilly scoffed. "He's kind to everyone, he's a wonderful friend."

"Friend, huh? That's not the vibe he gave in regard to you. Well, I'll leave you alone to get settled. If you need anything, just press any of these buttons"—she pointed at several buttons around the suite—"or dial this number on your phone." Jacqui left her card and exited the suite.

"Let's get you unpacked." Ben helped Lilly unload her duffel bags and within twenty minutes they were finished. "I hate to run, but I have a meeting at work. Will you be okay on your own?"

"Of course. Thanks, Ben."

"It isn't me you should be thanking," Ben reminded her before showing himself out.

Alone again, she thought. *It seems that's how I always wind up.*

Shaking off the doldrums, Lilly wheeled to the window overlooking the walking paths and made herself a mental promise that she would walk those trails before the month was over.

Ben was right. Jacob deserved a message of thanks. This was beyond kind and it needed to be recognized as such.

She pulled out her mobile, a chuckle escaping her lips. It was the second phone Jacob had purchased for her in less than two months. He was right, he should buy stock in the cellular company.

With trembling fingers, she composed her message.

'*I'm at Renaissance. I can't thank you enough for setting me up at such a renowned center. I hope you're well and that you and Victoria are making*'—Lilly paused, a tear rolling down her cheek—'*positive strides forward. I'll make this up to you somehow, Jacob. I'll pay back every dime once I'm on my feet again. I won't forget your kindness to me.*'

She sent the message and wheeled herself back to the living area, eyeballing the couch. The wheelchair was far from comfortable and she needed to elevate her leg. Jacqui had reminded her to call for help with transferring since her body was still weak, but Lilly was far more stubborn than smart at that moment. She could do this. She didn't need any help. Mind over matter… or uncooperative body.

"Here goes nothing," Lilly muttered, using her arms to push herself up from the wheelchair. For a second, it was bliss. That second ended too quickly.

Her 'good' leg was still unsteady—she couldn't support her weight. To make matters worse, the wheelchair slipped on the tile floor and Lilly landed on her ass with a thud, crying out as she hit the floor. "Shit!"

Her body might gain a bruise or two from the experience, but it was her pride that took the real beating. When the wheelchair rolled back a few feet, stopping just out of her reach, Lilly broke down, burying her head in her hands.

"I give up, I can't do this!" she sobbed to the empty room as despair overwhelmed her being.

She felt someone sit on the floor next to her, their arm wrapping around her shoulder and pulling her close. She could recognize Jacob's touch anywhere.

"Shh, don't cry angel. You can do this. I'll help you, Lilly," Jacob whispered, lifting her face from her hands. His thumbs brushed away her tears, his eyes radiating a desperate longing.

God, she wanted to fall into that azure stare and push away the nightmare of the last week, but her self-doubt yammered in her head. *You're not enough, Lilly. You'll never be enough.*

Lilly pushed against Jacob's chest as reality crept back into their moment. It was mortifying for this man—this symbol of human perfection—to see her so weak and desperate. Through everything, all the lies and heartache, she had maintained a facade of strength. But now, that facade had crumbled into rubble and left her exposed and bare.

"What are you doing here? You should be with Victoria and your baby."

Jacob's jaw twitched—the man was not happy with that statement. "I'm exactly where I'm supposed to be."

Lilly grabbed the couch, attempting to haul herself off the floor, but her body lacked the strength and she threw her head back, with a huff of resignation. "Damn it."

"Come on, let me help you—"

"No! I can do this myself." Lilly tried once more, in vain, to pull herself onto the couch. When she couldn't, the tears pricked her eyelids again.

"Christ, I'm pathetic," Lilly muttered, knotting her hands in her hair and willing her breathing to slow to a normal rate.

Jacob scooped her off the ground without warning and set her on the bed. His hand wrapped around her chin, forcing her gaze to meet his. "I'm going to tell you something, Lilly, and you'd better listen to me. If I ever—*ever*—hear you speak about yourself in that manner again, I'm spanking your luscious ass."

Lilly's jaw dropped. Was he serious? "Excuse me?"

Jacob smirked his signature sex on a stick grin, the one that melted Lilly's—and every other woman's—panties. He leaned down, his lips tickling her ear. "You heard me. Of course, I'll enjoy the hell out of it."

"Sadist," Lilly mumbled, staring at the floor.

He ran his fingers through her hair, placing a hand on her nape. "You only *think* I'm joking. Have you taken a shower yet?"

Lilly shook her head, sniffling through her tears. "Falling on my ass was the first event of the evening. I'll have to save slipping in the shower for another time. Can't have too much excitement in the first couple hours."

"Stay put, I'll be right back." Jacob dropped a kiss on her head and strolled out of the room.

"As if I have a choice in the matter," Lilly grumbled to the empty room, glaring at her wheelchair across the room. She swore the damn thing was taunting her, and she would take great delight in setting it on fire when she left the rehab.

Jacob returned within a few minutes, a basket of luxury bath supplies tucked under his arm. "They had about a thousand different varieties. I picked jasmine."

"I wear jasmine perfume."

His penetrating stare held hers. "I know. I love your scent." As if embarrassed, he cleared his throat and broke the gaze. "You'll feel better after a shower, I always do."

Lilly avoided looking directly at him, it was akin to staring at the sun. Jacob was tanned and tone, his white button-down taut across his chest muscles, his short hair golden from the summer sun. He looked downright scrumptious. Impending fatherhood looked good on him. That thought wrenched what was left of her heart, along with the idea that Victoria now stood in her stead, by Jacob's side.

Tucking a strand of hair behind her ear, Lilly offered up a rueful smile. "Thank you for fetching the supplies. I'll head in there once I'm done rallying up the courage not to fall again."

127

"You won't fall."

"Thanks for the vote of confidence but you were privy to my glorious maneuver just moments ago. I'm the epitome of grace."

He scooped her into his arms again, despite her protests and carried her to the bench seat in the Roman style bathroom. "You won't fall because I'm not letting you out of my sight. I'll protect you."

Fabulous, from lover to nursemaid. How mortifying.

Jacob's fingers moved under the hem of her shirt, sliding along her ribcage, his gaze never leaving her face.

Lilly jumped at his touch. "What are you doing?"

But Jacob was otherwise occupied as his hands caressed her sides. "I'm taking care of the woman I love. You have a problem with that?"

"I don't want you seeing me like this, please just go." Lilly stayed his hands, but he pushed past her, pulling the shirt over her head.

His sapphire eyes were bright as he pressed his forehead to hers, so close that their breath mingled. "This is the only place in the world I want to be. I want to help you—"

"You're not obligated—"

Jacob smacked the tile wall. "You're not an obligation, Lilly! I love you, damn it! Why can't you see that?"

"Jacob—"

"Perhaps you don't love me, but the sun rises and sets on you, Lilly. You're my entire world. So, I guess I have enough love for the both of us."

The pain in his eyes stabbed wounds into Lilly's heart, and the fight drained from her body. "I don't want to cause trouble with you and Victoria—"

Jacob's brows raised. "Victoria? I don't have anything to do with that woman."

"I don't understand."

"Clearly. I have one woman in my life, and she owns my entire heart. But she doesn't believe me...or love me anymore." He busied himself setting up the shampoo and shower gel, but the tremor in his voice belied his emotions. "It doesn't matter though, because I believe in her. I believe in our love."

"You do?"

"With every fiber of my being. Now, are you going to let me help you? Trust me, I'm going to enjoy stripping you naked." Jacob forced a smile but the hurt resonated in his eyes.

Lilly could continue fighting him, but he wasn't going to let her win. She was smart enough to know that much. Without another word, she let him undress her before shedding his own clothes and joining her in the shower.

Lilly's body relaxed as the warm spray soothed her aching muscles. "God, that feels good. I never thought a shower could feel so amazing."

"I told you. See? Sometimes I'm right." Jacob sat behind her, his hands massaging her shoulders and back with gentle strokes. "Your poor muscles are so tense. How's that feel?"

"Wonderful," Lilly moaned contentedly, forgetting anything beyond the warm water and Jacob's soothing caresses. His hands were magic, pure unadulterated magic.

He tongued her nape as his hands slid around her waist, pulling her closer to him. "How about now?" He whispered against her skin, his voice choppy. "God, I love touching you, Lilly."

"Jacob…" Lilly stiffened, her mind snapping back to the reality of the situation.

"I wish you could see what I see when I look at you." His voice echoed a deep longing as he pulled away and focused on helping her bathe.

But Lilly didn't want to know how he saw her anymore, or why he insisted on staying by her side. The truth was likely more than her poor heart could handle. All that resonated in her mind was Victoria's intimation that she won Jacob's affection by default—her injuries ensuring that he would remain bound by her side.

Jacob's hands moved over her body with such reverence. It felt like love, but she wasn't sure her body could tell the difference between love and obligation at this point.

"Feeling better?" His tone was guarded and unsure, such a departure for the usually confident man.

"Yes, thank you. I can finish, you don't need to stay in here." Lilly reached for the sponge, but Jacob held it fast.

"Please let me do this." His plea broke through her defenses, and she nodded, closing her eyes as his fingers massaged her scalp and neck. "How's your leg feeling?" Jacob moved over the scar on her thigh, still an angry red against her pale skin.

"It's sore and hurts like hell when I try to put weight on it. I hate the leg immobilizer, but I have to wear it for another couple weeks."

"Is that the big foam contraption?"

Lilly nodded. "Yeah, the one that is the height of fashion. But until my injuries heal, it's part of my daily wardrobe."

"You'll get there before you know it. Look at how far you've come already."

She knew he was trying to be positive, but screw optimism. Lilly released a bitter laugh. "Right. I'm making tremendous strides. Can't shower by myself, can't walk by myself, I look hideous—"

She gasped when Jacob reached out, his fingers pinching her nipple as his gaze kept her pinned. "Lilly, what did I tell you about belittling yourself? Are you looking to get spanked?"

His barely concealed smile assured her he was joking, but the combination of his banter and proximity reawakened the dormant swarm of butterflies in her body. "Promises, promises."

Jacob chuckled, swooping in to steal a kiss from her lips. "It is a solemn vow that I have every intention of upholding, if you misbehave."

Lilly returned the laugh. It felt good to release an emotion that wasn't anger or grief. Then she caught his gaze and saw every emotion living within those sapphire depths. When his fingers traced along her lower lip, she released a small gasp. She should pull away and break the moment, but she was drawn to Jacob like a moth to a flame.

He took her lips with his own, his kiss warm and welcoming. It demanded nothing except her acceptance. God, he tasted so good. She missed him so much. "Lilly," he moaned into her mouth, his hand cupping her head and pulling her closer.

With a start, Lilly pulled back. What was she doing? What was *he* doing? It didn't matter what her body wanted, her mind needed to stay in control.

With a chuckle, Lilly replied, "I'll behave, no spanking required."

It took a second for her words to sink in, but Jacob didn't laugh or even smirk at her humorous retort. Quite the opposite. Without warning, the smile faded from Jacob's face and he turned away from her, shutting off the water.

"Were you hoping I'd misbehave?" Lilly ventured, unsure what had caused the sudden departure from the earlier levity.

Jacob kept his back to her, his hands bracketed on either side of the faucet, his breathing ragged and head bowed.

Lilly felt the emotion flowing off him in waves but didn't know the origin. They had been fine—relatively so—only moments before. "Jacob?"

No answer, just more deep breaths.

Lilly placed her hand on his hip, her fingers wrapping around his waist. His breath hitched when her fingers grazed his skin. "Jacob, please tell me what's wrong."

A sudden chill blew over Lilly's skin, causing her to shiver, and Jacob snapped from his reverie.

CHAPTER TEN

Jacob

He knew he would have to turn around eventually, but his emotions were hanging by a thread at this point and he didn't know whether to laugh, scream or cry.

The last several weeks had been a tumultuous whirlwind of loss. Lilly was Jacob's saving grace but when she pulled her heart away too, he thought he might lose his last grip on sanity.

He hated seeing her like this; he didn't give a shit about the scars, they'd heal. But Lilly's shattered confidence and ego were heartbreaking. This beautiful woman was unable to comprehend that his entire world revolved around her.

The kiss only lasted a few moments, but it awakened every fiber of his being. Flames raced through him the moment their lips touched. Any touch from her drove him to the edge of madness, yet Lilly doubted her effect on him.

"Thank you for helping me with the shower," Lilly whispered, breaking into his reverie.

Willing his erection to settle, Jacob pulled a towel around his waist before grabbing another, drying her with gentle strokes. "Admit it, you feel better."

"I feel almost human. Thank you," Lilly made a grab for the towel as Jacob dried her hair. "I'm good."

"You're spectacular, angel," Jacob murmured as he wrapped a warm towel around Lilly's body. He knelt in front of the shower bench, pushing a few errant strands of hair behind Lilly's ear.

"Not anymore." Those two words fell like a lead weight into the moment.

He grasped her fingertips, pressing them to his lips. "Always. I know it's frustrating for you, Lilly. I know you hate this extended recovery and that you're tired and in pain…but all I think is how lucky I am that you're still here."

Lilly curled her fingers around his hands, an apologetic look crossing her features. "I know I should be grateful—and I am—but some days I just want to stay in bed. I know what you've lost, Jacob. I can't imagine how painful his death is for you."

Another wave of sadness crept over him at her statement. The grief seemed more powerful now than it had in the immediate aftermath, and Jacob had lost count of the number of times he had to hold back the tears lingering on the back of his eyelids. He didn't want to burden her with his pain. She had enough of her own. With a deep sigh, he shook off the feeling, shooting Lilly a smile. "Let's get you dressed."

But Lilly wasn't deterred. She knew him better than anyone, better than he knew himself, it seemed. Her hand raised his face to meet her gaze, radiating the warmth and understanding he always found there. "You need to let out the pain or it will eat you alive."

Her simple statement cracked open the door to his fractured heart. A few tears rolled down his cheeks as the emotions became more than he could bear. "I miss him so much. I still have Roger's number in my phone; I can't bring myself to delete it. I have a few voicemail messages too and hearing his voice brings me comfort...even when he's telling me what a blooming arse I am."

"That sounds like Roger," Lilly chuckled.

"Certainly is—was—*fuck*. I don't know how to talk about my best friend in the past tense. So, I keep his number in my phone because it's my last link to him. I've convinced myself that as long I keep his number, he's still on the other end of the line."

Lilly's fingertips traced the planes of his face. "I promise you, he's still there. If you talk to him, he'll listen and let you know he's heard you." She framed his face with her hands. "Your poor, dear heart. I wish I could trade places with Roger and bring him back to you."

Jacob's blood froze in his veins. He knew Lilly felt unwarranted guilt over Roger's death, but this was the first time she intimated she should have died in his stead. When that notion hit Jacob, he couldn't breathe.

Jacob grabbed Lilly's arms, tightening his grasp slightly. "Don't *ever* say that. I can't live without you. If you had died"—his voice faltered, recalling how close she came to death—"I would be lost. I don't want to be a part of a world you're not in."

Lilly's eyes sparkled with an emotion he hadn't seen since he returned to Santorini; the look she gave him when he told her something beautiful, and she believed him. Her expression lit up her entire being from within and convinced him Lilly's heart wasn't closed, just wounded. "I'm here. If you need me, I'm here. I'll always be here for you."

Jacob's head collapsed against her lap, his breathing heavy with emotion. She was a survivor of a terrorist attack, dealing with immeasurable pain and guilt, yet she was willing to take on his burden too. Jacob had never known a heart so generous and his love for her magnified with her offer.

"Do you know that I fall more in love with you every day? All I want—all I need—is for you to love me again, the way you used to love me. God, the way you used to look at me, it was almost more than I could handle." He lifted his head, his mouth twisting. "But you can't love me like that anymore, can you? I've ruined it, and I can't bring it back."

"You didn't ruin it, Jacob, time and circumstance ruined it. You made my life beautiful."

Her words gave him hope and he forged ahead. "Do you remember what I told you? That night before I returned to England. I said I wanted to lay you down on the grass and make love to you until you promised never to leave me—"

"Love me until we made a baby," Lilly whispered.

There's a chance. She remembers. "Exactly. That's what I want, I want that back, that insatiable, mind-blowing love that we share. Come on, let me take you outside, we'll find the most private garden and I'll make love to you for hours."

Lilly shook her head, her eyes staring at the tile. "Jacob—"

"Or we can stay right here. That bed looks amazing."

"Please stop. We can't do that."

But Jacob wasn't prepared to stop, he was ready to fight. "Did the doctors say you weren't allowed? Is it because of your leg? Your lungs? Why can't we do exactly what I just said?"

"The doctors didn't mention it, but I didn't inquire either. I'm sure, from a professional standpoint, it would be fine—"

Jacob shot her a cheeky grin. He had to keep her from dwelling in her thoughts of despair. "Then let's go."

Lilly stayed his hands as they rested on her thighs. "Jacob, no. I'm tired."

Her refusal deflated the minor high Jacob was experiencing. Her emotional barricade was still resolutely in place around her heart and she seemed intent on keeping him out. "When I returned to London, after you were attacked, and you told me you loved me too, I believed life couldn't get any better." He stood, defeat exiting his body alongside his breath. "I was right, those days with you were the happiest of my life."

"I miss those days too. They were like a dream—an exquisite, magical dream that I would gladly spend the rest of my life in—screw reality and all its pain."

"They can be our reality, Lilly."

Lilly looked away, her jaw setting as her eyes filled with tears. "We aren't the same people. Too much has happened, we can't go backwards."

"We don't have to go backwards, we move forward, together. You said you would let me spend the rest of my life adoring you. I can't do that if you don't let me near you."

"I'm tired, Jacob."

Conversation over. Jacob knew her words were an excuse, love like theirs didn't disappear without a second glance. Even though she was fighting him every step of the way, he wasn't going to give up.

Jacob carried Lilly to the bed, setting her down gently and easing her injured leg onto the mattress. "What do you want to wear?"

"I'm not sure. What matches that hideous immobilizer?" Lilly threw a glare at the blue foam device laying on across the table.

"You make everything look good."

"You're a bad liar, Jacob."

"I'm not lying. You're beautiful." He gripped the footboard to keep from reaching out to her, caressing her body. God, he needed to stay with her, curl up beside her warm body and feel alive again.

But no matter what he said, Lilly believed he was better off with Victoria, and he didn't know how to convince her otherwise. "Would you like to listen to some music?"

Lilly nodded and Jacob flipped on the radio, their gazes holding as their song—*their song*—sounded from the speakers. Perhaps the universe was trying to tell them something, at least that was how Jacob was taking it.

Her reasons for their separation flew out the window as Jacob slid into bed next to her and took her lips with his own. Her lips parted, but Jacob swallowed any objections with his kiss as his tongue claimed her, desperate for the feel of her body and the taste of her skin. He wasn't waiting for her to let him in again, he was taking back what was rightfully his.

Lilly's arms slid around his neck and he deepened the kiss, pulling her body against him, his hand running along her spine. Touching her was as essential as water and he wanted to drown in her, the rising passion in her kisses only further fueled the tempest until he feared he would lose all control.

Lilly tore her mouth away, resting her palms on his cheeks, her eyes bright with tears. "I'll be okay. I will get through this, Jacob."

His finger traced her lower lip as he pressed kisses to the corner of her mouth. "There isn't a doubt in my mind that you'll overcome this hurdle. But that isn't the point. I want to be with you every step of the way."

"You need to move on with your life, prepare for your future."

"What do you think I'm trying to do?" Jacob held her wrists to either side of her head, his mouth against her throat. "You are my life, and my future.

I'll keep telling you until you believe every damn word."

Words weren't working, he needed to up the ante. He'd show her how desperately he needed her, let every kiss soothe away the inner demons haunting Lilly's mind.

His fingers slid under the towel, feeling her warm, damp skin under his palm, his eyes never leaving her face.

"What are you doing?"

Without a word he lifted Lilly's fingers—one by one—from her grip on the towel, pulling apart the edges and exposing her body to him.

"Jacob—"

"Shh, I'm busy." Jacob's palms slid along her ribcage, cupping her breasts. He watched her chest heave with emotion before taking one taut nipple between his teeth and torturing it with his tongue. "Do you know how many nights I've dreamt about touching you like this, licking every inch of your body?" His mouth traveled down the flat planes of her stomach, his hands wrapping around her hips and holding her close.

"Please—"

Jacob smiled, dropping kisses along her stomach as his mouth moved down her body. "That's my goal. To please you."

"Jacob," Lilly gasped, her back arching as his tongue circled her clit. Christ, he missed touching this woman.

Moving his gaze along her body, he saw her hands hovering in midair, unsure whether to push him away or pull him close. He was going to make the decision for her—right here and right now.

"Lilly, stop fighting me. I need you, I need to taste you." He nuzzled her further open, dropping kisses along her thighs as his fingers teased her folds.

She moaned as his fingers slid inside her, stroking her slow and deep and when her hands came to rest softly on the back of his head, Jacob deepened his conquest. Careful to avoid her injured leg, his hands slid under her ass as his mouth lavished attention on every inch of her, his tongue conveying the depth of his need, his desire, his love with every caress.

Lilly's breathing was shallow and rapid as she pressed him against her body. Jacob kept her dangling on the edge of release—his tongue driving deep inside her, relishing her sweet taste, before moving upwards to suckle her clit, smiling as she writhed against him. He released a silent victory yell. She still wanted him.

"Jacob," Lilly panted, her fingers gripping his shoulders. He knew she needed to come, her body needed the sweet release, but Jacob wouldn't allow that happen until he was buried inside her.

Trailing kisses up her body, he captured her lips against his with a fervent urgency. Then he yanked his towel off, pulling her naked body to him. The feeling of her wet heat against his erection was so powerful he feared he would climax before he even entered her.

Just as quickly as Lilly's body softened, she stiffened again, her teeth biting her lip as she looked away.

Jacob nuzzled Lilly's neck and jaw, depositing soft kisses. "What's wrong, angel?"

"We can't do this."

Bugger, she's in her head again. "I promise, I'll be gentle. Let me make you feel good."

Instead, Lilly looked over his shoulder, not meeting his gaze. "I don't want you fucking me because you feel sorry for me."

Jacob drew back, her words gutting him like a knife. "I don't feel sorry for you, and I didn't plan on fucking you, Lilly. I've *never* fucked you. I plan on making love to you, for hours, until you comprehend how much I adore you."

Lilly turned away from him, pulling the sheet over her body. "You should go."

"What just happened, Lilly? You were enjoying it, I felt it. Why the sudden change?"

"I told you why."

"You think you're broken now, undesirable for some reason, but you're so wrong...on both counts. You're beautiful and strong and so damned stubborn. You're my everything."

"Please...go." Her voice was barely a whisper but the resignation in her voice made his anger flash.

"Why have you shut me out? Do you have any idea the agony I'm in because you won't let me near you?" Jacob heard the bite in his voice, but he couldn't control it.

Lilly's shoulders shook with silent sobs. "You need to go—"

Jacob wrapped his arms around her slight frame, enveloping her in his embrace. "No, I need to stay. Even if you don't want me to stay, I'm going to be selfish tonight because I need you. Do you hear me? *I need you.*"

"You have everything—money, looks, talent. You don't need me, Jacob."

His grip tightened around her, pulling her closer against his body. "Without you, I have *nothing.* You make me feel alive. The happiest days of my life are the ones I spend with you, Lilly."

"But—"

"We can keep arguing all night, if that's your preference. But I'm not leaving. So deal with it." If she wanted to be stubborn, two could play that game.

He had hoped for a small chuckle or hint of a smile, but she simply shook her head with a defeated sigh. "Why won't you forget me? Forget us?"

He pressed his face against the nape of her neck, inhaling her heady scent. "Because it's impossible to forget the woman that gave you so much to remember."

Lilly

H er mind told her to push Jacob away and send him back to Victoria and his glamorous life, far away from the realities of rehab and recovery. Her ego cautioned her that his affections were likely driven by pity and obligation. Her heart whispered of a love so true it stood resolute in the face of any obstacle.

But in that moment, reason didn't matter. Lilly needed Jacob, and he claimed to need her. Love, pity, obligation—those emotions could be sorted later. Right now, she wanted to forget her reality and dwell in his adoration, no matter how short the visit.

She pressed Jacob's hand against her heart as her body relaxed against him. "You'll always live here, no matter if we never see each other again. You'll always have a part of me."

"Never see each other again? That's *not* going to happen. I won't let it, Lilly. Besides"—Jacob splayed his fingers against her chest—"I'm not satisfied with just a part of you. I want all of you, every day, for the rest of our lives."

His words scorched her skin and Lilly bit back a whimper.

Jacob hands wrapped around her hips, pulling her tight against him, his mouth at the curve of her neck. "Let me love you. I'm begging you, my darling."

Lilly moaned as he kissed her neck and shoulders, tangling his hand in her short hair as he slid inside her before she could protest.

"Christ, Lilly. You feel so perfect." Jacob exhaled, his breath tickling over her skin. He began to move inside her, his thrusts slow and deep, ever mindful of her injuries. It seemed he couldn't get deep enough, close enough, and Lilly pushed her hips against him in response. All the while, his long fingers teased the hard nub of her clit, working her into a frenzy.

She tightened around him, earning a groan of approval as he stretched her, his cock pulsing inside her. Lilly felt every cell in her body come alive. It had been almost two months since they last made love, yet his touch felt so familiar, so welcome.

Any lingering doubts were silenced as Jacob filled her, reminding her that she belonged to him, that no one would ever fill her mind, body and soul the way he did. With each stroke, pleasure short-circuited her brain and stole her reason. All she knew was the building pressure within her, the fire only Jacob could extinguish. She tried to speak, but all she could manage was a series of moans that only spurred this delicious man on further.

She was so close, and with a final thrust, Jacob pushed her over the edge. Lilly screamed her release as her muscles spasmed around him, her release triggering his own.

Jacob collapsed against her back, panting against her skin, their bodies slick with perspiration and desire. "There is nothing sexier in this world than you, the feeling of you wrapped around me. Christ, I missed you." He pressed open-mouthed kisses against her shoulders, their bodies still connected on every level.

"I missed you, too."

"I can tell. You weren't exactly whispering just a moment ago."

Lilly chuckled and gave him a light jab in the ribs. "Aren't you sure of yourself."

He tongued her earlobe, sending a new set of tingles down her spine. "Not at all, but I'm sure of you."

"Now that your sexual hunger has been abated, what do you plan to do with the rest of your evening?"

She felt him smile against her neck. "Being inside you *is* my plan for the evening, so don't even consider kicking me out of this bed." His fingers trailed over her breasts and stomach, and within moments he was moving inside her again.

"Good morning, time to get you ready for therapy." A therapist in her mid-thirties, clad in khakis and a polo shirt, pushed open the door to the suite immediately after knocking. "Oh bugger...sorry. I didn't realize you had company. The door was unlocked." The woman's eyes gazed at the floor, her embarrassment evident at walking in on the lovebirds.

Lilly struggled to sit up in the bed, the sheet falling to her waist in her haste. "Crap, sorry. I must have overslept." She yanked the sheet up to hide her nude body.

"I guess I wore her out," Jacob commented with a chuckle, sitting up in the bed. "Good morning."

The therapist's eyes widened in recognition. "You're...you're Jacob Edmonton."

With a luxurious stretch and a knowing wink, Jacob responded. "Last time I checked. What's your name?"

"Meg-Megan." It seemed although Renaissance was an abode for royalty and celebrities, Jacob was in another stratosphere altogether.

"Pleasure to meet you Megan. This is Lilly, she's as stubborn as she is beautiful. Consider that fair warning. Oh, and she's a Yank too."

"Don't build me up too much, Jacob," Lilly muttered, running her hands through her rumpled hair.

Jacob ran his hand along the back of her head, smoothing down a few strands. "How did your hair get so messy, luv? What *were* you doing last night?" That world-famous smirk split his face and Lilly was tempted to remove it with a whack of her pillow.

"I can only imagine."

He bit her shoulder, seemingly oblivious to the therapist standing not ten feet away. "Do you need a refresher? Something to jar your memory?"

Megan cleared her throat. Poor woman, privy to Jacob's post-coital banter. "I'll come back in a few minutes. I have to grab…something."

"You don't have to rush out on my account, Megan. But, would you be a doll and turn around for a moment so I can grab my boxers?"

Lilly bit back a laugh at the look crossing Megan's face. Hell, she didn't blame the therapist—Jacob was delicious. "A few minutes would be wonderful, thank you Megan."

"What?" Jacob asked with an innocent look as Megan scurried out the door. "Was it something I said?"

Lilly shook her head, smiling as he pushed her back down to the mattress, his mouth wasting no time in finding hers. "You've got to go," she murmured against his lips.

"But I don't want to, I'm primed and ready for one more round with you this morning." Her body jerked in surprise as his hand drifted between her thighs, his fingers sliding deep inside her. "I knew it."

"Knew what?"

"You want me as much as I want you."

"How do you figure?" Lilly whispered, trying desperately to focus her thoughts. It was damn near impossible as he curved that talented hand around to caress her from the inside.

"You're soaking wet." His lips growled at her ear as he sank inside her, a low groan emitting from his throat.

Lilly's eyes widened at the unexpected maneuver, her fingers gripping his shoulders. "Jacob! We have to stop. I have therapy."

But Jacob wasn't listening. He was intent on making her come and his slow, deep thrusts were getting her there fast. "You're almost there, I can feel it."

"We need—"

"I'm not stopping until you come, angel. We can do this all day. Decision is yours."

Bastard. Cocky, arrogant, gorgeous, magical bastard. Lilly curled her lips up in a scowl, but any snarky remark was soon forgotten as he filled her, and her body quivered around him.

"That's it. God, you're beautiful," Jacob breathed as he angled her hips for deeper penetration.

For a moment she couldn't see or hear...she could only feel. The delectable pleasure of the man she adored filling her completely, releasing himself deep inside her. The mere idea triggered another orgasm and Lilly gave herself over to the blistering heat flowing through her body.

When she opened her eyes, Jacob's watchful gaze was focused on her, the corners of his mouth upturned in a satiated smile. "Marry me, Lilly."

Her heart leapt at his simple, heartfelt request but her mind butted into the moment, warning her against answering anything spoken in the thrill of the afterglow. Instead, she stretched, whimpering when her leg smarted in pain.

"Did I hurt you?" Jacob sat up, pulling the blanket down, his hands gently running along her injured leg.

"No, I just moved wrong. What you just did certainly didn't inflict any pain."

"I told you, I have skills."

God, she loved Jacob's sexy smirk, even if it graced a million magazine covers, even if he was lusted after by countless women, even if he'd bedded countless more. Because right after that smirk came the soft smile reserved for her, and the gentle press of his lips against her forehead.

"Let's get you dressed."

Just like that, the afterglow dissipated as her harsh reality charged back into the moment. Lilly's hands fisted in the sheet as embarrassment swept through her being. Gone was the independent, sexy woman who had captured Jacob's fancy. In her place remained a woman now broken and scarred. She pushed herself to a seated position, careful to pull the blanket over her injuries.

When her eyes rested on the scar on her thigh, she closed them, biting back nausea. Who was she kidding? There was no way this demigod still found her attractive. Jacob had women like Victoria begging for his affections. Women without flaws or limitations...women who didn't need help dressing or bathing or walking.

"Quit it. Right now." Jacob knelt by the side of the bed, his hand covering

141

the scar. "I know where your head's at, and I want you to stop."

Lilly bit back tears but shook them off. She had to pull herself together and rebuild her emotional wall, brick by brick. "I'm fine—"

"You're a terrible liar, Lilly."

"I'm not lying. I'm just tired. You wore me out." She forced a chuckle.

Jacob's azure gaze locked with hers and she read it in his eyes—he didn't believe her, but he wasn't going to push the issue this morning. He pulled on his boxers and pants and Lilly felt her body clinch at the sight of his long, sinewy muscles. What a glorious perfect specimen.

She averted her gaze, a flush of color staining her cheeks as she recalled her boisterous climaxes from the night before—and this morning. So much for willpower. Her body had caved to her primal urges, but the morning light showcased all her flaws which the shadows kept hidden. "Thank you for last night, and this morning. I didn't realize how desperately I needed…the release."

Jacob stopped in the middle of a button, his eyebrows raised. "Are you thanking me for making love to you?"

Lilly nodded, and Jacob sat next to her, pulling her onto his lap. "I plan on doing that every chance I get for the rest of our lives, so get used to it." Jacob stated between kisses. "You think *you're* stubborn? You have no idea how stubborn I am when I want something."

"Really? What is it that you want?"

His hand twisted in her hair, the slight pressure forcing her to meet his gaze. "You. You're the only thing I want in this world. If you think, for one second, that I'm giving up on you, you're crazy."

"Doesn't sound like I have much choice in the matter." Lilly gave a fake scowl, giggling when he tongued the seam of her lips.

"No choice at all. As long as you still want me, wild horses won't keep me away from you." His hands ran gently over her thighs, careful to avoid paining her injured leg. "Come on, let's get you ready for the day."

"Can't wait," Lilly muttered, taking the bra and tank that Jacob offered. "Thanks."

He knelt in front of her again, helping her slide on her underwear and sweatpants. "Hold onto my shoulders so I can pull them up."

Lilly felt a flash of mortification as she obliged his request. "You don't have to do this, Jacob."

"Don't start that garbage again, angel. I actually enjoy being of some use around you. You're so fiercely independent."

"I like being independent."

He released a chuckle before pulling her back onto his lap. "Perhaps you might consider taking on a partner in crime. Someone to do the grunt work."

"You have someone in mind?" Lilly tucked her hair behind her ear, forcing away the feeling of inadequacy.

"I do, and I think you'll approve of my choice." His lips brushed against hers, his tongue playing along her lower lip. "The next few weeks are a bit crazy, with the nomination proceedings and filming, so I'll be here a bit later in the evening. I'll bring us dinner."

Lilly's face lit up. She had forgotten about his nomination. "I'm such a jerk. Congratulations on your nomination! You're going to win this one, Jacob."

Jacob tightened his embrace, his nose nuzzling along her jaw. "I've already won the greatest prize. I've got you."

His words should have made her jump for joy, but her niggling doubt crept in again, squashing her happiness. "Why don't we take a step back?"

Jacob pulled away from her, his face drawn. "Why would we do that?"

He was right—Lilly *was* a terrible liar, but this lie was necessary—for everyone involved. "Just a temporary hiatus. You focus on the new movie, all your nomination interviews, and whatever Victoria needs in regard to the baby. I'll be here, regaining my strength and independence. Once the whirlwind is over, we'll both be in better places."

"This sounds like another trick, trying to push me out of your life again." Jacob studied her face, searching for the truth behind her lie. "Lilly, you're my number one priority. I want to be in this movie, but I'll gladly pull out of the role if you want me here. I'll stay by your side 24/7."

Lilly's heart flipped at his statement, but regardless of what she desired, he had a family. That family needed him. She would have to learn to get along without him. "You are *not* pulling out of Milieu of Madness after everything you endured to get that role! I'll beat some sense into you myself."

"Careful I may enjoy it." Jacob offered a wink as he nipped her neck. "I may not arrive until later in the evening, but I want to be here with you."

"I want us to remain focused on our end goals."

"You're my end goal."

His simple declaration made her lie feel even uglier. "You're going to be late."

"You really don't want me coming here tonight?"

Lilly shook her head, pulling his mouth to hers. "You're a distraction, a gorgeous, sexy as hell distraction. If you're here, the only thing I'll think about is how quickly I can have you naked—"

"I'm okay with that idea."

Lilly forced a laugh. "I'll call you though."

Jacob shot her a wistful look, his hand on her cheek. "You're killing me, Lilly. I'll agree to this ridiculous arrangement but only if you solemnly swear to allow me unlimited access to this body for the rest of your life."

Lilly smirked. "Is that all?"

"No. Once you're done with rehab, we get married and start trying to have a family."

Her breath caught at his statement, words she prayed to hear that now felt like knives stabbing her already slaughtered heart. "Jacob—"

Jacob stood, crossing his arms and shooting her a pointed stare. "Total agreement or no deal, in which case I'll see you tonight. To be honest, I hope you don't agree, because then we can start trying for that baby immediately. Practice makes perfect, you know."

What was one more lie? She had told so many this morning. "Deal."

Jacob shot her a fake glare before capturing her mouth in a kiss. "Why did you have to agree? I wish you'd said no."

She stroked his cheek, wishing she could fall into his arms and stay there forever. "I'm nothing if not difficult."

"Truer words were never spoken. I doubt I'll be able to stay away from you for a day, much less a few weeks."

Lilly wagged her finger in front of his face. "Your deal, you have to live up to your end. Now go."

"No promises. I'm weak where you're concerned. I love you, angel." He captured her lips in one last kiss, his hand cupping her head and holding her fast to him. He turned and walked to the door, offering up a brilliant smile for the therapist. "Have a great day, Megan. Pleasure to meet you."

Lilly's head swung up, noting the therapist leaning against the doorframe. How long had she been standing there?

"Lilly, did you lose your damn mind in the attack?" Megan remarked drily as she strolled toward the bed.

Great, she has jokes. Opting to ignore the pointed question, Lilly focused her attention on securing her leg immobilizer. Time to begin the grueling recovery process. It would be a quest of misery, of that Lilly had no doubt, but she could deal with the discomfort. She was going to get her independence back, come hell or high water.

"I repeat, have you lost your mind?"

"What is that supposed to mean?"

Megan jerked a thumb at the door. "What do you think I mean?"

"How much of my conversation did you hear?" Lilly inquired as she pulled her hair away from her face with a headband.

"Enough to know you're certifiable for pushing away a man like Jacob Edmonton. My ovaries damn near burst at the things he was saying to you—begging you to get married and have a baby. Never mind all the naughty things that gorgeous man was doing to you earlier."

"We weren't—"

Megan chuckled. "The walls aren't that thick, luv. Hey, I don't blame you. He's—"

"Perfect." Lilly finished her statement. Hell, it was the truth. She was sure Megan was shocked that a man like Jacob aimed his affections at a woman like her.

"Perfectly in love with you, that much is apparent."

"It's complicated." Lilly settled into the wheelchair with Megan's help. Hell on earth, day one, was about to commence.

"Life always is, but the heart wants what the heart wants."

It was the second time Lilly heard that statement with regards to Jacob. "Sometimes the heart can't have what it wants."

"That man is wrapped around your little finger."

"Not even close. He feels sorry for my situation and obligated to help me."

Megan leveled her with a dark stare. "What that man said to you wasn't from any sense of obligation. That was a mad, crazy love."

"It isn't—"

"Actions speak louder than *your* words, Ms. Lilly. I may not know the two of you, but I recognize adoration when I see it. Personally, I don't think you'll be able to run him off unless you pack up and move to Antarctica, and even then, it's not a guarantee. He'd likely buy a parka and join you."

"What about America?" Lilly mumbled, more to herself than to Megan.

"Warmer than Antarctica, but I suppose moving across the pond might deter him, emphasis on might. Of course, why would you want to push Jacob Edmonton away? He's delicious, and utterly devoted."

Lilly scarcely heard Megan's compliments regarding Jacob as her mind focused on one part of her statement. A return to the United States. She realized that Megan was joking about a move stateside, but she *had* been planning on going home after that press release aired. If she returned to New York, it was an undisputed signal that her relationship with Jacob was over.

The distance would allow Jacob to focus on Victoria and their baby whilst simultaneously alleviating any lingering feelings of obligation. The

145

idea of a life without the man of her dreams was agonizing, but this was so much bigger than either of them. Even though Jacob was in denial, it's what his daughter needed, a fresh start without another woman being involved to complicate matters. One day, he would look back and thank her for letting him go.

"Am I allowed off campus? Can I come and go as I please?"

Megan nodded, eyes widening at the sudden change in conversation. "It isn't jail, but we ask that you schedule off-site visits around your therapies."

Lilly pasted on a smile as a plan formed. "Not a problem. Now where do I get my hall pass?"

"Are you running back to America today?"

Lilly sent her a scathing glare. "Not hardly, and certainly not running. I have something to pick up, a very important gift."

Edward let out a low whistle when he walked into Lilly's suite later that afternoon. "Bloody hell, this is three times the size of my flat! And you don't have a stinky bald guy passed out on the couch, reeking of potted meat and crisps."

Lilly laughed and held her nose. "Phew, thank God for small favors."

Edward swooped in, planting a kiss on Lilly's cheek. "How are you, luv?"

"Getting better, but it's a slow, painful, uphill battle."

"You look better. I was really worried about you, Lilly."

He gave her hand and squeeze and Lilly smiled. Although an unlikely friendship, Lilly and Edward became close friends over the last few months. They shared a love of old films and sarcasm, along with an easygoing banter.

"I still can't get over this place," Edward muttered, shaking his head as he surveyed the suite.

"It's swanky, isn't it?"

"Are you a secret billionaire? How can you afford this place?"

"I can't afford a water glass in this place, but I have a generous benefactor. The entire month was paid in full."

Edward regarded her with a knowing glint in his eyes. "I see, and how is Jacob?"

"He's fine, ever the gentleman."

"Has he visited you recently? Never mind, I have my answer." He motioned to her neck, and Lilly wheeled herself over to the mirror, noting a mark from one of Jacob's more exuberant kisses.

Blushing, Lilly rubbed her neck. "He stopped by last night."

"Obviously. Have you two finally reconciled?"

"No, of course not."

"Surprising," Edward mumbled as his gaze fell to her collection of flowers and cards. He grabbed the sonogram picture, his jaw slackening. "Is this what I think it is?"

"It's a sonogram picture."

His exasperated sigh floated through the room. "No shit, Lilly. Why do you have Victoria's sonogram photo? Did Jacob bring this here?"

Lilly shook her head. "Victoria sent flowers and the photo was in the card, a not so subtle plea to send the father of her baby back to her."

"Fucking woman. I thought she had finally given up the ghost."

"Determination is one of her many gifts."

"I wouldn't call Victoria determined, I'd call her manipulative."

Lilly watched her friend's jaw twitch. This was the first time he'd ever intimated any animosity toward the great and regal Victoria. "I thought you two were friends."

"We were...we are...I don't know anymore." Edward stared at the image, his gaze narrowing. "I'll be damned."

"What?"

Something had intrigued him thoroughly, but Edward chose not to elaborate on the subject. "It's nothing."

"Liar."

He snorted. "The photo makes it real, that's all. Are you ready for our little outing?"

Lilly nodded, wheeling to the bedroom to grab her coat. "Thank you for taking me to the jewelers today."

Edward nodded, pushing her wheelchair towards the main entrance. "I'm thrilled you wanted to be out in public. I feared I would have to drag you kicking and screaming from these halls, worried you turned into a recluse."

Lilly chuckled. "Not quite yet, give it time."

The duo enjoyed a pleasant jaunt to Broad Street as Edward discussed his new role in Milieu of Madness. It was a huge break for his career. "I'm on set with Jacob—not all the time, since his role is much larger than mine. But we have a few scenes together."

"That must be nice, working with friends."

"We aren't friends, Lilly. We knew each other through Roger. Jacob's a good man though and dedicated to his craft. Dedicated to anything he feels passionately about."

Lilly nodded, remembering her shared passion with Jacob the night before. He had loved her body until she forgot her own name and didn't care if she ever remembered.

Edward looked at her, no doubt waiting for a response, but Lilly had no reply. "Victoria said she's disputing the DNA test, can't say I'm surprised. That is her last claw in Jacob's coat."

"Why would she dispute the test when she swears up and down Jacob is the father? The truth will come out either way, eventually. He isn't going to forget that he requested proof of paternity."

Edward's chuckle turned into a cough. "Come on Lilly, you know why she's disputing the test. Jacob isn't the father. My guess is she hopes she can string him along until he falls back in love with her, but that's a futile plan."

"Seems to be working so far."

"How so? Despite her best efforts, he doesn't want any part of her. The second he returned to London, Jacob ran straight into your arms, a place he never left, apparently."

"It's not what you think," Lilly huffed, aggravated. Why did everyone believe Jacob was so hopelessly besotted? They didn't understand the sense of duty Jacob felt towards her, the care of his dutiful and faithful companion, as Victoria termed her. "It was a pity fuck. He felt bad for me, and I guess he thought if he slept with me, I might forget my injuries for a while."

Edward pulled into a parking space, turning to face Lilly. "Are you daft?"

Lilly's eyes widened at his biting question. "Excuse me?"

"The situation isn't what *you* think. You're a fool if you believe Jacob came round to give you a pity romp. It's bloody obvious the man worships the ground you walk on—obvious to everyone but you. And he's not the only one, either. I know plenty of men who would give their eyeteeth for a chance with you."

Lilly's harsh laugh echoed throughout the interior of the car. "They're lined up down the street, waiting for a chance with me."

Edward leveled his gaze at her. "I don't know how you don't see it."

Lilly shook off the statement, maintaining her gaze straight ahead. "See what?"

Edward sighed. "How everyone looks at you. I guarantee even your buddies feel more than friendship for you. You have this ability to get under people's skin and change them…for the better."

Lilly opened her mouth but then closed it again, unable to think of one proper response.

"Don't try to figure out a reply. I know you don't agree with my take on the situation, but you're blind if you don't see how Jacob feels about you…or how you feel about him."

Lilly shook her head. "I'm not in love with Jacob."

"What a load of bollocks."

Lilly bit back tears of frustration. "What does it matter?"

"I'm certain it matters a whole lot to Jacob." Edward helped Lilly transfer to the wheelchair, moving up the pavement toward their destination.

"He's about to become a parent, a journey I can't take with him, and one that requires absolute devotion. Let's not forget my recovery ordeal. I refuse to usurp any more of his time with my rehabilitation."

"You'll be running circles around us in no time, you're getting stronger every day." Edward's voice held a gentle force.

"Jacob feels sorry for me, he feels obligated to help. Hell, he is helping me, Renaissance costs a fortune. He needs to be with Victoria and their baby, he doesn't need the burden of me hanging around his neck."

Edward sighed as he pushed her through the jewelry store entrance. "You're the only one who thinks you're a burden. It sounds to me like you're using this injury and his supposed love child as a way to keep him at arm's length."

Lilly ignored his statement, focusing her attention on Clive, the jewelry store manager, as he rushed to her side. "Ms. Lilly! Dear God, what in the world happened?"

"I was on the Tube that day."

"Oh no, you and Roger were together. I never suspected you were injured." He clasped Lilly's hands, his eyes soft with concern. "My deepest sympathies for the loss of your friend. He was a good and decent man."

"The very best," Lilly echoed, another round of tears threatening to break through her lashes. Would there ever be an end to her sadness? "I'm here to pick up the watch that Roger ordered, if I may?"

"The gift for your fiancée's birthday."

Lilly nodded, the title piercing her heart like an arrow. "It's a gift for Jacob."

Clive strolled into the back to fetch the watch, returning a few moments later and showing Lilly the engraving. "Does it suit?"

"It's perfect. He'll love it."

The jeweler packed the watch, looking at her hand. "Where's your ring?"

"I—I don't have it on." Lilly fumbled out the words. *Nothing like stating the obvious.*

149

"Jacob was so excited when he picked it up that day."

Lilly's brows raised in disbelief. "You remembered the day he picked up the ring?"

"How could I forget?"

"Of course, it was the day of the explosion."

"Yes, it was, but that's not why I remember it. He was full of nervous energy. He said he couldn't wait to tell the world how much he loved you."

Lilly smiled, surprised at the jeweler's revelation. "He said that?"

"That he did. I've never seen a man so in love. I wish you two the very best."

As Edward wheeled Lilly back to the car, her mind recycled Clive's words. "If only I hadn't been injured…"

"Pardon?"

"I was just thinking about what the jeweler said."

"About how deeply in love Jacob was with you?"

"Was, yes."

Edward sighed, running his hands through his dark hair. "Bugger. Bugger." He caught Lilly's hand, holding her gaze. "I need to know right now, did you mean what you said earlier? Or was it a load of shit?"

"What are you talking about?"

"Are you in love with Jacob? Do you still want to be with him? Marry him?"

Lilly sniffled and nodded. "I love him desperately, but I don't have anything to offer him—"

"I don't want to hear your excuses. I just want to know if you're in love with him."

"I am, but it's not enough."

"It's not for you to decide if it's enough."

"*I'm* not enough, Edward."

"That's where you're so very wrong, Lilly. But until you believe you're deserving of love, you'll continue to push it away."

Edward remained silent the rest of the ride, a look of stern concentration in his face. Lilly considered making small talk, but his white-knuckled grip on the steering wheel changed her mind. Whatever he was mulling in his mind, he didn't want to share.

Edward pulled up to the front entrance of Renaissance ten minutes later and helped Lilly into her wheelchair.

"Do you want to come up for some coffee? Or whiskey?"

"You have whiskey upstairs?"

Lilly chuckled. "Sadly, no. I thought my company might be enticing enough."

"I have to go."

"So soon?"

"I have to go," Edward reiterated brusquely, giving her a quick peck on the cheek. "I'll call you later."

What in the hell just happened? Lilly watched her friend drive away so fast she expected to see flames shoot from under his tires.

CHAPTER ELEVEN

Jacob

As he sipped his tea on the set of Milieu of Madness, Jacob couldn't remember if it was Monday or Wednesday; he felt like a hamster on a wheel. Thankfully, his interviews for the upcoming award show finished taping the day before; balancing the movie and promo spots damn near killed him. He usually enjoyed discussing film roles, particularly ones recognized by judging committees, but the mood over this season was subdued. Roger's death left a gaping hole not only in his heart, but Hollywood at large.

However, it wasn't Roger's death that was front and center on his mind. Lilly had made good on her end of their deal, successfully avoiding even his calls for the last three weeks. He received an errant text or two, where she claimed to be focused on her recovery, but Jacob wasn't born yesterday. His angel was pulling away again, and her absence left a gigantic void in his life. Without her, he moved through life like a robot. She was his reason for being, his entire happiness wrapped up in one and a half meters of the most stubbornly exquisite woman he'd ever known.

Within a month, Jacob would land in the City of Angels for the awards show. He wanted Lilly on his arm, and their love front and center as he introduced the woman who claimed his heart to the world. The tricky part would be convincing Lilly to attend, especially in the wake of her injuries. Janie agreed that Lilly would likely decline, so his baby sister was on standby as his date for the evening.

Victoria dropped countless hints about attending the show as his date, but Jacob set her firmly back in her place, reminding her that there was no relationship beyond his supposed love child. He didn't know whether to be appalled or amused at Victoria's obstinate attitude. She couldn't fathom that her denial to grant him a paternity test had ended any additional discussions.

The morning sun was brutal—an unusual heat wave had arrived in England and was taking no prisoners. Jacob sought relief under a tree, reading over his lines for the day. The character was a meaty challenge, a departure from his earlier roles and Jacob relished sinking his teeth into the part.

I'm so glad I listened to Lilly. The thought drifted through his mind, bringing his thoughts firmly back to the woman he loved. God, he missed her; they'd been apart more than together, and it was torturous.

"How's your morning?" Albert inquired, wizened from the heat. The movie director settled next to Jacob under the tree, offering a resigned chuckle as he blotted the sweat from his brow.

Jacob nodded, offering a generic reply.

"How's Victoria?"

Jacob huffed. "She's fine, I guess."

"Don't you know? I thought you two were engaged."

Jacob damn near spit out his tea. "God, no way in hell."

Albert's eyes narrowed in confusion. "Didn't you two hold a press conference announcing your engagement and impending arrival?"

Be careful Jacob. Tread lightly, you don't know how deep Victoria's hooks are sunk into Albert.

Jacob cleared his throat, giving himself a moment to collect his thoughts and reply with some manner of decorum. "We broke off our relationship, and I'm not positive about the paternity of Victoria's child."

"I thought that press conference sounded like a load of hooey. You looked shell-shocked the entire time."

"She caught me off-guard. I never proposed to her, I guess she wanted to force my hand."

"How romantic, regular Hallmark movie," Albert remarked drily.

Fuck, this conversation is traversing a dangerous path. "You no doubt think I should be grateful to Victoria, but I'm not in a gracious mood at the moment." *So much for decorum.*

Albert paused mid-sip as his expression segued into bewilderment. "Why would I care if you're grateful to Victoria?"

"I got this role because of Victoria—"

"What?"

Something in the world shifted, Jacob felt it as the hairs on the back of his neck stood at attention. "Victoria said you two were close friends and you only considered me for the role because of her recommendation."

Now it was Albert's turn to sputter on his drink. "She can certainly twist a story, I'll give her that much."

Jacob leaned back against the tree, his jaw twitching. "Yes, she can."

Albert stared at his coffee. "I'm afraid Victoria wasn't telling you the truth. She did speak to me about the film, but it was for her own personal gain. She seemed to believe she deserved the role of the heroine despite her complete lack of training or expertise."

Jacob snickered. "That sounds like Victoria. So, she never mentioned me and my desire for a role in this film?"

Albert cleared his throat, his gaze on the crew assembling the movie set.

"She told me you were desperate for the lead role, and I was excited to have an actor of your caliber pursuing the part, but Victoria didn't believe you were a good fit." He tapped his chin, recalling the memory. "How did she put it? Your experience vacillated between bedding models and selecting fine wines. She claimed you cheated on her multiple times, but she was kind enough to forgive you."

"That bitch," Jacob muttered under his breath. He straightened, realizing he spoke the statement aloud. "I apologize, I know she's your friend."

"We're not friends. I met Victoria only a week or so before I made your acquaintance. And you're spot on with the bitch comment. I saw through her immediately. I knew what she was trying to do, but I assumed from her statements that you two had reconciled. Who was I to question your relationship?"

Jacob rubbed his hand over his buzzed hair, willing his anger to settle. "I should have known she never tried to help me. So, when she said you weren't considering me for a role, was that all a load of bollocks as well?"

Albert could have been an actor, his face certainly parlayed every emotion known to man during their brief conversation. "I knew you were terribly talented, Jacob, but I didn't know if you would dig into a role like this one."

"So how did we get here?"

"You had an angel in your corner."

Jacob's eyes widened. "Who—"

"I shouldn't even be telling you this, she asked me not to say a word… but in light of Victoria's deception, I find it fitting that you know the truth." Albert released a deep sigh and chugged down the rest of his coffee. "I was in the hospital at St. Luke a couple months ago, a minor surgery."

Jacob's ears started ringing as his mind raced. Once he heard the name of the hospital, he knew exactly who had recommended him for the role. "Lilly."

"Yes, Lilly Staver. I met her during my stay, and she chewed my ear for an hour about all your merits as an actor…and a gentleman."

His darling Lilly struck again, and Jacob smiled at the thought. "She was your nurse?"

"No." Another loud, winded sigh. "My nephew fell in with an ill-advised crowd, one lad in particular. One afternoon, this hooligan decided to attack Lilly in the parking deck—"

Jacob's blood thundered in his veins as his fists clenched. "Your nephew was the monster who attacked Lilly?"

Albert raised his hands, easing Jacob down. "My nephew didn't touch her—Lilly swears to it—he actually attempted to stop her attacker. Earned a broken nose in the process. Still, she could have still pressed charges against him as an accessory, but she told me that if it hadn't been for my nephew… let's just leave it that the outcome would have been much worse."

Jacob buried his head in his hands as memories of her bruised body flashed through his mind like a movie reel on speed. "I still don't understand—"

Albert patted his shoulder. "I went to visit Lilly in Accident and Emergency. I was only there a few minutes but left my card. Within fifteen minutes, she was on the phone, asking that I return. I was certain she had decided to press charges, but the darling woman had one favor when she realized who I was—that I ignored everything Victoria told me about you and watched a few of your older theater pieces before I made a decision about the movie."

He felt nauseous, this story was getting more convoluted by the moment. "Christ, Lilly bribed you into giving me the part?"

"Absolutely not!" Albert shook his head. "*You* got you the part—you and your unbelievable acting talent. Lilly ensured my opinion of you wasn't tainted by what Victoria said and that I understood the full scope of your gift."

His emotions were in an uproar. At first, he felt extreme anger at Victoria, but it quickly segued to feelings of graciousness as the truth of the situation settled over him. All these months Victoria had been dangling this part in front of him, but she hadn't helped him one iota. Instead, it was the woman who had helped him more times than he could count, yet she never mentioned it. Just like her animal rescue, Lilly didn't support him for personal gain but because she knew in her heart it was the right choice.

Albert studied Jacob, a knowing smile on his lips. "Lilly didn't want me to tell you that we met. She knew you would think she somehow finagled me into giving you the role."

"My Lilly strikes again."

"Lilly believes in you, and she adores you."

"I adore her."

"I can see it in your face. Personally, I'm shocked she isn't married. She's the type of woman that when you find her, you scoop her up and marry her immediately. She's an anomaly, in the best possible sense."

"We were engaged."

"Were?"

"Victoria and her press conference happened right after Lilly accepted my marriage proposal. I thought by going along with Victoria's game that I would keep Lilly safe from harm, but I should have fought for her. She's always fought for me."

"Are you still speaking?"

Jacob nodded, finishing off his last swallow of tea. "She was injured in the attack on the Tube and is in rehab right now. I'm hoping she'll let me see her tonight."

"I can't speak for you, but if I had a chance to marry a woman like that, I would get on my knees and beg until she agreed to be my wife."

"Trust me, I've asked her several times since I returned to London…but she said no…or worse, she didn't say anything at all."

"So that's it, then? You're giving up? Seems to me, if you love her that much—and she loves you—I wouldn't stop asking until she says yes."

Albert was right. It was time to reclaim the woman he loved. "I plan on doing just that. She's fighting me every step of the way, my stubborn Yank."

Albert patted his arm. "Sometimes you have to keep fighting for what you want in this world even when the world seems to be fighting against you. I'm off to discuss some changes with the set director."

Jacob watched Albert depart before grabbing his phone. He dialed Lilly, not caring about the time. He needed to speak to her.

"Good morning, Jacob. Aren't you up early?"

He nearly dropped the phone when she answered his call, it was the first time in weeks that she hadn't let it go to voicemail. "I figured you wouldn't answer the phone any other time, perhaps I could catch you off guard early in the morning."

Lilly remained silent for a few beats. "I'm not avoiding you—"

"Aren't you?"

Silence. Ten seconds of screaming silence. Jacob took a deep breath and plowed ahead.

"I can't go any longer without you in my life, Lilly. I miss you so much it physically hurts. I know you wanted space but how much damn longer do you need?"

"I miss you too." Her voice was barely a whisper, but it oozed emotion. "Maybe you can come by—"

"Yes, whenever. All I want is to be near you."

"We need to talk, Jacob."

Christ, he hated that line, but he wasn't giving her time to continue in that vein. "Yes, we do."

"Oh, I'm…I'm glad you agree." But Lilly didn't sound pleased, she sounded disappointed, and that was all the room Jacob needed.

"Absolutely. We need to finalize the details on our wedding…I'm thinking Greece or Paris."

"What?" Lilly sounded dazed.

"Hmm, I think a beach wedding would be perfect. But no matter the location, I can spend the next several days after the wedding naked in bed with you. Then, nine months later…well, you're the nurse."

More silence, then finally a sign of hope—she chuckled. "You have our timeline all figured out?"

"Down to the last detail. Of course, I'd love your input, but only if you agree to the main proponents of my plan."

"Which are…marriage and a baby?"

"Exactly. You can select the flowers and whatever else one chooses for a wedding. Now, as much as I'd love to speak with you for the next several hours, Albert is shooting me dirty looks. Filming starts in a few minutes, but I will be there tonight. No later than seven." He paused, waiting for her retort. "What, no argument?"

Another chuckle. "Bring me ice cream?"

A genuine smile stretched across Jacob's face, the first one in weeks. "Only if I can eat it off your delectable body."

"Don't forget the whipped cream too, then." Her low voice flirted in his ear, making him immediately hard.

"Fuck Lilly…just wait until tonight. Once I have you in my arms, I'm never letting you go again."

"See you soon, handsome."

"I love you."

"I love you back." She hung up and Jacob sat back, a stupid grin crossing his face.

He felt elated, things were moving in the right direction. It was about damn time.

Jacob cleared his thoughts in time to see Edward heading his way and his good mood sank like a stone in water. He wasn't sure why he disliked Edward with such intensity, the man had never done anything to him.

Jacob assumed it was his relationship with Lilly that angered him the most. Edward held her trust in a way Jacob was unable to obtain, and that truth was a hot poker in his heart—and temper.

Edward's face was unreadable as he approached. Without a word, he thrust an envelope in Jacob's direction.

"Good morning to you too. What's this?" Jacob inquired, pulling out several documents.

"Your freedom pass. You can do with the information what you wish."

Jacob perused the papers. They were medical documents from Victoria's obstetrician. "I don't understand. What are these papers supposed to tell me?"

Edward jabbed his finger at a number on the baby's ultrasound image—a gestational age of sixteen weeks. Jacob did the math in his head…it didn't add up. The last time he slept with Victoria was over five months ago.

"I believed Victoria at first, when she told me you were the father of her baby. Then one night, she mentioned the last time you two were intimate was before you left for Santorini. I did the math and realized she was a month off in her dates."

Jacob was certain his jaw was on the ground, his heart racing a million miles a minute.

"I know you're waiting on the court order for the DNA test, but with this paperwork, you have your answer."

"Did Victoria admit the truth?" He held his breath, feeling as if he stood on a precipice over a bottomless cliff.

Edward paused before nodding. "It took some prying, but she finally came clean. You're off the hook, Jacob. You're not the father of Victoria's baby."

Jacob started laughing, his first real laugh in weeks. It felt like a two-ton boulder had been lifted from his chest and he could breathe again. Suddenly, every obstacle between him and Lilly disappeared. The world was his fucking oyster. "This is the greatest news I've ever received. So, who's the lucky dad?"

"Who the hell knows? She didn't exactly live like a nun." Edward ran his hand through his hair, clearing his throat. "There's a chance that I'm the father."

"What?" Jacob's jaw slackened. "You and Victoria slept together? When the hell did that happen?" *And what alternate reality have I fallen into?*

Edward sighed and shook his head, taking a seat next to Jacob. "I am not proud of my behavior these last several months. I was an utter git, and to two really nice people. For a long time, I was in love with Victoria…hell, I still adore the ice queen."

"I'm not following this conversation."

"I was her lackey and her lover, one of many men she slept with while you were dating. I was an asshole for doing that, you didn't deserve it."

"Don't worry yourself too much, she slept with half of Hollywood, apparently."

"I'm sorry I didn't respect your relationship with Victoria but I'm far sorrier for interfering in your relationship with Lilly."

Jacob's insides flipped at the statement. What the fuck was he talking about? "What the hell do you mean? How did you interfere?"

"I was in love with Victoria and would do anything she asked. Victoria enjoyed stringing me along, until she found out about Lilly…and how you changed after meeting her. She went ballistic, insane with jealousy that you were in love with someone and it wasn't her. So, she enlisted my aid."

"Your *aid*? What exactly did you do?"

"I reported back to Victoria everything I knew about you and Lilly. That's how she maintained tabs on you, kept showing up wherever you were."

"Jesus, man!" Jacob was shocked by Edward's confession, but relief about the pregnancy outweighed any lingering outrage.

"I know! Like I said, I was an utter git. I blindly believed that if I did what Victoria asked that she would choose me. But it got complicated because while I was keeping tabs on Lilly, we became friends. She's an amazing woman. She's kind and generous and beautiful—"

"I'm aware of my angel's many attributes. That's why I'm in love with her."

"I understand why you adore her…she's any man's dream."

Jacob's blood boiled at Edward's implied connotation. "Are you and Lilly together?"

Edward shook his head. "Are you crazy? She's head over heels for you."

"I wouldn't be so sure. Tonight is the first time she's letting me near her in three weeks. I worry I've fucked up too many times, that it's too late."

Edward leveled his gaze at Jacob. "Trust me, it's not too late."

"She said something to you?"

"She's dealt with a tremendous amount of crap from everyone, and emotionally she's still very vulnerable. She was embarrassed for you to see her at the rehab."

Jacob released an aggravated growl. "Why?"

"She feels she can't compare to Victoria and thank God for that fact. But she mainly pushed you away out of a sense of obligation."

"That doesn't make any sense."

"Lilly felt that as long as you were with her, you wouldn't be able to devote your time to being a father. She believed if she was out of the picture you would reconcile with Victoria. She thought she was robbing you of your chance to have a family."

Jacob felt a knot tighten in his gut as he listened to Edward. "Having her push me away robbed me of my happiness."

"It stole hers too, Lilly is miserable without you. Over the last couple months, I grew tired of Victoria and her games, tired of watching her hurt

159

decent people. When I visited Lilly, I saw the sonogram photo that Victoria sent and when I noted the gestational age, it all clicked. All of Victoria's lies came flooding back and I knew I had to act. I had to fix this fucking mess that I helped create. So, I stole the sonogram picture, confirmed the dates with a doctor friend and went to Victoria's house to play moment of truth."

"That doesn't sound pretty."

"Hardly. But I had physical proof along with the countless times she asked me to spy on you and Lilly. I confronted her, watched her squirm with a great deal of satisfaction, and finally got her to confess. I figured this bullshit had gone on long enough."

Jacob ran a hand over his head, barking out a laugh. "I could punch you for the shit you pulled and hug you for putting an end to it."

"I deserve the left hook."

"Nah, I'll you slide. Now I get to focus on winning back my Lilly. What are you going to do about Victoria? Are you two still friends after last night?"

"She's mighty pissed off at me right now, but for some stupid reason, I still love her. How is it possible to love someone and hate them at the same time?"

"I don't know. All I feel for Lilly is love, it's all I've ever felt for her. But with Victoria, I can understand the confusion."

Edward chuckled and motioned to the documents. "Are you going to talk to Victoria?"

"I don't think talking is the correct term, but yes, there will be a conversation, just as soon as we wrap for the day."

It was amazing how different the world could look in twenty-four hours. Jacob was finally free of Victoria. He drove immediately to her luxury rental after filming wrapped, eager to end this atrocious situation once and for all. Their final confrontation started with denial, progressed to anger and ended with Victoria's tearful admission. She tried to justify her actions, claiming her desire for Jacob to be the father as the motive behind her falsehood but her pleas fell on deaf ears and dulled emotions.

Jacob strolled out of Victoria's penthouse around nine, turning on his mobile as he reached his car.

His heart jumped into his throat when he went to call Lilly. He had written her a text earlier in the day, explaining his delay that evening, but the text never sent. Now he was two hours later than promised. "Bugger, bugger, bugger."

He dialed Lilly's number, fearing she wouldn't pick up the phone. "Hi."

"Lilly, I'm so sorry. I wrote you a text, but it never sent—"

"Did filming run late?" Her voice was unusually flat, and it sent chills of foreboding up his spine.

He could lie, but there had been enough untruths during the course of their relationship. "No, we wrapped on time."

"Hmm. So…where were you?"

It was as if this woman knew the answer before he spoke the words aloud. "I have great news, Lilly. I was with Victoria—"

"That's your definition of great news?"

Shit. "No! You don't understand, Lilly. It's about her baby. You and I need to talk—"

"You're right, we do need to talk."

Jacob started his car, backing it out of the space. "I'm only fifteen minutes from you. I'm leaving now. I'll be there before you know it."

"I don't feel like talking tonight. Perhaps some other time."

His stomach flipped. Lilly's wall was back in place, with reinforcements. "Please, I'll be right there—"

"I said no, Jacob." Her words were clipped, falling like ice against the phone receiver.

Christ, if only she would remove her emotional armor long enough to let him explain. "I miss you, Lilly. I need to see you—"

"Apparently not as much as you miss Victoria. Goodnight."

"Lilly, the baby isn't mine." But the words never reached Lilly. The line clicked and Jacob stared at the phone, jumping when a car honked behind him. "Fuck!"

Screw it, Lilly might be angry now, but as soon as he spoke with her, everything would be right with the world again. He drove to Renaissance and walked to the front desk. "Good evening, ladies. I'm here to visit Lilly Staver."

"Mr. Edmonton," a voice called out behind him.

Jacob turned and saw Jacqui standing there, a stern expression on her face. "Good evening, Jacqui. I'm just on my way to visit Lilly."

"May I have a moment of your time, please?"

"I really need to speak with Lilly—"

"And I need to speak with you *about* Lilly."

Jacob's heart sank. What was wrong? "Is she okay?"

"Come to my office." She escorted him to a small but tastefully decorated space, closing the door behind her.

Jacob paced the floor, his eyes widening with apprehension. "What's wrong with Lilly?"

"At this point, you are, Mr. Edmonton."

He willed down his anger. Who did this woman think she was? "Excuse me?"

"I know you've gone above and beyond to provide this care for her, and it is my obligation to ensure her recovery is as painless as possible."

"I'm not following you, Jacqui."

"I saw Lilly earlier this evening. She had been waiting for you for a couple hours…but you never showed."

"I got caught up in a situation."

Jacqui held up her hand. "I don't need the details. It's not my business, but Lilly is my business. She was terribly upset, even more so because she canceled her evening therapy to spend time with you. Rehabilitation is not strictly healing the body, Mr. Edmonton. It's also healing the psyche, and Lilly's emotional state is very fragile."

Jacob hung his head, releasing a huff of frustration. "I never meant to hurt her. I came here to explain everything to her, so if you'll excuse me, I'll go do that now."

"I can't allow you to do that, sir. She specifically requested no visitors after the incident tonight."

His jaw slackened. "But I *need* to see her."

"And I need to respect her wishes. I ask you to do the same."

"Jacqui, give me five minutes."

But the director was not to be swayed. "I abide by the patient's wishes, sir. Not yours. You can come by tomorrow and speak with her. Right now, she's trying to rest, and we both know she needs it."

He could tell by the set of the blonde's mouth that he wasn't arguing his way out of this scenario. He could throw around his status, but it would likely earn him an escort back to the parking lot. "This is bullshit," he grumbled, hitting the arms of the chair and storming out of the office.

Back in his car, Jacob dialed his sister and begged her to meet him at the pub. Janie would have the answers—she had to.

Thirty minutes later, Janie and Jacob sat side by side at the local pub, glasses of whiskey in front of them.

"Good riddance to bad rubbish," Janie proclaimed, watching her brother peruse the contact list in his phone. "Dear brother, you dragged me out of my pajamas to drink with you, but your nose has been stuck in that phone the entire time."

"Sorry, Little Bit, this is important."

"Who are you calling?"

"My publicist, I want a statement issued immediately."

Janie did a double take. "Wow, unusual turn for you. You normally remain quiet during media storms."

"It's time I stopped taking a backseat in my own life." He sipped his whiskey and dialed the number, relaying the story to the recipient on the end of the line. A few minutes later, he hung up with a triumphant smile. "Done, being issued as we speak. The truth of that horrible woman's actions will finally be revealed."

"It's about time she got her comeuppance." Janie raised her glass. "You have two reasons to celebrate. Congratulations on your nomination. Cheers, to your freedom and your future."

"My future...I feel like I have one again."

They clinked glasses. "Now it's up to you what to do with it."

Jacob knew exactly what he wanted to do with his future, every blasted second of it. But with his usual finesse, he had buggered the situation. Staring at his glass, he opted for a safe subject. "It's surreal being nominated but I doubt I'll win. The committees often have a favorite in mind."

"It doesn't matter if you win or lose; you were nominated. Out of all the actors, they chose five, and you're one of them; what an honor." Janie toyed with her drink. "So, when are you going to broach the topic?"

"What topic?"

"How to fix your latest fuck-up with Lilly."

Jacob laid his head on his arm and groaned. "She told you?"

"Not exactly. I was with Lilly earlier. She asked me to take her out shopping...for something special to wear tonight." Janie sipped her drink, her eyes lingering on Jacob. "Imagine my surprise when my brother calls me to meet him for a spur of the moment cocktail. I know you would never pass up time with Lilly, so it wasn't much of a leap to surmise you'd stepped in it again."

"I'm such an asshole."

"Jacob, what happened? Lilly's ego is far too fragile to handle any additional erratic behavior."

"I wrote her a text telling her I'd be late tonight for our date...but it never sent, and now she thinks I blew her off in favor of seeing Victoria."

"Why didn't you go over there after you spoke with Victoria? You should have gone there straightaway and explained the situation in person."

"I did, but she had specifically requested no visitors and the rehab police weren't making any exceptions. God, I'm a bloody idiot."

"It was a misunderstanding. She's upset tonight but you can make it up to her—"

"How? All she said is that we need to talk. You know how positively those conversations tend to go."

Janie choked back a chuckle. His sister apparently considered the situation a damn riot. He did *not* share her sentiment. "Do I have to do everything for you? Arrange a special evening for Lilly, then get on your damn knees and beg her to forgive you one last time. Then marry her before you have the chance to muck it up again." Janie wrapped her arms around her brother. "You love each other too much *not* to be together."

"I've never done anything right where Lilly is concerned. Even when I have the best intentions, she winds up feeling second-best."

"Then I suggest you try a different tact. Make certain she knows where your loyalties lie. She'll push back, you just need to push harder."

"She always seemed so strong, able to handle anything."

"Even the strong need a day off now and again, Jacob. Lilly is far more delicate than she seems, particularly where you're concerned." Janie finished off the last of her whiskey, sliding off the bar stool. "It's time for you to go sweep your lady off her feet, once and for all."

Jacob spent the majority of the night tossing and turning. He even got up half a dozen times, keys in hand, determined to drive to Lilly and fix this latest predicament. He knew he would have no problem sleeping curled against Lilly, his hands free to travel the planes of her body.

His common sense—and Jacqui's warning—stopped him. It was the middle of the night, his angel was sleeping, and she needed the rest.

But tomorrow was a different story. He had a day of filming in front of him, but he would go to Lilly immediately after wrapping. He wasn't certain how Lilly would react to his appearance, all things considered, but he was letting her push him out of her life any longer.

Lilly

"Why couldn't you let me walk here today?" Lilly grumbled, sending Megan a scowl as she wheeled her into one of the therapy rooms.

"Because, you already walked far more today than recommended."

"I thought the goal was *to* walk. I'm trying to get stronger."

"It takes time, Lilly. You're not supposed to be full-weight bearing on your right leg for another week."

"It's just sore now. I miss walking. I hate this stupid chair." Lilly glared down at the wheelchair in which she now sat.

"You'll be out of it in no time. Lord, you're in a mood today."

"Sorry, I'm just tired." Lilly lied, blinking away tears. She was tired, but it wasn't due to pain or exertion, rather hours of crying when Jacob stood her up the night before.

She felt so utterly foolish, buying lingerie and believing his promises, only to find out he'd been with Victoria. *Some fools never learn, and I am the queen of idiots.*

"How about some eighties tunes to liven things up?" Megan asked, turning on the radio.

"If you play 'Eye of the Tiger' one more time, I'm chucking my wheelchair at you."

Her therapist smiled, her dark ponytail bouncing as she nodded toward the therapy parallel bars. "Ready for some balance work?"

Lilly considered the dull ache in her leg and then looked at her despised wheelchair and nodded. Megan started to help her step onto the bars, but Lilly held up her hand, locking the chair. "I got this, let me do it."

Lilly had made terrific progress in the last few weeks, the wheelchair was only a crutch now. Taking a deep breath, she ran her hands through her dark hair while eyeing the bars with equal parts trepidation and loathing.

Some days Lilly wondered why she kept pushing herself. She'd always been a fighter, but her heart and body were so tired she wanted to take to her bed and stay there. *But today is not that day, Lilly. Get your ass moving.*

Pulling herself up with her arms, she stepped onto the bars.

"That a girl," Megan remarked, her gaze focused over Lilly's shoulder.

Lilly huffed. "I did exercise earlier. Perhaps I can get a pass?"

"Not a chance."

"You're all heart, Megan." She jumped as hands slid around her waist and lips nuzzled her ear.

An all too familiar voice whispered, "Hi, angel."

Lilly gripped the parallel bars, her heart racing as she breathed in Jacob's scent. "What are you doing here?"

Jacob chuckled, pressing his body flush against her back. His lips and tongue danced along her neck, leaving goosebumps in their wake. He could melt her with a single kiss.

"I fucking love you, that's what I'm doing here," Jacob whispered against her skin, sending chills up her body.

"Right, that's why you stood me up last night." If he would just stop touching her, she could focus on disliking him. No such luck. The man's hands were all over her. Had he suddenly morphed into a damn octopus?

"Lilly, I didn't stand you up. I came by last night, but your guard dog wouldn't let me through."

"You did?"

"I have something very important to tell you, something that's going to make your night."

Her heart leapt at his statement. What the hell did that mean? It was likely just another tactic to turn her attention away from the fact that when he promised—again—to be there, he wasn't.

"Let go of me, Jacob. I have to finish my therapy."

He nuzzled her ear, taking her lobe between his teeth. "Go ahead and act like you're not enjoying this, but your body is practically vibrating against me. You want me as badly as I want you."

Cocky bastard. Screw him for his arrogance, and for being right. "I want to finish my therapy." Hell, she couldn't even convince herself with that statement, and his chuckle confirmed it.

"Whatever you say, angel. So, if you want to get away from me so much, you're going to have to walk." More kisses, more chills, his hands firm on her hips. "But I'll be right behind you, following you wherever you go. You're not getting rid of me this time." His whisper echoed a fierce promise as he dropped one last kiss on the nape of her neck. "Now move."

Her body wanted to scream in protest when he released his grip, but she focused her attention on the parallel bars and the task at hand.

"Okay, let's get this torture over with." She felt his smile burning into her back as she walked the entire length. She certainly lacked the grace of a ballerina—or a water buffalo for that matter—but she made it.

However, in true klutzy fashion, Lilly overshot the final step. She had pushed herself too far that afternoon and her leg was done performing. She started to sink, but good to his word, Jacob was right behind her, scooping her into his arms before she hit the ground. "I've got you."

"Thanks," Lilly mumbled, a wave of embarrassment flooding her body as he settled her in the wheelchair. She focused her attention on the ground, but his hand lifted her chin, forcing her to meet his gaze. Christ, no one should be allowed to be that attractive, there had to be a law about it somewhere.

His blue eyes crinkled as his lips grazed hers. "I missed you, angel."

Lilly opened her mouth, all set to respond with a cranky retort, but Megan decided now was a great time to interject her opinion.

"Lucky woman, having such a dedicated man in her life."

Jacob turned his smile to her therapist. "I remember you—Megan, right?"

Megan blushed under his gaze, no one was immune to the good old Edmonton charm. "Right. I'd recognize you anywhere, even if you do have a few more clothes on this time."

"Oh god," Lilly muttered, mortified at Megan's brazen statement.

Jacob, however, was only too keen to maintain their banter. "Something I plan to remedy soon with this beautiful woman. I'm hopelessly addicted to her." His fingers traced Lilly's jaw, tangling in her hair when she attempted to jerk her face away. "How's she been doing?"

"Fantastic, except for the fact that Lilly doesn't listen and is stubborn as hell. She's been walking regularly with the walker, even though she's not technically supposed to—"

"You said I could walk in the courtyard."

"Not a dozen times around the courtyard!"

"It was ten times." Now Lilly was pouting. Wonderful, she was behaving like a petulant child.

Jacob knelt by her chair, an amused smile on his lips. "She's always been stubborn. It's a yankee trait."

"She's lucky we love her." Megan smirked, patting Lilly on the shoulder. "We're all done here, will you take her back to her room?"

"With pleasure. I have plans for this lovely lady." Jacob dropped one more kiss on Lilly's cheek before grabbing the handles of the wheelchair.

"Do I get a say in any of this?" Lilly inquired with a huff.

"No," Megan and Jacob replied in unison as he wheeled her out of the therapy room.

Jacob fell silent once in the corridor, but Lilly was tired and needed

167

answers. "What are you doing here?"

"I thought I'd stroll around Renaissance for a while, take in the sights. What do you think I'm doing here?"

"What do you want?" She tried to sound gruff and uninterested, but every cell in her body was firing simultaneously from Jacob's nearness.

Jacob wheeled her into her room, turning to her with a determined look. "I don't want to hear a word from you—"

Lilly opened her mouth to speak, but Jacob shushed her immediately.

"Are you kidding? You can't even be quiet for a sentence!"

Lilly shut her mouth and smirked. She was always quick to speak up, often without listening. "Fine."

Several seconds went by but Jacob said nothing, staring at her with an amused grin. Lilly opened her mouth to speak but Jacob silenced her with a quick, "Wait here." With that, Jacob turned on his heel, leaving the suite.

Lilly sat, twiddling her thumbs. When it hit seven minutes, she gave up and rolled over to her bed. A nap would be a welcome respite after last night. She had just transferred to the bed when she heard his voice in the doorway.

"Do Yanks never listen when they're told to do something?" His words were harsh, but his face belied his amusement.

Lilly chuckled despite herself. "Yanks aren't known for falling in line."

"I'm busting you out of here, for the night at least."

"Where are we going?"

"We're going home."

"Home? To the cottage?"

Jacob opened the dresser drawers, tossing yoga pants and a t-shirt onto the bed. "Where are you hiding that fancy lingerie?"

The bastard ignored her question, so she would ignore his. She responded with her best scowl.

"You'll want to get dressed, since you aren't going to tell me where the lingerie is." He crossed his arms, completely unfazed by her glare, his gaze darkening with desire as his eyes devoured her body. "No matter, I didn't plan on keeping you in it long anyway."

Lilly chuckled nervously, sending him a pointed stare. "Can you turn around and give me some privacy?" Her body felt as hot as lava, his gaze penetrated to her very core.

Jacob smiled and shook his head. "Absolutely not."

"You're just going to stand there and watch?" When Jacob nodded, Lilly scoffed in disbelief. "What if I refuse?"

Jacob's mouth twisted in amusement. "Then I'll come over there and do it for you."

Lilly knew the outcome of her next statement, but she couldn't hold back the words as they slipped from her lips. "You wouldn't dare."

But Jacob would dare. He lay on top of her in the next moment, his body holding her hostage as he held her wrists on either side of her face.

"What do you think you're doing?" Lilly asked, her eyes wide as she tried to appear disinterested.

Jacob bit her bottom lip, sucking it gently before slipping his tongue into her mouth. After several moments, he pulled away, offering her a smile that radiated pure sex. "What does it look like? I'm having my way with you." He nipped her neck, earning a low moan of approval. "Don't even try to tell me it doesn't feel good. I feel your heat through your clothes."

Lilly tried to free her hands, but Jacob held them firm. "I'm mad at you."

Another grin, before his lips made contact with her neck again. "No, you're not."

"I am—"

"And you know why you're not?" Jacob spoke right over her, his sapphire blue eyes holding her gaze. "Because you know that I love you more than life itself, and that I didn't stand you up last night. I worship you, Lilly, so if you want me on my knees..." He left the innuendo hanging there, another smile splitting his face.

Arrogant SOB. He was right though, she would sooner die than stop his sensual assault, and her soft purr spurred Jacob on. His hands released her wrists, moving to cup her breasts and Lilly pushed up into his hands, demanding his touch. God, she missed him. He lowered his mouth to one nipple, suckling her through her shirt as his hands grasped her hips, arching her off the bed to press against his erection.

Lilly pressed his head against her body, bucking her hips when he bit her inner thigh. He pulled her shorts to the side as his tongue teased her open, and Lilly cried out, writhing against his mouth, claiming every caress for her own.

Lilly's mind blanked as Jacob's hands and mouth waged a carnal war inside her and let out a hushed whimper as his lips found hers again.

When he pulled away, a fire smoldered in his eyes as the corners of his mouth lifted in that sexy smirk. "Now," Jacob began, dropping kisses along her ear and neck, "you can either get dressed, and we go home, or I finish ravishing you right here, unlocked door and all. Perhaps Megan will drop in unannounced again."

This was a different side of Jacob. He wasn't asking her, he was telling her. And Lilly really liked it. "I'll get dressed."

"Damn, I hoped you'd keep protesting. Guess I'll have to wait until tonight." His tongue played with her fingertips as he pulled her to a sitting position.

"What makes you think we're having sex tonight?"

Jacob's gaze made her insides quiver. "What makes you think we're not?"

Within thirty minutes, Jacob had them settled into the car and headed towards his home.

The man never did do things halfway, even the weather seemed to jump to his beck and call. In fact, Mother Nature was showing off that night—countless stars illuminated the sky as a warm breeze captured the scent of the night blooming jasmine planted in the gardens surrounding the courtyard of Jacob's home.

Jacob insisted on bringing the damn wheelchair, despite Lilly's protests, but she forgot about that earlier disagreement when he wheeled her into the patio area. It was as beautiful as the evening itself—flames crackled in the outdoor fireplace next to loungers draped with blankets and cushions. But the pies de resistance was the food: trays of fresh fruit, meats and cheeses sat waiting next to a bottle of Glenfiddich and two glasses.

"Oh my God, it's amazing. I haven't had real food or a drink in forever." Lilly clapped her hands, reaching for a grape. She yelped in surprise when Jacob swatted her hand away. "Hey!"

"Not so fast angel, there's a charge for food."

Lilly snorted, her gaze swinging from the fruit plate to Jacob. "You're going to charge me for the food?"

The corners of his irresistible mouth curled into a smirk. "I've got questions, and for every answer in the affirmative, you get a piece of whatever food you desire."

Lilly laughed, only stopped when she realized he was serious. "And what if the answer is no?"

"Then," Jacob murmured, kissing the back of her neck, "you lose one article of clothing."

"This is a joke, right?"

"Absolutely not—my house, my food, my rules." He poured them each a finger of scotch and his smoldering blue eyes regarded her over the glass, awaiting her next move. "Your choice, of course."

"You're going to hold out food on a person who's been in a hospital for over a month? That's a whole new level of cruelty!" Lilly feigned anguish, but she was enjoying his assertive stance and open sensuality towards her. It almost made her forget about her injuries…almost.

"No, it isn't, and the food at Renaissance is five-star."

"But they don't have scotch."

"True. If you would like some scotch, all you have to do is answer my questions—honestly, I might add."

Lilly smiled and bit her lip, running her hand through her hair, aware of Jacob's eyes burning holes into her body. "I have many shortcomings, but deception isn't one of them. I'll participate—on one condition—you have to play as well."

His grin widened as he took another sip of scotch, and Lilly realized how terribly unfair it was to the rest of the human race for anyone to be that attractive. "By all means. I can't let you have all the fun."

Lilly locked the wheelchair and transferred to the chaise, noting Jacob's gaze of admiration. "I told you I don't need the chair anymore."

"It won't kill you to take it easy for a few more days."

"It might." Now it was Lilly's turn to smirk as she pulled the blanket over her legs. "Go ahead, let's get this party started."

Jacob regarded her for a moment before breaking into a full smile. "I'll start off easy. Are you in pain?"

"A little, but this game of yours is keeping my mind otherwise occupied. However, since it's a yes or no answer, and I'm starving, we'll go with yes. Can I have a piece of food now?"

Jacob laughed, picking up a strawberry. "Come and get it."

Lilly leaned forward, closing her lips around the strawberry, her tongue flitting along his fingertips. If he wanted to play, she was game, and she smiled when his breath hitched.

They batted questions back and forth, the first few rounds peppered with painless inquiries as they feasted on the food and let the warmth of the scotch spread through their bodies.

Lilly closed her eyes as she bit a grape, the sweet nectar exploding in her mouth and she released a contented moan.

The cushion sank next to her and she opened her eyes to find Jacob only inches away, his azure eyes burning with an inner fire. "Have you slept with anyone else?"

Lilly startled at both the question and the effect his proximity was having on her body. She felt her insides clench as she refrained from reaching out to touch him. "Wow, right to the point, do not pass go. No, as sad as this fact may be, I haven't been with anyone else, there's only been you. I never wanted anyone else touching me."

"Good, because this delectable body belongs to me." Jacob's tone was light, but she saw the relief flash in his eyes at her answer. Had he honestly thought there was someone else? "Aren't you forgetting something?"

"What?"

"A piece of clothing."

"If I had known about this game, I would have worn layers. But wait, you picked out my outfit. Another unfair advantage."

"That's the breaks."

Lilly slipped off one flip-flop, tucking her foot back under the blanket, but Jacob shook his head. "First—both shoes and you can't hide under the blanket." He held up his hand when she opened her mouth. "And before you protest, no one can see you—no one but me, anyway."

She slid off the other shoe, pulling the blanket off her legs. "What if I don't want to know the answer to some of these questions? What if you don't want to know?" Lilly's stomach churned, wondering what secrets Jacob held close to the vest.

Jacob shrugged, his gaze unflinching. "It's time we knew all the answers."

Lilly sighed, he was right. The truth needed to be spoken, even if her heart got run over in the process. "I don't know…"

"Ask me anything, Lilly."

Here goes nothing. "Did you sleep with Victoria after you proposed to me?"

Jacob locked eyes with her and shook his head, slipping off his shirt. "Are you kidding? I'm so in love with you, I can't even look at another woman."

His words washed over her, drowning some leftover doubts like the sea drowns the reeds. Lilly wished it wasn't so hard to believe him, believe in his love. "It's your turn."

His fingers tapped against his legs—this did not bode well. "Did anything happen between you and Enrique? Besides that kiss?" He spit out the question, as if the very idea burned his mouth.

"He kissed me twice, but it never went further, and since I'm out of shoes—" Lilly paused, swallowing her feelings of self-consciousness. She pulled off her shirt, her breasts heaving. Jacob's eyes rested on the faint scar on her side and Lilly moved her hand to cover the area.

"Don't do that. You're beautiful, absolutely breathtaking. I want to see every inch of you."

There went those damn butterflies again. "I always gave you shit about the starlets in Greece, and there was that one woman who wanted you to skinny-dip—"

Jacob released a groan. "You mean Jackie?"

"I don't know her name, nor do I want to know. I didn't want to believe you were fooling around with them but…people surmised that might be the case. Did anything happen with Jackie or any of your many admirers?"

Jacob slipped off his pants, his sinewy frame relaxing against the lounger. "I already told you the answer to that question. You're lucky I'm a good sport."

Lilly's eyes wandered his frame, she couldn't help it, you just don't ignore sculpted perfection. "Damn you for having a perfect body. It's your turn, make it a good one."

He grabbed her hand, his fingertips tickling her palm and sending chills up her spine. "Have you changed your mind about wanting to have a baby?"

Lilly's breath caught. "Oh, wow, I can't believe you asked me that question."

She saw a brief flash of pain cross his face, but he covered it with a practiced smile. "Swinging for the fences."

She bit her lip as she unfastened her bra, her nipples taut with anticipation.

His fingers traced along the length of her arm, his eyes feasting on her full breasts. "Now who has the perfect body?"

"What do you plan to do with me tonight?" She had a laundry list of ideas and just the thought of them made her wet.

"That's not a yes or no question, Lilly." Jacob's gaze was always direct, but tonight it was piercing. He wouldn't let her hide from him anymore.

Lilly was done beating around the bush. As much as the next answer terrified her, not knowing was a worse torture. "Are you still in love with Victoria?"

Jacob shook his head, shedding his underwear and laying back in all his muscled glory. "I was never in love with Victoria, I know that now."

"God, you're gorgeous." Lilly breathed, unaware her words were audible.

Jacob propped himself on his elbow. "I'm changing the rules—"

"What? You can't—"

His seductive smirk would be the death of her. "My house, my rules."

Lilly crossed her arms over her breasts. If he wanted to play dirty, she would take away the view. "Fine. What are your *new* rules?"

"Next time you answer a question with a yes, you're naked and I get to do whatever I want, no protest—"

"Totally unfair."

"How? I'm already naked."

"So technically didn't I win?"

"You don't even know the rules." The firelight danced in his eyes, he was enjoying this far too much. To be honest, so was she.

"Well, you keep changing them, so I don't think even *you* know the rules."

Jacob chuckled. "Fair enough." His eyes locked with hers. "I don't give a shit about anyone else. I need to know about you. Do you love me, Lilly?"

She expected questions about sexual history and conquests, but Jacob had more important topics in mind. She blinked back tears and nodded, sliding off the last of her clothing as he pulled her against him.

"What—"

Jacob shushed her, his finger to her lips. "Are you in love with me?"

Lilly gasped, this was raw and personal as his hand held her jaw and forced her to look at him. But he wasn't done.

Kissing her, he murmured, "Do you want to be my wife and have a child with me?" He kissed her neck, his hands moving over her body. "I need to know your answers, Lilly."

Lilly moaned at Jacob's caress, so much for playing it coy. "The answer to all your questions is yes. Definitely yes." She had exposed all her secrets, all her truths were on the table. How would he react?

CHAPTER TWELVE

Jacob

acob released a breath he didn't know he'd been holding. Lilly wanted a future with him, and now there were no more roadblocks.

His lips claimed hers again as he sighed into her mouth, his hands running along her spine.

He still hadn't told her about his meeting with Victoria, but as his hand ran over Lilly's naked curves. He knew the news would keep for just a little while longer. Right now, he needed to touch her and remind her that she belonged to him, body and soul. The same way he belonged to her.

God, she was gorgeous, her fragile exterior covering the heart of a warrior. Lilly hated her battle scars, but Jacob saw them as the mark of a survivor. They were already faded and would soon be invisible to all but the most trained eye.

His lips brushed along her ribs, eliciting a soft squeal. "Ticklish?" Jacob smiled, nibbling her side.

"You know I am, now behave."

No way in hell was Jacob going to behave, his body was screaming for release, he was desperate for this woman. He pressed her breasts together, teasing each nipple as his tongue dipped into her cleavage, his leg nudging her open as he settled between her thighs.

"I thought I told you to behave," Lilly murmured. She wasn't stopping him, but she wasn't entirely comfortable either, her mind likely focused on her scars instead of his sensual invasion. Time to up the ante, get her mind back to pure pleasure.

"And I told you that you're mine and I get to touch you wherever I want." He took her wrists, placing her hands on either side of his head. "Keep them there." Jacob traced the lines of her abdomen, trailing his mouth lower to nip the inside of her thigh and tasting her hint of sweetness on his tongue.

"Jacob—" She wanted it, her body was on fire for him, but her mind kept her tensed.

"If you don't relax, I'll take twice as long."

Her chuckle sent a wave of relaxation through her body. She was back with him. "Promise?"

Lilly's fingers tightened against his scalp as her thighs fell open, allowing his mouth full access to her body. He ravished her, his mouth consuming every delicious inch of her, his tongue laving against her clit until her hips bucked against him, her body shattering underneath him.

Jacob kept his head on her leg, dropping soft kisses on her thigh. He was giving her a few minutes reprieve, but he wasn't done pleasuring her—not by a long shot. "I guess I win."

"How do you figure that? I am definitely the victor in this scenario. Now bring that gorgeous mouth up here." Lilly demanded, pulling slightly on his scalp.

"No way in hell, I'm not done with you." Jacob didn't give her a chance to object as his mouth latched onto her again, his hands sliding under her ass and holding her to him.

Lilly's second orgasm hit her with more force than the first, her body writhing underneath him, her cries bouncing off the courtyard walls. Christ, Hannah might come running from the cottage, thinking he was killing her, but he loved every second of watching her come undone.

He couldn't wait a moment longer—he slid inside her, burying himself to the hilt. Her back arched against him as she released a deep purr. She was tight around him, so warm and wet. "You feel unbelievable. I'm not going to last, Lilly," Jacob whispered, sucking her earlobe.

The look on her face was one he hadn't seen in months—the sensual vixen who knew exactly how her body affected him. She tightened around him, milking his shaft until he saw stars. "Show me how much you want me."

"Isn't it obvious?" Jacob choked out, his brain going on lockdown as his hormones raged.

Her lips brushed against his as she squeezed him again. "Show me."

He had been so delicate the last time they made love, afraid to hurt her, now she demanded more, and Jacob was never one to disappoint a lady. Especially not his lady. He grabbed her hips and took control, thrusting into her until he felt her shatter all over him, his own orgasm exploding a moment later.

Jacob collapsed on top of Lilly, their breath mingling in the night air. "Fuck, you're amazing. I love you."

Lilly nuzzled his mouth, her brown eyes warm and soft. "Can I tell you something?"

He smiled against her mouth, his tongue sliding along her lips. "Certainly."

Lilly took a deep breath, and holding his face inches from hers, she stated, "I lied to you."

Jacob rose up on his elbows, unsure what she had lied about and even more uncertain he wanted to know.

"I lied that day at the hospital when I said I wasn't in love with you anymore. I didn't want to obligate you, I didn't want to need you..." Lilly captured his lips, her caress echoing her emotion.

"Then tell me the truth now, tell me what you want from me." His heart hammered in his chest. Would she finally take down the wall and utter the words he needed to hear? Lilly might have said she wanted to marry him and share a life together, but that was in answer to his question. Now he needed her unbidden response. He nuzzled her jaw with his nose, willing her fears away. "Tell me, Lilly."

Her nails trailed lightly along his arms and even her benign gesture made him immediately hard. "I have an insatiable appetite...for you. Only for you. I want you to spend the rest of the night making love to me."

It wasn't the romantic declaration he hoped for, but it was a start. "Lucky for you, I have the same weakness. But I can't keep waiting weeks in between making love to you. I need this every day."

"Can we start with tonight?"

Jacob chuckled, nuzzling her neck. "Your wish is my command."

They lay together a couple hours later, the blanket and fire warming them against the night chill.

"You know, it's odd."

Lilly lifted her head from his chest. "Sex is odd?"

Jacob chuckled. "No, and definitely not with you. With you, sex is fucking amazing. But I just realized that today is the fourth and your monthly friend is normally paying a visit."

Lilly's eyes widened. "Is it the fourth? I guess the stress of the accident knocked my cycle off kilter. I didn't realize you paid that much attention."

"Where you're concerned, I always pay attention."

"I'm sure it's just stress. Besides, be happy that we could take advantage of my irregular cycle this month."

"I'm certainly not complaining, just pointing out a fact. I'm surprised *you* didn't notice...you notice everything."

Lilly licked her lips, focusing her gaze over Jacob's shoulder. "I'll probably get it tomorrow."

The gears in Jacob's head were spinning, she was being evasive. "You should have had it four days ago." He stroked her jaw, a small smile on his lips. "Nothing you need to tell me?"

"No, now can we not destroy the afterglow with any more talk of menstruation?" Lilly laid her head back on his chest, but he caught her expression. The woman had the world's worst poker face.

"Speaking of babies—" Jacob's smile widened.

"Were we speaking of babies?"

"We might be, in fact, we likely are because you are never late." His fingers traced the smooth skin on the back of her neck, the idea of Lilly being pregnant the best news he could imagine.

"I told you, it's likely stress." What a crock, and Jacob knew it. Her voice and expression both told the same story and her words wouldn't convince either of them.

"You're a terrible liar, Lilly."

She smiled when she gazed up at him, a flush creeping over her cheeks. "I'm not lying—stop giving me that look." She pressed a kiss to his chest. "What did you want to tell me about the baby?"

He couldn't stop the grin that split his face. "Guess who isn't the father of Victoria's baby?"

Lilly's jaw dropped. "Are you serious? Holy shit! When did you find out?"

"Your friend Edward—my new best friend—got the information out of Victoria two nights ago. He presented me with all the documentation and that's why I was late last night."

"You were confronting Victoria." Lilly chewed her bottom lip. "I thought you two—"

Jacob stroked Lilly's cheek before pressing his mouth to hers. "I know what you thought, but Lilly, it's always been you. I had to get closure on that nightmare chapter of my life."

Lilly threw her arms around him, squeezing his neck. "Are you okay with the news?"

"I'm bloody fantastic! I never thought I was the father, my gut was right all along."

"I think you would have been an amazing father."

"I think I will be. Hopefully soon, my angel." Jacob caught Lilly's lips again, loving the pink stain that crept across her cheeks. "That's not the only news I discovered yesterday."

Lilly propped her chin up with her hand, her fawn eyes soft and questioning. "There's more?"

"Albert sends his regards."

Lilly let out a small groan and buried her head in his chest. "He promised!"

Jacob chuckled. Leave it to Lilly to hate the attention. "Why didn't you tell me? It was you all along—"

"All I did was talk to him about how talented you are…because you *are* the most talented actor I've ever known. You deserved that role and I was afraid that Victoria would ruin your chance just to be spiteful."

Christ, he loved this woman. "I don't deserve you, Lilly."

"This isn't about me. It's about that part—*your* role—and you deserve it a thousand-fold."

"Everything in my world is about you." Jacob idly stroked her back as he considered how to broach the next topic. "The awards show is in a few weeks."

Lilly pushed herself to a sitting position, beaming at him. "I know, and I'm so excited for you. Wait there, I have something to give you." She scooted off the sofa, transferring easily into the chair and grabbing her purse.

"You're a regular Evil Knievel with that thing," Jacob stated, marveling at her increased strength and stamina.

"I wasn't lying when I said I really don't need it anymore. Want to see?" She locked the chair and stood up, walking—albeit unsteadily—back to the sofa.

Jacob's eyes widened, and he pulled her on top of him, peppering her face with kisses. He knew Lilly could walk with the support of a walker or therapy bars, but to see her moving without any assistive devices brought tears to his eyes. "That's wonderful! I knew you would do it."

Lilly smiled at him as she sat back up. "Can't keep a stubborn Yank down, not for long anyway." She handed him a box.

Jacob looked at the box and then at Lilly. "What's this?"

"Open it and see."

Jacob's eyes widened at the antique Patek Phillippe pocket watch inside. "This is exquisite. Lilly, you shouldn't have—"

Lilly grasped his hands, her eyes bright. "I didn't. This is from Roger."

"What?" His heart leapt into his throat at her statement.

"He and I ran into each other on the Tube, remember? He asked me to help pick out your birthday gift. He wanted to get you the most fabulous pocket watch so you would"—Lilly broke off, wiping away tears—"always be mindful of how precious time really is."

Jacob admired the watch, noting the engraving on the back. "Time is the longest distance between two places…Tennessee Williams, this sounds like you."

Lilly nodded. "That was my contribution. I know your birthday isn't until a few days after the awards show, but Roger would want you to have it now."

"I miss him so much." He traced the face of the pocket watch, feeling his friend there beside him, sharing in the moment.

"He'll live forever in your heart. Just remember to keep his memory alive."

Jacob snaked his hand into Lilly's hair, capturing her lips and pulling her down on top of him again. "Will you come with me to the awards show?"

Lilly pulled back, her face registering shock. "Me?"

Jacob laughed at Lilly's confusion. "Yes, you. I want you there with me. I *need* you there."

"Why would you want me there?"

Jacob's brow furrowed, that was an odd question. "Because you're the love of my life and I plan on marrying you immediately. You make me happier than I've ever been, Lilly. I want my wife at my side—not just that night, but every night."

"I can't attend but I'll be rooting for you. I'll watch every second of the show just to catch a glimpse of you. I know you're going to win, Jacob."

"I don't want you watching the show on the telly. I want to experience this together." Jacob ran a hand along the back of his head, trying to figure out his strongest argument. "Why can't you attend? Is it because of the wheelchair? At the rate you're going, you'll be running at that point!"

Lilly sat up with a deliberate sigh. "That's part of it, but I won't be here."

"At the rehab? I know, you're getting discharged next week."

"No, I'm going home," Lilly murmured, not meeting his eyes.

Jacob felt his heart drop but willed himself to remain calm. Perhaps he was being paranoid. Why was she being so vague? "I thought Ben had family staying at the cottage. I figured we would move into our country house, start finally living our life together. I've called the decorators to freshen up the paint and gardens before our arrival."

Lilly swung her head to meet his gaze, her eyes filled with tears, her lower lip trembling.

"Angel, what is it?"

"Tonight was goodbye, Jacob. I'm going home to America. I leave next week."

Lilly

illy watched the myriad of emotions flow through Jacob as his mind registered her statement. Disbelief, followed by shock, anger, and despair all slammed into his body. "You're what?" His words were no more than a guttural whisper, burning the air.

"I was going to tell you—"

Jacob stood up, jerking on his pants. "When? The day you left, drop me a note as you flew out? That's fucking great, Lilly."

"I have to return to the States. I'm not working anymore, so I have to go back before my visa expires."

Jacob paused and Lilly could see the gears turning in his mind. "So, we fly to New York, see some friends and stay for a show, then we return to England. You'll be good for another six months."

"That paperwork can't be completed in a few days."

Jacob smiled. "Then we stay a bit longer."

"You're in the middle of filming. You can't just up and leave for America for a couple weeks."

"I'll arrange something with Albert. Better yet, let me speak with my barrister and see if we can't get an extension on your visa—"

Lilly grabbed his hand, pulling him back down to the chaise. "Don't worry about it. I've got it covered."

"No way. I'm not letting you out of my sight again. If we have to go to the States, we go together. We bribe whatever politician we need to get your paperwork and we come home. By the time that six months is up, we'll be long married, and you'll hopefully be several months pregnant…you'll be forever legal."

God, he had a plan for everything, but it was too late.

Too much had happened and even though she now knew his reason for blowing her off the night before, the event nonetheless solidified her decision about leaving England. "Jacob, we can't get married."

His blue eyes widened as he knelt in front of her, taking her hands. "Why in the world not? There's nothing in our way anymore, no one can interfere—"

Lilly fought back her tears, trying to maintain some level of control. "There shouldn't have been anything in our way from the beginning, but there is a mountain of heartache behind us. Nothing but heartache interspersed with a few moments of utter joy."

"I know it hasn't been easy, but we're free to be together, Lilly. Don't you want to marry me? You told me earlier that you did. Was that a lie?"

The tears won their battle, spilling down her cheeks. "Every word I told you was the truth. I love you more than I'll ever love anyone, more than I believed it possible to love another human being. And I want to be your wife more than anything—"

Jacob kissed her fingertips, trying to coax a smile. "Then there's no problem, my angel. We both want the same thing."

Lilly stared into his deep blue depths and almost caved, but her mind won this time. There was too much pain, too much destruction. She couldn't trust that this scenario wouldn't play out with another woman in the future. "Jacob, I know you say you love me, but I don't believe you. Not anymore."

Jacob's jaw slackened as if she'd slapped him. "How can you doubt my love for you? After everything I've gone through to prove how much I adore you, how can you doubt me?"

For the first time, Lilly's anger bubbled to the surface. She was tired of taking it on the chin. "How can I doubt it? Are you serious? In our time together, I've been pushed to the curb more times than I care to count, for a myriad of reasons—a film role, your ex, your reputation, my safety—but not once did you consider how your decisions made me feel! I wasn't allowed to be involved in the course of our relationship—*our* relationship—you and Victoria held the reins and I was just a bit player in my own damn love life. How long did you expect me to live like that? I'm tired of being your runner-up, Jacob."

Jacob's face sagged as he stared at the ground, sighing. She knew he couldn't argue her points. "Lilly, you were never my runner up. And I know I've fucked up, so many times, but I'm here now."

"But for how long? You've asked me to marry you several times, but no one, outside of family, knows I exist. I don't need worldwide acclaim, but I shouldn't be your dirty secret either."

Jacob scrubbed his face, looking equal parts sickened and frustrated. "You were never a dirty secret. I just tried—"

"To protect everyone, right? The only problem is somewhere along the line you forgot to include me in that group. It's okay, I'm used to being overlooked." Lilly wiped her face with her hands and reached for her clothing.

Her heart broke watching the intense pain radiate across his face at her statement. "You're such a good man, Jacob, and I love you so much, but I can't take the chance of being pushed aside again. My heart won't survive it."

His hands framed her face, his expression desperate. "I would never leave you, not after everything we've fought through to be together. You're running away Lilly. You're scared, and I understand but let's fight this together. Don't run away from me, don't run away from us."

He was on his knees, but Lilly didn't want him to beg, she wanted his promises to be real. Barring that, she needed him to set her free. She would never heal from the loss of Jacob, but she would never survive it if he left her again.

Lilly kissed him on the mouth, her tears wetting his face. "Tolkien said it best that 'not all those who wander are lost'; our time has come to a close." She kissed his fingers, offering a sad smile. "It's time to get me back to the rehab."

The ride back was silent, save for one final plea as Jacob pulled up to the entrance of Renaissance. His words played in her head on a continual loop, and it was an exquisite form of torture. "How am I supposed to live without you? You're my reason behind everything. Life doesn't mean anything without you in it. Don't take your love from me, angel. I can't live without it. Give me one more chance, Lilly. Let me show you what it means to be worshipped and adored."

Her heart begged her to tear down the wall and let Jacob love her, but her mind reiterated that their love was not to be trusted.

"I'll love you forever."

"If you meant that, you wouldn't leave." His statement echoed Lilly's own words when he made a choice, choosing his career over her love. It cut just as deep on the receiving end.

After she kissed his cheek goodbye, he helped her out of the car, but wouldn't look at her or say another word. He drove off, taking her heart with him when he left. Lilly knew he was as devastated—as was she—but she had lost faith in Jacob's ability to stick it for the long haul. Another heartbreak and this time she'd never recover. It was time to figure out what her life looked like without Jacob Edmonton in it.

Lilly lay curled on her couch five days later, staring at the television, her month-long stay at the rehab coming to an end. She had chucked the wheelchair and was now using a cane for balance—she was determined to discard it within a week or two.

She hadn't heard from Jacob since that night at his house. His plea echoed in her bones. Christ, she wanted to believe him. She ached without him. Despite her decision to return to America, she needed to speak with him.

She'd almost called him a thousand times, but memories of all the times he hurt her, broke her, and left her behind stopped her from completing the call.

Her phone rang, and Lilly jumped. For a second she thought it might be Jacob, but it wasn't. It was Ben, and she wasn't in the mood for idle chit-chat. She declined the call, but her phone started ringing again immediately. Once again, she hit decline.

Not more than thirty seconds later her door was pounded with the enthusiasm of a first-year police officer and Lilly groaned at the intrusion into her pity party.

They're relentless with this therapy nonsense. The therapists had not let her slide an inch in the last few days, despite her fast approaching discharge date.

Throwing open the door, her eyes grew wide as she was greeted by Ben, Janie, and Sabina.

"Hi, what are you all doing here?"

Ben pushed past her into the suite. "No time for that, where is your television remote?" He searched the couch cushions and changed the channel, checking his watch. "We have five minutes, perfect."

"Perfect for what?" Lilly asked her friend, eyeballing the bottle of whiskey in his hand.

"The Brad Taylor Show, of course." Janie smiled at her friend, handing her a finger of whiskey. "You'll want to drink up. I hear it's been a rough few days."

"That's an understatement. Are all your televisions broken? Is that why you've descended on me to watch Brad Taylor?" Before they could answer, the show came on announcing Jacob Edmonton as one of the guests and Lilly groaned in resignation. "Or just a bit of amenable torture, I see."

Sabina led her friend to the couch. "You see nothing. Sit."

Lilly obeyed, bristling at the sudden bossiness of her friends. "Seriously, what are we doing?"

Ben gave Lilly a pointed glare. "You're being quiet if I have to duct tape you to achieve it."

Jacob walked out on stage, resplendent in a dark blue suit, his blonde locks closely cropped, his jaw chiseled. Lilly felt her heart clench as she watched him. He had such a confident public persona, yet she knew the soft underbelly that was Jacob. God, she missed him so much it hurt to breathe.

The interview began, and she listened intently as Jacob discussed his situation with Victoria. "I thought this was old news?" Lilly inquired, being shushed by all three. "Jeez. Sorry I asked."

Janie came around with the whiskey bottle. "Come on, luv. Drink up."

Lilly shook her head, ignoring the strange look Janie shot her. *I'll have to explain later, Janie. Right now, your brother has my undivided attention… some things never change.*

Then the interview segued—away from Victoria, the awards show and Jacob's acting career. Brad handed Jacob a magazine, inquiring about the mystery woman in London.

Lilly held her breath. "Oh, my God…"

How would Jacob respond? Would he dance around their relationship or deny its existence entirely?

She braced herself for the emotional onslaught she knew was coming, preparing her poor heart for one more round with the executioner.

But the executioner was no longer on duty, replaced instead by a man utterly devoted to the woman he loved.

Tears poured down Lilly's cheeks as Jacob confessed the truth about the love of his life and his intention to make her his bride. Lilly crawled toward the television, touching his image on the screen and feeling so overwhelmed she didn't know whether to laugh or cry.

And then her Jacob pulled out the ring, that beautiful ring designed especially for her and divulged his plans to propose that night.

When the interview ended, Lilly turned to her friends, her hands shaking. "I don't understand. Why now? Why is Jacob telling everyone now?"

Janie pointed at the screen as Brad Taylor appeared on camera in a different suit. "That interview was taped several weeks ago on the day of the Tube explosion. We wanted to air it sooner, but in light of Roger's death and Lilly's injuries in the attack, we thought it best to wait until the proverbial dust settled. I still haven't heard about the outcome for Jacob and Lilly, but I hope they found their happiness together. I can say without a doubt that man was more in love than anyone I've ever seen. Now, let's welcome our next guest."

Ben turned off the television, and three pairs of eyes stared holes into Lilly.

Lilly couldn't breathe. Her entire world was upending and everything she thought she knew was dead wrong. "Holy shit, he taped this weeks ago." Then it hit her, Roger's comment that Jacob had an interview that day. *'I wager he's got something grand planned.'*

Janie nodded. "I knew Jacob taped an interview, but I didn't know what he said until he told me it was airing tonight. I know it bothered you that he never came clean publicly about what you meant to him, but he tried to tell the world weeks ago."

185

"Why didn't he tell *me*?" Lilly's heart hammered in her chest, knowing she was leaving the only man she ever truly loved in two days. "If he had told me..."

"I asked him that too and he said he forgot about it with Roger's death and you being so ill. He was focused on everything immediately surrounding him." Janie took Lilly's hands. "My brother keeps his emotions close to the vest, but he wanted the world to know how much he loves you."

"Let's not forget how he sat by her bedside for four days," Ben interjected.

Lilly's eyes widened. "He did what?"

"He wouldn't leave your hospital room—at all—for four days while you were in the coma. He stayed right there day and night," Ben explained. "We all tried to get him to go home, even for a shower and a nap, but he refused. I've never seen such devotion."

Lilly buried her face in her hands. "I had no idea he'd done that for me. He never mentioned it."

"The same way *you* never mentioned speaking to Albert about Milieu of Madness?" Janie's smile was equally sad and knowing.

"That's different—"

"That's love," Sabina piped into the conversation. "When you love someone, you'd do anything for them—"

"Do anything to make them smile." Lilly repeated the words she told Jacob all those months ago. "He loves me. He really loves me."

"No, he doesn't love you, Lilly. He worships the ground you walk on. I told you that before." Janie sat next to her friend, stroking her hair.

Lilly couldn't catch her breath—there was a tornado of upheaval and emotions inside her body. "Jacob asked me to marry him the other night and I told him no because I thought he didn't really love me. I still believed I was his fallback." She glanced at the wall calendar and wailed, "What am I supposed to do? I'm leaving in two days!"

The friends exchanged a glance, shrugging.

"Whatever you plan, it better be amazing." Sabina eyed her friend's whiskey. "Are you pregnant?"

Lilly's eyes widened at Sabina's question. "What did you say?"

"You heard her. Are you pregnant?" Ben chimed in, picking up the untouched glass of whiskey.

Janie gripped her hands. "Are you?"

Lilly closed her eyes, the truth would come out eventually. "Yeah, I'm pregnant. I only found out a few days ago."

"It's Jacob's baby, isn't it?" Janie's eyes were wide and questioning.

Lilly nodded. "I haven't been with anyone but him."

"Oh my God, I'm going to be an aunt!" Janie threw her arms around Lilly, squeezing her. "I have to call him, he must be so excited!"

"Wait! I haven't told Jacob yet."

Janie paused, her face scrunched in confusion. "Why in the world not?"

"After everything that was said the other night…the last thing he's going to want is to be saddled with another unwanted pregnancy. I doubt he'll want anything to do with me or the baby."

Sabina slugged Lilly's whiskey and shook her friend's shoulders. "I love you, Lilly, but you're a moron if you don't believe Jacob adores you and will be over the moon about this baby. Now the question you have to ask yourself is, do *you* love him?"

"And if you do, how are you going to make it right?" Janie chimed in, grinning.

Lilly's mind rattled through a hundred ideas a second, before a huge smile crossed her face. It was risky, but Jacob was a risk worth taking. "I love him and our baby"—she placed a hand over her stomach—"more than anything in this world." She stood, ignoring the twinge in her leg at the sudden movement. "I've got a plan, but I'm going to need help. Are you in?"

CHAPTER THIRTEEN

Jacob

acob released a sigh when the pilot announced their descent into Los Angeles. How ironic that he followed Lilly's path back to the States only a few weeks after her departure.

He called her bluff, thinking she wouldn't really leave England. He left her alone for a week, and then drove to the cottage to tell the love of his life that he wasn't letting her walk away from him.

He expected to find her there, but instead he found Ben in the garden. Her friend verified that Lilly returned stateside right after her discharge, and Jacob's heart shattered with the news.

He couldn't fathom that she actually left him, boarded a plane, flew out of his life and away from their love.

To make matters worse, the mobile phone she used in England wasn't accepting calls and he didn't have any number for her stateside. She was, for all intents and purposes, gone forever.

Jacob could hire an investigator to track her down, but if Lilly wanted him to know where she was, she would have given him a way to reach her. She left without a word.

"I can't believe I'm in Los Angeles. I've always wanted to visit, see how the other half lives."

They called it the city of angels, but Jacob felt as if he were trapped in hell. It didn't matter that he was attending one of the most prestigious awards shows in the world and that he was a nominee; without Lilly, it meant nothing.

"Jakey? You okay?" Janie nudged him gently, stirring him from his reverie.

Jacob forced a smile. He felt awful being such a stick in the mud but every time he smiled it felt like his face would crack. "Tired. Damn jet lag."

"Well that's what hopping several time zones will do to you." Janie gave her brother a quick hug. "I've got a great idea, apart from sampling the mini bar in the hotel suite."

Jacob stood and made his way off the plane, his sister behind him. "And what is this great idea?"

"A vacation in Seychelles."

Jacob smirked. "I don't think so Janie, I'm not in a frolicking mood."

"But you might be, right? After your big win tomorrow!"

"Who says I'm going to win? Besides, it doesn't seem as important as it used to. Anyway, I can't go on vacation. I'm due back for filming in three days."

Janie chewed her lip, looking unconvinced. "What if I told you I spoke with your director and explained that with everything that happened, you needed a few days off to celebrate your birthday?"

"I would say it's a load of rubbish."

"Call him. Here, use my phone. Look under Albert."

Jacob scoffed as they walked to the limousine, headed for the Beverly Hilton. "Can we just focus on a few hours of relaxation before the melee begins?"

"Fine, but we're revisiting this conversation later."

Within two hours, the siblings sat lounging in their private hot tub in the luxury suite, whiskeys in hand.

"Now this"—Janie giggled—"I could get used to. This is the life, big brother. I believe I was always meant to live a life of luxury. Just look at this view!"

Jacob sipped his whiskey, studying the LA skyline. "I prefer the English countryside."

"Speaking of the country, when are you moving into the house in Gloucestershire? What an unbelievable sanctuary."

Jacob chewed the inside of his cheek, fighting to keep the tears at bay. The house, *their house*. The home he purchased for Lilly in a futile effort to buy her love when all his angel ever wanted was their love to be his top priority. "I don't think I'll be able to live there."

"Why not? You love that manor house."

He swigged back his whiskey, willing the alcohol to burn off some of the pain. "I bought that house for a future I'll never have. I've called the realtor about listing the property, but I'm not ready to sell it yet."

He doubted he would ever be ready to sell it. He would keep it forever, as a monument to a love he never deserved. But he couldn't live there, couldn't walk those floors knowing that Lilly's light and exuberance would never be a part of it.

"I think you should keep it. It's an amazing home. What a place to raise a family—" Janie ended abruptly, looking into her drink.

Jacob scoffed. "I would need a family first."

"Jacob—"

He shook his head, pouring another finger of whiskey. "And please don't tell me to start dating because I can't even consider that right now."

Janie squeezed his hand. "I wouldn't dare. Now, about Seychelles—"

"Janie!" Jacob groaned.

"We go, just for a few days. It will do you good to be somewhere peaceful and have no obligations beyond drinking mai-tais and lounging in a hammock. What do you say? Sun, sea, and miles of beaches?"

Jacob's blue eyes flashed at his sister. God, she was a persistent pain in the ass. "Here's the deal. If through some stroke of luck, I win tomorrow night, we fly to Seychelles the next day. But don't expect me to enjoy myself."

The water splashed over the rim of the hot tub as Janie embraced her brother. "You old spoilsport. You won't be sorry!"

"I already am," Jacob muttered.

Jacob adjusted the cufflinks on his navy tux the following evening, patting the pocket that held Roger's watch. The gift had become his most prized possession, second only to Lilly's ring that he carried in his breast pocket—always keeping a part of her close to his heart.

Janie walked in, letting out a wolf whistle when she saw her brother. "You are fit as hell, Jacob. If you weren't my brother and I wasn't a lesbian—"

Jacob laughed, kissing his sister on the cheek. "I don't want to explore that train of thought further." He twirled his sister, admiring her in a floor-length ivory gown. "You look beautiful Janie, you'll outshine any of those actresses tonight."

Janie smiled and admired the two of them in the mirror—both tall, slender, and blonde. "Not too shabby. We clean up good, don't we?"

"Mum would be proud."

"Do you have your speech ready?"

Jacob shook his head. "I didn't prepare anything."

"That should make for an interesting acceptance then, way to wing it."

"I appreciate the enthusiasm, but I think you'll be disappointed when the winner is announced tonight. Are you ready to go? I'll call for the limousine."

"Almost." Janie held out a small box. "This is for you."

"You didn't need to do this."

Janie's voice was barely a whisper. "I didn't."

Jacob's breath caught as he opened the box, his hands trembling. Inside were two platinum cuff links with an inscription: *Is ceol mo chroí thú.* He held them up to the light, unsure of the translation, but certain of the emotion behind the gift. "What does it mean?"

Janie wrapped her arm around his shoulder. "You're the music of my heart. It's Gaelic."

Jacob couldn't breathe as he sank into a chair, his hand covering his mouth. "Is she here? Is Lilly here?" Had his prayers been answered?

Janie's eyes were bright with tears. "No, but she wanted you to have them. A memory of that first night you two were together. Something about a song."

How could Jacob forget their song—the song that described true love, even when it ended. He stared at the ground, willing his heart to stop pounding like a jackhammer. "You know where she is?"

"Not at the moment."

"I need to speak with Lilly. You obviously have her phone number, and I need it."

Janie knelt by Jacob, squeezing his hands. "Settle down. She hasn't set up a mobile phone yet. When I get her number, I'll give it to you."

"I don't want to live without her, Janie. How am I supposed to do this? Maybe I was better off before, when I didn't give a shit about anyone—"

Janie grasped his chin, her expression stern. "No! You are the most amazing man now that you've opened your heart. Don't you dare close it again. Things will get better. You'll see."

"Time will heal your wounds and all that shit, right? I need a drink." Jacob stood, heading for the minibar in the suite.

"We have to leave, Jacob. You cannot be soused at the awards show. I promise I'll have a glass of whiskey waiting for you immediately afterwards. Look, if it's too difficult, you don't have to wear them," Janie offered.

Jacob put on the cufflinks, fingering the inscription. "Yes, I do."

Two hours later, Jacob and Janie sat smack dab in the middle of Hollywood royalty. Janie gazed around, admiring all the 'beautiful people' but Jacob's mind remained on Lilly. He wished she was there with him, holding his hand and shooting him those soft, warm glances that melted his insides. *Where is she tonight? Is she even watching?*

Before he knew it, his category was being announced, and Jacob realized if he did win, he hadn't prepared a thing and his mind was blank on what to say.

"And the winner is…Jacob Edmonton!" The crowd went wild, and Janie squeezed his arm like a vise.

"I told you you'd win! Congratulations, Jakey!" She threw her arms around him, hugging him tight.

Jacob smiled, shaking hands with a few colleagues on his way to the stage, feeling utterly flabbergasted. He accepted the award and stood at the podium, shaking his head in disbelief.

What in the hell am I supposed to say? Shit, talk about being naked in school without your homework. He sighed, suddenly feeling the weight of the watch and ring in his pockets.

Facing the crowd, he flashed his million-dollar smile and set the award down on the podium.

"I'm in awe at the moment. I didn't prepare an acceptance speech because I honestly didn't think I'd win." The crowd laughed appreciatively as he continued. "This film made me truly proud, not because of the box office earnings or the hoopla surrounding it or even the action figures which are beyond comprehension, but because of the people associated with it. Everyone from housekeeping to the production team made this a truly human experience."

Jacob picked up the statue, his eyes watering. "It's been a tough year, and I'm struggling to find happiness in such a time of loss. Throughout all these twists and turns, there has been one constant in my life, and I dedicate this award to her." Jacob looked right at the camera, speaking to the screen and hoping that somewhere, his angel was listening. "Lilly Staver, you stole my heart months ago, and not because you're 'normal' as you sardonically state but because you're exquisite, in every sense of the word."

With a fortuitous breath, Jacob continued. "I've never met someone with your bravery, who has stared into the face of death countless times yet still has a heart of gold. You have a depth of character that defies logic. You cling to your beliefs like a dying man to a lifeboat and you won't be wavered in the slightest. You love on a level I've never encountered. It's cliché to say you make me want to be a better man but it's the truth. You make me fearless, perhaps because your fearlessness is contagious or perhaps because you ignite that spark in people. Either way, I'm blessed to have the privilege of loving you, wherever you are now. You told me that not all who wander are lost, but I'm lost without you. I love you, angel."

The applause was thunderous as the crowd sprang to their feet. His speech was unlike any other that evening—brimming with raw honesty and devotion—and the admiration for the golden-haired actor ran rampant. But Jacob's pain was only more acute after the win and he walked offstage, his usually erect stature stooped slightly with the weight of losing Lilly from his life.

He had achieved his greatest goal, the pinnacle award, but it was a hollow victory without Lilly by his side to share in it.

After the awards ceremony, Jacob and Janie arrived at the afterparty at Spago, a veritable who's who of Hollywood. He had no sooner walked in the door when he was engulfed by well-wishers and newly minted fans.

He forced cordial humor as people complimented him on his win and his exceedingly touching speech. His sentimental statements were like catnip to the women and they flocked around him, offering their services in his time of need—offers Jacob had no difficulty refusing. A few inquired about Lilly's whereabouts, but Jacob only offered a sad smile, unwilling to disclose any further information.

After what felt like hours but was likely only thirty minutes, Jacob finally escaped the throng of people. He settled into a dark corner, intent on downing a few glasses of whiskey. His baby sister was chatting up a director and basically charming the pants off everyone she met. She was having a ball, and after the year she'd endured, she deserved every moment.

"Congratulations on your big win. Was it everything you hoped for?"

Jacob stifled a groan—Victoria. Christ, he hoped she wasn't there to cause any further damage. He couldn't handle any more of her games.

"Hello, Victoria. Enjoying the evening?"

She offered a brilliant smile, her small baby bump noticeable beneath her evening gown. "How are you?"

Shit, is she really asking *that* question? He swallowed his anger along with his whiskey before replying. "I'm grand, how are you? How's the baby?"

Victoria laid her hand on her stomach, a diamond engagement ring sparkling on her finger. "The baby is fine."

Jacob raised his eyebrows—this was a turn of events. "Engaged, are we? Congratulations."

Victoria nodded her head over her shoulder. "Turns out the man who worshipped me was right in front of me all along. I was just too blind to see it."

Edward walked up to the pair, extending his hand to Jacob. "Congratulations Jacob, that was quite a win, and quite a speech."

Jacob had to bite his tongue to keep from bursting into laughter. It was perfect actually, Edward and Victoria, they both spent months lying and scheming against others—now that energy could be focused on each other and give the rest of the world a much-needed break. God help their child if she inherited her parent's flair for the dramatics. "I see you two finally connected. Congratulations to you both, big days ahead. Are you ready to be parents?"

"We'll see," Edward chuckled. "I don't know if you're ever ready to be a parent, but it's going to be one hell of a ride."

Jacob wanted to inquire if Edward had actually obtained a paternity test but thought better of it. When both snakes are caught in the snare, leave them to their own devices. "Are you two planning to marry before the baby arrives?"

"No, I don't want to look like a beached whale for my wedding!" Victoria groaned, a genuine smile crossing her face when Edward placed his hand on her stomach. "We aren't staying—it's intolerable speaking with a bunch of soused individuals when I can't participate." She wrapped her arms around Jacob, her hug soft instead of clingy. "I know it won't change anything, but I'm sorry." She paused and met his gaze. "I'm sorry I tried to make you love me. The love you have for Lilly is a thing of beauty. I hope you two find each other again."

Jacob nodded, his emotions ganging up on him. He needed to escape. Even if Victoria was apologetic, her meddling led to this disaster and now she was happily engaged. Fuck this night. Fuck this town.

"Yes, I hope you two reconnect. Lilly is one in a million," Edward offered.

"Not much chance of that, she's left England, and I don't know where to find her anymore. If you'll excuse me."

Jacob strode outside, Janie close on his heels. "Jakey, are you okay? That bitch didn't upset you again, did she? I swear, if she weren't pregnant—"

"Victoria didn't do anything except apologize."

"That's rich. A day late and a dollar short."

"I need to leave Janie. I can't stay here any longer. I need to get back to England."

Janie nodded, sending for the limo. "Seychelles first, then England. Smile, you'll be on a beach within twenty-four hours."

"Great," Jacob muttered. "More time to think about everything I've lost."

Lilly

Some will think I am mad for this plan, Lilly surmised, pausing to take several deep breaths outside the lounge area and earning a few quizzical looks from passing patrons.

The lounge was part of the elite private island resort on Seychelles. Lilly rubbed her brow, recalling her shellshock when she handed over her credit card to reserve the villas. It was the biggest risk she'd ever taken, every card she owned was now maxed out, yet she hadn't a clue to the outcome of the day.

She arrived on the island the day before to prepare and arrange documentation, now came the hard part. She had to see if her plan would play out in reality as it had in her heart a thousand times before.

She steadied herself against one of the giant teak columns, her cane stashed against a wall in her villa. She hadn't used the blasted thing in a week, and her legs felt stronger than ever thanks to the rehab center—aka torture camp, as Lilly lovingly dubbed Renaissance.

With a final exhalation, Lilly smoothed her green chiffon sundress and felt for the orchids the resort beautician has skillfully woven into her short strands. Hopefully, her romantic appearance would bode well in the next few minutes.

Inside, the lounge was even more luxurious, all thick wooden tables and gold gilded decor. But Lilly wasn't able to appreciate the beauty just yet, her heart and stomach in knots as the moment of truth approached.

No time like the present, Lilly thought, her heart quickening as she spotted Jacob and Janie at the bar. He was dashing in a white linen shirt and slacks, his golden head bent over his drink.

Panic overtook her, and she glanced to the exit, considering a hasty escape. But Janie caught sight of her friend and a wide smile crossing her face. She blew Lilly a kiss before leaning in to whisper to her brother, and when Jacob turned in his seat, he caught sight of Lilly in the doorway.

His face changed from one of sadness to bridled expectation as she walked across the lounge.

"You're walking," Jacob murmured, his eyes welling when he met her halfway across the floor.

"I told you, you can't keep a Yank down for long." She took a deep breath and bit her lip, willing her heart to stop racing. "I bet you're wondering what I'm doing here." Talk about a fabulous opening line—all her planned prose flew out the window as she stared at his beautiful face.

Jacob swallowed hard; he looked as nervous as she felt. "This can't be a coincidence."

Lilly shook her head. "It's a carefully executed plan. Well, it had a lot of bumps along the way, but it began as a carefully executed plan."

"Did my sister arrange this plan?" Jacob tried to smile but looked away, his pain evident.

Lilly gulped air, her stomach flipping. *How am I supposed to get through this?* She reached up, her fingers grasping his chin and directing his gaze back to her. "I have some things to tell you. I'm terrified of how you'll react, but I need to say them before I lose my nerve and run out of here."

Jacob's eyes scanned her body, softening as they focused on her face. "You never have to be terrified to tell me anything. I'm listening." He leaned in, his lips caressing her cheek. "You're beautiful, Lilly. No matter what you have to say, I didn't want to forget to tell you."

His words gave her the courage she needed to open the door to her heart and tear the damn thing off its hinges. She didn't want to close her heart again—not to Jacob. "My darling, you've always been the beautiful one"—she held up her hand to shush him when he opened his mouth, no doubt to argue her statement—"but that's not why I'm here."

Jacob offered a small chuckle; it was a start.

"I was afraid of loving someone the way I love you, afraid it would consume and destroy me. But it didn't, being away from you did that. I thought I was second-best, your runner up, but I was so wrong. You never told me you stayed by my side when I was in the coma, when I was at my most helpless, you didn't leave me alone—"

A single tear slipped down her cheek, and she gasped as Jacob wiped it away with his thumb. "There was no way in hell I was leaving you. You're my angel, from the moment we met."

"I saw the Brad Taylor show. I didn't know you told the world how you felt about me—about us. I didn't know. I should have trusted you when you told me how you felt. I didn't want to be hurt again." The harder she tried to hold back the tears, the more they pushed through her eyelashes.

His hand reached out, tucking a stray strand of hair behind her ear. "I'm sorry it took me so damn long to realize what you needed from me. I'll never be that foolish again."

Lilly grasped his hands, and after a moment's hesitation, his fingers curled around hers. She sniffled, smiling up at his gorgeous features. He wrecked her, body and soul, and she was so damn grateful. "I'm so proud of you, winning that award. I told you that you'd win, and no one deserves it more than you."

"I hope you're not here to talk about the award," Jacob murmured as his face fell and he tore his gaze away, staring at the ground.

Lilly released a nervous giggle—time to open her heart and let Jacob in—if he still wanted to live there. "Definitely not, except for the fact that I was supposed to hand-deliver those cufflinks."

Jacob's face swung to meet hers, his eyes wide. "You were?"

"You weren't the only fool. I was letting fear rule my heart instead of love. So, I swung into action to get my life arranged before the clock ran down." Lilly wiped away her tears, offering a dry chuckle when Jacob immediately reclaimed her hands. "I'm fairly certain both the US and British governments now hate me, but I had to return to America and fight to get another British visa."

His fingers tightened around hers. "You're coming back to England?"

Lilly nodded. "That's where the love of my life lives, and I'm lost without him too." She willed away her tears. She had to get through this. "I finally got approval for my visa—I think they just wanted to get rid of me— and was set to fly to LA to surprise you. But the doctors wouldn't clear me to fly. They wanted to keep me grounded for another day."

Jacob cupped her cheeks, his face streaked with concern. "What's wrong, Lilly? Are you okay?"

She couldn't contain the smile spreading across her face. *Time for the big announcement.* "We're perfectly fine. But I wasn't able to fly that day, so I opted to fly straight here—"

His bright blue eyes widened as his fingers tightened on her shoulders. "You just said 'we're fine'."

"I did, didn't I? Well, they're the reason I couldn't fly to LA to be with you at the awards show. I wanted—"

Jacob's face broke into a huge smile. "Lilly, my angel, are you pregnant?"

Lilly nodded, putting her hand on her stomach. "We're pregnant…with twins."

Jacob swept her into his arms, twirling her around, pure joy radiating from his face. "I knew you were pregnant. I told you that night. God, this is glorious news."

Lilly giggled, a sigh of contentment escaping her lips as he nuzzled her neck. "Since I'm going to be big as a cow soon, I have something really important to ask you."

Jacob set her down, smoothing her hair back from her face. "You are *not* going to be as big as a cow—" His voice halted when Lilly pulled out a small box and opened it to reveal a platinum and diamond men's band inside. His eyes grew large, his face hopeful.

"This has been a rocky road, and we have overcome a ton of obstacles, but I'm hopelessly in love with you, and if you're still hopelessly in love with me, I thought you might like to get married." Tears glistened in her eyes, every cell in her body quivering with emotion. "Will you marry us, Jacob?"

His lips claimed hers in the next instant. As his tongue delved into her mouth, Lilly fell into Jacob's kiss, wrapping her arms around his neck. He lifted her off the ground, pressing her body tight against his.

Lilly pulled back an inch, smiling. "I'll take that as a yes?"

Jacob brushed her lips with the softest of kisses. "Are you sure you want to marry me?"

"You're my true north, my home. Marry me?"

Jacob smiled against her lips. "God, yes." He set her on the ground, trembling as he pulled Lilly's ring out of his shirt pocket. "Will you finally wear your ring?"

Lilly's eyes sparkled as she nodded, a fresh batch of tears on standby. "You carry it with you?"

He clutched her hand, sliding the ring onto her finger. "Everywhere. That way, a piece of you is always with me."

"You won't have to settle for a piece of jewelry anymore. Now I'll always be with you—your children and me."

A tear rolled down Jacob's face as he kissed her hard on the mouth. "You just made my life."

"You made mine."

The patrons in the lounge cheered, and Jacob looked up, a huge smile splitting his face. His jaw slackened as he gazed around the bar, realizing he knew every single person.

Ben, Sabina, and Enrique lounged against the bar, Sophie and Miriam raised their glasses in a toast, Hannah and her husband offered a knowing smile, his parents, sister, Audrey and Elizabeth clapped from a table to his left. Everyone he and Lilly loved was here in Seychelles.

"What in the world?" His eyes rested on Lilly, a mischievous smile on her face. "What have you got planned?"

"I brought everyone here to celebrate your birthday," Lilly replied haltingly.

"That's not the only reason," Audrey piped up.

Lilly giggled—damn her future sister-in-law. "The main reason is that the laws in Britain are so strict with marriages, and Seychelles is so accommodating. I brought everyone here in the hopes that you might want to get married."

Jacob's eyes grew as big as saucers. "Now?"

"Tomorrow would be the earliest since there's still some paperwork to sign." Her nerves took over, and she stammered, "We don't have to, we can wait—"

Jacob's finger went to her lips, the sexy smirk that melted her decorating his face. "I'm not waiting for a second longer than necessary to make you my wife. Just tell me the time and place, and I'll be there." He pulled Lilly against him, his mouth at her ear. "I do have one request, though, after we sign all the necessary documents."

Lilly felt the warmth spread through her body as his hands ran along her spine. Christ, she hoped he had the same idea she had for the next few hours. "What is that?"

"I want time alone with you—now."

Lilly wound her arms around his neck, offering up her seductive smile. "It just so happens that is exactly what I had in mind for the next few hours." She winked to their friends and family. "Jacob and I have some matters to discuss regarding our upcoming nuptials."

"Sure, you do," Sabina joked. "Go get busy. The birthday celebration doesn't start for another three hours. You think that's enough time for your *discussion*?"

Jacob scooped Lilly into his arms, flashing that million-dollar smile. "It's a start."

He carried her out of the lounge area to the sound of catcalls and cheers from family. His hands tightened around her slight form as he gazed down at her. "I missed you, angel."

Lilly stroked his cheek, feeling the slight stubble under her palm. "You never have to miss me again." She pressed a soft kiss to his lips and sighed against his neck. "It feels so good to be home. You don't have to carry me though. I can walk."

"No way in hell." Lilly quirked her brow at him, and Jacob chuckled. "My reason is threefold. You're still recovering, my legs are twice as long as yours—"

"What's the third reason?" Lilly grumbled.

"I can get us back to the villa faster...and that means I can be inside you sooner." Jacob slid the key card into the door and walked straight back to the bedroom, placing Lilly on the bed.

"Brilliant thinking, Mr. Edmonton," Lilly responded with a wink.

Jacob slid off her shoes, running his hands up her legs. "Lie back, angel. I need some quality time with this magnificent body."

But Lilly wasn't content to remain idle. She rose up on her knees and met Jacob's mouth in a fiery, blistering kiss as her fingers made quick work of the buttons on his shirt. "I feel like I can breathe again."

"Don't ever leave me again, Lilly."

She saw it in his eyes and heard it in his voice—he was terrified—terrified that she would walk away again. It was time to allay his fears, once and for all. "Never. I promise you."

His hand drifted to her stomach, as his lips captured hers, his tongue stroking against hers—owning, claiming. "Is it safe?"

Lilly giggled. "Not only is it safe, but it's also highly recommended. Now, get those damn pants off because I need you, Jacob. You always feel so good inside me."

Her affirmation stripped away any remaining hesitation. Jacob rained hungry kisses along her neck and collarbone, his hands pulling at the sheer material of her dress. "I love this dress, but I'm ready to rip it off you," he breathed against her mouth.

Lilly pulled down the zipper with a husky chuckle and let the dress fall from her body. "Better?"

"Getting there." Jacob unclasped her bra, chucking it across the room before shoving off his pants and pushing Lilly down to the mattress. "I promise I'll make love to you for hours later, but right now, I need to be inside you."

Lilly released a low moan as Jacob pulled off her g-string, his fingers stroking her slow and deep.

His gaze found hers and held her hostage, while his fingers continued their erotic assault. "Tell me you're mine, Lilly."

"I've always been yours. Now take me, I belong to you." Her hand stroked his erection, feeling him pulsate against her palm.

He didn't need any additional encouragement as he sank into her, her muscles spasming around his cock. Jacob groaned as his mouth nipped at the tender skin on her neck, driving himself deeper and deeper into her body.

Over and over, he thrust himself inside her, as her hips arched to meet him. Jacob was wild, pounding into her with a driving hunger, reclaiming her as his own.

"Come for me, Lilly," he choked out.

Lilly felt the familiar clench deep down in her core and shot him a seductive smile. "Make me, Jacob."

Jacob curled his hands around her hips, and Lilly's body vibrated as pleasure rippled through her. Her back arched as she trembled and moaned, lost in the moment. Her nails ripped down his back as she screamed out his name.

"You are the most gorgeous creature I've ever seen," Jacob whispered, gritting his teeth against his climax.

Lilly tightened around him, feeling him pulse deep inside her body as he came.

Jacob collapsed on his elbows, his breathing harried and heart racing. His lips claimed hers, but the caress was soft, tender. His gaze traveled over her face, and Lilly felt the all too familiar flush under his scrutiny.

"See something you like?" she joked, running her nails along his scalp.

"I see something I worship, my beautiful soon-to-be wife."

Lilly couldn't hold back her smile. "It took us long enough."

Jacob claimed her lips again in a searing kiss. "We still have forever, Lilly."

"Wait a second. It's only been two and a half hours. What are you doing back here, you slackers?" Sabina chortled when Lilly and Jacob entered the lounge area that evening.

"It was only round one," Jacob retorted, sending their friend a knowing wink. "As if you couldn't find something—or someone—to keep you occupied."

"I was busy with your party planning." The words sounded sincere enough, but the smirk on Sabina's face told a different tale. The woman was in love and judging from the gazes Enrique sent in her direction, the feeling was mutual.

Lilly gazed around the lounge area, her mouth watering at the delectable aromas drifting from the myriad of food trays. All manner of fish, rice, fresh fruit, and vegetables formed a colorful bouquet on the banquet table.

"This is quite a party, beautiful," Jacob whispered, nuzzling her neck.

"You're quite a man, Mr. Edmonton." Lilly would never tire of the smile that stretched across his face, knowing that she was the reason behind it.

"Would you care for some champagne?" A server inquired, holding a tray of Krug Vintage Brut in her hands.

"Do you have anything non-alcoholic?" Jacob interjected, wrapping one arm around Lilly's waist as the other one took the champagne glass she had

201

grabbed from the tray.

"A sip won't hurt." Lilly reached for the glass, but Jacob shook his head, that sexy smirk decorating his features.

"You're absolutely right." Jacob sipped the champagne before capturing her mouth with his own. "A sip won't hurt me, but we aren't taking any chances with you. My babies are far too precious."

Lilly smiled up at him and chuckled. Well, now she knew. He was going to be very protective during her pregnancy, and that suited her just fine. "May I have some sparkling cider instead?"

"Of course. As long as it's healthy, you can have anything you want. Just ask, and I'll give it to you."

That certainly opened up a world of options. "Sex every single day?" She bit her lip, sending him a mock worried glance. "Perhaps that's not healthy either, though..."

Jacob set down the champagne glass, wrapping his arms around her and pulling her close. "It's actually very healthy. In fact, I've been told it's recommended."

She released a laugh against his mouth. Sex every day with this delectable man? Yes, please. "Really? When did you become a doctor?"

"I didn't, but I am marrying a brilliant nurse who knows a brilliant surgeon. He'll back up my claim."

"Sorry to break up this magnificent moment, but the registrar has some paperwork for the future Mr. and Mrs. Edmonton to sign." Janie beamed at the couple. "Lilly, I assume you'll be staying in my villa tonight?"

"Why would she do that?" Jacob inquired, tightening his grip on Lilly.

Janie smirked at her brother's not so subtle gesture. "I'll give her back tomorrow. It's tradition, Jacob. You don't see the bride the night before the wedding. Bad luck and all."

"No. Lilly and I are starting a new tradition. My wife is staying with me tonight, and every night after."

Lilly felt her old familiar friend—that flush of color—race over her cheeks.

Jacob's thumb brushed over her cheek as he chuckled. "What did I say?"

"You called me your wife."

"Is that a bad thing? You will be in less than a day." He bent closer, his lips brushing her ear. "Lilly, I've wanted you to be my wife since that first night we spent together. It was always you."

"So, Lilly is staying with *you,* then?" Janie pressed, trying to suppress a laugh.

"Yes. We've already lived through ten lifetimes of bad luck, and I've lived far too many nights without Lilly by my side."

"Are you going to be like Paul and Linda McCartney? Rumor has it that they never spent a night apart."

"No," Lilly replied, wrapping her arms around Jacob's neck. "We'll be like Jacob and Lilly Edmonton—even better."

She wanted to freeze that moment, the smile that lit her fiancée's face, the feeling of being in his arms after everything that had transpired. He was right. They'd lived through their share of bad luck. They'd done their time in hell. Now it was time to begin the celebration—of life, of love and of their happily ever after. "Perfect," Jacob murmured, lifting her off the ground into a tight embrace.

"Perhaps you two *should* go back to your room. The nausea quotient is increasing every second," Janie remarked with a good-natured wink.

"Actually, I have to run out for a bit." Jacob ran his fingers along Lilly's jaw. "I'll be back soon."

"You're leaving?"

Jacob nodded, pulling her in for one more kiss. "I have a few things to take care of this evening."

Lilly nodded, squelching the old fears that still haunted her mind. "Let's sign those papers first?"

"Absolutely."

They walked over to the registrant, and Jacob took the documents. His eyes narrowed as he read over the paperwork. "What is this?"

Lilly glanced at the paper, offering a noncommittal shrug. "It's a prenup. Your lawyer said it's pretty standard."

"You want a prenup?"

Lilly wrapped her hand around his arm, squeezing it. "I want you. I don't want your money. That's what the prenup says. In the event of…divorce, I don't want anything."

A muscle twitched in Jacob's jaw, right before he took the piece of paper and ripped it into pieces. "There will be no divorce, and there will be no prenup."

Lilly's eyes widened—please don't let him change his mind now. "Your lawyer said he made this up months ago—"

Jacob nodded, offering a rueful smile. "He did, the first time I proposed marriage. I told him where he could shove his prenup then, too."

"You still want to marry me?"

Jacob didn't answer right away, his focus on the remaining paperwork, which he quickly signed before meeting her gaze. "More than I want my next breath. It's your turn, angel."

Lilly took the pen Jacob held out to her, signing her name next to his on the marriage certificate. "Easiest decision ever."

The registrant verified the information and left, taking the paperwork to be filed.

Lilly turned her face up to Jacob, grabbing his hands. "You're free to go, but you'd better return to me."

"Every second away from you is too long." With a final kiss, Jacob strolled out of the lounge.

"I swear, you two are sickeningly in love," Sabina remarked, wrapping an arm around her friend's waist and offering her a glass. "Don't worry, it's not alcoholic. Your future husband already gave me an earful about the danger to the babies."

"Sorry, he's just being careful."

Sabina kissed her cheek. "I'm all for it. He wants to dote on you, wait on you hand and foot. That works for me! Where did he go anyway?"

Lilly shrugged, offering a small smile. "I'm not sure. I hope he isn't getting cold feet. I did spring this whole marriage idea on him."

"Are you mad?" Janie interjected. "He's wanted to marry you for ages. He is *not* getting cold feet."

"I'm sure you're right." If only Lilly could convince her mind to pipe down for a moment.

Janie framed her face with her hands. "Lilly, trust me. Trust him. Most importantly, trust your love."

Lilly released a sigh, and with it, her fears. Janie was right. Jacob was wild about her, and he seemed thrilled about the babies. There was nothing to fear. "As always, the voice of reason. I have to return to the villa for a moment. I'll be back soon."

She stepped out into the balmy night, breathing deep of the sea air as she strolled the short distance back to her villa. As she rounded the corner, she heard Jacob's voice—he was speaking on the phone—and he sounded less than pleased.

"I don't care what it costs or what arrangements have to be made, but I need an appointment with the doctor as soon as we land in London."

Lilly's blood chilled in her veins. A doctor. He wanted to see a doctor as soon as possible, and she knew there could only be one reason for his insistence.

Jacob looked up and caught sight of Lilly, a smile crossing his lips.

"Make it happen, please. This is vital to me," he stated to the person on the other end of the line before hanging up. Within a few strides, he was by her side, tilting her face up to meet his azure gaze. "Did you miss me already?"

Lilly took a deep breath and forced a smile. "I'm sorry, I didn't mean to intrude. I forgot my medicine in the villa and wanted to fetch it before I ate."

"I'll walk with you." Jacob clasped her hand, but Lilly halted his movements. "What is it, angel?"

Lilly grabbed both his hands, giving them a gentle squeeze. "If you—if you want to wait to get married—"

His eyes widened. "What?"

"I overheard your conversation just now. I didn't mean to eavesdrop." She released a sigh. "I don't know why it didn't occur to me before."

"Why what didn't occur to you, Lilly?"

"That you'd want a paternity test."

His brow raised in shock. "Who said I wanted a paternity test?"

"You want to see the doctor as soon as we return to London. I need you to understand that I have no problem with providing a paternity test. I know what you've been through and…why are you laughing?"

Jacob chuckled, that sensual smile lit up his whole face. What in the world did he find so amusing? "For such a brilliant woman, you certainly are thick-headed."

Now it was Lilly's turn to guffaw. "Excuse me?"

He gathered her to him, dropping kisses on the top of her head. "I don't want a paternity test; I know they're mine. And I certainly don't want to wait to get married, but I am setting up appointments with the best obstetrician in England. I also plan on being at every single appointment, probably driving you out of your mind the entire time."

Lilly's face relaxed into a smile. "You're worried about the babies."

"Not worried, just…okay, fine, I'm worried. I want to hear firsthand that you're fit as a fiddle and my babies are healthy. I know I may have overstepped but—"

His statement was cut off as Lilly threw her arms around his neck, capturing him in a deep kiss.

His arms wrapped circled her waist, drawing her against his body. It didn't matter that they had made love only an hour before, she craved this man constantly.

"I'm never going to get my errands finished if you keep throwing your beautiful body against mine."

"I could apologize, but I'm not sorry," Lilly giggled, unbuttoning a few buttons on his shirt and tonguing along the muscular lines of his chest. "I can't control it. I'm a hopeless addict."

"It's about damn time," Jacob growled, jutting his hips against hers and eliciting a low moan from Lilly.

"Can your errand wait five minutes?"

Jacob's eyes twinkled. "Yes, but it will take that long to walk back to the villa."

"We aren't going to the villa." Lilly motioned over her shoulder at a small lounge with several overstuffed chaises, closed for the evening. "Come with me."

"I like this side of you, Lilly. Since when do you throw caution to the wind?"

"Since I need you so deep inside me that I don't know where I begin, and you end." Her erotic whisper produced the intended effect as Jacob picked her up with a primal growl and carried her to the vacant lounge area.

"Lay back," Lilly demanded, pushing against his chest and smiling as he sank back onto a chaise. She offered up a sexy wink as she straddled him, her fingers unbuckling his belt and loosening his trousers. Without waiting for an invitation, she lowered herself down onto his shaft, emitting a moan of satisfaction.

Jacob's breath hitched as she rode him, his hands sliding up under her dress to latch onto her hips. Lilly didn't care who saw them as she ground her hips against him. He was utterly at her mercy, and she wanted to hear him beg for release. Scratching her nails down his chest, she clenched around him, not giving him a moment's reprieve.

"Lilly…Lilly, fuck—"

Leaning over him, Lilly took his lobe between her teeth, a low giggle reverberating from her body. "Let go, Jacob."

With a desperate growl, Jacob slammed into her, and their bodies shuddered out their mutual release. She collapsed onto his chest, her breathing heavy, but her body sated. His hands stroked along her spine as their heart rates slowed.

"You're free to run your errands now, sir." Lilly pressed a kiss to his chest before buttoning his shirt again.

Jacob's laugh echoed in the night air. "What errands were those?"

Lilly smiled and climbed off him, offering him a hand up. "Did I make you lose track of time?"

Jacob gathered her into an embrace, tipping her chin up to meet his gaze. "Time stops when I'm with you. The world could come to an end, and I wouldn't care."

Lilly pressed a chaste kiss to his lips. "We'll build our own world, remember? Now go finish your business. I just wanted to give you a reason to hurry home."

CHAPTER FOURTEEN

Jacob

Ninety minutes later, Jacob strolled back into the lounge, making a beeline for Lilly, seated at a table with his parents. Judging from their besotted gazes, his Mum and Dad loved Lilly as much as he did…almost. "Come with me," Jacob whispered, grabbing Lilly's hand.

His request was greeted with that beautiful smile stretching across her face as she stood. "Gladly."

He led her outside the lounge, where the party was still rolling, their guests dancing and laughing as the night wore on.

They strolled down the beach, the warm water tickling their feet, fingers intertwined. Jacob couldn't keep his eyes off Lilly. Her every movement, every facial expression made him smile. She was gorgeous before, but now that she was carrying his children, she had attained a new pinnacle of beauty. She was radiant.

"I feel you looking at me." Lilly gazed up at him, her dark eyes dancing in the moonlight.

"Get used to it."

"I wondered where you had gone. I thought maybe you were high-tailing it for the airport," Lilly teased.

"No way you're getting rid of me. I told you I had a couple of errands to run."

"In Seychelles?"

"Yes. I needed to get a suit fitted for tomorrow."

Lilly reached up, her fingers brushing against his scalp. "And a haircut."

Jacob smirked. "I want to look good for you."

"You always look good. Seriously, you've never looked bad a day in your life. How am I supposed to compete with your Grecian god-like beauty?"

Jacob stopped walking, pulling Lilly against him. "You outshine me every day, angel." He waited for her to balk at his comment, but instead she stood on her tiptoes and pressed her mouth against his. "While I was with the tailor, the dressmaker said she could work late tonight to get your dress ready."

A flush crept over Lilly's cheeks. "I already have my dress."

Her simple statement hit Jacob like a train. "You do?"

Lilly nodded. "I brought it with me…that was a bit presumptuous, I suppose."

He tangled his hands in her hair, forcing her to meet his gaze. "Not presumptuous—hopeful. You believe in us...you finally believe in us."

The look of adoration crossing Lilly's face was a thing of beauty. "My heart always believed in us. I just needed my mind to get with the program."

Jacob pulled a light blue scarf from his pocket. "In that case, the evening can continue."

Lilly eyed the scarf with a confused stare. "What's that for?"

"You."

"Uh-oh. What have you got planned?"

"Close your eyes." Lilly obliged, and Jacob stood behind her, securing the scarf around her head. "No peeking."

"No promises," Lilly giggled.

His hands encircled her waist, sliding up to cup her breasts as his lips nuzzled her nape. "You'd better cooperate."

"Or what?"

"Or you don't get your surprise and trust me, you want it."

"Does it involve more of what you were just doing?" Her hands reached behind her, stroking his shaft.

"Lilly," Jacob hissed, bucking his hips against her palm. "Keep that up, and we won't make it another three feet."

"What am I doing? I'm just stretching." The little minx, she could turn him inside out and enjoy every second of it. God knows he loved every moment of it.

"Right, and I'm just holding onto these"—his grip tightened on her breasts—"for leverage."

"Fair enough." Lilly held out her hand to him. "Lead on."

Jacob scooped her into his arms, chuckling at the grumble she released. She had just started walking again, and the idea of any other mode of transportation other than her own two legs was less than ideal for his fiancée.

He stopped a few minutes later, setting Lilly back on the ground.

"Can I look now?" Lilly questioned, a bit impatiently.

"I suppose. You've been somewhat cooperative." He untied the scarf and took a step back as Lilly opened her eyes.

"Jacob," Lilly breathed, her hand over her mouth as she took in the surroundings.

His final errand of the evening was arranging a private moment for the two of them—in a secluded nook with a breathtaking view of the ocean and stars. Flames crackled in a brick firepit, and thick, fluffy blankets lay on the bamboo mats covering the sand.

"Do you like it?"

"It's gorgeous."

"You're gorgeous." He could tell by the expression on her face that she finally—*finally*—believed him. He filled two champagne flutes and handed one to her with a smile.

Lilly's brow quirked. "I thought I wasn't allowed to partake?"

"It's sparkling cider."

She offered up a wink before taking the glass. "You thought of everything."

Jacob nodded, holding out his hand to her. "Come sit."

They snuggled together on the blanket, lost in the quiet of the waves and the breeze, Lilly leaning against him as his arms held her close.

"Thank you. It's been an amazing day, but I adore the few moments I have alone with you."

"I don't want you getting too tired."

Lilly giggled. "Are you going to be an overprotective husband?"

"Yes," Jacob murmured, pressing his lips against her hair. Was she crazy? Just the idea of anyone looking at Lilly the wrong way made his blood boil. Overprotective was the understatement of the century. "I don't know how to be any other way around you, Lilly. I'll be an overprotective father, too."

Lilly clasped his hand, placing it over her abdomen. "I would expect no less. You'll be an amazing father."

He pressed his hand against her stomach. It was flat now, but soon, he would see the evidence of the lives growing inside her beautiful body. "Christ, you're exquisite, my angel. How did I get so lucky?"

She tilted her head, peering up at him through dark lashes. "*We* got so lucky."

"I wouldn't mind getting lucky," Jacob chortled when Lilly offered up a forced look of shock. "Hey, we still have some serious catching up to do. I do recall telling you that I wanted this magnificent body every single day. Considering the amount of time we've been apart, I think I've earned a few extra rounds."

"I see I'm not the only one who's addicted," Lilly joked.

Jacob's expression turned heated. "You are my only addiction." His flirtatious grin returned as he nipped at her shoulder. "Now, where was I? Oh yes, about to kiss every inch of your body." His hands stroked up her legs, under her dress, a guffaw of disbelief when she blocked his movement.

"It's a shame because I desperately want you to continue, but I suppose we will have to behave."

"Why in bloody hell would we have to do that?"

Lilly waved her arms around, motioning to the secluded cove. "We're in public."

"This coming from the woman who dragged me to a cordoned off lounge area not two hours ago?"

"I hardly dragged you."

But Jacob wasn't letting her change the subject. "This is a private cove, no one will find us…and even if they do, they'll just be jealous when they realize I'm making love to the most beautiful woman alive."

"So, what you're saying is that you'd appreciate some more personal attention?" Her fingers glided over his thighs, wrapped securely around her.

"I'm saying that where you're concerned, my willpower can only hold out for so long." He nuzzled her ear, dropping kisses down to her shoulder.

"Ulterior motive. I knew it, that's why you brought me out here," Lilly teased.

"Obviously"—Jacob stood up, kneeling in front of Lilly—"not."

Lilly's jaw slackened when he pulled a small box out of his pocket.

"I had grand proposals planned the first—and second—time I asked you to marry me, but life mucked up those plans."

"It all worked out in the end."

"It did, but you are far too spectacular not to have an out of this world proposal, so although it's last minute, I hope this will suffice." He opened the ring box, a smile splitting his face when tears formed in Lilly's eyes.

Nestled inside the box was a platinum and diamond infinity ring. "But you already gave me a ring," Lilly exclaimed, holding up her left hand.

"That is an engagement ring. This"—Jacob took Lilly's hand and slid the ring down her finger—"is a promise ring. I promise always to put you first, Lilly. I will love you from this life into the next, and I will spend the remainder of my years dedicated to your happiness. Everything I do from here on out will be to ensure that you feel safe and loved in every possible way. I would die to protect you." His hand moved to her stomach as tears backed up in his eyes. "I would die to protect our children. You three are my whole world, my reason for being. Will you let me take care of you for the rest of our lives?"

Tears streamed down Lilly's cheeks as she threw her arms around his neck, pulling him down onto the blanket with her. "Yes, a thousand times yes…but I do have a condition of my own."

Jacob swallowed and forced a smile. *Please let it be a simple request.* His heart couldn't handle any further upheaval. "A condition? Okay, let's hear it."

"That you let me take care of you in return, allow me the pleasure of loving you forever, of carrying our children and making you happy every day that you chose me. Let me always run to you because I'll never run away from you again."

"You are my forever choice." His lips captured hers as his hands tangled in her hair, his tongue moving against hers in a slow, sultry rhythm. The kiss continued—sucking, biting, tasting—as his hands worked the zipper down on her dress, sliding it off her body. "It's time to fulfill my other promise."

"What promise?"

"To kiss every inch of your body."

"I think you'll have to wait."

"Why?" His erection was straining against his pants. He needed to sink deep inside her and tame the fire that threatened to rage out of control.

But Lilly was more focused on unbuttoning his shirt than conversation, her hands splaying across his pecs. "It's my turn. I could spend the next several hours exploring every inch of you."

Jacob's body jumped to life at her statement. Lilly was rarely so forthright, and he loved this fearless side of his future wife. "Feel free."

Lilly rolled him over, straddling him. "I'll never pass on an opportunity for unbidden caresses." She lowered her head to his neck, delivering a series of nibbles as her hands worked their way south across his abdomen.

She continued further down his body, tonguing her way from one nipple to the next, delivering an erotic blend of bites and licks. Her hands unfastened his pants, and she pushed them down until he lay naked and fully aroused in front of her.

Her fingers wrapped around his erection, earning a grunt of approval as his shaft pulsated against her touch. She slid her hand along his length, her tongue flitting against his tip.

"Lilly, Christ that feels amazing."

"I'm just getting warmed up. It's been entirely too long since I've been allowed to do this. We'll have to make certain you never go this long without proper attention again."

Fuck, he was all for that scenario. He released a low groan when Lilly took him deep into her mouth, flattening her tongue and licking him from base to tip. His fingers knotted in her short hair as she stroked him; she was relentless in her pursuit.

Without warning, Jacob pulled her up against him, flipping her over as he covered her body with his own.

"Hey," Lilly balked, "I wasn't finished."

"Don't you worry that pretty head of yours, I'm going to finish…after I reciprocate the pleasure." With a swift yank, he pulled the dress over her head, his breath catching at the sight of her nude body. Even now, when he had possessed Lilly, time and again, her body was the most exquisite gift he'd ever received.

His tongue skated the curve of her breast and down her abdomen, pausing to press kisses on her stomach. Jacob laid his head against her as he wrapped his arms around her slender frame. Everything he loved in this world was right here, encased in Lilly's petite form.

"While you're down there—" Lilly broke into the moment with a smirk, her fingertips tracing his scalp.

Jacob smiled against her skin—this highly sexual version of Lilly would give him a run for his money. "I have every intention of continuing my journey." He dropped kisses along her hips, delivering a bite to her inner thigh. "Open."

"Yes sir," Lilly replied, letting her legs relax and granting him access to her every part of her body. But it was more than the gesture that caught Jacob, it was the look in her eyes. Instead of the hesitation that so often lingered in her gaze, there was now only pure, unadulterated desire.

Swiping his tongue along her folds, he felt her hands tighten their grip on his shoulders. She was ready, willing, and eager for him to continue, and that idea made his cock throb. He slid a finger deep inside her as his tongue teased her clit, working her open and driving her wild with abandon.

"Jacob…it feels so good," Lilly moaned as she writhed against him, arching her hips against his mouth.

Christ, he loved touching her, the taste of her on his tongue, the feel of her body in his arms. He was going to explode if he didn't sink inside her soon. How he'd managed to go weeks in between loving Lilly, he didn't know.

"I want you inside me," she choked out, but Jacob was intent on making her shatter first, and within moments, he felt the waves of her orgasm rip through her.

Jacob moved back up the length of her body, claiming her mouth, the need in her kiss spurring him on further.

Lilly reached down between them, stroking his shaft. "Mine. Now."

Jacob chuckled, teasing along her folds with the tip of his cock. "Was there something you wanted?"

Lilly wrapped her legs around his waist, locking him in her embrace. "Don't tease. Deliver."

He didn't know if it was the fire in her eyes or the hunger in her voice,

213

but Jacob wasn't making either of them wait for a second longer. She was wet and ready, her body begging for him as he surged inside her.

"You want more?" Jacob asked, moving to his knees and lifting her hips, deepening his movements.

"I want everything," Lilly replied, her eyes closing on a sated sigh.

"I'll give you everything." He quickened his pace as she met him thrust for thrust. She was so deliciously tight around him, and he couldn't get deep enough. He wanted to fill her and possess her utterly. "You feel perfect, Lilly."

Her only answer was a series of heated whimpers as her climax pushed her over the edge, taking him with her into the ecstasy.

Jacob fell against her, attempting to catch his breath. He gazed up when he heard her chuckle. "What's so funny?"

"You brought me out here to rest…instead, I got the workout of my life."

"You started it."

Lilly released an incredulous laugh. "I did no such thing. This was all you, sir."

Jacob dropped kisses along her neck and shoulder. "Will you forgive me?"

"Hmm…I suppose. On one condition."

"Another condition? How many of those damn things do you have?"

Lilly wrapped her arms around his neck, her tongue tracing along the seam of his lips. "Two."

"Fine. What is it?"

"You have to promise to love me like that every day for the rest of our lives."

Jacob smiled down at his future wife. He'd never negotiated an easier deal. "With pleasure, my angel."

Lilly

"Come on, sleepyheads, we've got a wedding to attend." Janie's voice carried through the villa, stirring Lilly from her slumber.

Opening her eyes, she glanced up at Jacob, meeting his smile as he gazed down at her. She had slept sprawled across him, her leg and arm thrown over him in a possessive gesture. "Last chance to run."

"Are you crazy? Do you know how hard I've fought to be here with you?" Jacob's eyes widened as he pulled her into a deep kiss, his tongue caressing every corner of her mouth. Lilly shifted her weight, straddling him and allowing for greater contact.

"Are you two still—oh for god's sake, give it a rest for an hour, will you?" Janie lounged against the door frame, chuckling and shaking her head.

"Morning Janie," Lilly and Jacob replied in stereo.

"I know you'll fight me on this, Jacob, but I actually need the bride. No negotiations."

Lilly glanced back at Jacob, offering a chuckle. "Can she steal me for a bit?"

Jacob put one hand behind his head, the other gently tracing the lines of Lilly's face. "Only for a little while. I'll meet up with you this afternoon. One o'clock?"

"You've got a deal. I'll be easy to spot…I'll be the one wearing all white." Lilly teased his mouth open with her tongue.

"Do I really have to wait that long?"

Janie cleared her throat behind them, and Lilly pulled back with a smile. This man—this gorgeous, spectacular man—was going to be her husband. "I'll be out in five minutes, Janie. Let me grab some clothes."

"You look so happy. So does Jacob. I've never seen him so content." Janie wrapped her arm around Lilly's shoulder as they strolled to a nearby villa.

"It's surreal. Looking back at everything we've overcome, and here we are. Getting married, having a baby—"

"Babies. Wow, I can't wait to see how my brother handles two at once!"

Lilly giggled at the mental image of Jacob trying to change two diapers simultaneously. "I think he'll do just fine…with a minor learning curve."

"He'll do fantastic. I can't believe it's the same guy. This time last year he was arrogant and self-involved and now—"

"He's my dream come true."

Janie's eyes brimmed with tears. "Thank you for saving him, Lilly. Thank you for loving him."

Lilly squeezed her future sister-in-law's fingers. "We saved each other." She nodded toward the villa patio. "Are you joining us for breakfast?"

Janie shook her head. "No, I'm going back to chill with the groom, get him all gussied up."

"Don't make him too pretty. I don't want him outshining me!" Lilly chortled.

"No promises," Janie retorted, blowing her a kiss as she left.

Lilly meandered through the villa, following the sound of laughter from the lanai. She pulled out a chair and sat down, listening to Sabina, Enrique and Ben prattle on around her.

She eyeballed the eggs and vegetables, but her stomach was tied in knots.

"Let's go, you have to eat something," Sabina insisted, handing her a plate of fruit.

"I'm not very hungry."

"She's nervous," Ben commented, ruffling Lilly's hair. "Don't be, this is everything you've ever wanted."

"It is, he's my reason for everything." Lilly put her hand on her stomach. "Well, Jacob and these guys here."

"I can't believe you're having twins. I can barely handle having one." Sabina shook her head, spearing a bite of pancake.

"I don't think two babies would be so bad if you have dedicated parents." Enrique's remark was to Lilly, but his gaze remained locked on Sabina.

Lilly hid a smile behind her hand. If she were a betting woman, she would wager that Sabina and Enrique would be welcoming their own bundle of joy within a year. There was no denying the devotion flashing between the couple.

"It will be an adventure, but let's face it, life has been ever since I've met Jacob."

"A good adventure?" Ben inquired.

"The very best. Ben, I have a favor to ask."

"Anything. Does it involve jetting off to another tropical paradise because then I'm all in."

Everyone at the table snorted, but Ben was right, this wasn't the worst way to spend a few days.

"Maybe for the next wedding." Lilly offered a pointed stare in Enrique and Sabina's direction, laughing at the embarrassed looks crossing their faces.

"That's what you had to ask?" Sabina inquired, shooting her a scowl.

"No, just placing bets on the next betrothal." Before Sabina could retort, Lilly turned in her chair and grabbed Ben's hand. "Since my Dad isn't here, I don't have anyone to walk me down the aisle. Would you do that for me?"

Ben, usually gregarious and jovial, fell silent for a moment and Lilly feared he wouldn't want the task. Looking up, she saw his eyes bright with tears. "It would be my honor, Lilly."

Lilly blinked back her tears as Sabina gave her a quick hug. "Don't get her crying Ben. She doesn't want to be red-rimmed for her wedding."

"Doesn't count if they're tears of joy," Ben retorted with a wink.

"Tell that to the makeup artist," Sabina grumbled.

Lilly's heart was full. She was a lucky lady, surrounded by love and laughter. Taking her glass of juice, she raised it in preparation of a toast. "To each of you, thank you for always being there for me. The world is a lonely place without the comfort and love of friends. To friendship."

"To friendship," they echoed, glasses clinking.

Lilly let out a small gasp when she arrived at the oceanside chapel. It looked like a painting, the turquoise waters lapping against the white sand beaches.

Lilly was equal parts excited and terrified. Everything she ever dreamed of was coming to fruition, but what if Jacob had a change of heart at the last minute?

"You need to relax," Sabina joked, securing the flowers in Lilly's hair. "You look so beautiful. He won't be able to keep his eyes—or hands—off you."

Lilly took a deep breath, rolling her shoulders and forcing a smile. "What if he doesn't show? What if he changes his mind?"

Ben nudged Lilly, pointing towards the chapel. Jacob stood at the front door with his sister and parents, resplendent in a beige suit, a glow of happiness emanating from him. "He's already here. He's been waiting for you, luv."

Lilly smiled, the duality of Ben's statement clear. "Do I look okay, Ben? Do you approve?" She twirled in her gown, the georgette fabric ruffling in the breeze.

"You look like a princess—no, a queen. A regal, elegant, and gorgeous queen." Ben kissed her cheek, pulling her into a fierce hug. "Are you ready to finally marry that man?"

Lilly smiled as the first notes of music played, signaling the start of the ceremony. "God, yes."

Ben escorted Lilly up the aisle to where Jacob waited for her, and the look of love on her fiancée's face wiped away any lingering doubt in her mind. From now on she was listening with her heart.

"You're exquisite, my love," Jacob whispered, tears in his eyes as he beamed at her, his lips nuzzling the back of her hand.

Lilly caressed his jaw, her smile radiating her inner happiness as she finally allowed herself to bask in Jacob's adoration. "So are you. Ready to get married?"

"I've been waiting forever for you, Mrs. Edmonton."

The ceremony was simple but beautiful, as Lilly and Jacob voiced their devotion in front of family and friends, their song lilting in the background. They had loved, lost, and loved again, and now, no one could tear them apart.

Lilly knew there wasn't a dry eye in the chapel, but her gaze remained locked on Jacob as he slid a platinum band on her finger and proclaimed his undying love for her and their unborn children. She believed him, believed in his love and now understood how the power of that love could save them all.

"You wanted to say a few words, miss?" the preacher inquired, and Lilly smiled, nodding in his direction.

Grasping Jacob's hands, the trembling within her body quieted when she felt his warmth. He was her strength, her safety.

"I believe Jacob will remember this quote from Rumi. I sent it to him when I realized he was the love of my life, and it's truer now than ever. 'The minute I heard my first love story, I started looking for you, not knowing how blind that was. Lovers don't finally meet somewhere. They're in each other all along.' Thank you for showing me how to be loved. There is no greater pleasure in this world than being loved by you."

Then Jacob's lips were on hers, their cheeks wet with tears. "En sa beauté gît ma mort et ma vie. You are the music of my heart, Lilly."

When the pastor pronounced them husband and wife, the guests cheered and clapped. Everyone present realized how arduous a journey this had been for Jacob and Lilly, but one look at her husband and Lilly knew—beyond a doubt—it was worth every moment.

"I love you, my beautiful wife." Their gazes held before his lips found hers, and she knew she was finally home.

Jacob and Lilly didn't dally long at the reception. They had needs—pressing needs. Their desire to be together overpowered any reception etiquette. Besides, the guests seemed fine with entertaining themselves amongst the gourmet food and top-shelf liquor.

Jacob carried her into their villa, laying her on the bed and looking at her with such ardor Lilly thought her heart might burst.

She released a contented sigh when his weight was on top of her, his mouth on hers, and she knew that he belonged to her and no one else.

Jacob slid off her dress, littering her body with kisses. He paused at her stomach, wrapping his hands around her ribs and lowering his mouth to press against her skin. "I love you—I love you all so much."

He was going to be an amazing father; he was already an amazing husband. Lilly pulled him to her, reclaiming his lips as she slipped her arms around his neck. "Make love to me, my darling husband. Love me every day," she whispered as he slid inside her, capturing her lips again.

"That's a promise," Jacob answered.

EPILOGUE

Three months later...

Lilly stood at the window, watching the snow cover the gardens of their country home with a dusting of white. Everything looked so enchanting underneath Mother Nature's blanket. "I think I'll put on my boots and take a walk. Want to join me?"

Jacob walked up behind her, wrapping his arms around her waist—well, what used to be her waist. She was now twenty-two weeks pregnant and felt like an overstuffed aardvark, despite Jacob's constant affections. "I would, but I have plans for us."

Lilly turned in his arms, smiling up at him. "You do?"

He nodded, pressing his forehead against hers. He'd been good to his word, and they hadn't spent a night apart in the three months since their wedding. Jacob even turned down several movie roles in lieu of staying by her side during the pregnancy. "I've got our bags packed—"

"You packed my bag?" Lilly asked incredulously, eyebrows raised.

"Hannah helped."

"Whew. I was worried for a minute. Where are we going?"

Jacob's eyes twinkled down at her, a smile on his lips. Without a word, he fished a lock from his pocket. "I think it's time we placed this lock. What do you think?"

"You're taking me to Paris?" Lilly felt the tears back up, and she palmed the lock, her finger tracing the engraving on the back. "Mon ange, tu me manques."

"My angel, you are missing from me."

"Not anymore."

Jacob captured her lips in a fierce kiss, his hands framing her face as their tongues danced a slow, sensual dance. "Thank God. I promised I would take you to Paris, my angel, I figured what better time than Christmas?"

A few hours later, the private jet touched down in Paris, and Lilly planted her feet on French soil. The air was cold and crisp, her breath hanging in the air as she bundled her scarf around her neck. "The air even feels different here."

"It's all the flour in the air from the French pastries," Jacob joked, grasping her hand as they walked towards the limousine.

"Speaking of pastries, I'm starving."

"Angel, when are you not starving?"

Before she could retort with a snarky comment, he'd pulled her against his chest, his hands cupping her belly. "I know, you're eating for three."

"Don't you forget it." Lilly wound her hands around his neck, standing on tiptoe and pressing her lips to his. "You're the reason I'm now as wide as I am tall. I told you I'd look like a cow."

"You're gorgeous, and when we get to the hotel, I plan on showing you just what I think of you."

"Promises, promises," Lilly teased, a favorite joke between them.

The limousine weaved through the streets of Paris, and Lilly knew she was the epitome of a tourist as she squealed with delight, pointing out all the sights. Jacob kept his arms wrapped around her, chuckling every time she clapped her hands at yet another restaurant or bakery. "I know, I have an insatiable appetite."

His lips brushed her ear, his breath sending sparks throughout her body. "So do I, ever since the first day I saw you."

It never failed. It didn't matter that she was now Mrs. Jacob Edmonton and assured always of his love. Every time he intimated what she meant to him, her heart melted.

The driver slowed, opening the partition separating them. "Monsieur, we are here." He then opened the door for the couple, and Lilly's heart seized with joy.

The Pont des Arts bridge, the bridge of lovers.

She wanted to say something profound, but words escaped her, she was overcome with emotion as she stared at the gray waters of the Seine. Her hand moved to her chest as fat tears rolled down her cheeks.

"Angel?" Jacob tipped her chin up, wiping away her tears with his thumbs. "What is it?"

"We made it, Jacob."

Then she saw it, the bright sheen in his sapphire eyes—he was equally moved by the moment. "The first of many promises to be fulfilled, Lilly. Are you ready?"

Lilly nodded as her husband opened the padlock with a key and then directed her hand to cover his. They found a spot near one end of the bridge and looped the lock through the metal.

"From this lifetime into the next, Lilly. I will always choose you. I will always love you."

Lilly squeezed his hand and nodded. "My forever choice."

With those words, they snapped the lock shut, but their eyes never strayed from one another. They each took a key and with a smile, tossed them into the river below.

Their love could never be undone now...or so states the legend. But Lilly knew better. Lock or no, nothing would come between their love again.

Seeking out his wife's lips, Jacob slid his tongue into her mouth, his touch hungry and yearning. Despite the cold temperature, Lilly's body surged with warmth as the kiss deepened, his hands sliding up into her hair.

"Let's go get you warmed up, beautiful." Jacob held out his hand, leading her back to the limousine.

A short while later, the limo pulled up in front of the grandest building she had ever seen, and Lilly couldn't hide her shock. "Wow, what is this place?"

"Le Meurice. This is where we'll be staying for the next few days."

Lilly's eyes widened. "Here? It looks like a palace."

"Fit for my queen."

The luxuriant air was not reserved for the exterior of the hotel—every inch of the interior reeked of refinement. A bellhop escorted them to one of the suites—a palatial expanse of wood paneling and marble baths. Lilly wandered from one room to the next, shaking her head at the opulence.

"Jacob, this is spectacular. Have you stayed here before?" Her high faded slightly when he nodded. Of course, he had, he was a superstar celebrity—he had experienced everything the world had to offer—and then some. "No wonder you wanted to return."

Jacob knew his wife well, and a knowing smile split his face as he led her to the balcony. "Look at this view."

"It's beautiful," Lilly murmured as she gazed at the Parisian landscape. Beautiful didn't do the panorama justice. It was breathtaking...much like the man standing next to her.

His arms wrapped around her as his chin rested on her head. "What are you thinking right now?"

Lilly shook off the doldrums. Her husband had gone above and beyond for this trip. Any self-doubt needed to sit down and shut up. "How glorious all this is."

"You're a bad liar, my angel."

Lilly turned to face him, her eyes wide. "I *do* think it's glorious."

"But..."

With a resigned sigh, Lilly realized she wasn't getting out of this conversation. Jacob knew her too well. "You've seen everything, experienced all that life has to offer. I want to give you something in return, but there's nothing I can give you that you haven't already done—why are you looking at me like that?"

Instead of looking despondent, her husband could barely contain his amusement. "As I've told you numerous times before, for such a brilliant woman, you certainly are thick-headed."

"What is that supposed to mean?" Lilly inquired, feeling a bit prickly at his cavalier grin.

His fingers traced along her jaw, threading through her hair as his lips caught hers. "You still don't get it, do you?"

"No, you'll have to fill me in," she replied with a grumble.

"You've given me everything I never knew I wanted. You've given me the world—love, and passion"—his hands cupped her stomach—"and a family. All I've given you is a hotel room and some flights on a private jet. So, if anyone has fallen short, it's me, angel."

She didn't know if it was the hormones, the season, or his statement but tears spilled down her cheeks. "You see? That's where you're wrong. You gave *me* the greatest gift."

"A luxury suite?" Jacob joked.

Lilly pressed her lips to his, smiling against his mouth. "Far better. You gave me you."

Fifteen months later...

rad Taylor greeted Jacob as he walked onstage, offering up a warm handshake. "Welcome back to my show, Jacob. It's been a while. Eighteen months or so?"

Jacob nodded, smiling at the host and then at the audience chanting his name. "About that, yes."

"You're causing quite the stir in the London theater world."

"I'm enjoying myself thoroughly."

"You're also nominated for Best Supporting Actor in Milieu of Madness. What an achievement. Critics are calling it your finest work."

"I have to agree. It was a step outside my comfort zone, one I would never have considered a few years ago."

"So, what made you take the leap of faith? Spread your wings, so to speak?"

Jacob ran his hand along his jaw, smiling at the talk-show host. "The same person who turned my entire life around a year-and-a-half ago."

"In more ways than one."

Jacob laughed. He knew what track this interview was taking. "It's been a year of many firsts."

"Well, I'd have to live in a cave in Antarctica not to know about you and your beautiful wife, Lilly."

Jacob couldn't help it. He grinned like an idiot at the mention of her name. "She's amazing, isn't she? I think people tolerate me simply because they're enamored with my wife."

Brad nodded, laughing. "I can't say I fault their taste, mate. She's an exquisite woman, a true lady."

"She's the best thing that ever happened to me—well, one of the best things."

"Ah yes, how is fatherhood treating you?"

"I haven't slept in months, but I think that's normal, right?" Jacob asked the question more to the audience, who laughed in agreement.

"How old are your boys now?"

"Ten months."

Brad tapped the desk with his pen, a smile lighting up his face. "You didn't waste much time after our last show together, did you?"

At first, Jacob bristled at the forthright question. He didn't like inviting

225

the outside world into his sanctuary with Lilly, but Brad's jovial wink ensured it was just friendly banter. Might as well play along. "Do you blame me? Have you seen my wife?"

"I don't know how to answer that question without getting in trouble," Brad chortled, flushing slightly. "Lilly's beautiful—inside and out. So, your family has permanently settled in England? I know she's from New York originally."

"We visit the US at least once a year, but Lilly considers England home. We own a house in Gloucestershire and one here in London. Lilly prefers the countryside and wants the boys to spend as much time there as possible."

"How is that working for you with your theater run? That's a bit of a commute every day."

"It would be the commute from hell. We're staying in London during the run, but we'll be headed back to our country home within the month."

"So, there's a highly romanticized rumor that you two never spend a night apart."

Jacob held back a growl. They hadn't spent a night apart...until Lilly left on a trip to the north of England to visit a location for another animal sanctuary. She had been gone for four nights, but to Jacob, it seemed like forever. "Well, we didn't until earlier this week. Lilly had a trip up north, and I couldn't go with her. So, I haven't seen her in almost a week."

"You make it sound like an eternity."

"I'm addicted to my wife, so one day is too long without her." The audience let out a collective sigh of appreciation. "She was supposed to fly home tonight, but her plane was delayed, so it's one more night alone."

"Maybe not," Brad mentioned with a nonchalant grin, and before Jacob could inquire, he felt hands slip over his eyes.

"Guess who?"

He knew that Yankee accent anywhere. He practically dove over the chair, pulling Lilly into a fierce hug. "Hi, my angel."

"Hi yourself, did you miss me?" Her smile undid him, and he claimed her lips, his tongue sliding in to taste her mouth; something the audience enjoyed thoroughly.

Jacob intertwined their fingers, leading her to the adjoining chair. He marveled at how his wife grew more beautiful every day—the royal blue dress played off against her fair skin, her dark hair fell against her jaw, her brown eyes bright with affection. But it was the small bump that truly sent him over the edge. He placed his hand on the swell of her belly, knowing his baby was safe and secure.

"Did we surprise you? Brad was inquiring about the animal sanctuary and thought an impromptu visit might be nice," Lilly asked with a chuckle, giving the audience an embarrassed wave when someone screamed out their love for her.

Jacob captured her lips again, nibbling her bottom lip. "Much more than nice."

Brad laughed, bringing the couple from their loved-up reverie. "My wife is going to demand flowers after this display." He nodded at Lilly's baby bump. "I see you two have been busy. When are you due?"

Jacob laughed. "We've still got a while, another four months."

"Three children under the age of two. You are one brave couple," Brad joked.

"Together, we can do anything," Lilly replied, earning another kiss from her husband. "Except sleep. Sleep is not in the cards."

"If you keep having babies, it never will be." The audience chuckled at Brad's barb.

"We're done after this," Lilly assured the talk-show host.

Jacob squeezed her hand, offering up another sparkling smile. "We'll see." His gaze met Lilly's, and he felt his heart clench. He loved this woman on a level he hadn't believed existed. "Right now, I'm just enjoying every moment with my wife."

The audience cooed their approval as Lilly leaned in, pressing her mouth against his.

"Well, I am thrilled to see how your story turned out; almost like a fairytale," Brad added.

Jacob smiled at Lilly, bringing her hand to his lips. "Better than a fairytale."

Not the End, but the Beginning of a beautiful life together…

Hello again lovelies,

I hope you've enjoyed Jacob and Lilly's journey—I know that creating this series was a labor of love and I will forever be indebted to these characters for teaching me so much about myself, the world, and most importantly, love.

I hope their story made you laugh, cry, and sometimes want to throw the book across the room. Life—and love—is often like that, but in the end, it's always worthwhile.

I love to hear from my readers and encourage you to subscribe to my newsletter or to email me at m.l.broomeauteur@gmail.com. If you have questions, ideas or suggestions, I'm all ears!

It would be great if you could spread the word about this book, particularly if it touched you in some way. Reviews on sites like Amazon, BookBub, and GoodReads are very welcome and appreciated.

Best wishes for a life well-lived. Until we meet again.

M.L. Broome

ALSO FROM M.L. BROOME

Unguarded Moments, A Series of Moments Book Two
http://bit.ly/MomentWeMet
Beautifully Broken Moments, A Series of Moments Book Three
http://bit.ly/brokenmoment

Connect with M.L. Broome —sign up for my newsletter!
Website
https://www.mlbroome.com/
BookBub
https://www.bookbub.com/profile/m-l-broome
GoodReads
https://www.goodreads.com/author/show/19088931.M_L_Broome
Facebook
https://www.facebook.com/ML-Broome-350211855703261/
Instagram
https://www.instagram.com/mlbroomeauteur/
Amazon Author Page
http://bit.ly/MLBroome

A SERIES OF MOMENTS

Beautifully Broken Moments

M.L. BROOME

About the Author

I'm a bohemian spirit with a New York edge. I adore dressing up and kicking back, a nice glass of wine with an equally stunning view, and experiences that make the soul--and mouth--water.

When I'm not writing or holding one-sided arguments with my characters (spoiler alert—they always win), I love losing myself in nature on my North Carolina farm, one of my rescue buddies at my side.

Life is beautiful...so are you. Don't forget to look up. Peace, love, & magic.

"YOU'LL CLIMB AS HIGH AS YOU DARE BELIEVE YOU ARE CAPABLE. THE STARS ARE ONLY AS FAR AS WE IMAGINE THEM TO BE, AND TIME IS NEITHER FRIEND NOR FOE. MAGIC IS EVERYWHERE. LIFE IS A THING OF BEAUTY."